AF520952

ZUBAAN

PENGUIN BOOKS

MATRIARCHS, COWS AND EPIC VILLAINS

Suniti Namjoshi is a poet, fabulist and children's writer with over forty books to her name. After a stint in the Indian Administrative Service, Namjoshi moved to Canada, where she earned a PhD at McGill University, taught at the University of Toronto for many years, and then moved on to doing what she loves best—writing. A selection of her works is published in *The Fabulous Feminist* (2012). Her books include *Suki* (2013), a memoir about her beloved cat; *Foxy Aesop: On the Edge* (2018), which asks point-blank whether it is the function of writers to save the world; and *Dangerous Pursuits* (2022), which contains 'Bad People', the first part of the trilogy about Ravana and his siblings.

PRAISE FOR THE AUTHOR

'There is something about the authorial "voice" which recalls the Indian *katha* style of narrative . . . The "voice" is there, helpfully warm, wrapping around us in a friendly tone. It is our own Indian *katha* tone, telling us fables'—**Lakshmi Kannan, *Times of India***

'What Namjoshi's entire work—poems, fables and novels—taken together conveys clearly is a strong resistance to the status quo of oppression, be it gender-based, race-based or class-based'—**C. Vijayasree, *Suniti Namjoshi: The Artful Transgressor***

'Suniti Namjoshi is one of the most brilliant living writers I know . . . Namjoshi's host of fabulous creature-protagonists . . . constitute perhaps the most engaging dimension of her work'—**Ruth Vanita, *Tulsa Studies in Women's Literature***

'Suniti Namjoshi is an inspired fabulist: she asks the difficult questions—about good and evil, nature and war—unfailingly bracing her readers with her mordant humour and the lively play of her imagination'—**Marina Warner**

'In her prose, Namjoshi's questions about an "absurd" world's assumptions are turned into subversive statements, delivered with cool wit . . .'—**Kathleen Jamie, *Times Literary Supplement***

'Here were stories deftly pointing out the absurd ways in which human beings insisted on categorizing anything strange as Other and Worse, on preferring their own cosy visions to harsh reality, on trying to save and convert each other rather than leaving each other alone'—**Michèle Roberts, *New Statesman***

'I do not know a poet more skilled at appropriating and reshaping classic myths and folktales from East and West than Suniti Namjoshi'—**Diana Brydon, 'Beyond Orientalism', *Canadian Literature***

matriarchs, cows and epic villains

New and Selected Fables and Poems

SUNITI NAMJOSHI

With an introduction by Gillian Hanscombe

zubaan

PENGUIN BOOKS
An imprint of Penguin Random House

ZUBAAN

128B Shahpur Jat, 1st Floor, New Delhi 110 049, India

Zubaan is an independent feminist publishing house based in New Delhi with a strong academic and general list. It was set up as an imprint of India's first feminist publishing house, Kali for Women, and carries forward Kali's tradition of publishing world-quality books to high editorial and production standards. *Zubaan* means tongue, voice, language, speech in Hindustani. Zubaan publishes in the areas of the humanities, social sciences, as well as in fiction, general non-fiction, and books for children and young adults under its Young Zubaan imprint.

in collaboration with

PENGUIN BOOKS

Penguin Books is an imprint of the Penguin Random House group of companies whose addresses can be found at global.penguinrandomhouse.com

Published by Penguin Random House India Pvt. Ltd
4th Floor, Capital Tower 1, MG Road,
Gurugram 122 002, Haryana, India

First published by Zubaan Publishers Pvt. Ltd and Penguin Random House India 2025

10 9 8 7 6 5 4 3 2 1

ISBN 9788194253396
eISBN 9788194721864

Typeset in Bembo Std 11/13 by Jojy Philip
Printed at Replika Press Pvt. Ltd, India

www.zubaanbooks.com

www.penguin.co.in

MIX
Paper | Supporting responsible forestry
FSC™ C016779

Contents

Acknowledgements

The Conversations of Cow was first published by The Women's Press, London in 1985; and *The Mothers of Maya Diip* was first published by The Women's Press, London in 1989. 'Birds' appeared in *The Four Quarters Magazine*, Online ISSN: 2349-6061, Vol. 4, No.1, April-May, 2015; 'Superstars' in *CONVERSE: Contemporary English: Poetry by Indians* ed. Sudeep Sen (UK: Pippa Rann Books & Media, 2022); and 'An Honest to Goodness Fairy Tale' in *Live Encounters* Online magazine, Feb. 2018.

Introduction

Indian fabulist Suniti Namjoshi is well-known for the satirical wit and feminist viewpoint embodied in her prose narratives and lyric poems. She is often described as an Indian feminist writer, owing both to the autobiographical content in *Goja* and *O Sister Swallow*, and to the reference framework of the *Ravana Trilogy*, comprising *Bad People*, *Shupi's Choices* and *Kumbh*. The Trilogy shows the absurdity of trying to apply so-called 'heroic' norms to twenty-first century lives, while at the same time satirising how we think and behave. Further Indian elements in her work have more to do with sensibility than with straightforward content: she is a story-teller, for instance, because she comes from a nation of story-tellers. In Indian contexts, points made in conversation are often illustrated by stories or anecdotes, rather than by abstract argument or formalised debate. And the irony typical of her work is characteristic of Marathi, her mother tongue. Further, her Hindu background is an endlessly rich reference framework, helping to energise the abandoning of the many arbitrary identities with which we try to shore ourselves up. Feminist influences in the development of her style come from the women writers who preceded her: Virginia Woolf, Kate Millett, Adrienne Rich, and so many others. Their work created the cultural context which made it possible for others to write from a woman's viewpoint.

Although Suniti Namjoshi's feminism is uncompromising, there are some writers from the mainstream canon whose works echo again and again in her own fables, poems, and narratives.

The way her mind moves has affinities with Jonathan Swift and Lewis Carroll, and indeed with Aesop whom she has conjured as the main adventurer in *Foxy Aesop*. Such affinities align with a highly developed sense of the absurd. When something that is normal or conventional or taken for granted is put into a different setting or framework, its inherent lack of logic, or its arbitrariness, or its absurdity, reveals itself. This is what makes the fabulist a skilled mythmaker: we would not want to do without Lilliput and Brobdingnag, or Wonderland, or the talking beasts of Aesop, for instance.

A fabulist can't avoid satire altogether, however gently it's done. And as a feminist, Suniti Namjoshi is keenly aware of the absurd ways in which women are regarded and treated in societies that take male norms and double standards for granted. When asked whether she would rather make a good point or write a good fable, she has always chosen the fable, but has added that she would rather do both. She has also said that she doesn't necessarily want to tell people what to think, but that she does want them to think. The fable is a didactic form because questioning is inherent in it, so for Suniti Namjoshi as a feminist writer, it has been a wonderfully useful genre. As she has often said, 'Myths mutate. That is their power.' When asked, as she has been so often, why she writes fables and poems, her answer usually is 'It's the way my mind works.' For example, in her version of 'The Mouse and the Lion', the irony of the mouse ever being able to do the lion a favour is doubled when the mouse is called upon to help the lion and tripled when the mouse points out that it hasn't killed the lion. After all, refraining from killing it is the only favour the lion has done the mouse. *Feminist Fables* showed how the power of myth, and of storytelling in general, could upend common sexist assumptions by retelling a story. Having once acquired her retelling skills, Suniti Namjoshi has gone on to explore particular themes. In *The Conversations of Cow* she examines how enforcing and developing an identity works; in *The Mothers of Maya Diip* she questions why feminism has had so little to say about motherhood; in *Saint Suniti and the Dragon* she probes the problem of wanting to be good, but not too good, given how difficult and hard that is; in *Building Babel*, she asks how we put together the building blocks of culture; in *Goja* she probes the huge polarities between the rich and the poor in India; and in *Foxy Aesop* she wonders whether writers have a duty to save the world, and if they do, how it might be possible.

Two other works hover over her writing and inform her imagination: Shakespeare's *The Tempest*, and Ezra Pound's *Cantos* (the subject of her doctoral dissertation). *The Tempest* is the play that many poets return to again and again, most notably W.H. Auden, perhaps because it speaks both of the poet's task and of the poet's limitations, or perhaps because its imagery is so rich that it permits infinite exploration. In 'Snapshots of Caliban' we're given a lesbian Caliban, and in 'Sycorax', a dying Sycorax is centre stage. In 'The Dream Book' Suniti Namjoshi explores the dream imagery of each of the characters in the play, and discovers that

Their dreams and decisions, their warring egos
were as pretty and pitiless as glass shards.

The question follows, 'How are we to dream well?' Our idealisations and utopias have come to nothing, our theories and inventions have resulted in impending disaster. This is a preoccupation in her later work, *Dangerous Pursuits* and *The Good-Hearted Gardeners*.

Ezra Pound may seem a bizarre influence: Pound the racist? Pound who gave broadcasts over Radio Rome for Mussolini? Pound whose *Cantos* hardly make sense? In defence, Suniti Namjoshi might quote from one of the later *Cantos*: 'It coheres all right/even if my notes do not cohere'. What she likes is his belief that paradise is possible here and now on earth; and what she admires without reserve is his skill as a poet when he is at his best. Poetry matters intensely to her. For her, it is when we think like poets that we stretch our thinking and our language, allowing ourselves to formulate what we have not been able to otherwise.

If asked how she sees herself now, Suniti Namjoshi might say, 'As someone who tried to do good work'. She might even quote Ezra Pound:

But to have done instead of not doing
this is not vanity
...
Here error is all in the not done,
all in the diffidence that faltered... *Canto LXXXI*

Gillian Hanscombe

Feminist Fables

Feminist Fables was a breakthrough for me. On my sabbatical in England in 1978-79, I discovered feminism—or rather I discovered that other feminists existed. It gave me the confidence that I would be heard and understood. For a writer that's particularly important. A poem or a fable exists between the writing of it and the reading of it.

It's not possible to grow up in India without seeing the different kinds of disparities in power all around. The fables, because of their form, speak to these imbalances. To be oppressed, whether because of caste, class, wealth, gender or sexual orientation, isn't shameful, it's doing the oppressing that is so very wrong.

If *Feminist Fables* is about any one thing, then that is what it is about. I've tried to use the very power of language and the literary tradition to expose what is absurd and unacceptable.

From the Panchatantra

In the holy city of Benares there lived a brahmin, who, as he walked by the riverbank, watching the crows floating downstream, feeding on the remains of half-burnt corpses, consoled himself thus: 'It is true that I am poor, but I am a brahmin, it is true that I have no sons, but I, myself, am indisputably a male. I shall return to the temple and pray to Lord Vishnu to grant me a son.' He went off to the temple and Lord Vishnu listened and Lord Vishnu complied, but whether through absent-mindedness or whether for some other more abstruse reason, he gave him a daughter. The brahmin was disappointed. When the child was old enough, he called her to him and delivered himself thus: 'I am a brahmin. You are my daughter. I had hoped for a son. No matter. I will teach you what I know, and when you are able, we will both meditate and seek guidance.' Though only a woman, she was a brahmin, so she learned very fast, and then, they both sat down and meditated hard. In a very short time Lord Vishnu appeared. 'What do you want?' he said. The brahmin couldn't stop himself. He blurted out quickly, 'I want a son.' 'Very well,' said the god, 'Next time around.' In his next incarnation the brahmin was a woman and bore eight sons. 'And what do you want?' he said to the girl. 'I want human status.' 'Ah, that is much harder,' and the god hedged and appointed a commission.

Case History

After the event Little R. traumatized. Wolf not slain. Forester is wolf. How else was he there exactly on time? Explains this to mother. Mother not happy. Thinks that the forester is extremely nice. Grandmother dead. Wolf not dead. Wolf marries mother. R. not happy. R. is a kid. Mother thinks wolf is extremely nice. Please to see shrink. Shrink will make it clear that wolves on the whole are extremely nice. R. gets it straight. Okay to be wolf. Mama is a wolf. She is a wolf. Shrink is a wolf. Mama and shrink, and forester also, extremely uptight.

Nymph

The god chases Daphne. Daphne runs away. Daphne is transformed into a green laurel. What does it mean? That that's what happens to ungrateful women? Daphne says, 'Yes.' She says, 'Yes. Yes. Yes.' Apollo is pleased. Then he gets bored. Girl chases god. It is not very proper. Daphne gets changed. Into what is she changed? Daphne is changed into a green laurel. What does it mean? That that's what happens to ungrateful women. Daphne says, 'Yes.' Then she keeps quiet. Her timing is right. Daphne gets changed. Into what is she changed? Daphne is changed into a green laurel. And what does it mean? It means, it obviously means, that trees keep quiet.

The Princess

And so it was settled that she was a genuine princess. They had brought the equipment: seven thick mattresses stuffed with eiderdown, a magnificent bed, and a small green pea, which was placed with some care under the mattresses. They made up the bed and the princess lay down, but she couldn't sleep because of the green pea. The proof was conclusive. The pea was removed, and the royal parents embraced their daughter. She was very beautiful and exceptionally charming, and, of course, her sensitivity was such that it was absolutely amazing. If anyone cried, she would suffer so much that no one was allowed to cry in the palace. If anyone was hurt, she would take to her bed and be ill for weeks. In consequence, no one who was hurt was admitted within. Sickness sickened her, and she could not bear to see anything that was in the least bit ugly. Only good-looking people and those in good health were allowed to be seen. The king, her father, and the queen, her mother, did their best for her, and the people of the city were quite proud of her—she being a princess and the genuine thing; but it soon became obvious that her skin was such that she was allergic to everything. Cotton was too coarse and silks too heavy. The king levied taxes and all the people were made to work hard at spinning and weaving. They worked very hard and grew very tired, but it wasn't any use, and finally, the princess caught a cold and died of it.

The Female Swan

And then there was the duckling who aspired to be a swan. She worked very hard, studied the history and literature of swans, the growth of their swanhood, their hopes and ideals, and their time-honoured customs. In the end, even the swans acknowledged that this duck had rendered them a signal service. They threw a banquet (no ducks invited) and gave her a paper, which stated clearly that thereafter she would be an Honorary Swan. She was highly gratified, as were some of the ducks, who began to feel that there was hope for them. Others just laughed. 'A duck is a duck,' they said, 'and ought not to aspire to be a swan. A duck, by definition, is inferior to swans.' This seemed so evident that they forgot the matter and paddled off. But there were still others who were angered by this. 'Those ducks do not think,' they said. 'But as for the learned one, she has betrayed us to the cause of swans. She is no longer a duck. She is a swan.' This too seemed evident. They turned to Andersen. 'Well,' he said, 'there are a great many ducks and a great many duck-ponds.' But that didn't help, so he tried again. 'The thing is,' he said, 'you are beginning to question the nature of ducks and the values of swans.' 'Yes,' they said. 'We know,' they said, 'But where will it end?' 'I don't know,' said Andersen, 'You're learning to fashion your own fables.'

A Moral Tale

The Beast wasn't a nobleman. The Beast was a woman. That's why its love for Beauty was so monstrous. As a child the Beast had had parents who were both kindly and liberal. 'It's not that we disapprove of homosexuals as such, but people disapprove and that's why it grieves us when you think you are one. We want you to be happy, and homosexuals are not happy, and that is the truth.' 'Why are they unhappy?' 'Because people disapprove...' The Beast considered these arguments circular, but she discovered also that she was unhappy. Boys didn't interest her. She fell in love with a girl. The girl disapproved, and she found that she was now the object of ridicule. She became more and more solitary and turned to books. But the books made it clear that men loved women, and women loved men, and men rode off and had all sorts of adventures and women stayed at home. 'I know what it is,' she said one day, 'I know what is wrong: I am not human. The only story that fits me at all is the one about the Beast. But the Beast doesn't change from a Beast to a human because of its love. It's just the reverse. And the Beast isn't fierce. It's extremely gentle. It loves Beauty, but it lives alone and dies alone.' And that's what she did. Her parents mourned her, and the neighbours were sorry, particularly for her parents, but no one was at fault: she had been warned and she hadn't listened.

The Monkey and the Crocodiles

A monkey used to live in a large jambu tree which grew along the banks of the river Yamuna. The fruit of this tree was unusually delicious and a bit like plums. At the foot of the tree lived two crocodiles. The monkey and the crocodiles were very good friends. The monkey would feed the crocodiles plums, and the crocodiles, in return, would make conversation. They also protected her—though she did not know it—by keeping a watchful eye on her. The day came when the monkey began to feel more and more restless. 'I'm off,' she said, 'to explore the world.' 'Here, jump on my back,' said one of the crocodiles, 'and I'll ferry you over.' 'No,' she said, 'I don't want to go to the other river bank. I want to follow this river to its ultimate source.' 'That's dangerous,' said the crocodiles. 'Why?' said the monkey. 'There are beasts along the way. They'll eat you up.' 'What sorts of beasts?' asked the monkey suspiciously. 'Well, they are long and narrow with scaly hides and powerful jaws.' 'I don't understand,' said the monkey. 'Don't go,' said the crocodiles. 'But I want to find out and see for myself.' 'Beware of the beasts,' said her friends, the crocodiles. The monkey set off. Seven years later she hobbled back. She had lost her tail, six of her teeth, and one eye. 'Did you find the source of the river Yamuna?' 'No,' said the monkey. 'Did you encounter the beasts?' 'Yes,' said the monkey. 'What did they look like?' 'They looked like you,' she answered slowly. 'When you warned me long ago, did you know that?' 'Yes,' said her friends and avoided her eye.

The Giantess

Thousands of years ago in far away India, which is so far away that anything is possible, before the advent of the inevitable Aryans, a giantess was in charge of a little kingdom. It was small by her standards, but perhaps not by our own. Three oceans converged on its triangular tip, and in the north there were mountains, the tallest in the world, which would perhaps account for this singular kingdom. It was not a kingdom, but the word has been lost and I could find no other. 'There wasn't any king. The giantess governed and there were no other women. The men were innocent and happy and carefree. If they were hurt, they were quickly consoled. For the giantess was kind, and would set them on her knee and tell them they were brave and strong and noble. And if they were hungry, the giantess would feed them. The milk from her breasts was sweeter than honey and more nutritious than mangoes. If they grew fractious, the giantess would sing, and they would clamber up her legs and onto her lap and sleep unruffled. They were a happy people and things might have gone on in this way forever, were it not for the fact that the giantess grew tired. Her knees felt more bony, her voice rasped, and on one or two occasions she showed irritation. They were greatly distressed. 'We love you,' they said to the tired giantess, 'Why won't you sing? Are you angry with us? What have we done?' 'You are dear little children,' the giantess replied, 'but I have grown very tired and it's time for me to go.' 'Don't you love us anymore? We'll do what you want. We will make you happy. Only please don't go.' 'Do you know what

I want?' the giantess asked. They were silent for a bit, then one of them said, 'We'll make you our queen.' And another one said, 'We'll write you a poem.' And a third one shouted (while turning cartwheels), 'We'll bring you many gifts of oysters and pearls and pebbles and stones.' 'No,' said the giantess, 'No.' She turned her back and crossed the mountains.

Broadcast Live

The Incredible Woman raged through the skies, lassoed a planet, set it in orbit, rescued a starship, flattened a mountain, straightened a building, smiled at a child, caught a few thieves, all in one morning, and then, took a little time off to visit her psychiatrist, since she is at heart a really womanly woman and all she wants is a normal life.

The Fox and the Stork

One day a fox invited a stork for a visit. As soon as Stork arrived, Fox started saying that she, herself, was a very progressive fox and intended fully to respect Stork and Stork's individuality. 'Thank you,' said Stork. 'Now,' said Fox, 'I do not wish to make any assumptions, and so I must ask you: do Storks, in fact, eat?' 'Yes,' said Stork. 'How extraordinary,' said Fox, 'and do they eat food, or do they eat some amazing and unlikely dish?' 'We eat some amazing and unlikely dish,' said Stork. 'How delightful,' said Fox, 'how absolutely charming.' 'And tell me,' she added, 'have Storks ever been known to drink?' 'We drink on the fifth and seventh of each month, except in a leap year, when we drink on the third and fourteenth respectively.' 'How curious,' said Fox, 'how very interesting. And can Storks speak? I mean, I see that you are speaking, but are Storks fluent in ordinary speech?' 'No,' said Stork, shaking her head sadly, 'we ration words, and I've used up mine for at least three centuries. I must be leaving,' and left abruptly.

In her work on Storks, Fox has computed that the average stork utters seventeen words, exactly seventeen, in every century.

The Oyster Child

Once upon a time there was an oyster child. She never said a word, didn't give a damn, just lived quietly at the bottom of the ocean, and did what she could, which in effect meant doing nothing and keeping very still, to protect herself. This required constant effort and she developed an ulcer; but she kept on at it, protecting herself from within herself and keeping her mouth shut tight. Then one day, a diver found her and cut her open. Inside the oyster was the most beautiful pearl anyone had seen. Its near perfection, its extraordinary size, its gentle lustre were absolutely amazing. Everyone came from far and near solely to admire it. And was the oyster pleased? She was probably pleased, but for obvious reasons, she said nothing.

Question: Why did the oyster say nothing?

a. From habit
b. Because by this time she was already dead
c. Out of sheer modesty.

Further Adventures of the One-eyed Monkey

One sunny afternoon when the one-eyed monkey had wandered into the forest behind the river, she came across a woman meditating fiercely. The monkey recognised the famous ascetic—she was the wife of a brahmin who was even more famous—so she leapt into the branches of a large peepal and sat very still, not wanting to disturb her. Suddenly she heard a tremendous crashing, and the god, Indra, fell through the treetops and landed in the clearing. The woman ignored him, but the god knocked her down and proceeded to rape her. Then the god disappeared, and the brahmin appeared. He understood at once that his wife had been raped, so he petitioned the higher gods to avenge the wrong he had thus suffered. Lord Vishnu appeared and asked if there were witnesses. 'Only a one-eyed monkey,' said the brahmin. The monkey was asked to describe what had happened. Now the monkey had a great deal of respect for the woman sage, so she gave her testimony as accurately as possible. When she had finished, Lord Vishnu declared that the god, Indra, had committed a great sin, in that he had sinned against a brahmin. It was necessary for the god to purify himself by performing a sacrifice. Indra was summoned, and performed the sacrifice that requires a stallion. And so it came about that a horse was killed, a god purified, a brahmin appeased, a woman ruined, and a monkey left feeling thoroughly puzzled.

The Mouse and the Lion

One day, a lion caught a mouse. 'Spare me,' said the mouse, 'I am so little and you are so big; but, who knows, perhaps some day I will be able to do you a favour.' The lion thought this funny and let the mouse go. But a few days later the very same lion was caught in a net. After a while the mouse came along. 'Help,' called the lion, 'Help, little mouse. Chew through these ropes. Remember, after all, that you owe me a favour.' The mouse started chewing and then suddenly stopped. 'Why have you stopped?' roared the lion. 'Well, I just thought of something,' said the little mouse, 'You see, I think I have already done you a favour.' 'You haven't,' roared the lion. 'Yes, I have,' said the mouse. 'What?' roared the lion. 'Well, you see,' said the mouse, 'I haven't killed you.'

Svayamvara

Once upon a time, there was a little princess who was good at whistling. 'Don't whistle,' said her mother. 'Don't whistle,' said her father, but the child was good at it and went on whistling. Years went by, and she became a woman. By this time she whistled beautifully. Her parents grieved. 'What man will marry a whistling woman?' said her mother dolefully. 'Well,' said her father, 'we will have to make the best of it. I will offer half my kingdom and the princess in marriage to any man who can beat her at whistling.' The king's offer was duly proclaimed, and soon the palace was jammed with suitors whistling. It was very noisy. Most were terrible and a few were good, but the princess was better and beat them easily. The king was displeased, but the princess said, 'Never mind, Father. Now let me set a test and perhaps some good will come of it.' Then she turned to the suitors, 'Do you acknowledge that you were beaten fairly?' 'No,' they all roared, all except one, 'we think it was magic or some sort of trick.' But one said, 'Yes.' 'Yes,' he said, 'I was beaten fairly.' The princess smiled, and turning to her father, she pointed to this man. 'If he will have me,' she said, 'I will marry him.'

The Saurian Chronicles

Two lizards on a rock are sunning themselves. It's early in October. The rains have just stopped. The younger lizard, wishing to be amiable, says to the elder, 'O wisest of lizards, O long-lived one, tell me once again—if you think it is proper—of the world's beginning.' The Old Lizard's tongue flickers for a moment. Her eyes cloud over. She opens her eyes, and begins, 'Know then, that the sun is a lizard, a fire-breathing dragon, and the earth is an egg. The sun warms the earth. That, my dear, is the essential wisdom. In the very beginning, as the Great Mother Lizard warmed the earth, rocks split open, mountains cracked, and the Giant Lizards, our First Ancestors, saw the light of the sun. Imagine, if you can, their gigantic proportions, their fiery energy, their tremendous strength. Continents were their playing fields. They flew through the skies and sported in the oceans. The eggs that they laid gleamed like domes on the world's horizons. They were the Mothers, the First Mothers; and all would have been well had the Mothers not asked the Supreme Mother for male companions. The Sun in Her bounty granted their wish. At first, the little fellows were playful and happy, but in time, they turned to mischief and turned the Mothers from the worship of the One. Then She grew angry. Her wrath was terrible. She punished the Mothers. And that is why, my dear, we have all been reduced to such diminutive proportions.' The Old Lizard stopped. The Young Lizard squirmed. There was something about the story that he didn't really like, but what could he say? It was the Ancient Wisdom.

The Authentic Lie and From The Bedside Book of Nightmares

These were both difficult books to write. My father was a test pilot and was killed when his plane crashed in December 1953. I was about twelve and traumatized by his death. A recurrent dream in which he's only lost, not gone forever, didn't help. It wasn't till many years later that I could write about any of it.

In *From the Bedside Book of Nightmares* I was, in part, trying to investigate family relationships. In the first section of the book, 'From Baby F with Much Love.' the basic relationship is between daughter and mother. The little creature knows that it is not always lovable, that it can be a nuisance, that it is often disobedient and displeases its mother; but it wants to survive and it would like, if possible, to please.

The third section, 'Snapshots of Caliban,' explores the relationship of the 'children', Miranda and Caliban, to Prospero in *The Tempest*, a play I would return to again and again for inspiration.

From Discourse with the Dead

He died when she was ten in a distant country
and therefore the dreams wouldn't stop.

She made nightly journeys,
        climbed out of bed,
walked to the shore.
        Who is that sleeping giant?
Not your father—of his bones
        are coral made.
She examined his body—his gills
                were slits—
then heaved him up quickly
                on the palm
of one hand
        (like a gigantic balloon,
        like a bloated whale)
                hurried home with him.

'Discourse with the Dead'

Glass Coffins

There were two glass coffins, the prince was in one and Snow-White in the other, and though the sun glared and the leaves fell, the glass was undamaged. They were like pretty marionettes in cellophane wrappers, waiting to live. And the dwarfs were not miners, they were cybernetic experts, wise wiremen doing their damnedest to trigger the dream. Then a thought leaped an arc. A sudden impulse: 'Cough up that apple.' Snow-White coughs. 'Break through the glass.' Her fist crashes. The dream begins. Stepping so gingerly, so timidly on grass she approaches the prince. He has snow-white hair. This is no prince. This is the king. He died in his sleep. She buries him. Then 'Cough up that apple.' Snow-White coughs. 'Break through the glass.' Had she time to consider, she might prefer not to dream.

Snow White and Rose Green

Once upon a time there were two sisters and one got married and one didn't. Or, once upon a time there were two piglets and one went to market and one didn't, or, one was straight and one wasn't. The point is, whatever they did or failed to do, they were a great disappointment to their poor mother. Luckily for them, the two sisters loved one another. When they saw that their mother was growing more and more unhappy, they proposed to her that she cut them in half and out of the two good halves make one splendid one. Their mother refused in high indignation, but she was so wretched that the dutiful daughters went to a surgeon. The surgeon obligingly sawed them in half, then interchanged halves and stuck them together. But there were still two of them. This was a problem. So they went back home and said to their mother, 'Now choose the good one.' But their mother was furious that they had even thought of such a scheme. 'You did it to mock me,' she told them angrily. 'You are both bad children.' When the two sisters heard her say this, the Good One wept, but the Bad One smirked.

'From Baby F With Much Love'

From Caliban's Notebook

They dreamed it. There was no storm,
no shipwreck, nobody came. Prince Ferdinand
was a rock or a tree. M dreamed it.
She said to the tree, 'Bow gracefully,'
and the tree bowed with Ariel in it.
As for revenge—the old man's dream—
even in his dream he could not change them,
not utterly; they still plotted, still schemed—
as though in a play—until Ariel once again
was sent to intervene.
                    And they never got away,
for here we all are, M and myself
and doddering P, still islanded,
still ailing, looking seaward
                    for company.

'Snapshots of Caliban'

Prospero

I made them? Maiden and monster
and then disdained them?
Was there something in me
that fed and sustained them?
Are they mine or their own?
I dare not claim them.

'Snapshots of Caliban'

The Jackass and the Lady

I never met P. Lal, but hoped that I would meet him one day and acknowledge my debt of gratitude; but now he's gone and it's too late. He published my first book of poems in 1967, and after that he published more poems. 'Homage to Circe' is perhaps the first really good poem I wrote. 'From the Travels of Gulliver' takes its imagery from Swift, of course. For him, the giants were yet another means of reflecting on the unpleasantness of humans; but here the metaphor is used for celebration.

Homage to Circe

... this frame wee looke upon, hath been upon our trenchers;
In briefe, we have devoured our selves.

Sir Thomas Browne, Religio Medici 36

She rewards her lovers at random
    like Circe feeding tit-bits to mice,
    almonds to bears,
        and whatever's handy
to miscellaneous swine.
The snake curled about Circe's shoulder
    tracing the whorl of her perfect ear
        with an agile tongue.
The little dog barked,
was a good little dog,
        burrowed
its nose in her warm thighs.
The dog, who barked
        and laughed,
had bright eyes.
I am all animals to you?
I could sit cat-like and gaze
        sisterly.
I am all animals to you,
        could offer myself
            on a wide lily-pad,

drink from your cup and eat from your lip,
turn bird for your purpose, feed
from your hand—disarm the wary.
She draws the birds from the trees,
they would say, she tames the hungry.
                                        Circe,
all animals adore you,
you are all things to each
in the tutelary garden, at the continuous feast.

From the Travels of Gulliver
(revised edition)

And I fell in love with a woman so tall that
when I looked at her eyes I had to go star-gazing.

Tall treasure-houses, moon-
maidenly silence ... Someday I'll teach you
to smile on me. She sways, sighs,
turns in her sleep. Did a feather fall?
Thor's hammer blow makes no effects.
I'm told that it's unnatural
to love giantesses.

In the mornings small dogs bark.
Giantesses strut, fell trees like toothpicks,
while we just stand there, gaze up
their thighs, foreshortened, of course,
but astonishingly pretty.

One day she picked me up off the floor and set
me on her nipple. I tried to ride, but consider my
position—indubitably tricky.

To sleep forever in my fair love's arms,
to make of her body my home and habitation ...

She keeps me about her like a personal worm.
She is not squeamish.

Once,
the giddy and gay were gathered together.
Then she brought me out, bathed me
and kissed me. She put me in a suit
of powder blue silk and set me to sail
in a tepid cup of tea. There
I fought out the storm of their laughter.
I performed valiantly.

I love to hear her laugh,
would not see her grieve,
but a teacup of brine would have seemed
more seemly. I could sail in such a cup,
be swayed by her sighs.

She gluts me on the milk
of healthy giantesses:
'Poor little manikin,
will nothing make you grow?'
I grow. I am growing. You should
see me in her dreams.

The Blue Donkey Fables

The first blue donkey fable was inspired by a card with the Chagall painting of a blue donkey on a bright red bridge and a vase of flowers. The figure of the blue donkey persisted and produced more and more fables. For me a fable often starts with an image. The creature looking out is so eloquent that once the creature starts to speak, the fable develops its own logic. The conventions of the traditional storytelling form and its powerful rhythms generate a momentum, and that momentum can be used to startle the reader with an inevitable but surprising conclusion. Sometimes a stray remark can spark a fable or a poem. The process of writing also involves just waiting to find out what's ready to be written. And the rest is patience and drudgery, drudgery and patience. There's not much to be said for a writer's life? Well, there's the immense satisfaction when the work finds its right shape.

The Blue Donkey

Marc Chagall, *The Blue Donkey*

Once upon a time a blue donkey lived by a red bridge. 'Inartistic,' said the councillors who governed that town. 'A donkey who lives by our bright red bridge must be of the purest and silkiest white or we must request that the said donkey be required to move on.' The matter soon turned into a political issue. One party said that donkeys never had been and never would be white and what was asked of the donkey was grossly unfair. If, on the other hand, the donkey were required to be a nondescript grey (instead of a loud and laughable blue), they would be prepared to accept the solution as a reasonable way out. But the opposing party found a fault in their logic. 'Just because donkeys have never been known to be white,' they pointed out patiently, 'it does not follow that a donkey is incapable of achieving whiteness. Your argument imposes an arbitrary limitation on the creature's potential.' 'Good heavens!' cried the others. 'Are you suggesting that the donkey's blue-ness may be a matter of culpable willfulness rather than a mere genetic mischance?' 'Yes,' responded the logicians. 'Let us confront the creature and you can see for yourselves.'

They approached the donkey, who happened to be munching a bright pink carrot which clashed most horribly with the bright red bridge. 'O Donkey,' they said, feeling they had better get it over with at once, 'we'd like you to turn an inoffensive grey or else move on.' 'Can't and won't,' replied the donkey. 'There you see,' cried half the populace. 'Obviously wilful!' 'No, no,' cried the other half. 'Patently flawed!' And they began to dispute among themselves. The donkey was puzzled. 'I'm a perfectly good donkey,' she said at last. 'What exactly is the matter with you?' 'Your blueness troubles us,' wailed the citizens. 'It clashes with our bridge, as does the pinkness of your carrots. Oh what shall we do? We cannot agree among ourselves.' 'Look again,' advised the donkey.

And so they did; they looked and argued and squabbled and argued and after a while most of them got used to the blueness of the donkey and didn't notice it any more. But a few remained who maintained strongly that blueness was inherent, and a few protested that it was essentially intentional. And there were still a few others who managed to see—though only sometimes—that the Blue Donkey was only herself and therefore beautiful. These last occasionally brought her a bunch of blue flowers which she put in a vase.

The One-eyed Monkey Goes into Print

It was winter. The sun was shining like anything. It was pleasant, it was cool. The temperature was about seventy degrees. The one-eyed monkey was feeling mellow and middle aged. 'I have travelled,' she said. 'I have seen the world. I have lost my tail, six of my teeth and one eye. I have lived. It's time I wrote down what I think about it.' But her friends, the crocodiles, appeared not to have heard.

'Ahem,' she said loudly. 'I'm going to write a book.'

'What for?' murmured one crocodile and went on dozing.

'What about?' muttered the other crocodile and went on basking.

She ignored the first crocodile and addressed the second exclusively.

'About me,' she said strongly.

'Oh,' replied the crocodile. 'Will I be in it?'

'Well, I don't know,' she answered. 'Why would a book about monkeys have crocodiles in it?' But she saw that his eyes were beginning to close, so she added quickly, 'But I'll put you in it.'

'Me as I am?' he asked, stretching out his tail luxuriously.

'No, you as you are in relation to me.'

'Oh.' He sounded dubious.

'And you have to help me,' she put in quickly.

'Help you to write it?' He sounded interested.

'No, no, I can do that. To tell you the truth I've already done it. I want you to help me get it published.'

'Oh.' He thought for a moment. 'Well, I have some contacts with the animal rights people. Send it to them and see what they think.'

So she wrote to them and they wrote back that her title was lacking in human interest. That's what makes a book sell. People are interested in people, you know, they pointed out perfectly pleasantly. But they enclosed the addresses of a few publishers who were non-mainstream.

The one-eyed monkey had a crisis of conscience. Should she change the title? She changed it. It had been called *The Life and Leanings of a One-eyed Monkey.* She went through the text. Wherever the word 'monkey' appeared she put in 'blank'. *The Life and Leanings of a One-eyed Blank.* She said it out loud. She persuaded herself that it had a ring to it. 'I speak in parables,' she told herself bravely. 'The intelligent will know how to read in between the blanks and will appreciate my true, my native, my deliciously malicious monkey wit.'

She sent it off to the publishers. Some wrote back and some misplaced it. Those who wrote back told her bluntly, 'The syntax slithers and the vision is monocular. Who is talking to whom, may we ask? We regret to inform you that your work is entirely lacking in clarity.' The one-eyed monkey felt disheartened. She brooded for days. Then she re-submitted the manuscript with the word 'monkey' typed in clearly. And the miracle happened. A smaller publisher wrote to her saying that they were intrigued by her manuscript and would like to publish it. But please, they begged her to remember that an audience of exclusively one-eyed monkeys was hard to find; could she help to pay for it?

The one-eyed monkey tore her fur in utter despair. Her friends, the crocodiles, happened to notice.

'Oh, all right,' they said. 'We'll help you to rewrite it.'

'But it mustn't be about monkeys and it mustn't be about crocodiles.'

'No,' they agreed. They made suggestions and the monkey rewrote it.

In the end the book achieved a moderate success under the title *The Amorous Adventures of a One-eyed Minx*. 'Is it autobiographical?' the reviewers wondered. 'No,' declared the monkey quite truthfully, 'I do not recognise myself in it.' But her publishers beamed. They patted her back. 'Art transforms,' they murmured kindly.

Dusty Distance

One of the stories the Blue Donkey tells—there's a controversy raging about whether to classify it as fact or fiction—is about the first time she set off on a long, dusty road to make her fortune. In no time at all she met a woman who offered her a carrot, a place to stay and an occupation. 'No thank you,' replied the Blue Donkey. 'You see, I'm a poet, and I have a long way to go.' 'What is a poet?' enquired the woman. This so disconcerted the Blue Donkey that she muttered and mumbled and managed to utter a hasty goodbye and marched onwards. In consequence she nearly ran down a fellow wayfarer.

The Blue Donkey apologised profusely, and to show that she was genuinely sorry and genuinely interested she asked him who he was, and what he was doing and what was his purpose. 'Oh,' he answered sternly, 'I'm on my way to encounter Life. When I find her, I shall take her by the throat and grapple with her.' 'And then?' asked the Blue Donkey, enthralled by this account in spite of herself. 'And then I shall bind her hand and foot and take her home.' 'And then?' The Blue Donkey was almost whispering now. 'And then,' he responded magnificently, 'I shall chop her up and grind her down and put her into delicate mince pies which shall go on the market at four-pence a dozen.' His teeth were gleaming. He turned on her. 'And who are you?' he enquired suddenly. 'Oh, I'm only a poet,' the Blue Donkey murmured with what she considered suitable modesty. But her fellow traveller grew highly indignant. 'Rubbish!' he cried. 'I am a poet. Why you, you are only a bit of Life.' As he said this, his eyes grew round with speculation. The Blue Donkey didn't wait for more. She says that her readers can call her a coward if they like, but she galloped off fast and left him behind in the dusty distance.

Eventually the countryside grew greener. There were landscaped gardens, immaculate woods, and in one of these woods, there was a Beautiful Lady reclining gracefully against a convenient tree trunk. She was reading a book. As the Blue Donkey approached, the Lady looked up and smiled at her. 'Hello,' said the Blue Donkey. 'What are you reading?' 'Poetry,' sighed the Lady. 'I think poetry is so beautiful. I feel I could live on poetry and fresh air forever.' The Blue Donkey edged closer. 'Well, as it happens,' she ventured diffidently, 'I am a poet. Perhaps you would like me to recite some of my verse?' 'Oh. Oh no,' the Lady replied hastily, then she recovered herself. 'The fact is,' she explained, 'that though I have studied many languages and my French and German are both excellent, I have never mastered Blue Donkese. And though I have no doubt whatsoever that your poems are excellent, I fear they would fall on untutored ears.' 'But please, I speak English.' The Blue Donkey could hear herself sounding plaintive. 'Oh,' murmured the Lady. 'But surely as a Blue Donkey, integrity requires that you paint the world as it appears to you. And consider: what have a lady and a donkey in common?'

'Nothing at all,' said the Blue Donkey sadly and she turned away and retraced her steps. At last, she came to the door of the woman she had first encountered. 'Please,' she enquired humbly, 'would you settle for a part-time worker for half a carrot?'

Cythera

Small rivulets ran about her feet
    and backwards to the ocean.
I knew who she was,
    but she walked through the waves
and sat down beside me.
        I stayed very still.
She said that it was hot.
I didn't say anything, but I thought
  to myself I would make a poem
  out of this, of how I sat on a beach
  and gossiped with a goddess, and of
  how kind she was and friendly.
Her movements were slow. 'She's lazy,'
  I decided. 'Olympians have the time
  and are therefore unhurried.'
I wondered how I looked, but she was
  combing her hair. I waited quietly.
  And then she smiled. I was
  very ashamed. She was my friend
  and I had made her a goddess:
          that shamed me.

The Bride

Once upon a time there was a proud young prince, and he had reason to be proud. He was heir to the kingdom, he was handsome and healthy, he had been extremely well educated, and all the social graces that could reasonably be taught had been carefully inculcated. What was more, his father was a king, and his father's father, and his father before that, so that his right to rule was undisputed. Now, when it was time for this young man to marry, he said to his father, 'Father, you have always said that only the best was fit for me. I have the best falcons, and the best hounds and the best stallions in all the world. But where will you find a bride who is worthy of me?' The king didn't think that this would be much of a problem. He had contests instituted throughout the kingdom. There were contests for beauty, and contests for strength, and contests for knowledge and intelligence and wit, and there were skill-testing contests for all sorts of things such as archery and music. When the tests were done, the winners of the contests were presented to the prince. He looked them over. Their credentials were good. Indeed, he began to be afraid that some of their credentials were better than his. 'These women have excelled,' he said to his father, 'but they seem to be lacking in the womanly qualities.' 'Well, of course,' said his father. 'I have weeded these out. You can now choose from those who did not compete.'

Look! Medusa!

Medusa living on a remote shore
troubled no one: fish swam, birds flew, and the sea
did not turn to glass. All was as before.
A few broken statues lay untidily
on the lonely beach, but other than these
there was nothing wrong with that peaceful scene.
And so, when the hero Perseus came to seize
the Gorgon's head, he thought he might have been
mistaken. He watched for a while, but she turned
nothing to stone. The waves roared as waves will,
till at last the hidden hero burned
to be seen by her whom he had come to kill.
'Look! Medusa! I am Perseus!' he cried,
thus gaining recognition before he died.

To Be a Poet

Saying that this was what it felt like to put
the right foot forward, and then the left, saying
that this was the taste of morning porridge,
that of milk, and this other of a niggling
but persistent pain, saying –
that, I suppose, was what was distinctive –
being unable to keep my mouth shut,
my mind from working. But a poet lives
like any other creature, talks perhaps
more than is normal, her doom no brighter,
nor her death less dismal than any other.

Saint Suniti and the Dragon

Here, as in *The Conversations of Cow*, the well-meaning, but faintly ridiculous central figure has my own name. It makes her Indian background clear. It also allows me to place the struggle to be good in three contexts: the private world in which the would-be saint is struggling, the world of the writer in which these efforts are being described, and the outside world in which various atrocities occur all the time. In 'The Trials of the Saint,' her only 'trial' is a mawkish monster, Grendel, who demands more than she is willing or able to give.

'The Solidarity Fables' were added to the Saint Suniti sequence to make the whole long enough to form a book. 'Beauty Incarnate and the Supreme Singer' gently mocks a certain kind of romanticism and harks back to Oscar Wilde's story about the nightingale and the rose.

Section IV
The Trials of the Saint

It so happened that as St Suniti was walking down the street, absorbed in thoughts concerning the complications of a saintly life, she was suddenly confronted by Grendel and his Mama. The old hag leered at the saint. 'Hey Sunny!' she called. 'We're going to have to eat you, you know. It's not for myself, you understand, but Sonny Boy here is starving to death and I've got to feed him.' Suniti glanced at Grendel, a long adolescent with hungry eyes; she looked away quickly. It was a difficult situation: could she talk her way out?

'Please Madam,' she began tentatively, 'as a fellow woman you are surely unwilling to fatten your son by victimising me?'

'Willing or unwilling, don't really matter,' the Mama replied. 'He's got to be fed and that's about it.' Then she looked cunning, and in a fair imitation of Suniti's voice, added slyly, 'But surely, Sunny, as a fellow woman, you ought to be willing to aid and abet?'

Suniti was stumped only for a moment. 'I am,' she replied. 'Come with me and I'll help you to find him something to eat.'

Now as the saint and the mother, with Grendel in tow, stalked the streets, the women ran away or hid in their houses, as did most of the men, though there were one or two who were either too drunk or too brave to take any notice. 'Eat them?' Suniti suggested. Mama glanced at Grendel inquiringly, but Grendel just stood there and looked obstinate. His mouth quivered. It looked as though he was getting ready to howl.

'Poor darling,' his dam explained. 'He has a strong preference for female flesh and he's getting hungry.' She looked at Suniti appraisingly. 'You had better find him something quickly,' she said.

By now they had reached the outskirts of the town and the saint was getting desperate. Only a few days ago she had resolved to take a vow of abstaining from meat; but surely in an exceptional situation an exception might be made. 'Besides, I needn't partake,' she told herself.

'Wait here,' she told the two monsters. She left them huddled by the side of the road and set off rapidly across the fields. Almost immediately, she saw a rabbit; but by the time she had bent down to pick up a stone, the rabbit had vanished. She took the precaution of picking up a number of stones, but saw no more rabbits. Time was running out, and she hurled a stone at a passing cat. She chased it briefly. At the second try she hit her target, but she could not find the corpse.

She was cross with herself, 'I should have cajoled it.' Still, there was no time to waste worrying about what she ought or ought not to have done, or about whether or not she had actually killed the cat. In front of her was a field of cows. Her eyes brightened. A cow would do! She was sure that a cow couldn't run very fast. Indeed, some of the cows were approaching her. But the stones in her pocket would just bounce harmlessly off a cow's back. She looked about for a large rock with which she might be able to brain a cow. She had heard that if you hit cattle in exactly the right spot, they fell down dead. But she couldn't see any rocks, and in any case she didn't know the right spot. Perhaps if she had a sharp stone, she could slit the cow's throat and take the blood to Grendel—as appeasement, so to speak? Then bring Ma and Grendel back and let them finish the job?

Just as she began to sort through the stones, she heard a crashing in the hedgerow. Time had run out. Grendel and his Mama had come to attack. The saint summoned all her fortitude. 'Hello,' she called out cheerfully. 'I was just coming to get you two. Look, here's a whole herd of cows that you can have.' For some reason her words weren't producing the right effect. Grendel and his Mama were glaring at her.

'I—I was just about to slit the throat of that cow over there and bring you her blood. The thing is,' she attempted a quick, embarrassed smile, 'I haven't a container...'

Her voice trailed away. Grendel's Mama took a step forward. 'My son,' roared Mama, 'only eats human flesh.'

St Suniti gave up at this point. She waited for Grendel to tear at her body. But Grendel was sobbing in the background somewhere. In between the sobs she heard him say, 'She's not a proper woman. I'm hungry, Mama. I need a woman's flesh.' For a moment Suniti couldn't understand what was happening. She saw Mama turn, and in the dim light she saw her begin to suckle Grendel. Aware at last that the monster had rejected her, Suniti walked away and left them to it. She wasn't quite sure what she felt, though of one thing she was certain: her sainthood was in shreds.

Beauty Incarnate and the Supreme Singer

For Oscar Wilde

'Look,' said the wren to the iris. 'I'm not a nightingale. You're not a rose. But we too have a tale to tell, a song to sing, that sort of thing.'

The iris was startled. She hadn't noticed the wren. She was engaged in letting the sun shine through her translucent skin, shaping and concentrating so that she glowed blue, with here and there a deep purple, modulating into darkness. 'What do you mean?' she said.

The wren was taken aback. She had thought that her meaning was clear. 'Well,' she began, 'you are not Beauty Incarnate like the rose—'

'I am beautiful!' The iris was irritated.

'Well, yes, that's just what I was getting at,' replied the wren. She hadn't meant to annoy the iris; just the reverse. 'What I was saying was that I am not a Supreme Singer, and you, of course, are not a rose—'

'Don't want to be a rose!' snapped the iris.

'No, of course not,' soothed the wren. 'You are not a rose, but you are very beautiful, and I would very much like to sing your praises.'

'Oh. Go ahead then, but I'm busy at the moment.'

'It's not that simple.' The wren explained. 'Don't you remember? The nightingale sang all night long—'

'*Not* all night,' said the iris firmly.

The wren ignored the interruption. '—with her heart pressed against a thorn—

'I haven't any thorns.' The iris gazed down her long, green stalk, her smooth green leaves, with a certain smugness.

'—and bled to death,' the wren finished triumphantly.

'Why?' asked the iris, jolted at last into proper awareness.

'Because she was suffering. In order to sing you have to suffer,' the wren told her.

'But you're not suffering, are you?'

'I am a little,' replied the wren modestly.

'Are you going to bleed?' By now the iris was thoroughly alarmed.

'Not if you're nice.'

'I am nice. I'm very nice,' the iris assured the wren earnestly. 'And please, you don't have to sing my praises. I don't really care for poetry much.'

'Now you're being cruel.'

'No, no. I am not cruel. And I am not a rose!' the iris protested.

But the wren wasn't listening. She had already begun her plaint.

Sycorax

During the period that these fables and poems were written, there were several deaths. My beloved cat, Suki, died in 1997, as did a favourite aunt. Two dear friends, Anna Mani and Mary Meigs, died in 2001 and 2002. My mother was aging, as was I myself. The sequence, 'Sycorax', is in praise of a bloody-minded old woman. It's also an attempt to follow her to the point of death in order to keep her company and also perhaps to allay my own fear.

Epilogue

O keep the blue wave from closing
over her head,
the foam from dissolving, the wind
from carrying all traces away.

From 'Sycorax'

Deaf Eurydice

For Suki d. 27 July 1997

Sometimes the murmur of longing is so
tentative, and the thought of a caress so
tangential, that the senses strain to hear what,
after all, cannot be said.
                                        And it's then that
the temptation arises: to write a lie
on the water, scribblings on sand, or to descry
from the way the leaves moved and the light
fell what shadows portend. This is twilight
time, Orpheus time, Demeter time, when they
call the long dead, and deaf Eurydice
struggles to hear and hearing nothing falls behind
till her footfall makes no imprint, save on the mind.

For Anna Mani

(1918–2001)

As a young student Anna worked under Sir C. V. Raman. After she retired from the Indian Meteorological Service, she continued to work at the Raman Institute in Bangalore as long as she possibly could .

The brave women I knew have grown old.
Each was like a tree, or like a lighthouse,
or like a gull circling the lighthouse,
or like a dolphin, circling the gull, who
circles the lighthouse, as my thoughts circle
inadvertently.

The Conversations of Cow (abridged)

If *Feminist Fables* was my way of exploring feminism, then *The Conversations of Cow* was my reaction to feeling I had to toe the party line. It was written as bedtime reading for Hilary Clare (aka Christine Donald), who had been the one to introduce me to feminism in a palatable form. I used my own name in the text because I thought that if I was going to make fun of earnest lesbian feminists, it was only fair that I start with myself. *The Conversations of Cow* is not an anti-feminist book, but everyone is absurd sometimes, particularly when zealously pursuing a cause.

I had a logical difficulty with both women's liberation and gay liberation. Questioning gender stereotyping was a central tenet. But if I questioned gender stereotyping, then labeling various groups 'men', 'women', 'heterosexual', 'homosexual', didn't make good sense. It's true that politics often requires simplification, and that a certain amount of generalisation is inevitable in that language has nouns, but I was uncomfortable with it, and particularly with the notion of a rigid identity.

It's difficult for someone with a Hindu background not to think of identity as, to some degree, arbitrary. Even the crudest version of transmigration—you are who you are in accordance with how well or badly you did in your last life—suggests that. And we're told as children—whether we understand it or not is another matter—that the ultimate aim is not to achieve a particular identity, but to divest ourselves of the particulars of identity. It's this that allows me to put the poor Suniti character through various situations in which she feels confused, indignant, and sometimes very foolish. Suniti is intelligent enough to know that who she is depends on who she is in a particular relationship and also on how she is perceived.

Contents

I
The Manifestation

I'm down on my knees, waiting for the goddess to manifest herself. When I open my eyes, The Cow of a Thousand Wishes is standing before me on green turf. Daffodils and crocuses grow at her feet, though, incongruously enough, the cow herself is a Brahmini cow. I like her for that. But what exactly am I to do with this goddess? Make a friend of her? A travelling companion? I look dubiously at her bony back. I pat her shoulder. I rub her forehead, the area between her curving horns. At last the cow betrays that she is alive. She blows on my shirt. I take a step or two back.

'O Cow,' I say, 'would you care to be my travelling companion?'

'What are the terms?' inquires the cow.

'Negotiable,' I answer. 'Perhaps as we stroll we might discuss the matter?'

We would like some information about our future partners, but where to begin?

'When did you come to Canada?' I ask.

'Oh, a few years ago. How did you know I was an immigrant cow?'

How not to be personal?

'Well, it's your horns,' I tell her. 'That astounding curve. It is not typical of Western cows.'

'Yes,' she says complacently.

'Well, what shall we do?'

'Let's go to your place and talk.'

'Sure.' But I'm thinking about the furniture. It was constructed primarily for humans.

'There are steps,' I venture.

'That's okay. I can handle steps.'

I note that she uses certain Americanisms. We amble along.

*

A week later. Cow drops in for a drink again: scotch and water, very colonial—but in a finger bowl.

I am trying to find out how she survives.

'What do you live on?' I blurt it out.

'Welfare,' she replies. 'Not as good as the pickings in India. There, one is supposed to be worshipped as a god, not that one is—but the climate is warmer.'

She proposes to me that I go with her to visit some friends.

'They're cows,' she says. It's a statement of fact. I resolve to make a good impression.

'Borrow a van. They live in the country.'

She might have said 'please', but I rent a van and we drive east till we come to a field of Hereford cows. The Brahmini cow leaps a fence and skips up to them. I feel an absurd surge of national pride. She looks so graceful compared to them. I wait to be called. There is much nuzzling and nodding among the cows.

At last she returns. 'Have you any credentials?'

'Driver's licence? Credit cards?'

'No, stupid. SPCA, Greenpeace, membership of the zoo, that sort of thing.'

I haven't. We're stuck.

'You might tell them I'm wholly vegetarian?' I make the suggestion diffidently. Cow gives me a sharp look.

'All right,' she says, turning abruptly. We start walking towards the others.

'I ought to tell you,' Cow informs me, 'that this is a Self-Sustaining Community of Lesbian Cows.' So, Cow and I have something in common.

The largest cow says 'Hello' to us. 'I ought to tell you …' she begins.

'Yes, I know,' I say. Have to watch these interruptions. But let's get on with it. 'How do you manage about children?'

'AI.' Well, there's brevity.

'What about property rights?'

'We're fighting it in the law courts.'

'How,' I begin—how not to be rude?—'How did you acquire the land in the first place?'

'Willed. Once upon a time there was a strong-minded lesbian who was determined to leave her all to A Good Cause.'

This is cow number two. It's time for introductions.

'I'm Suniti,' I say.

'Su? What?'

I tell them again. They get it wrong.

'Well, we'll just call you Sue for short, just as we do Baddy here.' Her real name is Bhadravati. I look at Cow, who looks away. Later she says to me, 'Well, you have to adjust.'

But right then and there I say distinctly, 'No, you will not call me Sue for short.'

There's an awkward pause. They tell me their own names.

'I'm Boudicca,' says the largest cow. Perhaps she detects the beginnings of a smile. 'I liked the name,' she says simply. I'm quite disarmed.

'I'm Cowslip,' says the second cow. 'I do the negotiating for this community of ours.' She looks like a very cow-like cow.

'Hi,' I say. 'Very pleased to meet you, Cowslip.'

'Very pleased to meet you too, Snooty.' My jaw muscles tense. I'm a little surly with the other three cows. Their names, it transpires are Lou-Ann, Ariadne and Sybilla—Sybbie for short.

'So, you're both from India,' says Lou-Ann. 'That's really great.'

'Why is it great?'

'Why, well, it just is, you know. You must tell us all about it.'

'It's very nice,' I say with deliberate inanity. I think I intend to be slightly insulting, but they don't notice.

'I've always wanted to go to India. I dream about it. Only last night I had a really beautiful dream.' Sybilla, of course.

She tells us about it—at some length. The only thing that is at all clear is that she plays a prominent part.

Boudicca decides it's time to be gracious. 'Why don't you have supper with us and stay overnight?'

My heart sinks, but Baddy is looking hugely delighted. Baddy and Sunny—where will it end?

'Sure,' she says. 'Thanks.' I conjure up visions of boiled dandelion soup. No, not even boiled. The fact is I am not a vegetarian. But this is not the time for confessions.

Supper is as bad as I expected. I can eat almost nothing. I watch Baddy hoping she won't notice and guess the reason, but she's engaged by Ariadne. They seem to be flirting. I become increasingly bad-tempered. It occurs to me to ask for some milk. But as I glance up at the cows, I'm suddenly overcome by an odd shyness. I say nothing, and try to swallow some oats and cold water.

At last Lou-Ann notices. 'I have a package of rusks. Perhaps you would like them?'

I accept gratefully. Boudicca and Lou-Ann express concern, 'You ought to make sure you get plenty of greens …'

We talk about food. I am very careful; I think it would be better to discuss something else. I make the attempt, but Sybilla interrupts.

'I had a dream the other day,' she tells us calmly, 'in which I had turned into a Carnivorous Cow. The odd thing is, I really enjoyed myself.'

'I had a curious dream too,' I put in nervously. 'About a Glyptodon … an extinct mammal …'

'What did you eat?' Baddy asks. No one is listening to me. We are all waiting for Sybbie's answer.

'A birthday cake.' Poor pathetic Sybbie. I feel relieved, but Baddy is relentless.

'What was it shaped like?'

'Well,' Sybilla looks vague, then she points at me. 'It was shaped like her, except, of course, it was pink and white.'

My hands and feet have grown icy cold. The best offence is defence, I decide. No, the other way about.

'And did you carve her up?' My tone is inquiring.

'No,' says Sybbie. She sounds perfectly innocent. I can't tell whether she means to be malicious or is merely stupid.

But Lou-Ann has decided it's best to get it over with.

'And then what happened?'

'Well, we all sang happy birthday and I nibbled her toes.'

'And then?'

'Then I woke up.'

Ariadne seems strangely excited. 'What did her toes taste like, Sybbie?'

'They tasted salty,' Sybilla says thoughtfully, 'like peanuts.' Oh, Sybilla.

The others are now willing to let the matter drop, and Baddy has moved over to sit beside me, but I no longer want her sympathetic looks. I am very cool. I speak to the cows in my most detached (but authoritative) manner: 'As you know, cows are generally regarded as a herbivorous species. Any change in their habits would certainly be disastrous.'

'Yes,' Baddy says nastily, 'It would change the world balance.'

Boudicca takes charge. 'It's time to clear up and find a bunk for our guests.' There's a slight emphasis on the last word. Baddy and I try to make ourselves useful. I think I've behaved badly, but it doesn't seem fair. I feel cross.

Baddy and I are supposed to sleep next to each other. I move as far away from her as I can, but later it gets cold. I curl up closer. She puts a hoof lightly on my shoulder.

⋆

'Baddy,' I say casually the next morning, 'I'm hungry. I'll just run into town and get some breakfast.'

'My name is Bhadravati,' she answers formally.

'I'm sorry,' I reply. 'I'll just …'

'I'll go with you.'

How to explain that I do not want Bhadravati to go with me?

I acquiesce. We drive to a pizza place, walk in and sit down, B as best as she can.

'I would like a vegetarian pizza, please. Anything for you?' I ask B politely.

'Yes,' she says, 'I like pizzas.'

'Two pizzas, please.' What I really wanted was a juicy hamburger …

The pizzas arrive, and so does the manager.

'Everything all right, sir?'

'Yes, thank you, but I am not a "Sir", I am a lesbian, and my friend is a cow.'

'GET THAT COW OUT OF HERE!'

I draw myself up to my full height. (He's still a foot taller.) 'That cow is a citizen of planet earth. If you throw us out, I shall complain about you to the Human Rights Commission.'

But he's thrusting his chest into my face. Cow gets up. I slink past. He stands in the doorway yelling at us. I feel beaten.

Inside the van I discover that B has appropriated the pizzas. We eat them silently and return to the farm. We tell the cows what happened to us.

'Oh,' says Cowslip. 'You said who you were. You must learn how to pass. Let me explain.'

We're in for a lecture. Cow and I settle back.

'The world is neatly divided into Class A humans and Class B humans. The rest don't count. How they look, walk and talk depends on television, but there are some factors which remain constant for years. For example, Class A people don't wear lipstick, Class B people do. Class A people spread themselves out. Class B people apologise for so much as occupying space. Class A people stand like blocks. Class B people look unbalanced. Class A people never smile. Class B people smile placatingly as often a possible. Now, it's obvious that cows have all the characteristics of Class A people. Our size and shape take care of that. Your best bet is to let them assume you are one.'

'Is that what you do?' I ask Cowslip.

'Yes,' she says, clipping the word, and stands there with her four feet firmly planted.

I essay a smile, but Cowslip's face remains expressionless. It's a demonstration. I am impressed, but not convinced. She seems to be suggesting ... I'd like to question her, but do not dare.

As we drive back, Bhadravati is quiet.

'What are you thinking about?'

'Oh nothing,' but finally she tells me. 'I'm wondering whether cows are really like men.' The thought doesn't please her.

'Perhaps they have more in common with women?' This seems to please even less.

*

B spends the night at my place. At about six in the morning I hear her knocking about in the kitchen downstairs. 'Looking for oats,' I think sleepily. There's a tremendous crash. I discover B in a pile of cans. Now I remember the corned beef. B is furious.

'You're an unscrupulous liar,' she tells me briefly. Then she walks out.

I dress quickly, gulp some tea, and set out after B. I walk up and down the streets. I ask people, 'Have you seen a large white cow anywhere?' Most of them pretend not to have heard me. A small brown woman in desperate search of a large white cow —I suppose, in their terms, it is weird. I walk into a restaurant. The only other occupant is a large white man chomping away at the edge of a pizza. I stare at him. The set of his shoulders is somehow familiar …

'Baddy!' I shout. I clap him on the back. Baddy glares at me. 'Baddy, I swear I'll never touch beef again. I was corrupted in North America. You know quite well Hindus don't eat beef …'

The waiter comes up. 'Give the lady a hamburger,' Baddy growls.

'Yes, sir.'

The hamburger arrives. I leave it untouched. Baddy finishes the entire pizza. I give her my wallet, Baddy pays, and I follow her out. Outside the restaurant she winks at me, then she remembers she's angry with me. She frowns.

'Baddy,' I plead. 'We've got to talk.'

She grunts and sets off down the street with an appalling swagger. She jostles everyone; one or two people are knocked off the pavement. I follow in her wake. At the lights Baddy crosses on a flashing green. A sports car comes to a screeching halt. The woman driver yells something. Baddy yells back, 'You fucking cunt!'

I'm horrified. I'm no longer sure I want to talk to Baddy, but we're at my house.

'Baddy,' I say to her, 'You're not a man, you're a lesbian cow. How could you say that?'

'Who are you calling a fucking cow? Ha!' Then she grins. 'Did you see her face?' she asks mischievously.

I did see her face, and I am not amused. I repeat my question, 'Why did you say that?'

'It was part of the role.' She looks uncomfortable.

'There are all sorts of men, Baddy. If you had to pass, why couldn't you have passed for a gentle one?'

'Haven't got the money.'

'That's no answer.'

'Yes, it is. Okay,' she says, tossing her horns carelessly, 'next time I'll be a real gent.'

'Your manner, Baddy, is less than penitent.'

'So's yours, Sue. So's yours. What about that mess in the kitchen there?'

This reminds me that I'm still hungry. I put all the cans of beef into the garbage and open a can of asparagus.

⋆

For the next two days Baddy and I don't speak; but on Wednesday I discover a number of packages on my desk. Cow stands by and grins at me.

'These are for me?'

Cow nods.

'How did you get them?' There's something about my tone she doesn't like.

'Waal, Sue,' she drawls in a parody of I don't know whom, 'I just strolled into a drugstore and told the salesgirl —'

'Saleswoman,' I interrupt.

'Yeah,' Baddy is imperturbable. 'I told the cute little salesperson that I wanted my girl, Sue, to make herself smarter, you know, start looking like a real woman; and so, would the cutie please help me to buy some make-up. No, I didn't say "please", I just told her, and she started scurrying about.'

I wait till Baddy finishes. Then I pick up the parcels and impale them on her horns. Lipsticks roll about. Face powder cascades over Baddy's face and a trickle of eye-liner runs down one ear. She looks extremely funny. I begin to laugh. At the same time I notice she is crying.

'Look, Bhadravati, I'm sorry,' I say. 'It was just your manner. It put me off.'

I fetch damp paper towels and wipe her face. We sit down and drink some tea. She's still sniffling, but I'd like an explanation.

'It was sweet of you to get me these presents,' I say patiently, 'but—by the way, how did you pay for them?'

'Your credit cards,' she mutters. I let that pass.

'As I was saying, it was sweet, but what was the point?'

'I was trying to make you into a Class B human.' She says it just like that. It's obvious, but still shocks me somehow.

'Why, Bhadravati? Don't you like me as I am?'

'Of course I do.' Bhadravati is entirely serious. 'But you see, we have to survive. And I thought if you dressed up as a Class B human and I dressed up as Class A, we'd manage better. Won't you consider it?'

I do consider it. I sulk for an hour, then sneak up to the bathroom and try on the make-up. I even begin to enjoy myself. When I'm satisfied, I descend the stairs and show myself to Bhadravati.

'How do I look?'

'You look charming,' she says.

I preen a little.

'But your skin is still brown.'

'Yes?' I say, challenging her, but Bhadravati is in a good mood.

'It's all right.' She winks at me. 'You'll pass.'

'Bhadravati, let's try it out. Let's go for a walk.' I'm very excited.

B rises. She opens the door elaborately for me. We set out. An elderly gent tips his hat to us, his elderly wife beams at us. Everyone seems to approve of us. I feel so good, so safe, so respectable ... I belong!

That night my conscience bothers me. 'B,' I say, 'Aren't we being false to ourselves?'

'What?' She turns down the TV. 'It's all right,' she says, 'identity is fluid. Haven't you heard of transmigration? And you call yourself a good brahmin.'

I don't, but I let that pass.

'But, B, aren't you really a lesbian cow?'

'That seems rather exotic ...,' she says. 'What's wrong with being a white man?' But she sees I'm upset and stops teasing. 'All I ever wanted,' she says seriously, 'was to be an ordinary animal.'

'Oh, but you are. You're perfectly ordinary —' I stop short and try again. 'When I first saw you, B, standing foursquare in that green field, I thought you were a goddess.'

'And so I am,' she says complacently. I'm stunned.

Her mood changes. 'Go on,' she says, poking me in the ribs. 'You're putting me on.'

It's hopeless to try to carry on the conversation. 'Good night,' I say. I go to sleep, and dream that Bhadravati and I have undergone plastic surgery. We have the faces of women and the hindquarters of cows and we wear top hats like true gentlemen. We're walking through a forest, looking for something. At last, we sit down and villagers approach us and put garlands of flowers around our necks. They want our blessings. Bhadravati blesses them lavishly and also gives them our top hats. Then our wings slide out and we drift heavenwards. I can feel the sun warming my back and have the strongest possible sense of good-will towards everyone and everything.

When I repeat my dream to B, she chortles happily, 'Now we know who you really are—Saint Suniti without her top hat.'

*

Three days later B confronts me. 'Suniti, you're a dreamer, but dreams and conversation are not enough. Let's do something. Have you any money?'

'Sure,' I say. 'I work for a living.'

B is curious. 'What do you do?'

'I teach English Literature.'

B laughs.

'Just because I'm a woman and a foreigner, it does not follow I cannot be a university professor.'

'And a lesbian,' B adds, looking mischievous. 'But really,' she goes on, 'English Literature?'

'Onlookers,' I tell her loftily, 'often see more than participants.'

B isn't listening. 'If you have money, we could do something. Money is power. Money transforms.'

'I haven't much,' I interject hastily. 'What do you mean, money transforms?'

B shrugs. 'Super Cow today has an independent income.' It's obvious she has been watching TV again. For the moment she offers no elucidation, but a couple of hours later she returns to the subject.

'Suniti,' she says, 'will you give me some money?'

I hedge. 'What do you want it for and how much?'

'I want to go on a journey. I want 500 dollars.'

I'm not sure that B understands money. 'How far can you go on 500 dollars?'

'Oh, one can do a lot with 500 dollars.'

'What?'

'One can hire ten women to work ten hours a day for ten days at 5 cents an hour.'

'That's 50.00 dollars, B. What good is that?'

'You buy their time and add it to your own. and extend your life by one thousand hours.'

'What nonsense!'

'Can't you understand that money is power? You can fly through the air. You can treat a supermarket like a giant treasure trove. You can have three wishes and a bit left over. You can, if you like, become invisible. You can buy life, time and energy. You can make people do what you want.'

'Within limits.'

'Of course. It depends on how much you've got.'

'B, if money is power, why should I give it to you?'

'Because you like me.'

I try again. 'If money can do all that, isn't it better to use the money to buy more?'

'More what?'

'More money.'

'Miser!'

I explain to B that I sell my time, in other words, my life, to make money. I want to save some so that eventually I'll have an independent income. B nods.

'What will you do with your time then?'

'Write.'

'Dreamer!'

'What's wrong with dreams?'

'They make nothing happen.'

B goes away, but soon returns and sits there looking patient.

'This life you're leading,' she begins, 'has it occurred to you that it's too sheltered?'

I temporise. 'Perhaps. Let's do something.'

'What?'

'Let's think of a project. A realistic dream. World Peace. Non-discrimination Against Lesbians. Vegetarianism...'

'Do you think that's funny?'

'No, sorry. It was almost a kind of despair. What is needed is a transformation.'

B relents. 'You're just not practical.'

'What about something specific,' I venture, 'like the single-minded pursuit of personal happiness?'

'Be serious!' B is getting angry again.

'Sorry, B. I am trying to be serious, but I'm frightened.'

'Of what?'

Doesn't she know? I'm terrified of people.

'B,' I say suddenly, 'let's throw a party. Let's have fun.'

B is mollified, but I'm in for it now. She's smiling. She doesn't realise how awkward it's going to be. What am I to say? 'Friends this is Cow, Cow this is Friends'?

*

It's a small party. I've invited three colleagues, mostly white—I am not colour conscious—and entirely liberal.

Peter arrives first. Sometimes he drives round the block or waits in his car till the exact hour. A real gent—an example to Baddy. I wonder how he and she will get on.

I introduce them. B has decided to be gracious. She smiles. They talk solemnly about the joys of the country, the pleasures of pastoral. B occupies the entire sofa. She has thrown a turquoise and gold Benarasi stole across her shoulders. She looks magnificent. Peter, as usual, is being shyly gallant.

I think about dinner and hope no one comments about the food being vegetarian. But when Julia arrives, the first thing she wants to know is what's for dinner and congratulates me on my newly found vegetarianism. B doesn't look at me. She and Julia discuss salad. Peter looks on benignly.

I needn't have worried. Cow evidently has considerable charm. They don't seem to have noticed that she is a cow. Perhaps they all have excellent manners? I, myself, feel rather excluded. I go into the kitchen and toss salad. We drink more wine. Julia says she is getting hungry, so does Cow. Peter, as usual, looks patient. I explain that we are waiting for Kate. The telephone rings. A domestic disaster. Kate is going to be very late. We should start dinner.

They all eat hungrily and say how much they're enjoying the food. I toy with the salad. Halfway through Kate rushes in. She gives us a vivid account of her freezer overflowing. The food-supply people brought too much food. Cabbages and cutlets cascaded down the pavement. 'Oh,' I think, 'Cow isn't going to let that pass.' I flee into the kitchen. When I return they're deep in a discussion about cryology. Cow is saying that she doesn't envy the frozen mammoth. It's immortality she would not want.

Then Kate speculates, 'I wonder if the flesh of the mammoth was still fresh?'

Now surely there will be a row. Don't they realise that Cow is an animal? My palms are clammy. I feel a little sick. By the time I recover, Cow and Kate are happily discussing mutual consent: whether it's all right to eat meat if there's mutual consent between eater and eaten.

I decide to stop worrying, until over coffee I hear Cow expounding an obscure version of the Theory of Reincarnation. One becomes what one has eaten. For example, if one has eaten a great deal of beef, or a great many snails ... They are charmed by the concept. As Peter says, 'It offers a measure of self-determination.' And Julia adds, 'And constant control, the sense that destiny is in one's own hands.' Kate is looking wistful—undoubtedly concocting an exotic diet.

At last they leave. Cow has been a great success. My nerves are in shreds.

★

The following day Cow is in an excellent temper. 'That was a pleasant party.' She beams. 'Let's have some more. Haven't you got any other friends?'

'Sure.' I pretend my mouth is full of porridge. Luckily, she drops the subject. As she's in an expansive mood, I take advantage.

'B,' I say casually, 'were you ever in love?'

A reminiscent smile crosses her face. She leans back to talk, but it wasn't her reminiscences I was leading up to. I interpose a question. 'And did all your affairs end happily?'

'No,' she admits, 'in that they ended, it was an unhappy end if you see what I mean—in that an ending is an unhappy thing.' I like to see her stumble occasionally. She looks less smug. We brood for a moment.

'B,' I say suddenly, 'I think I'm becoming a misogynist.'

'That's rather awkward,' she replies, 'since you are yourself —'

'A woman. I know. Sometimes I think there's been a mistake. The wrong soul in the wrong body.'

'Who do you think you are then?'

'A cow?'

'A male cow or a female cow? A lesbian cow or a heterosexual one? Pedigreed or non-pedigreed?'

I look at B to see if she's mocking me, but she's merely looking politely interested.

'Perhaps not a cow,' I say hastily. 'Perhaps I'm a snail.'

'A snail?'

'Yes, they're bisexual.'

'And as a snail, do you like other snails?'

'I like eating them.' It's an honest answer and has slipped out before I could think. To my horror my mouth is watering, and I can taste garlic butter.

Cow's gaze remains dispassionate. After a while she asks, 'Why do you hate women?'

'Because they hurt.' That slipped out too.

'What? All of them?'

'No, only if one happens to fall in love.' I stare at my hands.

When she speaks, her voice is gentle. 'Suniti, what's wrong? What is the matter?'

'Oh, I got involved with someone. Didn't work out. Broke up. The usual thing,' I mumble rapidly.

B's voice is still gentle. 'Suniti,' she says, 'what do you want?'

'A drug, a dream, a facile perfection.' By this time, I am so embarrassed I take myself off to bed and eventually fall asleep in a terrible temper.

In the morning I apologise to Cow for being childish. She merely points to a bottle on the table. It seems to be filled with vitamin pills.

'What's that?'

'An aphrodisiac.' Is she joking? 'You take one a day. Then you and the world fall in love with each other.'

'Just like that?' I'm slightly shocked by the lack of discrimination.

'It isn't that good and doesn't always work. But it's quite good. Try some?'

'Have you tried it?'

'I eat it by the handful.'

I suspect that Cow is teasing me. 'How,' I say at last, 'does one know when it has worked, whether, in fact, it has worked or not?'

'That's the beauty of it. One doesn't.'

She smiles. I try to smile back, but I feel angry. Cow has been mocking me. I stalk out of the house. When I return, Cow tries to talk to me.

'Why are you angry?'

'I'm not. Just tired.' I'm not going to expose myself to such silliness further.

'Oh come on, Suniti. Don't be absurd. Tell me why you're angry.'

'Life is absurd. As for being sensible, let's drop the matter.' I try to sound quiet and dignified.

'Don't be so cross. Come and sit down and talk to me,' she coaxes.

I say wearily, 'There really isn't anything to talk about. We're both tired. Let's go to sleep. Good night.' I make my exit feeling very patient, long-suffering and serious.

*

That night I dream. Cow has transformed herself into a woman. She is wearing a sari and sitting on the lawn of a large house under a banyan, feeding chipmunks. A crow squawks somewhere. I can hear sparrows. I sit there, gazing at Bhadravati. I feel such admiration and love for her. She smiles at me. I approach closer. She ruffles my fur. I feel very clean and alive and healthy. I'm a well-kept poodle. I sit at her feet and look up at her. I'm an excellent animal. When she rises to go into the house, I walk beside her up to the door; but since she hasn't called me, I stay outside and chase chipmunks.

II
Bhadravati

When I wake up, I resolve not to say a word about the dream. I feel vulnerable.

She's sitting at the breakfast table, wearing a sari. The April sun is shining on her hair. She's beautiful. I recoil a little, though my body keeps walking. I enter the room. I don't want to deal with this. Why did B have to change into a woman?

'You've changed?' I say non-committally.

'Do you like it?'

'Yes, well.' I'm dithering. 'But, of course, B, you are always you, whoever you are—if you see what I mean.'

B is smiling. 'Come and sit down. Would you like some tea?'

'Yes, please,' I answer. I must pull myself together. B is obviously in charge. I can't let her have it all her own way. I must say something, be something. What's the right tone? I decide to be formal.

'Thank you,' I say when she brings me my tea. 'Did you sleep well last night?'

'I dreamed,' she says, smiling at me full in the face. Her beauty gives her so much assurance.

I manage to ask, 'And what did you dream?'

'I was in India again, playing with the chipmunks. I had a dear little poodle ...'

Is she mocking me? She isn't even looking at me. She's staring into space, seeing herself in the sunlit garden.

I decide to be brave. 'What was the poodle's name?'

'Let me think. Su-, Suzanne! That's right. Her name was Suzy. She was so loving, so intelligent.' B smiles as she thinks about Suzy.

My mind is made up. Whoever I become, I'm not going to be a poodle. If necessary, I shall be churlish. But what stance should I take? I wish B wasn't quite so beautiful. I feel resentful. What happened to Cow? Where's my friend Baddy? If only she wasn't so very attractive. Perhaps I should be Baddy? I decide to be myself: simple, sincere, earnest Suniti.

'B,' I say looking at her frankly. 'Why have you decided to become a woman?'

'Because I felt like it.'

I try again. 'Don't you see how awkward it is?'

'Why is it awkward? It's usually much easier to explain away a woman than to explain a cow.' Her voice is so reasonable, her smile so friendly.

'B,' I say in sudden exasperation, 'if you're going to be a woman, I'm going to be something else.'

'What would you like to be?' She seems genuinely interested.

'A goldfish!'

'Are you really sure you'd like to be a goldfish? It seems so confining.'

I push back my chair and stand up. 'I have to get to work,' I say shortly.

All day long I think of B. Why is there a problem? What difference does it make that she is no longer a cow? I feel resolute and angry. I decide to do nothing. I shall treat B exactly as though she were B, which she is, who she was, well as she would have been...

When I get home that evening, I slap her on the back, 'Come on, B. Let's eat out and go to a movie.'

'Suniti,' B says, 'since when have you adopted this hearty manner?' She isn't angry, just puzzled.

I feel sheepish, then catch myself. First a poodle, then a sheep. Where will it end?

'I was just being friendly,' I say lightly

'I've made dinner,' she informs me. 'Let's eat and then I want to talk to you.'

Dinner is excellent, though it is vegetarian. I find myself thinking, 'Though she's no longer a cow, she's still vegetarian, and still Indian, is she still ...?' I break off the thought and eat. B helps me to more rice. 'I feel like a guest in my own house,' I think bitterly.

'Dinner was excellent,' I say politely. 'Thank you.'

'Good,' she replies. 'Now let's talk.'

I brace myself, then say I need a drink. 'Would you like one?'

'No thank you.' Oh Baddy, Baddy, gone are the days when you downed your whisky and talked fake American.

I sit down. 'What did you want to talk about?'

'About you, Suniti. You haven't really been yourself today. You're behaving so oddly.'

'I'm very much myself,' I say in feigned surprise. 'See, same person, same body.' That last remark is intentionally pointed. B ignores it.

'You seem distant somehow. Are you hiding something?'

'Oh, you know me. 'Tis my secret sorrow. I'm an incurable romantic.' I'm not sure who that was supposed to be. I'm losing control.

B puts a hand on my arm—oh wicked B. 'Suniti,' she says, 'what's the matter with you? Why are you pulling away from me?'

'Just have a headache, feel a bit bearish,' I growl. I get up, and slouch about. So now I'm a bear? She fetches aspirins.

'Sit down. We really have to talk.' I sit obediently. 'Now, why did you say you wanted to be a goldfish?'

'Oh, I don't know. It's an experience.'

'But a goldfish, Sue?' Why is she calling me Sue? Suddenly I'm angry.

'Why are you calling me "Sue"?'

'I'm sorry, Suniti. It just slipped out. Don't be so sensitive.'

'Perhaps I should be a pachyderm?'

'Well, yes, that's a possibility. What else have you thought of?'

'A bear, a sheep and a poodle!' I shouldn't have said that. It's time to take this conversation by the horns, so to speak, and steer it around.

'Why did you decide to stop being a cow?' I say to her.

'So that's what's bothering you. I see.' Her voice trails away. 'I see...'

I wish I was something small and fluffy. I wish I could hide in B's sari, bury my face in B's shoulder. I wish B would cradle me. I feel like crying. Then to my horror, I am crying. That's not what I meant to do. That's not who I meant to be. B cuddles me.

After a while, I wash my face and blow my nose. 'I feel like a fool,' I tell B.

'Never mind, love,' she says comfortably. 'These transformations are always hard. You'll get used to it.'

That night I dream that Cow has returned to tuck me in. As she sits there, I hear her murmuring, 'I had forgotten you were a misogynist.'

⋆

But it's B who wakes me. 'Come on,' she calls. 'Wake up. We're going.' I dive under the bedclothes. I know I look scruffy in the morning.

'Where?' I mutter from under the bedclothes.

'On a holiday.'

I get up and dress. I decide I might be better off as a thick-skinned herbivore.

'Where are we going?' I ask.

'To see a friend. She's wise and kind and lives in the country.'

'Who else will I meet there?'

'My sister.'

'Your sister!' How to ask B whether her sister is a cow or a woman? 'B, what's her name?'

'Charlotte.'

'How can her name be Charlotte, if she's a Hindu?'

'She's English. Do get ready.'

'But, B,' I persist. 'What's going to happen? Are we going on a quest?'

'A what?'

'A journey of exploration. We undergo ordeals, and then I find out who I really am.'

'As far as I'm concerned, we're merely stepping into the next province to visit friends.' She smiles. 'Still, it's just possible you'll get what you want ...'

I dare not ask any more questions.

★

At first I'm glad I'm driving; I cannot look at B, I have to look at the road ahead. We stop for coffee. While the car's being filled, the garage mechanic chats with B. I feel resentful. Why do I have to do the driving and pay for everything? Inside the café I complain that my neck hurts.

B is sympathetic. 'Shall I drive?'

B takes over. She's a far better driver than I am. I stare out of the window. When we get to Montréal, we check in at a hotel, and B pays. I hope she hasn't been reading my thoughts. We walk about the city, have dinner and spend the evening at a lesbian bar. B makes friends with half a dozen women. I sit down and feel like a lump. I understand only a tenth of the French. B is being kind to me; she introduces me to the other women. They decide for some reason that my name is Sulky. What a nice name. I'm patted on the back, then ignored. After a while we return to the hotel.

'This can't go on,' I tell myself. 'You should never have agreed to this trip, but now that you have, pull yourself together and try to be pleasant.' I breathe regularly, count to five hundred, and fall asleep.

The following morning, I feel cheerful. The sun is shining, B is still B, I am still me and the people we're going to meet might prove interesting.

B has changed into slacks and a shirt, and looks more ordinary. What am I saying? But she does. I am less in awe of her. And driving through the countryside has put me in a good humour.

At the farmhouse, Charlotte is standing outside the door ready to greet us. She is tall—at least six feet two inches—and fat. Her blue eyes laugh, her blonde hair blazes in the bright sun. She and B embrace one another like long-lost sisters. I can't understand how they can be sisters, but they seem to be. I stand there awkwardly. When we are introduced, Charlotte gives me such a friendly smile that I smile back at once. We troop into the house.

Margaret is also tall, but slender like an egret. She smiles at us shyly. I feel we have interrupted her, but she makes us welcome. Suddenly I hear music, just a bar or two, bird-like and clear. It enters the room, stays for a minute, then exits abruptly. I look at Margaret.

'That's Madeleine,' says Margaret. 'She's very elusive. You'll meet her at dinner.'

B has disappeared. Margaret indicates the open window. B has changed into Cow again. She and Charlotte are walking in the garden. Charlotte has her arm about B's neck. They look peaceful. I don't know what to do with myself. Margaret sets me to chopping vegetables.

Charlotte dashes in and grabs a sandwich. She calls out something over her shoulder. Margaret explains, 'She and Bhadravati haven't seen each other for a very long time. They're lunching together.'

Margaret and I sit down at the table. Margaret smiles.

'Madeleine probably won't be joining us. You see, she's in love.'

There's a pause. I ask, 'With whom is she in love?'

'That's uncertain,' says Margaret. 'Sometimes I think she's in love with the weather. The important thing is that she is in love.'

I tell Margaret about Baddy's love philtre. Margaret listens attentively. I like Margaret. She makes me feel sensitive and intelligent.

⋆

At dinner that evening, B has changed into a sarong and kurta. She looks fresh and clean, like a wood nymph. It's easy to imagine her in the wooded valley below the house. She also looks more mischievous. Margaret's face is as kind as ever, as is Charlotte's. The empty place is for Madeleine, who still hasn't appeared.

B says in a conversational voice, 'Suniti is a misogynist.'

And I had so wanted to make a good impression. Margaret turns her slow blue gaze inquiringly at me.

'Do you hate all women all the time?' she asks.

Charlotte nods encouragingly. 'It must be hard work,' she murmurs.

'No,' I mumble. 'Only some, some of the time.'

I feel miserable, but they're not going to let the matter drop.

'How do you feel about men?' Charlotte asks.

'And birds?' Margaret inquires.

'And wood nymphs and goddesses?' B continues.

'I don't like men very much. Birds are okay. And I don't know much about nymphs and goddesses.' I reply sullenly. They're never going to like me now. I want to say, 'I don't care if they don't like me because I don't like women.' I feel stupid and absurd.

'At which times do you dislike which women?' Charlotte again.

'When they make me feel stupid. When they hurt.' I know I'm making a fool of myself.

'There, there.' Margaret pats my shoulder.

'Suniti is very sensitive,' B murmurs.

When I've stopped snuffling into my napkin, they turn on me again.

'Suniti thinks she would like to be a cow,' B says as though in explanation.

'She thinks that cows are thick skinned,' B adds.

They study me intently. They're asking themselves whether or not I would make a good cow. I can feel myself fading under that threefold gaze. I make an effort.

'It doesn't really matter whether or not I would make a good cow,' I tell them firmly. 'The point is, do I want to be a cow?'

'Do you?' they ask simultaneously. At this moment they seem to me like three witches. I'm saved by Madeleine. She dances in rather than walks in. She takes her place and smiles enchantingly. I forget everything. I am dazzled. I would stare unblinkingly, but the light seems to flicker whenever she moves.

B kicks me under the table. 'Suniti, do wake up. You look exactly like a little owl.' I smile vaguely.

Madeleine laughs. 'It's the light,' she says. 'When one comes in out of the dark, the light dazzles.' I don't explain that I haven't been in the dark.

'Where's X?' Margaret asks.

Madeleine's golden eyes lose their light. 'X is gone,' she says blankly. Then her eyes light up. 'But she'll be back tomorrow.' I try to imagine X.

'I would like,' I say suddenly, 'to be a mysterious stranger.'

'Oh, Suniti,' Margaret is kind. 'You are very exotic.'

'I don't want to be exotic, only mysterious.'

'How mysterious?' Charlotte wants to know.

'Exceedingly, excessively mysterious.' I feel light-hearted. Anything can happen. Anything is possible. When I look again, Madeleine has left. I feel despondent.

'Who is X?' I ask casually.

B and Charlotte seem to be waiting for Margaret to speak. At last she does.

'No one quite knows. It's generally believed she is Madeleine's lover.'

'But who *is* X?' B kicks me, and I realise I'm persisting to the point of rudeness. I don't care. I ask again, '*Who* is X? What does she look like?'

Charlotte says, 'No one really knows. It's generally thought she's supremely beautiful.'

For the moment I have no more questions.

When we've finished dessert, Margaret clears her throat. 'It's time,' she says.

They're all looking at me. B kicks me under the table. I turn on her. 'B, that's the third time this evening you've kicked me. Please don't do it.'

B merely says, 'We're waiting, Suniti.'

'Waiting for what?'

'Your transformation.'

'My what?'

'Your quest for being. That's what you've always wanted, isn't it? To Be Someone?'

I didn't know that that was expected. I thought we were merely on a pleasant weekend.

'Well, what am I supposed to do?' I feel helpless.

'Make an intelligent wish, a well thought out one.' Margaret answers. Unlike B, whom I suspect of mocking me, Margaret looks serene and gentle. She also seems to be entirely serious.

'Can I do it tomorrow?' I suggest feebly.

They appear surprised, but they don't say 'No'. I have till tomorrow. What have I got into? What was B's intention?

*

B and I are sharing a room. She takes the large bed and I take the small cot near the window. It gets chilly. I complain. Also, I'm worried and can't sleep. At last B takes pity on me and lets me into her bed. It's warm and comfortable, but I don't know whether or not I can put my arms round her. I still can't sleep. I get out of bed and walk about.

One of these days I'll deal with B. Right now, I need to know what's going to happen.

'B, this wish I'm supposed to make, what's it about?'

'Who you are and who you'd like to be. What it is you really want. What you're always moaning about.' B is mumbling into the pillow.

'But, B, I'm thoroughly muddled about who I am.'

In answer, B grunts.

'B,' I plead, 'please help me.'

'Oh, all right,' B sits up. 'Now, what do you want?'

'That's just it, B. I don't know.'

'You'd like to be someone else, it that it?'

'Yes, or different. Bigger, and better and stronger.'

'What's stopping you? Be all that.'

'It's hard work.'

'Then that's not what you want?'

'B, if I make this wish, will I get what I want?'

'You can say what you want, we'll try to corroborate you.'

'Like indulging a lunatic? If I say, "I am Napoleon," all of you will say, "Yes, dear, and so you are!"'

'No, it's more like a play. If you have costumes and props, and the setting is right, for a while you have a functioning system.'

'Well, but what if I'm Napoleon, and you're Baddy, and Charlotte is an Englishwoman, and Margaret is a Brahmin, and Madeleine is an ambience, then what? What happens?'

'You have an arbitrary order. For pity's sake, go to sleep, Suniti!'

'B?'

'Yes!'

'I don't want to be Napoleon.'

*

The following morning Margaret takes me for a short walk. I trot along like a small dog. It's possible that I am one. I'm glad Margaret doesn't make conversation. That would require me to say something, choose an attitude, a tone, an inflexion. I toy with the idea of being a talking dog, the life of the party, a prize poodle. I decide in favour of being a strong silent one.

Then I see some water. I would like to be a duck. I try to tuck my head into my shoulder and catch Margaret watching me. 'I feel very duck-like,' I inform her. Margaret smiles her acquiescence.

After lunch I lie down on the grass. I'm convinced that the grass doesn't mind being crushed. I decide that Margaret, Charlotte and Bhadravati are daisies and Madeleine is the yellow sun. X is a shadow. Just as I've almost fallen asleep, I hear voices. Charlotte and B are nearby. I wonder if they're going to talk about me? I scold myself for being an egoist. They do talk about me.

'Where on earth did you find her?' 'Her'—they must mean me.

'In a park in Toronto. She was kneeling on the grass. She looked so peculiar that I walked up to her. We got into conversation.' B giggles. 'She thought I was a goddess.'

'And so you are.' This from Charlotte.

'Not in the sense she thinks I'm one.'

'What do you propose to do with her?'

'I don't know. She's not a bad sort really.'

'She's prickly and difficult.'

'She's all right when her ego's unruffled.'

'But that's all she is—a transparent ego and some sensations and impressions.'

'She has potential.'

'For being someone?

'No—'

I sit up and glare at them.

'I am *not* merely a transparent ego.'

'That's true enough,' Charlotte smiles pleasantly.

'On occasion, you can be quite colourful—"a woman of colour".'

'That's racist!'

'I'm sorry,' says Charlotte penitently. 'I couldn't resist the play on words.'

'I must be someone,' I point out to them. 'You can't have had a conversation about no one, can you?'

'No, dear,' B's voice is soothing. It makes me furious.

'Aren't we all an accidental conglomeration of arbitrary particulars, duly supplied with a functioning ego?'

'Suniti, what a good description!' I stare at Charlotte. She really means it. I feel mollified. I smirk, then remember to frown.

We go in to tea. Charlotte and B ply me with chocolate cake, which I don't particularly want. Still, it's a nice gesture. After several cups of tea, Charlotte asks gently, 'Have you thought about who you'd like to be?'

I look at her cunningly. 'Could we have a practice run?'

That's not what either of them wants, but they think they owe it to me.

'Certainly,' they say. 'Go ahead.'

'Well then,' I tell them, 'I would like to be a Lover.' I had hoped to startle them with sheer effrontery, but they seem unsurprised.

'Whose lover would you like to be?' Charlotte, politely.

'I'm not sure. I would like a choice.'

'Like a proud potentate with a largish harem?'

'No-o.'

'Well?'

I look them in the eye. 'From whoever's available.'

They begin to understand and I think they'll be angry, but they're laughing.

B says, 'You mean you want us to lie about while you strut up and down and make your choice?'

'Not exactly. B, you're not angry, are you?'

'What for?'

'For suggesting ...'

'That one of us might be your lover? Was it intended as an offensive suggestion?'

'No.' I stare hard at the floor. 'But these things can be offensive.'

'Why?'

'Cultural context. It's a way, you know, of humiliating women.'

'Do you, as a misogynist, wish to humiliate your fellow women?'

'No. I am one. I don't wish to humiliate anyone ...' I mutter confusedly.

'Well, what do you want?'

'A lover,' I mumble.

'Do you mean you want a lover or you want to be one?'

'She means both,' B says briskly. 'Come on, Charlotte, let's get on with it.'

They drape themselves on the living room sofa. B points to a large cushion. 'That's Margaret over there. She's busy at the moment. And if you want Madeleine, she'll have to be imagined.'

I just stand there and stare at them.

Charlotte gets impatient. 'Come on, Suniti, get on with it. Behave like a lover.'

'What? In front of everyone?'

'At least it will give you a sense of audience. How can you know that you've done something unless the thing is seen to be done?'

I don't understand this, but I force myself to walk over to B.

'You're very beautiful,' I say inanely.

'Yes. Well.'

'B,' I snap at her. 'You're not co-operating. What am I supposed to say if you just say, "Yes, well"?'

'All right. What should I say?'

'You should say something reciprocal.'

'So are you.'

'So am I what?'

'Beautiful.'

I can't think of anything to say to that. I throw up my hands. 'B, it's hopeless. I don't feel like a lover; I feel like a fool.'

'It may be,' B answers, 'that is the kind of lover you are.'

I feel utterly dashed. I sit down. Charlotte walks over and puts her arm around me.

'You look so very like a damsel in distress,' she says, 'I will be your lover. I will carry you off and lock you in a castle and protect you from everything forever and ever.'

I'm startled. 'I don't want to be abducted and imprisoned for life. Who would?'

'Sorry,' says Charlotte, 'I was only being gallant.'

I turn on them. 'Where do you get your notions anyhow?'

'We get them from you. This practice run was your idea.'

'Well, where do I get them from?'

'I suspect,' says Charlotte, 'you get them from being a student of literature.'

They both seem amused. I'm close to tears. I go for a long walk. When I come back in time for dinner, at least I'm prepared and a little in control.

Towards the end of dinner, Margaret asks the inevitable question, kindly enough, but there's no evading it. 'Well, Suniti, have you decided who or what you want to become?'

'Yes,' I answer smiling happily. 'You'll find out tomorrow.' I grin at them. 'I already am. Tomorrow I become.' I feel so cheerful, I dance like Madeleine, I flutter like a bird. 'I can be anything, anyone.' I collapse on the floor in a small huddle, I peer at them coyly. 'Or no one.'

Margaret, Charlotte and Madeleine clap. I make a note that even no one can be a good performer. Bhadravati helps me up, and we go for a walk. She disappears among the trees. I follow her.

III
Interlude

The air seems tangible. I can smell it and breathe it. It has colour, it's the solid night permeated by the moon. I can hear Bhadravati ahead of me. A leaf rustles, a twig cracks.

'B,' I call out, 'B, don't walk so fast. You're losing me.' She calls back something, but I can't understand it. I stumble after her.

I don't know whether or not I am happy. I don't know whether I'm supposed to follow her. I sit down under a tree, I rub my cheek against the bark. It's an evergreen of some sort, not a tamarind or a peepal, but the bark is pleasant and rough. I think I am happy. I listen to the night sounds. There's a light breeze. A cricket nearby is making a racket. I think I can hear B's voice. I lie down on the ground. Stars overhead. When I look through the trees again, I can see her watching me. She is beautiful. She is like the trees.

She comes and sits down close beside me. 'Suniti,' she says, 'what is the cricket saying?"

I tell her, 'The cricket is shouting. The cricket is saying how beautiful you are, how beautiful it is. It is saying, "I want to come close and lie down beside you." It is saying, "Pick me up, Suniti. Pick me up in the palm of your hand and stroke and caress me and I'll sing for you."'

'What nonsense. Crickets aren't eloquent.'

'Yes, they are. They say anything and everything. Do you know, I like this tree I'm sitting under.'

'It's a pine,' she says factually.

'A pine, a cricket, a moon, a forest, two women … Who am I, B?'

'Sometimes I think you're a baby.'

'All right, I'm a baby. I'm an intelligent baby with a transparent mind. Tell me a story intended for babies.'

She shifts slightly so that my head now rests in her lap. I'm not altogether sure whether it's B or the night that holds me so close.

'Once upon a time,' she says quietly, 'there was a Spindly Cow. Her taut white hide was stretched across a bony frame. She was large and reasonably good-looking, but she was hollow inside. There was a blackness inside her, an incessant craving. She decided that it would be her mission in life to assuage that darkness, to become substantial. So she ate everything she saw, pots and pans, kettles and crayfish, cabbages and turnips, articles of clothing, houses and furniture—just ordinary things one sees all the time.'

'Did she eat animals?'

'Yes, animals too—men and women, pigs and parrots, tiny little babies, tigers and terrapins, everything. Luckily, she was a careless animal and short-sighted too, so that she left a great many things only half-eaten, and then there were a great many more that she didn't even see. Still, she was persistent and she crunched steadily. The earth began to lose its shape and looked more and more like a pock-marked lump. At last the creatures who were left decided it was time to say something. "O Cow," they said, approaching her as closely as each of them dared.'

'Did they all speak together?'

'Yes, you mustn't interrupt, particularly not when it gets exciting.'

'Sorry.'

'"O Cow," they said, all of them at once, "you have now consumed a fifth of the planet. Is the hunger within you at all assuaged? Are you satisfied?"

'"No," said Spindleshanks, because that was her name. "No," she said with her mouth full, because that was her nature. "It's become a habit. But I'll tell you what I'll do. I won't eat you as long as you give me something else to eat."

'So the creatures went away and ploughed the earth, and built factories, and in times of scarcity, cast lots among themselves in order to decide who should be sacrificed. But casting lots didn't work well, and there were arguments among the creatures, and disputes and discussions, and a few minor scuffles, then a great deal of fighting and finaly huge wars, through all of which Spindleshanks chomped her way steadily.

'At last there was only a handful of creatures left and only a small patch of earth for the cow to stand on.'

'Oh, well, then she must have realised what she'd been doing and stopped doing it—when she saw the blackness of space underfoot.'

'No, she didn't. And you really mustn't interrupt.'

'But surely the few remaining creatures must have been driven to do something?'

'No, they weren't. The Cow ate them up, the very last handful and the last clod of earth.'

'And then?'

'And then there was nothing. Only Spindleshanks. Spindleshanks and Nothing. Nothing and Spindleshanks. She felt terrible. She began to scream. She screamed and screamed until she burst and turned herself inside out. Then the world spilled out of her, all higgledy-piggledy, and not quite the same world as it once had been because it had been processed by Spindleshanks and Spindleshanks permeated everything.'

'And the blackness?'

'The blackness was now both outside and inside. And Spindleshanks herself, fragments of Spindleshanks were a part of the world.'

'Then what happened?'

'The world carried on, but a different world.'

'Thank you for telling me the story, B.' But B is quiet. 'Has it a moral?' I ask slyly.

'No, no moral.' Her voice sounds sad.

I don't say anything. I caress her lightly, so lightly that I think perhaps she will think it's the breeze. When I sense that her sadness has lifted a little, I ask her gently, 'B, if you cut me open, what would you find?'

She smiles. 'Crickets and cockroaches, the carcasses of dead animals, pine trees and peepal trees, giraffes and ostriches, forests and rivers, entire bestiaries.'

'Do you mind, B?'

'No, I don't mind. I'm glad of it.'

'But you've forgotten something.'

'What?'

'The watch-dog, a poodle or a puppy, or even a cow, but functioning always as a guardian or a lackey, a self-appointed porter, and always with the same question, "Is this thing good or bad for me?"'

B laughs. 'And getting it wrong most of the time. If you were to cut me open, Suniti, what would you find?'

'Blood and guts, a functioning body, a living creature.'

'Will it do, Suniti?'

'You know it will.'

That night, B and I become lovers. The birds wake us up the next morning. They're hunting for food. They are very noisy. They are celebrating the fact ... well, they are celebrating the world.

IV
Bud

For the next two weeks I live in a daze. My soul, such as it is, seems to be extended over the entire countryside. My ego, vigilant as ever, but careless now of its old duties, is concentrated entirely on Bhadravati. She's in the air I breathe, the taste of water. I know this cannot go on for ever, but time seems to have turned into a golden haze. The sun and moon are our friendly companions, as are Madeleine, Charlotte and Margaret, who is a kindly host and offers the comforts and convenience of her house.

On the fifteenth day I find myself asking, 'B, what are we going to do next? What are we going to become?'

'Become?'

'Oughtn't there to be a logical pattern? One significant event following another? Now that we are lovers, ought we not to get married, for example?'

'Two women can't get married. You're being carried away by literature.'

'No, by life. Ought we not to settle down and have children?'

'Ought?'

'It's usually done.'

'Do be sensible.'

'I am being.'

'You're being conventional.'

'What's wrong with that?'

'It's arbitrary, my dear. Who would we be?'

'We could be Mr and Mrs Suniti, for instance.'

'What?'

'Canadians can't tell the difference.'

'So you'd like to be Mr Someone. What do you know about being a man?'

'In theory quite a lot. That's what literature is all about—the nature of man. In practice very little. I've come to the conclusion that men are aliens.'

'But you'd like to be one?'

'I didn't say that. I was just looking for a possible pattern. Well, what do you think?'

'I think we ought to explore the matter, the Men from Mars, the Unearthly Aliens.'

I don't pursue the conversation. The golden haze seems to have dimmed. I'm aware that we've stayed with Margaret for over a fortnight. We came for a weekend. We cannot go on living here for ever.

⋆

At dinner that night Margaret and Charlotte look as usual. Madeleine has disappeared. B looks different, still recognisable, but—dare I say it?—less beautiful.

She says casually, 'Suniti thinks men come from Mars.'

Charlotte is interested. 'Do you think they're a different species? Different from women or cows or poodles?'

I'm in for it. 'I mean they did not originate on planet earth.'

Margaret looks up. 'How did they get here?'

'Spaceships.'

'What happened to the spaceships?' Margaret persists.

'Broke down. It has taken all these centuries to build new ones.'

'In what capacity did they arrive on earth?' Charlotte wants to know.

'Invaders. This may be deduced from their subsequent behaviour.' I have adopted my driest and most academic manner.

Charlotte is amused, but Margaret has a question. 'How did they adjust?'

'Not very well.' I'm feeling confident now. 'But well enough by means of mutation and biological manipulation and a massive mythologisation of the planetary purpose.'

Charlotte is staring at me. 'What first led you to the formulation of this theory?'

I grin at her. 'The study of literature. As you know, man himself is at the centre of the literary universe. Pigs and poodles, bats and babies, women and children, the earth itself, are always "the other". How explain this inexplicable division, this perverse passion to make "the other" conform to the requirements of man's desire? It doesn't make sense, unless one postulates that men are really Martians. Then the pieces fit together.'

There's a pause. Then B says, 'Suniti was saying only this morning that she'd like to be a Martian.'

'That wasn't quite what I said.' Damn B anyhow! Why does she always have to spoil things? Just when I thought I was impressing the others? They're waiting for me to explain myself. 'I was just saying to B,' I mumble sheepishly, 'that perhaps we should get married...' I feel like a fool. 'It was only a shadow of a suggestion...' I trail off incoherently.

'That does not necessarily involve being a Martian,' Charlotte points out. Oh, what have I got into? They're obviously not going to drop the matter.

'Suniti wanted us to be a Mr and Mrs Someone, a Martian and His Maiden,' B puts in.

I must stop this. 'B,' I say loudly, 'I do not, I have never wanted, to be a Martian.'

'Why not? Then I suppose I'll have to be one.'

'What?'

'A Martian. We could call ourselves Mr and Mrs Bhadravati. It has a ring to it.'

'B.' I say, enunciating each word, 'I do not want to be married to a Martian.'

'We can live in sin then. More modern. You can be my mistress. We could call ourselves The Man from Mars and His Reluctant Companion.'

'B, you must be joking? How could you possibly turn into a Man from Mars?'

'Quite simple—a little padding, a little make-up and a great deal of confidence.'

My heart sinks. I have difficulty swallowing my dinner.

Margaret asks gently, 'Why does the idea distress you?'

'Are you a misanthrope?' Charlotte asks. Her deep blue eyes are smiling blandly. 'In the same way as you're a misogynist?'

'Not in the same way.' I keep my answer short, but I seem to have admitted that I am a misogynist. Best to let it go.

'These Aliens, these Men from Mars, aren't you interested in them?' inquires Margaret.

'Have to be,' I mumble. 'They occupy the planet, but I prefer to observe them from a safe distance.'

'Are you afraid of them?' B, of course. 'Why do you keep a safe distance?'

'Because they bite,' I snap.

'Martians bite?' Margaret sounds like an avid naturalist.

'Well, no. They rope you in, in accordance with their mission.'

'And what's that?'

'The domestication of the species of planet earth.' There, perhaps that will silence them.

B again. 'If the Martians are in charge, wouldn't there be some advantage in an alliance with a Martian?'

'What?'

'Easy access to Martian circles. Besides, consider how much safer you'd be if you ventured out tomorrow under the full protection of an honest-to-goodness Martian.'

I try pleading with her. 'Please, B?'

'It's no use, Suniti. My mind is made up.'

When Charlotte and Margaret kiss me 'Good night', they seem particularly gentle, like mothers and sisters at a wedding or a funeral.

*

At breakfast B has turned into what is unquestionably a Martian. I scowl, then turn my back. B seems impervious. When Madeleine comes in, B jumps up, hovers about her, and tries to see she has everything she wants. That B is making her comfortable in her own house doesn't escape my notice.

B suddenly sticks out a hand. 'I'm Bud. And this is Suniti.' He pushes me forward.

'I believe we've met,' I say feebly. Madeleine blinks, smiles and disappears.

Bud and I are left facing one another. 'I'll just bring down the suitcases.' he says. 'Then we're ready to go.' He doesn't wait for an answer.

When Margaret and Charlotte walk into the room, I leap to my feet.

'Margaret,' I expostulate, 'you've got to stop this. Bud has taken over.'

They understand exactly what has happened, but they don't seem alarmed.

'What has he been doing?'

'Drinking coffee and fetching the suitcases.'

'That's helpful, isn't it?' Charlotte offers.

'It's the way he's been doing it.'

Just then Bud comes down, kisses Margaret and Charlotte rapidly, says, 'Thanks for everything,' grabs my elbow and rushes me out, shouting, 'Come on, Suniti, let's go.'

He has started the engine before I can stop him.

This is really too much. I go back to the house.

'Margaret, Charlotte, Bud has turned into a Man from Mars. What shall I do?'

'You don't have to go with him,' Charlotte says.

'He has my car keys. He's revving up the engine.'

'Ask him for the car keys,' Charlotte suggests.

'That means a confrontation ... Oh, Margaret.'

Margaret comforts me. 'It's all right, Suniti. He's still B. Why not play along and see what happens?'

'All right,' I answer, but I have my misgivings. I kiss them good bye. I go up to Bud and demand the car keys.

'Sure,' he replies. 'You don't have to be so uptight about it.'

I put the car into gear and drive off. Bud beside me wears a stolid face, he looks immovable. After an hour or so, when we've had some coffee and I've paid for my own, I feel better, though his letting me pay seems a kindly concession. I remind myself that B is lurking in him somewhere, but he seems hopelessly alien.

When we get to Montreal and stop at a hotel, I try to check in while Bud looks over my shoulder. The clerk at the counter addresses him exclusively. Allying himself with a fellow Martian? But what am I to make of the waitress at dinner who behaves as though only Bud existed and I was furniture?

At last it's over. We can go to our room. I shall talk to Bud. Surely in the end B will emerge?

'B,' I say severely, 'this has gone on long enough.'

Bud puts his arms around me and gives me a kiss.

'Stop it!' I exclaim.

'Why?' he asks.

'It's not what I want.'

'Is that important? You don't have to do anything. Just lie back ...' As I'm about to lose my temper, his face breaks into a mischievous grin.

'B,' I cry gladly, 'You're back!' But when I put my arms around her, there's an incongruity—B's head and Bud's body.

'What have you done?'

'Nothing,' B says. 'You look so perplexed, and all day long you've been so bad-tempered.'

'But your body ...' I begin.

'Don't you like me as I am?'

'Yes, no.'

'The trouble with you is that you're very conventional.'

'That's not fair, B. When I'm with Bud in public, I become an appendage, a secondary person.'

'Why not look at it differently? You share in his status. When we return to Toronto with Bud at your side, you'll be a different person.'

I hadn't thought of that.

'B,' I wail. 'How am I to explain Bud?'

'Nothing to explain. You've caught yourself a live Martian. It's normal.'

'B,' I plead. 'Please dispense with Bud. When Bud is around, I feel uncomfortable.'

'That's your problem, not Bud's,' she says.

'But he takes advantage of his superior status.'

B draws herself up. 'Bud, I'll have you know, is a nice person. And you, my friend, are a snob and very status conscious.'

Perhaps B is right. I feel awful. Privately I think there isn't much to choose between B and Bud.

Suddenly B turns gentle. She puts an arm around me. 'Would you like to be Bud?'

'No, I wouldn't!'

'You see, it's hard being Bud. It's generous of me to agree to be Bud.'

This is so outrageous that I can't think of an answer. I manage to ask, 'What are the duties and obligations of Bud?'

'Being strong, successful, right and noble.'

'And the duties and obligations of Bud's partner?'

'You mean Sue's? The complementary ones—being weak, incompetent, uncertain and inferior.'

'That's nonsense. An incompetent Sue would be useless to Bud. Anyway, I don't want to be a Sue or a Bud!'

'Yes, dear.'

'Who was that?'

'Whoever you like, dear.'

'No, tell me, who are you at this moment?'

'If you can't tell the difference, how does it matter?'

I adopt a weary and patient tone. 'Of course it matters. Bud is a Martian, B isn't.' But even I can't keep a straight face over this piece of evasion. Bud is giggling, and I join her.

I don't sleep well. What difference does it make whether B is B or B is Bud? It makes a difference to me. B is just B. When Bud does something, he's backed by the forces of the Martian Empire.

'B,' I mutter, prodding him in the back. 'You're backed by the forces of the Martian Empire.'

B grunts.

*

That night I dream that the Jovians have invaded. They're unthinkably gigantic and unbelievably monstrous. Buddy and I are comrades in arms and giving battle. As we cower in a cave together I feel a sudden upsurge of fellow feeling.

'Buddy,' I exclaim, throwing an arm about his shoulders, 'compared to the Jovians you don't seem at all alien.'

Buddy responds by punching me lightly. 'You're a good chap, Suniti. Sometimes I forget you're not a Martian. When the war is over, why don't you take out the proper papers? Become one of us? We'd have a good time together—two gay Martians exploring the world.'

I'm annoyed. I want to say, 'Perhaps there isn't much difference between Martians and Jovians.' But it's the wrong time to say it. The Jovians are upon us.

*

I had half-hoped that B might have tired of being Bud. I glare at her. But Bud is being pleasant.

'Good morning,' he says nicely. 'How are you feeling this morning?'

'Terrible, thanks. I would like Bud to go away and B to return. I don't dislike Bud, but he tends to bully me. B is much nicer.'

'That's not true. B reduced you to a small poodle, whereas all I do is make you irritable.' He looks vulnerable and hurt. I wonder if he's about to start crying. I put an arm about his shoulder.

'Since you're B anyway, I'll treat you exactly as though you were B. Then I'm sure we'll get on together.'

'All right, but only in private. In public I have to uphold the ancient traditions of the Martian Empire.'

'Oh to hell with you!' I don't care whether I lose B or Buddy or both.

Buddy capitulates. 'All right. I won't uphold the ancient traditions, but don't blame me if we get into trouble. The Martians don't like it if any of their number goes native. There are severe repercussions...'

I see his point, but I'll be damned if I concede it. 'It's your own fault then for being a Martian.'

Buddy looks glum. 'Yes, Suniti, it's a terrible burden.'

We breakfast in silence.

'What shall we do?' he asks at last.

'We can't go to a lesbian bar. You wouldn't be welcome.'

'It's not fair,' he says. 'Haven't you any friends who would make me welcome?' He has that little boy look again.

'Several,' I mutter. I'm thinking of Amy Rose-Blossom. She would dote on him. I telephone her.

'Come on,' I tell him. 'We'll look around the city, and pay a visit later. We've been invited to lunch.'

We walk about. He makes a point of being conspicuously ungallant. I find it tiresome.

Eventually he asks, 'Who are we visiting?'

'Someone who will like you. She likes Martians.'

'What, without discrimination?'

'Yes. She runs a home for them.'

'For the discarded and disabled?'

'She thinks all Martians are in some way disabled. Something to do with the Jovian Wars. She thinks they need to be nursed and coddled.'

'I'm not at all sure I'll get on with your friend ...' but they get on famously. Amy makes a fuss about him, and Bud simpers and smirks.

I leave them together after telling Bud I'll meet him at the hotel. It's the first time in days I've been by myself. I feel luxuriously anonymous.

⋆

When I return to the hotel, I find that Bud is already back. He grins at me, 'Mrs Rose-Blossom's treatment does a world of good. You should try it.'

'The full treatment is for Martians only. Amy says women don't need it, women are tough.'

I feel relaxed and reasonably good-tempered. We go out to eat and are nice to each other. As we're leaving the *maître d'hôtel* says, 'Bring her again. She's beautiful.'

'There, Suniti. Aren't you pleased?'

'No. If you went into a parking lot with a foreign car, it's exactly what the attendant might say to you.'

Bud's face falls. 'You're very hard to please.'

'So are you. You'd be pleased if I were pleased. What you want is a happy acquiescence.'

'Why not? I could spend my life trying to please you, and you could spend yours being pleased. We'd live happily for ever.'

'What you need is a stone companion, smiling forever.'

'What I need is a metal one, smiling when I push a button.' Buddy grins suddenly. 'There must have been times when you've wanted a robot too.'

I consider. 'Be one then. Your function is to please, isn't it?'

'Only when it's convenient. And not as a robot. Why don't you be one?'

'You'd be bored, Buddy. What would you do for conversation?'

'I'd seek out the society of my fellow Martians.'

'And what would I do?'

'Join the local branch of the Robots' Club.'

By this time we're back at the hotel.

'Buddy,' I tell him, 'I am not a robot.'

'Suniti,' he answers, 'I am not an alien.'

'Who are you then?'

'I'm probably a woman. I would like to be one. It's less difficult.'

'What's to stop you? Be a woman then.'

'Do you think I would make a good one?'

'No. You have the wrong habits.'

Bud seems depressed, but he quickly recovers.

'Are you a good woman?'

'No,' I tell him, 'I'm an unsatisfactory one.'

Suddenly B is grinning—it is B, isn't it?—she puts an arm about me. 'Suniti,' she says, 'I'll tell you a secret, I also am an unsatisfactory Martian.'

'You do very well.' I pat her on the back.

She feels I haven't been suitably impressed. 'I'll tell you another thing, and this is a well-guarded secret— all Martians are unsatisfactory.'

I laugh. 'That's well-known.'

She looks put out. 'At least you'll concede that you and the Martians have something in common.'

At last I ask, 'Are you saying that Men from Mars are really women?'

'You've got it at last.'

'Then why do they behave so differently from women?'

'Lack of opportunity and education, my dear.'

B is grinning, I grin back; but late that night when B asks me, 'Suniti, what would you really like?' all I can say is, 'I need to be by myself for a bit; I would very much like to be left alone.'

V
Conjuring Cow

When I wake up the next morning S2 is lying in bed beside me. We open our eyes in unison. We lie there wondering whether it's possible to converse with one another.

'Suniti,' we say turning simultaneously, then fall back.

'This needs practice,' we say together.

I make an effort. 'I will be me, and you can be "you",' I say to S2.

S2 demurs. 'From my point of view—'

'I am me,' I finish for her. 'Well, let's take turns.'

We get up and dress ourselves. This constant contiguity is a nuisance. I know S2 is worthwhile in herself, but I'm not happy with this needless duplication. Still, we ought to get on. Our relationship will no doubt be amicable. We smile at each other, but both S2 and I are uneasy. We decide to have breakfast in our own room and return to Toronto.

'What shall we have?' I ask politely. I already know, but one might as well be courteous even with oneself.

S2 surprises me, 'Scrambled eggs on toast.'

'S2,' I say, 'you know I never have eggs for breakfast.'

'The truth is we seldom have breakfast, but since we decided to order some …'

'I never have breakfast when I'm alone.'

'I'm not alone. I am breakfasting with a charming woman …'

'You know perfectly well I'm not charming—not before breakfast.'

We order toast, and eat in silence. I have misgivings which are increased at the check-out counter. She uses my credit card to pay the bill, and produces a flawless signature. I realise that for whatever she does, I am accountable. I hope she turns out to be sensible.

'At least we can share the driving,' I console myself.

'True enough,' S2 replies. 'I'll drive first.'

When it's my turn to drive, I find I'm as stiff and tired as S2 herself. 'This is empathy,' I think. 'True fellow feeling. At last I'm experiencing genuine compassion, but it's something I could do without.'

I suggest that we stop at Cow Farm. S2 agrees readily. I know she is hoping to get news of Cow. It's late when we arrive.

'Hi, we were just passing by and thought we'd look in.' I feel awkward, but Boudicca and Cowslip make us welcome.

'This is S2.' I'm afraid Cowslip is about to say 'Neat', but she doesn't.

We head towards the barn. S2 and I keep peering into the dark.

'What are you looking for?' Boudicca asks.

'Cow,' S2 answers.

'Cow?' There are at least five or six cows on the farm.

'For Buddy,' I explain.

'Do you mean Baddy?' Cowslip inquires.

'Bhadravati,' S2 answers.

'What does she look like?'

'She looks like you,' S2 says.

'She looks like us,' I put in.

Boudicca and Cowslip stare.

'You must be tired. Come in and rest for a while. Have some oats.'

'No, no thanks.' But we do go in and sit down.

'Have you seen Cow?' I ask.

'You mean Baddy, don't you?' Boudicca answers. 'She's always about. She comes and goes. She isn't here now.'

All I wanted was a straightforward answer to a simple question. I get up to go, but Lou-Ann, Ariadne and Sybbie walk in.

'Hi, Sue,' they greet me cheerfully.

'My name is not—'

S2 interrupts me and introduces herself. I stare at her. She's positively beaming and they're smiling back.

'I've heard so much about you from Baddy,' she murmurs. To call Bhadravati 'Baddy' so effortlessly! I retreat into a corner and scowl.

'What have you heard?'

'About your friendliness and warmth,' she tells the cows. 'And about your dreams,' she adds turning to Sybbie.

This is crass flattery. I dissociate myself completely from her.

'I had a dream the other day,' Sybbie begins.

'What was it about?' Trust S2 to ask.

Boudicca and Cowslip have excused themselves to prepare supper. I resign myself and try not to listen.

'It was really weird. It was about a Cow. Everything was in colour except the Cow and some of the other cows, except me, of course.'

'What colour was the Cow?' I ask.

'Her left side was white and her right side was black.' Sybbie stares at me. 'You were in it too,' she says suddenly.

'And what colour was I?' I ask unpleasantly.

Sybbie doesn't notice. 'You were no colour at all. You were looking for a Cow. We took you to where the cows were. But you couldn't find her. The Black and White Cow was right there—you looked at her for a long time—and near her there were some zebra-striped cows, and lots of grey ones mixed, and dappled ones and ordinary brown ones like me. It was a grand sight. But you started crying. So Ariadne and I comforted you.'

I'm furious with myself for encouraging Sybbie. As I clear my throat to say lightly, 'What an absurd dream,' I find that S2 is giving Sybbie a hug and saying to her, 'Oh Sybbie, you're a dear.' Both Sybbie and Ariadne look smug and even Lou-Ann is smiling complacently. I keep quiet.

After a mercifully light supper, we leave. In the car, as we're driving home, S2 says, 'I'm glad we stopped, aren't you?'

'Yes,' I mutter, but after a while I lose my temper. 'You're a hypocrite,' I tell her.

'And you're a boor.'

*

The house seems unchanged. We both walk about looking for B; there's no trace of her. We make ourselves a cup of tea and sit down.

'It's lonely without B,' I say at last. 'Well, we have each other,'

S2 sighs heavily. I wish she'd cheer up. It isn't pleasant to have a despondent companion.

'Yes.' She doesn't sound enthusiastic.

'Don't you like me?'

'You're all right, Suniti, but rather self-absorbed.'

'In what way?'

'You just sit there, and behave exactly as though you were all alone.'

'We are all alone. I like being alone. What's the matter?'

'It isn't very pleasant having a despondent companion.'

I get to my feet. 'Come on, we're both tired. Let's go to sleep, and if possible, don't snore so much.'

Later that night I ask S2 'Do you think B will return?'

'I don't know, I wish I didn't miss her quite so much.'

'Perhaps we'll dream about her.' But we don't.

*

We have a nightmare instead. Bit by bit the world is stripped away, the blue carpet, the walls. It all peels off like so much paint. At last there is nothing left, except a small, transparent something. It's shapeless and composed of terror. It cannot penetrate the blackness around it. It cannot make any sound. But it's shrieking with the intensity of its own terror.

Luckily, I wake up. I don't know who I am. After a while I see S2 beside me sitting up in bed. Then I remember. I'm supposed to be Suniti, that particular person with those preoccupations. That's all right then. We fall asleep without further trouble.

*

In spite of the nightmare, S2 and I are cheerful the next morning. We skip breakfast, but make ourselves a large pot of tea, and get to work. We're well-supplied with pens and paper. We've arrived at the same conclusion.

I write down neatly: 'Conjuring Cow'. S2 nods approval.

'Now you have to address her,' S2 says.

'Using the vocative,' I mutter to myself. 'How's this? "O Cow, Baddy, Bhadravati and Bud".'

'It's not enough,' says S2, 'you have to put in all her names, some of them anyway. Here.' S2 starts writing.

I read it aloud: 'O Cow of a thousand faces and a thousand names, O Julia, Peter, Madeleine and Kate, O Margaret, Charlotte, Amy and S1, O Boudicca, Sybilla, Cowslip and S2, O Ariadne, Lou-Ann and Madame X, O Cow who manifests herself in a thousand shapes and a thousand wishes …'

'Well?'

'All right, but that's just the calling upon Cow.

'So now we put in the flowery epithets? Like "O Celestial Surabhi, Gentle Source of Food and Fragrance"? That sort of thing?'

'No, just what we know about her. Her attributes and qualities, what she has done and said.'

'How's this? "O you who have appeared in my dreams at times with a garland of flowers about your neck, you who have sported in the woods with me, and laughed and mocked and been my friend, O you who have slain a thousand Jovians ..." And so on. Will it do?'

'It's a bit personal.'

'Prayers are personal.'

'It's a bit poetic also.'

'You said "flowery epithets".'

'No, you said it. You haven't put in her darker aspects.'

'All right. "O you who have slain a thousand Jovians, kicked up the dirt and trampled the planet; O you who have reduced me to almost nothing, then made me a present of the world and myself; O you who contain a terrible hunger, ever assuaged and feeding itself—"' I break off. 'S2, are we suggesting that Cow is Spindleshanks?'

'Why not?'

'She mightn't like it.'

'Cow has a strong stomach. She won't mind.'

'It savours of dualism or Manichaeanism …'

'For pity's sake, Suniti. This is no time for theological disputation!'

'All right. If we've put in enough epithets, can we make our request?'

'One or two epithets more. Flattering this time.'

'All right. "O Cow whose tender muzzle feeds on snow peas, whose curving horns toss the sun; O Cow of the delicate bones and gentle eyes, grant us our prayer. Please return".'

'One long sentence, and one short one—It will do.'

We both sit on the floor in the semi-lotus position and meditate hard. Our wills and minds merge. After a while there's a clattering of hoofs like the sound of thunder. I jump up to answer the door. I fling it open. It's Cow, standing there grinning at me. I throw my arms about her neck.

I feel so very, so extraordinarily happy, I can't concentrate at all. Cow lets herself in and makes a pot of tea. I help her. We take it into the garden.

I watch the way the light glides along her flanks, the way the short thick hairs grow on her forehead. I admire her knees, her legs, her enormous rib-cage and the shape of her head. Finally I stare at her dusty hoofs.

'Cow,' I tell her solemnly, 'I think you're a goddess.'

Cow seems amused. 'So are you, Suniti.'

I'm appalled. 'Oh no,' I exclaim. 'I make no such claims. I, really—I don't have the energy.'

'You can't help it, Suniti. You're alive, you know.'

I can see that determined look in her eye. I don't want to argue. 'Oh, all right, but only a minor and obscure one.'

B hasn't been listening. She's thinking of something entirely different.

'What were you talking about?' she asks.

'The weather. How pleasant it is. How good it is to have you here.'

And then Cow startles me. She says, 'I like you, Suniti.' My eyes widen.

'I like you,' I tell her with complete conviction.

'Even when I'm B or Baddy or Bud?'

'Even then,' I reply and add quickly. 'Even then I find you wholly engaging.' It occurs to me she might vanish.

'This isn't just a visit?' I ask anxiously. 'You won't go away?'

I think she's going to tease, but she speaks quite kindly. 'There have been times, Suniti, when you've regarded my presence as a visitation.'

'You can be quite awful.'

B just grins. '"The Cow of a thousand faces and a thousand manifestations who walks rough-shod over fields and forests, and falls asleep when her day is done..." I'm misquoting, aren't I?' she adds penitently.

I smile at her. 'You know I'm going to write this down.'

'What? "The Conversations of Cow" faithfully recorded by her scribe Suniti?' B is laughing at me. I don't really mind. I go inside and get to work. On the lawn Cow grazes in the summer sun.

The Mothers of Maya Diip (abridged)

In *A Room of One's Own,* Virginia Woolf says that it would have been nice if our mothers and foremothers had made money and then left it for our education. But if they had done that, she continues, 'there would have been—that was the snag in the argument—no Mary.' In the first part of *The Mothers of Maya Diip* I set out to explore how women would cope with 'the problem of children' in a matriarchy. In Part II of *The Mothers of Maya Diip*, I consider how a civilised solely male society might work. And Part III depicts 'Paradise', a society divided into two 'genders', which are dependent on the role an individual chooses to play. A person can either be a Mother or a Gallant. It's hardly surprising that in 'Paradise' there's a shortage of Mothers. Few want the responsibility.

I was trying to explore what feminism had to say about mothers and who was going to help women raise children. I was also trying to demonstrate how the stories, the imagery, the rituals and the iconography of a culture work together to construct its orthodoxy. I dedicated the book to my maternal grandmother, who was something of a matriarch herself.

The Mothers of Maya Diip (abridged)

'Let Looking Glass creatures, whatever they be
Come and dine with the Red Queen, the White Queen,
and me!'

Contents

PART I

'What would you do if you were the Red Queen?'

'I would make everybody behave themselves,' Alice said firmly.

'How?'

'Well,' began Alice—

1
A Proper Matriarchy

Of all the princely states of India there was one in which a matriarchy bloomed unashamedly. Perhaps it was the soil, perhaps the climate, perhaps it was the location and the accidents of genetic history. Perhaps it was the goddess (whom feminists in the west beseech intermittently), or the happy line of competent queens.

When the Blue Donkey received an invitation from the Ranisaheb to visit the principality, she felt gratified and then dubious. Was this a joke or had she been recognised? There were rumours that a matriarchy did exist, but no one was sure whether it was a fact, a legend or a dream. The thought made feminists tremble. They spoke in hushed voices and exchanged scraps which they said were messages from the Maternal Deep. When it was discovered that some feminists had been circulating their own work cleverly disguised, the uncertainty and the excitement multiplied.

The Blue Donkey only told her friend, Jyanvi, about the invitation. Jyanvi was an Indian and a feminist and a poet, and might take it seriously.

'Well done,' Jyanvi said. 'Where are the Maternal Deeps?'

'Off the west coast of India. Surely you've heard of the Ma Deep?'

'Oh. You mean Maya Diip. "Diip" means a lamp, not a deep or a dip. And "dwip" means an island or place of refuge. Yes, I've heard of it.'

'And what does "Maya" mean?' asked the Blue Donkey.

'Compassionate or illusory.'

'Well, accompany me. It says I can bring a friend provided she is adult and civilised.'

Jyanvi lowered her eyes modestly. 'What are we going to do there?'

'Recite poetry. The inhabitants of Maya actually like it, according to the Queen.'

'If it's a matriarchy, are they allowed to have queens?'

'There have to be matriarchs.' the Blue Donkey shrugged. 'It says right here, "Ranisaheb", and even I know that means Queen. It does not mean the Feminist Poetry Collective.'

'In that case ought we to go?'

'Yes,' said the Blue Donkey unhesitatingly.

At Bombay airport they were met by Saraswati. She greeted them with her hands joined together. Jyanvi fell in love instantly.

'What does "Saraswati" mean?' asked the Blue Donkey.

'Saraswati is a goddess,' Jyanvi whispered.

The Blue Donkey snorted, but said nothing.

They were taken to a yacht. It was brilliant October, gulls flew about, the waves were playful. Saraswati smiled. 'Arms, legs and limbs/the curve of your throat/ when the goddess made you ... Shut up,' Jyanvi told herself fiercely. 'These are unpolished lines, and their standards are probably high.' She tried to look capable of the wry rejoinder, the witty aside, the lifted eyebrow and the deprecating smile. She was ready.

'And how are your children?' Saraswati asked.

Jyanvi blinked, but the Blue Donkey took it in her stride. 'In my youth,' she informed Saraswati, 'I took a vow of celibacy.'

'What has that to do with children?'

'I see your point. The fact is,' the Blue Donkey went on cautiously, 'neither Jyanvi nor I have any children.'

'At least she didn't say I dislike the little beasts,' Jyanvi thought uneasily.

'If neither of you has attained motherhood, how did you achieve adult status?' Saraswati was startled into asking.

'Are all the adults on Maya Diip mothers?' asked the Blue Donkey carefully.

'Of course. Ah. I take your point. You must have thought I meant Grade A status. Please forgive me. I have rushed in and trampled on griefs which take time to heal.' She put her arm around Jyanvi, half in supplication, half in affection. Jyanvi could smell the flowers in her hair, the sandalwood on her skin. 'Please,' she heard Saraswati say, 'do say it's all right.'

'It's all right,' mumbled Jyanvi. 'And how are your children?' she asked politely.

Saraswati beamed. 'So far I have only been permitted one daughter. Her name is Sona. By the grace of the goddess, she has done well in the tests and is thought to be promising.'

The Blue Donkey decided they had better learn more before asking questions. 'We are tired,' she murmured, 'after our long journey, and would like to rest.'

2
The Maternal Spirit

In the palace, Gagri the Good was on the rampage again. She had kicked and screamed, had been hauled away and had howled unceasingly for more than an hour. Everyone had a slight headache, except the Ranisaheb, who went on munching a plateful of pakoras, receiving visitors, granting some favours, refusing others and acceding to a few unmade requests. What made the Matriarch hard to handle was her incalculability. Some attributed this to her extreme intelligence. Others saw it as a political ploy. The Five Great Families were getting tired of it, but there was little that the Lesser Matriarchs could do. By a judicious use of the permissions and prohibitions licensing motherhood, she had manipulated the kinship patterns so that the flow of loyalties all led to her. She was a Grade A mother three times over and was herself the product of a Grade A mother. She had magnificent teeth and an excellent appetite. She usually prevailed.

Her present visitor was her friend, the Lesser Matriarch, Malini Devi. Malini Devi was tall and thin, fair for a Mayan. She adjusted the folds of her grey sari and began, 'If a friend betrays a friend, are debts and obligations immediately cancelled?'

The Ranisaheb knew that Malini Devi was furious with her. Why couldn't the woman accept that, in this instance, she would not bend the rules?

'No.' She answered Malini Devi in her grandest manner. 'The

vows of friendship are eternal and not to be shaken by small disagreements.'

'This can hardly be called a small disagreement!' Malini Devi expostulated. She altered her tone. 'Won't you grant my niece Grade B status?'

'Malini, I will not change the laws of the state. Sarla Devi has Grade A status with the proviso that she may not be a biological mother. To have the bar removed, she must resign her office.'

'Why should she have to resign?'

'You know why. Ever since the feud between the Third Matriarch and the Chief of the Temple, the Chief of the Goddess' Guild may not bear a daughter, and no daughter of the Mayan Matriarch may enter the Guild. Come, don't presume on our friendship.'

'She needs to have a child!'

The Ranisaheb lost patience. 'Then let her have a boy!'

Malini Devi flinched 'No!' she cried out.

The Matriarch sighed. 'Malini, why does it matter so much? My daughter, Shyamila, has already pleaded with me on Sarla's behalf. When Shyamila bears a daughter, Sarla Devi will be her co-mother. Then she'll have a child.'

'It's not the same thing.'

'Why not? I gave you Saraswati, my own daughter, to adopt. You've said yourself that you couldn't have loved her more had she been your flesh and blood. And Saraswati has a daughter who promises well. Your house won't die.'

Malini Devi clutched the Ranisaheb's sari. 'If my niece has no child, my bloodline will die!'

The Ranisaheb turned away. 'All children are the gift of the goddess.' It was a dismissal.

Anger and frustration drove the Lesser Matriarch to her feet. 'You have an heir!'

Just then, Gagri the Good rushed into the room. She paused when she saw the Lesser Matriarch. Malini Devi ignored her. With a perfunctory gesture, she began to walk away. The Ranisaheb summoned her back.

'Sit down. You haven't been given permission to leave. Why does it trouble you that I have an heir? You have one too.'

'It's not the same thing. You want to make sure that if Shyamila and Sarla ally themselves, the children of that alliance will be your granddaughters.'

The Matriarch laughed. 'Don't be absurd. Why should I care?'

'Because you want the next Matriarch to be of your descent.'

'I, who exiled my own daughter?'

'You had no choice. Your daughter, Asha, blasphemed against Maya itself.'

Gagri the Good listened avidly. They were talking about the Forbidden Subject. But then the grown-ups glanced at her and nothing more was said.

The Ranisaheb regarded the Lesser Matriarch. 'You forget yourself. You may leave now.'

Malini Devi realised she had gone too far. She tried to excuse herself. 'You don't know what it's like to be childless.'

'Isn't Saraswati your daughter?' The Matriarch enquired icily.

'Yes,' she retorted bitterly. 'But she's also yours!' With that, Malini Devi left.

Gagri the Good burrowed into the folds of her grandmother's sari. She liked the feel of the fine cotton. Her grandmother always smelled of mogra flowers. Gagri felt safe and warm. She had forgotten about her mother. She began to play with the green bangles and the gold ones on her grandmother's wrist.

'You're a darling, aren't you?' the Matriarch murmured.

Gagri the Good wriggled happily. 'Yes,' she said.

She ran away to climb the drainpipes. Two Grade C mothers followed quickly. Five minutes later the howling and screaming began again. She had fallen into a fishpond while jumping across it and one of the Grade C mothers had immediately insisted that she get changed. Her grandmother liked to see her impeccably dressed.

'Amuse me.' The Matriarch smiled at her daughters.

Dinner was over. The Matriarch had presided, her enormous bulk clad, as usual, in a green sari. She had made a genial host, but the Blue Donkey wondered if the others were a little afraid of her, all except Gagri the Good. The servants had cleared the table, and Jyanvi and the Blue Donkey were now sitting in the drawing room with the others. They had been settled in the palace and introduced to Valerie, a western immigrant, and to the Matriarch's daughters, Shyamila the Civil and Pramila the Poet. Gagri the Good had been sent to bed after half an hour of bribes and promises. Saraswati had returned after putting her own daughter to bed. The Matriarch glanced at her fondly. There were times when the Matriarch wished that she had kept Saraswati and packed off Pramila the Poet instead. She saw Pramila getting ready to recite. 'Guests first,' she said sharply. Pramila subsided.

Valerie rose. ' 'I have written a poem in your honour:

Here by the grace of the Mayan Queen

I can be at last who I've always been.'

'Who have you always been and why are you able to be her now?' The Matriarch asked.

'Because, Your Majesty, now at last I'm a woman amongst women.' Valerie looked so moved and upset by her own lines that it would have been a cruelty to question her further.

Shyamila the Civil smiled at Jyanvi. 'Your turn now.'

Jyanvi hadn't realised she'd be expected to improvise. Saraswati was looking at her—Saraswati the Beautiful, in pale printed silk. Jyanvi swallowed and blurted out briefly,

'Children may howl and children may squall.

The Maternal Spirit rides over all.'

'May I suggest,' murmured Pramila, 'that you delete the "and" in the first line, and reduce the syllables in the second? Perhaps "embraces" would be better than "rides over"?'

'That's a different poem,' protested the Blue Donkey.

'So it is.' Pramila looked around the room owlishly. The light glinted off her spectacles. Jyanvi thought she seemd anxious to gain her mother's approval. Even her sari did not hide her angularities. Jyanvi glanced down at her own jeans. Valerie in her sarong was better dressed than she was. She felt scruffy. But the Ranisaheb was nodding to Saraswati.

Saraswati threw Jyanvi a mischievous glance. She said,

'Two strangers came to our shore.

They asked one question and asked no more.'

'What did they ask?' demanded the Matriarch.

'Whether all the adults on Maya were mothers.'

The Matriarch seemed amused, but Shyamila the Civil said courteously, 'We know that in the patriarchies, matters are different. Ask what you wish. We will try to answer.'

Jyanvi felt reckless. 'Why are children glorified here? Don't the lives and longings of women matter?' She risked a glance at Saraswati; Saraswati appeared unoffended.

It was Valerie who protested, 'It's not like that at all. In the patriarchies, the children govern; and though to be a woman is bad, to be a mother is usually worse. Here on Maya the Rule of the Mothers is just, gentle and generous.'

The Matriarch smiled, Pramila muttered that the alliteration was just a little overdone, and Shyamila, seeing that Jyanvi and the Blue Donkey looked puzzled, said to them, 'I will tell you a story.

> *There was once a child who did not wish to grow up. She played with the pretty boys all day long. Her dolls gathered dust. She fished and swam and climbed tall trees. She explained to her mothers, 'You have made a mistake. I should have been a boy. Look how I run and dazzle in the sun.'*
>
> *Mother A said, 'You are a foolish child. The goddess has graced you. Some day you will grow into your full womanhood and you will embrace the sea and the air and the goddess herself and your daughters to come and be a woman amongst women.'*
>
> *And Mother B said, 'I prayed for a daughter, and when you were in my belly I fed and sustained you so that your bones would knit well and my line carry on.'*
>
> *And the C mothers said, 'We clothed you and cleaned you, we taught you and trained you. Was it all for nothing? There must come a day when you gather about you the robes of womanhood and we know that our work was well done.'*
>
> *But the little girl stamped her foot. 'I do not want to be a mother,' she told all her mothers. 'It's a thankless task and a lot of work. Being a child is much more fun.'*
>
> *Mother A groaned, Mother B moaned and all the C mothers winced and frowned. It was no use. The little girl refused to become a womanly woman. The years went by. She did no lessons, she failed her tests, the boys she had played with dived into the sea and turned into foam; but she continued eternally young. And then one day she*

turned fifteen. Her mothers informed her that for better or for worse their work was done. Suddenly she discovered that though still a child, she belonged to no one.'

'What happened to her?' Jyanvi had been listening intently.

'Nothing. If you see an elderly woman walking the streets who begs to be mothered—that's her.' Shyamila shrugged. 'A pitiful spectacle.'

Neither Jyanvi nor the Blue Donkey had much to say. Soon the company retired. Valerie had helpfully pointed the moral: 'This society has no use for childish women.' It perturbed Jyanvi, and then she was cross with herself for being perturbed. That there had been extra warmth in Saraswati's manner when she said good night made matters worse. She slept badly that night and dreamed that she and Saraswati had married each other. They had entered a great house, but they could not lie down; it was crammed with children.

3
Being a Mayan

In the palace garden, Valerie was sounding out the Blue Donkey, trying to arrive at her political affiliations and which side she was likely to choose on the Question of the Succession. The Blue Donkey was being agreeable. She liked gardens. She looked around her at the great banyans, the tamarinds and the neem trees and at the small mogra bushes. Because of the monsoon everything was green. It had rained earlier that morning. The air was gentle and felt benign.

'How do you like it here?' began Valerie.

'It's very pleasant.' The Blue Donkey was not to be drawn.

'And what do you think of our Matriarch?' Valerie continued.

'A formidable figure.'

'Now that you are here, do you think you'll stay?'

'Surely that depends,' murmured the Blue Donkey, 'on whether we're asked.'

'You'll be asked. The Matriarch likes you. I've lived here for the past ten years.'

The Blue Donkey decided that it was her turn to ask questions. 'Is the Ranisaheb an absolute monarch?'

'Oh no. She's only the head of the Mayan Council. The other members are the Five Lesser Matriarchs, but she can always outwit them. They're all related to each other.'

'Isn't the Council answerable to anyone?' the Blue Donkey inquired.

'To the Chiefs of the Guilds,' Valerie replied. 'The Guild of Poets, the Guild of Builders, the Guild of Servants, the Guild of Mathematicians and so forth. All Grade C mothers are members of a Guild.'

'And Grade B mothers?' the Blue Donkey asked.

'They're biological mothers,' Valerie told her. 'Usually all Grade A mothers are automatically given Grade B status.'

'I don't quite follow,' said the Blue Donkey politely.

'Well,' Valerie explained, 'Grade A mothers are the chosen few. They pass all the tests and go on to become the Chiefs of Guilds etc. They can have daughters right away and usually bear their own daughters, but not always. Take Sarla Devi, for instance. She's a Grade A mother, but isn't allowed to bear her own daughter because she's the Chief of the Guild of the Goddess' Servants.'

Valerie carried on. 'Grade B mothers are just means biological mothers. And Grade C mothers do the work. When they've worked long enough and can pay to have a daughter, they can apply for Grade A status. All mothers are members of Guilds, except, of course, the Matriarch.'

'I think I understand,' the Blue Donkey said to Valerie. 'But where do Blue Donkeys fit in?'

'For the time being you're an honoured guest. If you plan to stay on, you must find a Matron.'

'What is a Matron?'

Valerie sighed, but in a way she was enjoying her role as native guide to this benighted foreigner. 'A Matron is just a person, usually a matriarch,' she explained. 'If you are her client, you look to her for help and support, and in return you owe her your allegiance.'

'It sounds like a protection racket,' muttered the Blue Donkey.

'Oh no,' Valerie protested. 'It's almost maternal and does honour to both.'

'Have you a Matron?'

'I am under the protection of Pramila the Poet.'

'Is she a matriarch?'

'No, but she is a princess. She's also the Chief of the Guild of Poets. I could put in a word for you...'

They had been strolling along, but the thought of Pramila the Poet as her Matron made the Blue Donkey halt. 'Oh, that is kind,' she said. 'I'm still very confused and need time ...'

Valerie let it drop. They entered a coconut grove and saw Gagri the Good up a coconut palm, trying to shake loose a few coconuts.

'Isn't that dangerous?' enquired the Blue Donkey.

'It's all right. There are two Grade C mothers holding a net under her.'

'Surely two grown-up women have better things to do?' the Blue Donkey remarked.

'Under the Rule of the Mothers,' Valerie murmured, 'children prosper, especially if the child is the Matriarch's granddaughter.'

'Which of her daughters is Gagri's mother?' asked the Blue Donkey. 'Is it Shyamila? They didn't behave like mother and daughter.'

'Shyamila and Pramila have no daughters yet. Gagri's mother, Asha, was the Matriarch's eldest daughter.'

'What happened to her? Is she dead?'

'She was debarred from the succession and sent into exile for being a heretic. She said that the pretty boys deserved better.' Valerie blurted this out quickly. ' 'The Apostasy of Asha is not a subject a good Mayan should ever discuss. Let's talk about something else.'

The Blue Donkey could see that Valerie was upset. They walked back slowly. After a while the Blue Donkey asked, 'Who is likely to be the Matriarch's Successor?'

Valerie shrugged. 'It's a vexed question. The Matriarch's getting on. She favours Gagri the Good, but the child is only eight.'

'Does her Successor have to be her daughter or her granddaughter?'

'In theory, no; but in practice the bloodline has been unbroken for seven hundred years.'

As they approached the palace the Blue Donkey asked, 'Who controls the army?'

'We have no army, just the Therapists' Guild. They're the police. They deal chiefly with crimes of passion, rivalries and jealousies, non-conformity with Mayan customs, and, of course,' she nodded in the direction of Saraswati and Jyanvi, who were having a heated discussion in the middle of the courtyard, 'the problems of lovers.' They saw Jyanvi break off angrily and hurry to the palace. Saraswati followed at leisure.

'And who controls the police?'

'Shyamila the Civil. They're all trained in therapy. She is the Chief of the Guild of Therapists.'

'Is that the most powerful Guild?' the Blue Donkey enquired.

Valerie considered. 'Yes, that and the Guild of the Goddess' Servants. Shyamila's lover, Sarla Devi, is the Chief of that.'

The Blue Donkey realised it was a significant remark. She didn't know how to respond. 'It's a complex society,' she ventured.

Valerie grinned. 'That it is. No individual isolated and each woman bound to the others by ties of kinship, accepted loyalties and professional affiliations.'

'I can see why one would need a Matron here,' the Blue Donkey muttered. 'Why didn't you choose the Matriarch herself?'

'One has to be chosen. I made the mistake of reprimanding Gagri a few years ago. The child was making a nuisance of herself. I said something. Then I fell out of favour.'

The Blue Donkey didn't quite know how to phrase her next question. At last she said, 'Don't you find this currying for favour a bit difficult?'

Valerie shrugged. 'I was married and divorced before I came here. Coping with the mothers isn't that hard. At least they think they ought to behave like responsible adults.'

'Thank you for explaining these difficult matters,' the Blue Donkey said gently.

Valerie laughed. 'You'll soon get the hang of it. See you at the Festival.' She turned back to add, 'By the way, your friend, Jyanvi, is aiming pretty high. Saraswati belongs to the Five Great Families. The Matriarch is her biological mother. Next to Gagri, it's generally believed the Matriarch favours her.'

The Blue Donkey looked at Jyanvi sideways as they walked to the Festival Pavilion. Cows jostled them, children ran about, women eddied along and bicycles and an occasional car went past. At last the Blue Donkey said, 'What were you and Saraswati arguing about this morning?'

'I told her I was in love with her,' Jyanvi mumbled. 'And she said that she would carefully consider my application to be one of her lovers. She may have been teasing me, but I got angry. I said I didn't want to be just one of her lovers, I was serious.'

'And she?'

'She asked me if I was asking to take on the co-mothership of her daughter, Sona. What did that have to do with anything? But I asked what it involved. She said it meant joint responsibility for the raising of the child.'

'And then?' the Blue Donkey probed gently.

'I asked how old Sona was. She said that was irrelevant. We seemed on the verge of quarrelling, so I walked away.'

'That was a bit rude.'

'I couldn't very well say I wasn't interested in her child, only in her, could I?'

After a pause the Blue Donkey said quietly, 'Jyanvi, you do realise who you've been dealing with? Very possibly the Matriarch's Successor.'

'I don't care,' muttered Jyanvi. She sounded miserable.

As they drew near the Festival Pavilion the Blue Donkey cautioned, 'You're reciting this evening. Be careful.'

They entered the great hall. Someone put a garland around Jyanvi's neck and pushed her towards the platform. The Blue Donkey settled down near Saraswati. On stage there were two other poets besides Jyanvi, and behind them a group of musicians: a tabalji, a veena player, and a third with a tamboura. The tabla sounded. Pramila the Poet took centre stage, splendidly dressed in a brocaded sari, emerald earrings studded her ears. The other women were more modestly dressed. Jyanvi had exchanged her jeans for a cotton sarong and an embroidered shirt. She looked as though she almost belonged, but something about her was not quite Mayan. The smell of coconut hair oil hung like a cloud.

'May the goddess smile upon us!' Pramila cried out.

'May the goddess rejoice!' the audience returned.

Pramila introduced the poets. 'I will recite the first poem.' She smiled archly. 'That will set the mood, the tone, and the theme for the contest. It will remain for each of these poets to improvise a piece that fits in with the first.' She cleared her throat.

The Song of the Grade A Mother

First I worked hard,
Then I worked harder,
Then my daughters came.

They sang and they yelped.
My sisters all helped.
Life was never the same.

Now my daughters are mothers.
They look to the others.
They are gentle and just and sane.

The audience clapped. Pramila looked gratified. The three poets frowned and thought hard. At last the younger of the Mayans rose.

Song of a Grade B Mother

That first wrench hurt —
when they took her from me.
The other mother raised her.
Daily she grows
in strength and beauty...
and I,
who never had her
(yet I made her),
am as content
as is necessary.

The audience sighed and applauded. The second Mayan stood up and recited.

Song of the Grade C Mothers

Other women's children—for whom
we care.
Snotty-nosed darlings—dream
and despair.
Shall these daughters grow? We trim
and we pare
the unfinished young we did
not bear.

This effort was less well-received, but still, it was clearly acceptable. Jyanvi trembled. What was she supposed to do? She got to her feet abruptly. At her first words the tabla sounded ominously. Jyanvi plunged on.

Song of a Non-Mother

I loved my love with passion.
She said, 'Will you marry me?'
I said, 'Is that the fashion?'
She said, 'It is indeed.'

I cooked and cleaned and scoured.
I worked myself to the bone.
Her little children devoured
my labours every one.

They were clean and quick and sprightly.
They scampered in the sun.
'I must go,' I said politely,
and left true love alone.

In spite of the preposterous title, the Mayan mothers had let her finish, but now there was a moment of silence. 'In the name of the goddess, clap!' whispered Saraswati. 'Otherwise she's in trouble.' The Blue Donkey and Saraswati led the applause, others joined them; but the Blue Donkey noted that neither Shyamila the Civil, nor Sarla Devi, the tall, hawk-nosed woman who accompanied her, were among those who applauded. For the time being, the crisis had been glossed over. An interval followed. Jyanvi stumbled from the stage. Saraswati and the Blue Donkey were kind to her, but she seemed numbed.

4
Children are Wonderful

The following day Jyanvi was locked up. The Blue Donkey had contrived to get permission to visit her. Jyanvi's cell was clean enough. It had a wooden bunk, a small table, a barred window and a concrete floor. A potted rose had been placed in a corner, where it was trying to grow.

'Why am I in prison?' Jyanvi demanded.

'You're not in prison,' the Blue Donkey told her. 'You're in "hospital". They think you need therapy for disliking children.'

Jyanvi paced up and down. 'All I've ever said is that children, by definition, are unsatisfactory adults, and that they're a lot of work. These women as mothers know that. After all, they spend half their time making the children grow up!'

The Blue Donkey shook her head. 'Don't argue with me. I haven't put you here. Try to understand you're in serious trouble.'

'What have I done?' Jyanvi asked more quietly.

'You've sinned against motherhood—against their core identities, their religion, and their family structure. Isn't that enough? Have you heard of Asha the Apostate—Gagri's mother, the Matriarch's eldest daughter? She was exiled for heresy.'

The Blue Donkey had at last got through. 'I'm sorry,' she said. 'What's to be done?'

'Saraswati pleaded for you before the Matriarch that you did not fully understand their codes and conventions, and perhaps they had misunderstood yours. Perhaps your poem was intentionally ironic, and that, in any case, poetry was not simply self-expression.'

Jyanvi smiled. 'What did the Matriach say?'

'She asked Saraswati what it was she wanted her to do. Saraswati requested a Special Hearing. She didn't dare ask for anything more. The Special Hearing is at noon, today. The Matriarch is likely to preside. Try to think through what you will say."

'I shall say that children are wonderful!' Jyanvi replied scornfully, then recovered. 'Sorry,' she said. 'Thank you for helping and please thank Saraswati for me.'

After the Blue Donkey left, Jyanvi paced her cell. She noticed the rose in the corner and gave it the rest of her drinking water. The rosebush did not revive instantly, burst into bloom or say 'thank you'. 'Sensible thing,' Jyanvi muttered. She settled down to reconsider her views on mothers and children.

Jyanvi was taken to the palace by two large policewomen. They were kindly, almost maternal. Jyanvi drew herself up and tried to look as grown up as possible.

It was to be a semi-formal hearing. The Matriarch sat in a large chair with Malini Devi and Saraswati on either side; Shyamila the Civil and Pramila the Poet occupied the flanks. Valerie and the Blue Donkey were confined to the sidelines. Jyanvi faced the semi-circle. 'Like a family gathering,' she thought. 'I, of course, am the outsider.' She greeted them formally.

Shyamila began. 'Given that you were a grown-up woman, with a reputation as a poet, we assumed you had achieved adult status long ago. That should be cleared up. Are you now, or have you ever been, a Grade A, B or C mother?'

'Your Highness, I've been a Grade C mother for fifteen years.' Jyanvi knew that Shyamila was not entitled to be called 'Your Highness', but thought it would please her.

Shyamila's face betrayed nothing. She continued soberly, 'Then why have you never applied for Grade A status or at least Grade B? After fifteen years of service you're entitled to that.'

'Your Highness, due to my age I did not apply for Grade B status. I did apply for status as a co-mother. Unfortunately, because of the structures of my society, I was rejected on the grounds that a father would be much more useful.'

'What is a "father"?' interrupted Malini Devi.

'In patriarchal societies,' Shyamila explained, 'the pretty boys grow to a larger size and attempt to rule. Many of them then take up, after a fashion, the functions of co-mothers.'

'As a Grade C mother, did you train many daughters and did they grow up into responsible adults?' the Matriarch asked.

'Your Majesty,' replied Jyanvi, 'in our societies the pretty boys are trained alongside our daughters.'

There was a murmur among the Mayans. 'That must result in chaos!' Malini Devi expostulated.

'Your Ladyship,' Jyanvi answered with a sad smile, 'it frequently does.'

Shyamila the Civil looked thoughtful. 'In that case your Grade C status is questionable.'

'If you say so, Your Highness, but it was achieved under difficult conditions.'

'She has a point,' the Matriarch intervened. She addressed Jyanvi. 'If you choose to remain in Mayan society, you must have a function and you must have some status. Do you so choose?'

Jyanvi trembled. She had hoped not to have to decide so soon. She searched Saraswati's face. Saraswati seemed to be pleading with her. Jyanvi took a deep breath. 'I so choose,' she said clearly. Her head roared. What had she let herself in for?

'Very well,' she heard Shyamila reply. 'What is your function?'

'I am a poet.' Was that the right answer?

Pramila the Poet cleared her throat. 'As Chief of the Guild of Poets I must inform the company that there may be some difficulty in admitting Jyanvi as a member of the Guild, owing to her performance last night.'

'What else can you do?' Shyamila asked.

'I can teach poetry.' Jyanvi hesitated. 'And I can cook, clean and look after children.'

The Matriarch took matters in hand. 'Very well. You are provisionally admitted to the Guild of Servants as a Grade C mother. Should you do well, the question of your status may be reconsidered.'

'Who will employ her?' Malini Devi queried.

Shyamila looked blank, and Pramila looked preoccupied. Saraswati tugged at the Matriarch's sari. 'I will employ her,' said the Matriarch at last, 'as personal servant and Grade C mother to Gagri the Good.' She glanced at Jyanvi. 'No doubt your considerable experience will stand you in good stead. You will, of course, be paid.'

For a moment Jyanvi thought that the Matriarch was having a joke at her expense, then she realised that the Matriarch was serious and that she, Jyanvi, was expected to be grateful. 'Thank you,' she murmured.

Later the four of them crowded into the Blue Donkey's room. Jyanvi sat slumped in a corner. Saraswati had her arm about her.

'I told you it doesn't do to displease Pramila the Poet.' Valerie sounded smug. 'I'll do what I can. It will take time to placate her.'

'Will it be my turn next?' asked the Blue Donkey. 'What will they do about my status?'

'You're quite safe,' answered Saraswati, 'provided what you told me about having taken a vow of celibacy is true.'

'It's true enough, but how is it relevant?'

'Celibates are sacred. They occur so rarely that none of the rules apply to them. You can remain an honoured guest as long as you like.'

'So, I'm all right. What about Jyanvi? Will she survive?'

Nobody answered.

5
An ordinary woman

Saraswati and Jyanvi walked along the beach. The waves pounded. An obliging moon shone down. Saraswati was being kind and tender, but Jyanvi frowned.

'Tell me about money,' she said abruptly, scuffing the sand with her sandal and letting it trickle over her toes.

Her tone jarred, but Saraswati answered amiably. 'What do you want to know?'

'Do you have money? And does everyone have the same amount?'

'It's roughly distributed according to rank.'

'That isn't fair!'

'What good is rank if you don't have the money to back it up?' Saraswati was genuinely puzzled.

'And what does a woman's rank depend upon?'

'On birth and merit,' Saraswati replied. 'Why are you so cross?'

'I'm not cross! In a just society everyone ought to be equal.' She sounded petulant.

Saraswati tried to take her arm and unruffle her, but Jyanvi shook her head fiercely. 'No, don't try to soothe me. Just answer a few questions. I've got to understand how things work.'

Saraswati sighed. Perhaps Jyanvi's mood would change once her questions had all been answered.

'Right. Now, where does the money come from?' Jyanvi demanded.

'From the coffers of the Guilds and the Five Great Families and the Matriarch, of course,' Saraswati replied.

'Where did they get it from?' Jyanvi persisted.

'From the mothers of Maya for services rendered and goods supplied.'

'I see,' said Jyanvi, though she wasn't sure she saw at all. 'Look, if an ordinary woman—someone like me —needs to make a little money, what does she do? What are the sources of income?'

Saraswati thought for a moment. 'She sells her skills, and then, if she has any children, there are the bonuses that accrue from the children. If the children do well, the bonuses are substantial.'

'Do you have to pay to have a child?'

'The state insists that Grade A mothers and Grade B mothers have a child, so the state pays. Where the state does not insist, only permits, you have to show that you can pay.' It was like explaining to someone that the sky is blue, but Saraswati remained patient. 'That's why so many Grade C mothers have to work for years to alter their status.'

The whole system seemed unfair to Jyanvi. She tried again. 'Do Grade A mothers sometimes raise Grade C daughters?' she asked.

'All mothers who raise daughters have to be Grade A,' Saraswati responded.

'I mean the ones who are born Grade A.'

'No one is born Grade A. We have to pass tests. Though it's true that in certain houses there's a high proportion of potential Grade As. The genes are better, and these Grade A mothers can hire a number of Grade C mothers. It all helps.'

Saraswati caught Jyanvi's hand. She would have liked a change of subject, but Jyanvi was relentless. 'Do you mean the Five Great Families and the Matriarchy itself?'

'Yes. Jyanvi, why do you worry so much? The Matriarch likes you. If you do well with Gagri the Good, you can apply for Grade A status as co-mother of my own daughter. It will be all right,' Saraswati coaxed.

'I'm not a mother,' Jyanvi cried passionately. 'I'm a poet!'

'Everyone's a mother,' replied Saraswati placidly. 'As soon as all the fuss subsides, you can re-apply to the Guild of Poets.'

She smiled at Jyanvi and Jyanvi attempted to smile back. They watched the waves roll in one after another, but Jyanvi could not detect a usable pattern.

Gagri the Good was sitting astride the Blue Donkey and pounding her shoulders when Jyanvi returned from fetching a toy.

'Get off!' yelled Jyanvi. She hauled her off the Blue Donkey's. The child kicked and screamed and rolled into a puddle.

"You shouldn't let her bully you,' Jyanvi reproached the Blue Donkey.

'I don't mind,' muttered the Blue Donkey.

'I mind. I'm responsible for its manners, morals and misdemeanours.'

The Blue Donkey glanced at the small creature, who, by now, was covered in mud. 'What about her appearance?'

'I'll have to clean her. Come on,' she said to Gagri the Good. The child wouldn't move.

Jyanvi sat down wearily. 'It's hopeless,' she complained. 'The Matriarch, who is quite clear-headed on every other subject, is utterly contradictory about Gagri the Good.'

'What do you mean?' asked the Blue Donkey, though she could make a guess at what Jyanvi meant.

'The Matriarch thinks the child is perfect, and at the same time she thinks it must be made to grow up. A child, by definition, is an imperfect person.'

'The thing is, you're supposed to love her,' the Blue Donkey suggested cautiously.

'Why should I?' Jyanvi growled.

'If for no other reason,' replied the Blue Donkey, 'then because not to love children is sacrilege on Maya.'

'Look at it.' Jyanvi indicated the child. 'It's hardly lovable.'

'Why do you call her "it"?' asked the Blue Donkey.

'She's an amorphous lump!'

'Who will one day grow into a beautiful woman.'

'Another Matriarch brow-beating everyone!'

'Try to be nice to her,' the Blue Donkey protested. 'She has no mother.'

'The whole island is swarming with mothers!''

'Her real mother, Asha the Apostate, was sent into exile.'

Jyanvi remained unimpressed. 'The Matriarch more than makes it up to her.'

'Try to be nice,' the Blue Donkey repeated. 'Sometimes bribes succeed where threats don't work.'

'I've tried all that,' answered Jyanvi. 'She's used to people being nice to her. She takes it as her due. Besides, she knows damn well that the real source of power lies with the Matriarch. When she wants anything, she just asks her.'

'Well, look,' said the Blue Donkey reasonably, 'you've got to get on with Gagri the Good. Otherwise you're done for.'

'I know.' Jyanvi got to her feet and tried to pick up Gagri bodily. The child bit her. Jyanvi barely stopped herself from giving her a whack.

The Blue Donkey intervened. 'Come on,' she said to the child kindly. 'I'll give you a ride so that you can get cleaned up.' The child leaped onto the Blue Donkey's back.

'Wonderful!' muttered Jyanvi. 'First they're horrid and then you reward them for being less so!'

'Children aren't rational,' returned the Blue Donkey apologetically. 'Try to be patient. See, Gagri the Good is going to be good now, aren't you, Gagri?'

'Yes,' replied Gagri smugly. 'I'm always good.'

Jyanvi snorted. The Blue Donkey looked at her warningly. 'Please, Jyanvi. Pramila has agreed to let you re-apply to the Guild of Poets. They want you to submit a brand new piece immediately. Can you do it?'

'How?' asked Jyanvi. 'Gagri eats up all my time.'

'You must. Do calm down and try to be sensible. Once your skills have been reclassified, you'll be free to live with Saraswati as co-mother with Grade A status.'

'Yes,' said Jyanvi. She shuddered.

The children played in Malini Devi's garden. Saraswati and Jyanvi sat in a bower. Creepers of jai, jui and jasmine trailed above them. The scene ought to have been idyllic, but the children kept interrupting them. Sona was younger than Gagri. Even when the children didn't interrupt, they remained the centre of attention.

The Blue Donkey had told Saraswati about Jyanvi's difficulties. Saraswati wanted to help, but felt uncertain.

'Gagri is only eight,' Saraswati began. 'Just a little difficult, and must be handled carefully. She's promising child.'

Jyanvi turned on Saraswati. 'I'm not interested in the welfare of the child. I'm interested in my own welfare. Why should my life and time be given up for the wretched child? Let her flourish—but at somebody else's expense.'

'The Matriarch helped you when you were in trouble,' Saraswati pointed out.

'And in return must I chop up my life and toss it in gobbets to the hungry child?'

Saraswati recoiled 'Jyanvi, you're dramatising. Do you dislike children?'

'Yes! They take everything and give nothing.'

Saraswati glanced involuntarily at her own daughter. 'You expect Gagri to behave like a miniature adult. She's only a child,' she said reasonably.

'Yes, an imperfect adult,' Jyanvi retorted. 'But she demands services and privileges even adults haven't got, and she has none of the responsibilities.'

'That's my point. She's not an adult. She has to be looked after.' Saraswati couldn't understand why it made Jyanvi so furious.

'Then let her behave like a proper dependant,' Jyanvi decreed, 'and say "yes" and "no" and be grateful.'

Saraswati was doing her best to understand Jyanvi's point of view. 'Children didn't ask to be born,' she pointed out.

'If they dislike having been born, there's a remedy available.'

Saraswati was shocked. 'That's harsh!' she exclaimed.

'I did not ask to have Gagri the Good or any other children,' Jyanvi declared.

'What about the future? It's the duty of every Mayan to sacrifice herself for the welfare of the children,' Saraswati protested. She was finding it hard to remain patient.

'And what about the children?'

'They, in turn, sacrifice themselves,' Saraswati replied.

'Don't any escape?'

The bitterness in her voice startled Saraswati. 'No Mayan would want to escape,' she said quietly.

'There's still a lot of hypocrisy about,' Jyanvi muttered. 'The Matriarch's responsible for Gagri the Good, isn't she? I don't see the Matriarch sacrificing herself!'

'She loves the child!' Saraswati was getting increasingly annoyed. She drew herself up. 'Please remember, you're now discussing my biological mother.'

'I like and respect her,' Jyanvi replied. 'But can't you see that the more powerful mothers hire other women to care for their children?'

'Why does it make you so angry? It's natural for a mother to want the best for her child.'

'At the expense of other women,' Jyanvi pointed out.

'Naturally a mother loves her own children best. But every woman on Maya is a caring mother,' Saraswati explained. 'To be allowed to care for a Mayan daughter is a great privilege.'

Jyanvi got up suddenly. 'To be allowed to slave for a snivelling child is not a privilege, it's a bloody bore!'

By now Saraswati was also angry and upset. She rose to her feet. 'I see. To help me look after my child would not be a privilege, but only, as you put it, a bloody bore.'

'Can't you see it's you I want, not your daughter!' Jyanvi was beside herself.

For some reason this mollified Saraswati. 'So you do want me?'

'Yes.'

'Then be reasonable. We're not just two women who can live by ourselves, we're members of a society with a part to perform.' Why couldn't Jyanvi see the obvious?

'And we must pay our dues by raising children?'

'If you want to put it that way, yes,' Saraswati replied.

Jyanvi sat down. 'And to make the tasks of mothering easier we can hire the services of Grade C mothers?'

'Well yes.' Saraswati hesitated. 'It's good for the children. They all go to school where Grade C mothers are paid to teach them.'

For a while Jyanvi said nothing. At last Saraswati asked, 'Jyanvi, you're not going to do anything silly, are you?'

'No. I'm just figuring out how to get Grade A status.'

Saraswati looked hurt. 'Is that all you want?'

'No, I want to write verse, and I want you. But I also want my life.'

The children played. The two women remained silent.

After a while Jyanvi said, 'There's a favour I wanted to ask you.'

'Yes, certainly. What is it?'

'There's a potted rose in the cell I was locked in. Could you get it for me, please?'

'I suppose so. Why do you want it?'

'In order to congratulate it,' Jyanvi replied, 'on having gained its freedom without having to be grateful.'

6
A Little Preview

Ordinarily the testing would have been done at the Training Centre, but an exception was made for Gagri the Good. The Chief of the Guild of the Servants of the Goddess was conducting the examination herself. Sarla Devi, with her hawk nose and cold grey eyes, exuded authority. She had made it clear she was in charge. The Matriarch and Gagri's aunts could watch from a distance. They were seated in a row against a wall, and Jyanvi, Valerie and the Blue Donkey stood beside them.

The Examiner's assistant set out equipment on a large table, gave Gagri a friendly wink and retired. Gagri the Good was left facing the Examiner. The Examiner took out a wooden doll.

'Here is a doll,' said the Examiner. 'You are supposed to look after her. What is the first thing you are going to do?'

Gagri looked up at the Examiner. She was scrubbed and clean and had on a brocaded blouse and skirt. She knew she was must give the right answer, but she didn't know what it was.

'I'm going to put her to bed and send her to sleep. Then I'm going out to play,' replied Gagri.

'But the doll isn't sleepy. The doll is crying. What are you going to do?'

'I'll just tell her to stop crying.' 'Stop crying,' Gagri said to the doll.

'The doll hasn't stopped crying,' the Examiner informed Gagri.

'I'll put her to bed then.' Gagri was getting bored. 'In the end she'll stop crying and go to sleep.' She put the doll down horizontally.

'The doll is hungry,' said the Examiner. 'If she goes on crying, she'll make herself sick. What are you going to do?'

Gagri the Good looked exasperated. 'If the doll is hungry, why doesn't she eat? Why do you ask me what I'm going to do?'

'The doll is too little to feed herself. You'll have to give her food.'

'All right,' agreed Gagri impatiently. 'I'll give her some food, but then she had better go to sleep, because I want to go out and play.' She looked around. 'What does it eat?' she asked the Examiner.

'Boiled milk, but you'll have to boil it first and then cool it down so that the doll can drink it.'

Everyone thought that Gagri was about to revolt, but the Matriarch had warned her that the one thing she mustn't say was that she wouldn't. Suddenly she brightened. 'It's all make believe.' She waved her hand. 'There, the milk has been boiled.' She waved her hand again. 'Now, it's cooled down.' She pretended to feed the doll. 'The doll has been fed. Now it's gone to sleep and I'm going out.'

The Matriarch smiled broadly. Even Jyanvi was amused. The Examiner remained impassive.

'As you say, that was make believe, now see what you can do with a real baby.' With that the Examiner opened another case, it was padded and equipped with air holes, and produced a baby.

Jyanvi started forward. Valerie restrained her. 'Don't interfere,' she whispered, 'or Gagri will be disqualified. It's one of the pretty boys. He'll be all right.'

Gagri gaped at the filthy baby. Its nose ran. It had soiled its clothes. The Examiner held it out to her.

'It's dirty,' Gagri's voice was barely above a whisper.

The Examiner thrust it at Gagri. 'Well, then you'll have to clean it, won't you?'

Gagri clutched the baby. The baby howled. Gagri clutched the baby harder; the baby's howling increased. Gagri looked up despairingly. 'How?'

'Put it down on the table carefully, and take off its clothes.'

Gagri put the baby down and struggled with its clothes. They fell to the floor in a dirty heap. 'Now what?' Gagri stared at the wriggling baby, terrified it would roll off the table. '

'Bathe it.'

With the help of the Examiner's assistant the baby was put in a basin, washed, dried and dressed in clean clothes. It had cried unceasingly. Gagri looked at the Examiner. 'Is it over?'

'Now it must be fed.'

The assistant gave Gagri a bottle. Gagri fed the baby. The baby smiled. For a moment Gagri felt triumphant. Then the baby wet its nappy. With the assistant's help Gagri changed it. 'Now will it sleep?' she asked the Examiner.

'Yes,' said the Examiner. 'It will sleep for a while.' The assistant lifted it into its crib and shut the lid.

'Pick up its clothes and put them into this basket,' the Examiner directed Gagri.

Gagri looked at the pile with distaste, but did as she was told. She looked up at the Examiner. Had she done well? The Examiner only said casually, 'You may go.' Gagri the Good ran straight towards the Matriarch; but the Matriarch shook her head and Gagri swerved and ran out of the room.

The Matriarch and her daughters surged forward. Sarla Devi kept them waiting. 'Did she pass?' asked the Matriarch anxiously.

Sarla Devi looked at the Ranisaheb for a second. 'Just. She'll do.'

Shyamila stepped forward. She took Sarla Devi's arm. For a moment Sarla hesitated, then linked arms and together they walked out.

There was celebration in the palace that day, rituals and ceremonies to mark the passing of Gagri's First Test. The goddess was worshipped with milk and honey and garlands of flowers. In a week or two, Gagri the Good would be sent to school and the Matriarch would receive a substantial bonus.

Jyanvi walked away thoughtfully. The Blue Donkey caught up with her in an inner courtyard. She was contemplating a spindly rosebush. 'Do you think it will thrive?' she asked gloomily.

'There's plenty of light and it's sheltered here,' the Blue Donkey replied. 'Listen. Tonight would be a good evening for a preview of your piece for the Poet's Guild. Saraswati has made sure you're dining with the family.'

'But I haven't written it.'

'Write it this afternoon.'

'I have to mind the child.'

'I'll mind her for you. But write that piece. And Jyanvi—It would be appropriate if it somehow commemorated Gagri's success.'

The Ranisaheb and her daughters had flung shawls around their shoulders. The weather had turned cooler. Jyanvi was reminded of her first evening at the palace. Had anything changed? She felt sad and uncertain, though everyone else was in a good mood. Saraswati kept giving her encouraging glances, but Jyanvi kept her eyes down. The Blue Donkey nudged Jyanvi. 'Have you written it?' she whispered urgently.

'Yes, but—'

'This is your chance. Gagri goes to school in a few days. The Matriarch is in a good mood.' The Blue Donkey signalled to Saraswati; and as soon as the opportunity arose, Saraswati said, 'I believe Jyanvi has a piece she would like to read to us.'

The Ranisaheb smiled her permission.

'It's a story to mark the occasion,' said Jyanvi.

'What is the title?' enquired the Matriarch.

The Matriarch was being affable. Jyanvi realised that the old woman had been genuinely worried about Gagri's test. 'Well, perhaps she's human,' Jyanvi thought. Aloud she said, 'It hasn't got a title yet.'

'Read it. Perhaps we can help you find a title.'

With that Jyanvi read out the following story:

It so happened that there was once a young woman who did not want to have a daughter. This was her secret and her secret was so dreadful that she kept it to herself. But her genes were good, her background irreproachable, and she herself was not unintelligent, so that it is not surprising that she passed all her tests and was accordingly given Grade A status. It was requested of her that she bear a daughter. There was no help for it, she had to exercise her privilege. During the long months of pregnancy, the young woman prayed day and night and invoked the help of the Great Goddess. Now the ways of the goddess are hard to understand and it isn't entirely clear what it was for that the young woman prayed.

Whatever the mystery behind the matter, the fact remains that as soon as the young woman's daughter was born, the child spoke and apologised to her mother that she was as yet so entirely helpless. It was apparent at once that the child was a prodigy and had somehow been born with the wisdom and experience of the goddess herself. In a day or two she was walking about, within a week she was feeding herself, and within two weeks she had taken over the management of the entire household and was feeding her mother and herself.

They named her Shanta, because despite all her abilities she was gentle and peaceful. The mothers of Maya watched in amazement this strange reversal of the roles proper to mother and daughter; for as Shanta Devi grew in power, her mother declined in strength and health, and at the end of four weeks the mother was dead.

'What does it mean?' the mothers of Maya asked one another. They felt afraid. Only Shanta Devi remained unperturbed. With her customary calm she performed the rites for her mother's funeral, and when the pyre had been lit, she faced the populace. 'What does it mean?' the mothers of Maya demanded of her. 'Are you a Destroyer? Do you carry death?' But Shanta Devi only smiled. 'You know in your hearts exactly what it means. Within a fortnight I, too, shall be dead.' And that is what happened. The mothers of Maya declared her a saint and they built a shrine to honour her, but for weeks afterwards they would look anxiously at their own daughters to make sure that they, at least, were not racing ahead.

Jyanvi stopped. Pramila the Poet looked puzzled. 'The meaning is a little obscure,' she commented. Shyamila the Civil said nothing, but a slight frown creased her forehead. The Matriarch's expression was unreadable. Saraswati and the Blue Donkey trembled for Jyanvi.

'So, you call yourself a poet?' the Matriarch demanded.

'Yes, Your Majesty.'

'And you wrote this tale to please me?'

'Well—'

'But it does not please.'

'No, Your Majesty.'

'On the other hand, it does contain an element of truth.'

Jyanvi relaxed a fraction, but the Matriarch wasn't done with her. 'What is the function of poets?'

'To tell the truth, Your Majesty.'

'Do they know the truth?'

'Whatever little they know, Your Majesty.'

'And is the truth useful?'

'I don't know, Your Majesty.'

'You don't know!' returned the Matriarch. 'Has anyone told you you were a fool?'

Pramila felt it was time for her to say something. 'I fear you have misunderstood the nature of poetry—'

The Ranisaheb cut her short. 'Be quiet, Pramila. I have said she was a fool; she is also a poet. You will admit her to the Guild. I herewith appoint her my Personal Poet.' She turned to Jyanvi. 'You will wait on me in my dressing chamber tomorrow at eight.'

Shyamila the Civil rose to her feet. 'Mother, if you're dispensing favours tonight, it ought to be remembered we're indebted to the Guild of the Goddess' Servants.'

The Matriarch looked at Shyamila. 'Are you suggesting that without Sarla Devi, Gagri would have failed the test?'

'Well, perhaps not. But if you are bending the rules, you might bend them in a worthier cause.' She said this with indignation, and regretted it instantly.

The Matriarch's mood had changed. 'It was you and Sarla Devi who were foremost in insisting on the letter of the law when Gagri's mother was exiled,' she said.

Pramila sucked in her breath. It was the first time since her eldest sister had been exiled that the Matriarch had referred to the event. The Blue Donkey tried to think of something harmless to say, but the Matriarch was speaking again. She glanced at the company. 'You tire me,' she said.

They had been dismissed. They dispersed uncertainly, and the Ranisaheb went to bed.

7
Well, Poet?

The Ranisaheb was combing her hair. It had been washed with coconut milk, coconut oil and natural soap, and dried above a coal fire with burning incense. A servant was carrying away the little iron stove which contained the coals. Jyanvi looked at the Matriarch and saw an aged woman, overweight and determined. Then she noticed the fine hands, the thinning hair and the lines on her face. For a moment she liked her enormously.

'Well, Poet? What varnished truth can you offer today?'

'Varnished, Your Majesty?' Jyanvi queried. She didn't want to risk giving offence.

'Any fool can tell the truth, and, at court, only a fool sometimes does,' the Matriarch replied. 'It's the varnish that distinguishes fool from poet.'

The Matriarch seemed to be in a good mood. 'Well, now that I've told you something about the nature of poets,' the Matriarch continued, 'it's your turn to tell me something about the nature of matriarchs.' The Matriarch finished tying her hair in a bun, stuck in a few pins and looked quizzically at her personal poet.

Jyanvi had remained standing. She replied gravely, 'To be a matriarch is a difficult task, filled with responsibility. It needs the wisdom and experience, which, happily for Maya, Your Majesty possesses.'

To this the Matriarch responded with disgust. 'Any courtier could have told me that. Most of them do at least once a day. Pull yourself together, woman. You sound like a parrot. I asked for a poet.' She got up, examined the saris laid out for her and picked up one. She unfolded it, held it against herself, glanced in the mirror and let it drop to the ground. Then she selected a dark green one with its matching blouse. She put on the blouse and began tucking the sari into her petticoat.

While the Ranisaheb pleated and tucked and draped the sari around herself, Jyanvi had had a chance to think. She didn't know what to say. At last she mumbled, 'Your Majesty, I'm only a poet sometimes, that is when I compose a poem. I can't turn it on and off.'

The Matriarch looked her full in the face. 'And am I the Matriarch only sometimes? Can I turn it on and off?' She began to stamp on the edge of her sari in order to make the length even.

Jyanvi answered slowly, 'No, you can't turn it off.' She found she was kneeling at the Matriarch's feet trying to help her adjust the length.

'You can't switch on, and I can't switch off. And why is that?' the Matriarch demanded.

Jyanvi rose to her feet. 'Because, Your Majesty, the institutions of Maya are too well made.'

The Ranisaheb chuckled. 'That will do. Sit down. A truth a day. You're earning your keep. What's the going rate for poets?'

Jyanvi realized that the old woman was having a game with her. She ventured a smile. 'Payment is generally for keeping quiet or telling lies. A monarch who pays for the truth is like—'

'A poet who does not complain. A rarity. Now. Today is the Day of Oracles. We're going to the Cave Temple. Saraswati will be accompanying us.' The Matriarch paused and when she saw Jyanvi brighten, she added thoughtfully, 'Our kinship system is complex. In future you may call me Aisaheb.'

Jyanvi wasn't quite sure what to make of it. 'Thank you,' she said.

The Matriarch smiled. 'Oh, and go and find the Blue Donkey. On the Day of Oracles the Matriarch of Maya receives instructions from the goddess herself. These instructions are sometimes hard to interpret.'

Though mystified, Jyanvi hurried off on the Matriarch's errand. She found Valerie and the Blue Donkey with Gagri the Good in the coconut grove. Gagri was up a tree again. Jyanvi almost felt sorry for her. All this must soon end.

'The Aisaheb would like you to accompany us to the Cave Temple,' she informed the Blue Donkey.

'Who?' asked the Blue Donkey.

'The Matriarch. She told me to call her Aisaheb,' Jyanvi replied.

Valerie had been listening. 'Do you know what that means?' She had an odd expression on her face.

'Well, "Ai" means "mother" and "Saheb" means "Ladyship" or "Mistress". I thought it meant she was pleased with me.' Jyanvi looked anxious. 'Does it mean something else?'

'It means'—Valerie pronounced each word distinctly—'that she has decided to become your Matron.'

'Oh.' Jyanvi felt a smile spread across her face.

'You're lucky,' went on Valerie. 'Comes of being a lesbian, I suppose. It's easy for you. You relate to women. It took me a long time just to adjust.' She could not quite suppress a trace of envy. 'Anyhow, well done!'

'Are you heterosexual?' The Blue Donkey enquired carefully.

'Of course, I am,' Valerie replied. She felt a sudden urge to confide in the Blue Donkey. 'You don't know what a relief it is to talk to someone who actually understands what the word means!'

'It must be difficult,' the Blue Donkey murmured. 'Aren't there any men at all on Maya?'

'No. Not that I have much use for men, but, well—' Valerie broke off.

'What about the pretty boys?' enquired the Blue Donkey.

'That would be like having sex with children or with creatures of a different species. The mothers of Maya would put me in jail!' Valerie replied. 'But it's not just the sex,' Valerie continued. 'It's the Mayan attitude. They don't even want to understand who I am or what I've been.'

'It must have been very hard to fit into Mayan society,' said the Blue Donkey understandingly. 'You've done well. But tell me, how do the mothers conceive their children?'

'They milk the pretty boys.'

'What?' asked Jyanvi and the Blue Donkey simultaneously.

'They milk them of semen before the boys dive into the sea and turn into foam,' Valerie elaborated.

'This "turning into foam"—' Jyanvi hesitated. It was a question which had been troubling her for some time now. 'Is that a euphemism or —'

'Sort of,' Valerie grimaced. 'The thing is, the pretty boys go mad at fourteen. They become aggressive. They fight…' It was a subject she found distasteful, but Jyanvi and the Blue Donkey were intrigued.

'That sounds normal for boys that age,' Jyanvi put in.

Valerie looked at her. 'Boys aren't the norm on Maya Diip. The boys fight among themselves. The mothers of Maya let them. Eventually there's nothing left to fight, only the waves. So they fight the waves, turn into foam, so to speak...'

'What a waste,' Jyanvi couldn't help saying.

'Asha the Apostate protested,' Valerie said wearily, 'and look what happened to her. The Mayans say that to keep the pretty boys alive would be wasteful. They think that except for the semen the lives of pretty boys are pointless.'

'Why don't the pretty boys turn against the mothers?' Jyanvi asked.

'I don't know. They're not organised? Haven't any weapons? They turn most of their aggression against themselves. There aren't very many. The mothers of Maya don't regard them as children—just as necessities.' Valerie shrugged. 'The Princess Asha went around saying that if they were treated differently, they would be different. They might never reach the stature of normal women, but within their limitations, they could be helped to grow up.'

During Valerie's explanation, Gagri the Good had slithered down the tree and crept up behind them. She had meant to give them a start, but had stopped when she caught her mother's name.

'It wouldn't be much fun being a man on Maya,' Jyanvi muttered. She hesitated. 'If you don't like it here, why did you stay?'

'Because it's even less fun being a woman Outside!'

'Could you have gone with the Princess Asha?' enquired the Blue Donkey.

'To what purpose? She was sent off into the forest.'

'Did she have much support?'

'She had a little. That's why she was exiled.'

'By her own mother?' Jyanvi asked.

'Shyamila and Sarla Devi had a hand in it,' Valerie replied thoughtfully. 'The Guild of the Servants of the Goddess declared her a heretic and the Therapists' Guild pronounced her incurable. The Matriarch didn't have much choice. Look, it's a forbidden subject. I shouldn't have said anything. Last night was the first time I heard the Matriarch mention it.'

'Boo!' shouted Gagri. Unable to understand what the grown-ups were saying, she had got tired of eavesdropping.

Valerie jumped. The Blue Donkey said to Gagri gently, 'You mustn't do that, dear.'

Gagri grinned. 'Look at all the coconuts I got!'

'That was very clever, dear.'

'I am clever,' Gagri agreed, and tried to pick up all the coconuts.

'Thank you for telling us these things,' the Blue Donkey said to Valerie soberly. 'Just one question. Why do they call the pretty boys "pretty"?'

'Out of kindness,' Valerie replied.

8
Day of Oracles

Sarla Devi, the the Chief of the Guild of the Servants of the Goddess, and her acolytes, were waiting for them at the top of the cliff. She greeted the Matriarch with formal politeness. She glanced at the Matriarch's entourage. 'Has the Princess Shyamila not accompanied you?' she asked, her voice carefully uninflected.

'No,' replied the Matriarch. 'The Princess Shyamila has not accompanied us.'

On the face of it there had been nothing sinister in this interchange, but Jyanvi felt nervous. Behind them the sea pounded against the cliffs. Below them a crowd of Mayans had gathered to watch the Matriarch descend to the Cave Temple. When the Matriarch re-emerged, she would have the answers to the questions which most troubled the Mayans. Each of the mothers had sent her question to the Goddess' Guild, and the three most frequently asked had been picked out. The process was supposed to be automated, but Sarla Devi's grey eyes glinted as she presented the Matriarch with the 'Important Three'. The Matriarch took them. The crowd cheered. Then the Matriarch read them out:

1. Who will be the Matriarch's Successor?
2. Will Maya Diip prosper forever?
3. Under what circumstances may a Mayan mother disobey the Mayan Law?'

The crowd sighed, drums thundered. Jyanvi could just see the cave mouth halfway down the cliff. The slow descent to the cave began. At the cave the Matriarch paused and thanked Sarla Devi. She was forced to remain outside. To enter the cave with her chosen companions was the Matriarch's prerogative.

Saraswati now led the way through a short corridor to an open space containing a large temple. The walls of the cliff rose around them. Towards the top, the side facing the sea had been broken off, and it was through this opening that daylight entered. Every square inch of rock had been carved and polished and depicted the exploits of the goddess.

Jyanvi felt dazed. The goddess was everywhere, among her friends, her lovers, her warriors, her servants, her enemies and her babies. And she was there in all her aspects: grim, giddy, tender and maternal, languid and luxurious, asleep and waking, austere and amorous, warlike and proud. Jyanvi ran her fingers over the basalt. This was stone made flesh. She was overwhelmed.

The Matriarch spoke. 'Come with me into the inner temple and there we will meditate and seek guidance regarding the three questions.' Her eyes held theirs conveying an implicit understanding. Saraswati's nod in the direction of the entrance made matters clearer. Without further questions, Jyanvi and the Blue Donkey followed the Matriarch.

The inner temple was dominated by a figure of the goddess dancing. They touched her feet, and lit the lamps set down before her. They then sat down and contemplated the goddess. The limbs moved and did not move. The pattern had been caught, held in motion.

After a while, the Matriarch asked, 'Has the goddess spoken?'

It was Jyanvi who answered.

'She who shall reign in the goddess' name
must suffer change, yet stay the same.'

The Matriarch looked at Jyanvi sharply. 'Interpret it,' she commanded the Blue Donkey.

'Your daughter, Saraswati, bears one of the goddess's names,' the Blue Donkey replied, 'She was adopted by Malini Devi and has suffered change, yet she remains your daughter in her fidelity, affection and resemblance to you.'

The Matriarch nodded thoughtfully. She looked at Saraswati for a long time. At last, the Matriarch spoke. 'So be it.'

Jyanvi was startled. Could the future be fixed so easily? The Matriarch had already moved to the next question. 'And shall Maya Diip prosper forever?' she asked.

The Blue Donkey considered for a moment. 'The Mayan Lamp shall remain undimmed,' she told the Matriarch, 'till there are no more mothers, only daughters.'

'That can never happen!' Saraswati exclaimed.

'Do you think so?' The Matriarch's voice was indulgent. 'The goddess has vouchsafed you a good answer,' she said to the Blue Donkey. 'And now, my dear,' she turned to Saraswati again, 'when you are Matriarch, under what circumstances will you allow a Mayan to disobey the laws of this island?'

'When you are Matriarch'. The words reverberated in Saraswati's head. She took up the challenge. 'When that Mayan ceases to be a Mayan.'

Jyanvi and the Blue Donkey suddenly felt cold. It was only a draught, the lamps had flickered; but they knew that the situation on Maya had changed. Soon, the mothers of Maya would hear the instructions of the goddess. Decisions had been made and they had helped to make them. To have their words become a part of a functioning structure seemed strange, and somehow uncomfortable. The problem of the Oracle had only been a challenge. They had found the words that would fit gracefully. Shouldn't they be pleased? Surely poetry ought to make things happen? Jyanvi and the Blue Donkey felt uneasy. The Matriarch had risen. They followed her.

In the broad daylight Jyanvi blinked. Sarla Devi's bearing was impeccably correct—and antagonistic. She set the pace relentlessly on the climb back to the summit. The Matriarch was forced to pause for breath. Jyanvi felt concerned, then silly. Was there any need to worry about the Matriarch? Hadn't the old lady just manipulated them—and with such ease?

When they reached the top, a great cry rose from the crowd. The Matriarch presented them with a moving combination of majesty and humility. The instructions of the goddess were given to the mothers. They cheered and roared, riding on a crest of Mayan pride. Saraswati had always been popular, they saw her now as her Mother's Daughter and the two together as the supreme embodiment of their noblest dream. The Day of Oracles had been a great success. Only the Servants of the Goddess seemed less than gratified.

PART II

‘Did you succeed?’ enquired the Cheshire Cat.
‘Succeed in what?’
‘In persuading the mouse that I’m essentially quite an amiable cat.’
Then it did a slow fadeout.

9
Being Eater or Eaten

In the forest no creature harmed them. The birds and beasts were amiable enough, and the trees provided food for everyone. Shyamila the Civil, not quite able to bring herself to commit matricide, had exiled them. The Matriarch and Saraswati had been made to retire and Jyanvi and the Blue Donkey accompanied them. Gagri the Good and Saraswati's daughter had been left behind, presumably as hostages.

The trouble had begun as soon as the Matriarch had returned to the palace from the Cave of the Goddess. Both Pramila and Shyamila had wanted to know why they had been disinherited. At first the Matriarch had been amused. She pointed out that the Succession was only an administrative matter. They had wanted to know why this administrative detail had not been settled in their favour. 'Am I less your daughter than any of the others?' Shyamila had asked, and Pramila had said, 'Doesn't poetry matter?' Gagri the Good hadn't said anything, but she had been more demanding than usual.

'Be quiet,' the Matriarch had commanded. 'The matter is settled. My daughter, Saraswati, shall be my successor, and after her the succession passes to my granddaughter, Gagri the Good.'

At this Saraswati had demurred. 'Would it not be enough just to settle the matter of your successor?' She had to consider the interests of her own daughter. Shyamila and Pramila had seized on this at once.

'Gagri the Good as the eldest daughter of the eldest daughter is the rightful heir,' Shyamila had declared. 'Let her be appointed your Successor and I will serve as her regent. As for Saraswati, she was adopted by Malini Devi and isn't even our sister.'

'You are all equally my daughters,' the Matriarch had told them wearily; but Pramila and Shyamila had remained unconvinced and could not understand why Saraswati had been chosen.

'In what way is she better qualified?' Shyamila had demanded.

'She is less your daughter than I am,' Pramila had added.

In the end the Matriarch had told them to pull themselves together and behave like grown-ups, then she had dismissed them. The following morning, she was arrested. The Guild of the Servants of the Goddess in conjunction with the Therapists' Guild and the Poets' Guild had informed the mothers of Maya that the Matriarch, together with her entourage, had taken herself off to the Forest of Retirement. Shyamila the Civil and Sarla Devi would jointly take care of the administration of Maya in her absence.

And so the matter rested. The Blue Donkey glanced at the Matriarch. Was she hurt? Depressed? And hiding it all? She had seated herself under a large banyan. She looked tired, but not discontent. That Saraswati was angered by the loss of the matriarchy and anxious about the welfare of her daughter was obvious. She walked up and down while her mind worked on a plan of campaign. Jyanvi kept in step with her. The Blue Donkey settled down beside the Matriarch. After a while the Matriarch asked, 'Well, is your prophecy fulfilled? Are the Mothers of Maya only daughters and no longer mothers?'

'Not especially, Your Majesty,' replied the Blue Donkey. 'The daughters of Maya are only trying to look after their own interests and the interests of their daughters.'

'I am no longer "Your Majesty",' returned the Matriarch. 'One can't be a matriarch without a matriarchy. In a forest every creature is only itself. You are a donkey and I am an old woman.'

'All right,' agreed the donkey. 'What happens next?'

'I think Shyamila will send a deputation,' the Matriarch replied.

'What will you do?' the Blue Donkey asked.

'I don't know.' The Ranisaheb of Maya smiled at the Blue Donkey companionably. 'I quite like this forest.'

Just then Shyamila the Civil and Pramila the Poet, accompanied by several armed followers, burst into the clearing.

'Well, Mother, have you reconsidered?' Shyamila began boldly.

'Reconsidered what?'

It was extraordinary how the Matriarch had managed to make her seat under the banyan seem like a throne, and the banyan itself like a great canopy protecting her. It made Shyamila feel that she was a petitioner, or at best a naughty little girl. She reminded herself she had the upper hand. She answered evenly, 'Have you reconsidered the matter of the succession. I am more your daughter than any of these others. It's only fitting that I should be the next Matriarch.'

'In what way are you more my daughter?'

'I am most like you,' Shyamila replied with conviction. 'I have your strength and your intelligence.'

Pramila stepped forward. 'But I have your love of poetry. And that matters most.'

The Matriarch's glance travelled slowly from daughter to daughter. It rested on Saraswati. 'What is your claim to being more my daughter than any of these others?'

Saraswati hesitated. 'Like you, and unlike them, I have borne a daughter.'

The Matriarch sighed. 'So you feel that whichever one of you is most like me should rule in my stead?'

Shyamila confronted the Matriarch. 'Yes, Mother. That's what we think.'

The Matriarch turned to the Blue Donkey. 'The sight of my grown-up daughters behaving like children discourages me. Explain to them why they ought not to behave like children.'

The Blue Donkey considered. She said soberly, 'I will tell them a story.'

Several hundred miles from Maya, in the middle of the ocean, there was once an island where it was the general practice for the women of the island to eat one another. It was not that they were cruel or unusually savage or even suffering from a shortage of food, it was just that their digestive tract had a peculiarity which enabled them to acquire the essential virtue of any creature they happened to ingest. It followed then that the more evolved the creature, the greater the benefits derived from it. And it was for this reason that the women of this island began eating each other.

When they first made this discovery, murder became such a commonplace occurrence that the population of the island began to decline. Their Matriarch, who was, of course, a prime target, did her best to put a stop to it. Everyone agreed that the mandatory penalty for attempted murder and for murder itself should be death, but a controversy raged about what to do with the resulting bodies. There was a general consensus that the body of the victim should be chopped up carefully and distributed fairly among the populace; but there was some disagreement about what was fair. Some women argued that the children of the victim should be given the lion's share; but others pointed out that the possibility of a gain as large as that was only putting temptation in the way.

Discussion concerning the murderer's body was more ferocious. One group said that the real issue was whether to waste or not to waste. Others argued that to eat the murderer would inevitably make the murderer a part of themselves and that this would be improper. In a sense, it would make the murderer immortal, and vice ought not to be rewarded. It was decided in the end that each woman should be allowed to choose for herself.

Since life was still dangerous, all the islanders made out wills bequeathing their bodies either to their children or to the state, and, in some instances, to their lovers and friends. As for the bodies of the murderers, they were chopped up and placed in the marketplace. Those who wished to, were able to partake, but to be seen doing so resulted in disgrace. As a result, though there was a small black market in the bodies of murderers, most of the remains were thrown away. Gulls and vultures and scavenging animals fed on these remains, and in time these creatures acquired the skill and cunning of the women they had eaten. No woman was safe from marauding gulls, no gull was safe from the attack of vultures. Soon a general massacre prevailed. Every creature was eating every other as fast and as furiously as it possibly could. And that was how it happened that life on this island destroyed itself.'

The Blue Donkey paused, and surveyed the women assembled there to see what effect her story had had.

'That isn't logical,' the Matriarch commented. 'In the end there ought to have been one creature left. Which one was that?'

'Everyone and no one,' the Blue Donkey replied. 'It's true that in the end there was one glob left, but the essential virtues of all these creatures so warred within its mass that it died before it was born of self-hatred.'

The Ranisaheb nodded. 'Yes, that will do. It satisfies.'

Jyanvi protested. 'Weren't there any among these creatures who were kind and gentle, so that when they were eaten the Eater was changed?'

'There was one,' the Blue Donkey responded gravely, 'but faced with the terrible choice between being Eater or Eaten, she jumped into a well right at the outset. It's true that the fish in the well ate bits of her body, but this so changed them that they were no longer able to feed themselves. The well acquired a bad reputation and was known to the creatures as the Well of Death.'

Shyamila the Civil interrupted angrily, 'Tall tales and poetry make nothing happen. Are you or aren't you going to change your mind?'

'I am not going to change my mind.' The Matriarch sounded weary.

'But Mother,' Shyamila burst out in exasperation, 'what difference does it make which of your daughters rules in your stead?'

Suddenly the Matriarch smiled. 'Perhaps you're right,' she said.

'Then you agree to name me as your successor?' Shyamila could not keep the eagerness out of her voice.

'No.'

Shyamila frowned. Why was the Matriarch being so unreasonable? Couldn't she see that agreeing to their demands was mere common sense? 'Mother,' Shyamila tried to be patient, 'can't you see that the effective power is in our hands? In making any concessions at all, I'm being generous where you're helpless! I came in spite of Sarla's objections.'

The Matriarch glanced at her daughter. 'You are tedious,' was all she said.

For a moment Shyamila the Civil wanted to stamp her foot; but she managed to make herself answer quietly, 'With due respect, so are you, Mother.' She summoned her followers and left.

10
But She was a Heretic

'It's absolutely essential that we march into Maya, depose Shyamila and get the matriarchy back.' Saraswati was exasperated. Why couldn't the others see this? That her mother should appear so indifferent made no sense at all. The Matriarch was lying down in a crude shelter of leafy branches the others had made for her. She had said that the events of the past two days had tired her. It was Jyanvi and the Blue Donkey whom Saraswati was addressing. 'It isn't like my mother to be so resigned. Is she simply going to let Shyamila have her own way?'

It was on the tip of Jyanvi's tongue to say, 'Yes, why not? What does it matter?' But she managed not to say it.

'Perhaps the Matriarch is upset by the spectacle of her daughters quarrelling among themselves,' the Blue Donkey suggested.

'I can't let the matter rest,' replied Saraswati. 'Will you help me?'

Jyanvi and the Blue Donkey did not answer immediately. Which of the Matriarch's daughters ruled didn't really matter to them. Or did it matter? Jyanvi had begun to think that life in the forest had distinct advantages. She would be able to think in peace. She would have Saraswati to herself, and both Gagri and Sona would be far away, being looked after by somebody else. Jyanvi also realised that this was not a point of view Saraswati would share. Why start an argument which could only offend? She said she would help. The Blue Donkey was more disinterested, but she liked Saraswati. 'Yes,' she agreed. 'But it depends on the Matriarch.'

'Oh, the Matriarch will come round.' Saraswati continued briskly. 'What we need is a plan of action. What do you suggest?'

Jyanvi thought fast. She had to been seen to be doing her best. 'Let's ask Asha the Apostate for her help. She was exiled to this forest, wasn't she?'

'But she was a heretic!'

The Blue Donkey murmured quietly, 'Does it matter under the circumstances?'

As Saraswati was considering this, they found themselves surrounded by fifteen young men. Each carried a short, wooden rod. 'Please accompany us,' said the leader gravely.

Saraswati was outraged. 'Since when do pretty boys make requests?'

The young men looked puzzled. The Blue Donkey examined them. They were only boys, and very pretty in their light kurtas and bright sarongs. Their rods were elaborately carved. Toys or weapons? Two or three of the boys had wooden dolls. Were they playing a game? 'What happens if we refuse?' she enquired.

'Then we must go back for instructions,' answered one of them.

The noise had woken up the Matriarch. 'Who sent you?' she asked them.

'Our mother,' replied the leader, 'the Princess Asha. She was exiled from Maya for saving our lives.'

The young man had said this in all seriousness. The Matriarch didn't know what to make of it. She found herself asking, 'Do you always do what your mother tells you?'

'Yes!' he replied.

In spite of herself, this reminded the Matriarch of Gagri the Good. 'Well,' she told him, 'go and tell your mother that her mother has summoned her here.'

The fifteen young men gaped at the Matriarch. 'Are you the Matriarch of Maya Nagar, the fabled city?' asked the leader incredulously.

'Yes,' the Matriarch said briskly. 'I'm your mother's mother. Now, do as you're told.'

The boys were having trouble taking it in. It was as though

a fabled creature had appeared among them. They stared at the Matriarch a few seconds longer, then filed away into the forest.

Before the others could say anything, the Matriarch informed them that she was still tired and intended to rest. The Blue Donkey settled beside her and dozed off as well. Jyanvi felt uneasy. Anything could happen. Didn't the Matriarch and the Blue Donkey care? Saraswati, at least, looked suitably worried. Was she really going to ask for the Apostate's help. Then what? Would they march into Maya with an army of young men and Asha at their head? Armed with wooden rods? It would be stupid. On the other hand, was staying in the forest really a good idea? She would have liked a bath, but the brook was hardly adequate. And though the berries and fruits had been delicious, there was something to be said for hot meals, comfortable beds...

Jyanvi kept her thoughts to herself and waited. When the leaves rustled and twigs cracked, it wasn't Asha and her troops, it was Valerie looking flustered and distressed.

'Where's the Matriarch?' asked Valerie. 'I have a message.' She stumbled towards the Ranisaheb and fell at her feet.

'Your Majesty, the Princess Pramila craves your pardon. So does Malini Devi, the Lesser Matriarch. They asked me to tell you that Gagri the Good and Saraswati's daughter are quite safe. The Guild of Poets and the supporters of Malini Devi are at your disposal. They beg you to return from the forest.'

The Matriarch sat up and examined Valerie sleepily. 'Thank you for bringing news of the children. Just why do Pramila and Malini Devi want me to return?'

'They are troubled by the tyranny of the Princess Shyamila and of her consort, Sarla Devi, Chief of the Guild of the Servants of the Goddess.' It was a rehearsed speech.

'I understand the rhetoric,' the Matriarch told her. 'Now give me a proper explanation.'

Valerie got to her feet slowly. 'Well,' she said awkwardly, 'they're going to disband the Guild of Poets, merge it perhaps with the Goddess' Servants. According to them, poets are useful, but shouldn't be autonomous. The Princess Pramila is very upset.'

'And why is the Lesser Matriarch troubled?'

'The Princess Shyamila has ruled that that particular house has no legitimate heir after Malini Devi and that all their privileges and properties revert.'

'To whom?'

'To the Matriarchate, which in turn, it is rumoured, intends to hand them over to the Chief of the Goddess' Servants. That would make Sarla Devi a Lesser Matriarch—'

They were interrupted by the sound of conch shells. The fifteen young men, now accompanied by many others, marched into the clearing, divided into two rows, came to a halt and waited, while a dozen other young men brought in a palanquin upon their shoulders. Then they all fell on their knees, bowed their heads, flourished their rods and cried out loudly, 'The Empress Asha is here!'

A middle-aged woman climbed out carefully. She wore a white sari with a purple border, which had been washed and ironed, but looked old. She had a pleasant face. She bowed slightly to the Matriarch. 'Well, Mother?'

'Well, daughter? What is the meaning of this?' The Matriarch indicated the bowed heads.

Asha the Apostate smiled. She appeared unembarrassed. 'Oh,' she said, 'the boys like it. It's only a game. They say it gives them a sense of cohesion. Would you like me to send them away? Or will you come with us so that we can make you more comfortable?'

'We will come,' the Matriarch replied.

'Wait, Mother!' Saraswati interrupted. 'Oughtn't we to find out a little more?'

Asha the Apostate turned to Saraswati. 'You must be Saraswati. You were only a little girl when I last saw you. Welcome to the forest.'

Saraswati looked at her eldest sister doubtfully. 'Thank you,' she said. 'May I present Jyanvi and the Blue Donkey? And this is Valerie. Perhaps you remember her?'

'How do you do?' Asha the Apostate greeted each one of them in the friendliest possible way. 'Will you accompany us?' she asked politely.

The Blue Donkey agreed with alacrity. She found Asha congenial. The others were uncertain, but accepted the invitation with more or less grace.

11
A Loyal Mayan

Ashagad, or the Fortress of Hope, was some distance away. Once they left the forest, the terrain became hilly and barren. On some of the rocks it was possible to see the concentric rings made by the lava long ago. Overhead, the sun blazed and hawks circled on the thermal currents. The Ranisaheb was enjoying herself. She looked about her with huge interest. When she tired, the pretty boys carried her in a palanquin. Saraswati had her doubts about whether any of it was advisable, but there was little choice.

After a steep climb, they reached the stronghold. Even Saraswati was impressed. The inhabitants of Ashagad had cut splendid chambers in the cliff face to house themselves. Below them lay their fields and the broad stream which irrigated them. The general effect was neither impoverished, nor uncivilised. Jyanvi and the Blue Donkey were reminded of the Cave Temple, though these chambers had been constructed much more recently and there were only a few carvings here and there. These appeared to celebrate the Empress or perhaps the goddess. The female figure was usually surrounded by a group of young men, and just occasionally by a little boy and a little girl. Nobody offered a comment.

After the visitors had refreshed themselves, they were invited to dine. 'Would it please them,' the Apostate enquired, 'to be entertained with a dance recital first?''

'That would be most agreeable,' the Matriarch replied.

The dancing was good and the music excellent, it was just the story that was a little obscure. The principal dancers consisted of a tree and two young men, who seemed to be imploring the tree to give them something. The dancer who played the tree expressed the tree's indifference by subtle gestures. When the two young men had almost given up, the tree relented and appeared to shed a blessing on them.

'Beautifully done,' the Mayans murmured and congratulated Asha on the skill of the dancers.

Asha the Apostate turned eagerly to her mother, 'Now will you admit that boys can be civilised?'

The Matriarch looked up in surprise, 'Whether or not they can be civilised was never in dispute. It's just that it was never considered particularly worthwhile.'

For a fraction of a second Asha looked as though her mother had slapped her, but she said lightly, 'We won't argue now. Tomorrow I'd like you to meet Mohan and Madhu. Perhaps they'll convince you better than I can.'

'Who are Mohan and Madhu?' enquired the Matriarch.

'My eldest boys.' Was there a touch of defiance in Asha's manner?

'You call them yours?' Saraswati had been startled into speaking before she could stop herself.

'Yes, I call them mine.' Open hostility had replaced defiance.

Before any further damage was done, the Blue Donkey said quickly, 'I greatly enjoyed the dance performance, but I'm not sure I understood it. Who were the two young men, and why were they beseeching the tree?'

'The two young men were mothers and they were beseeching the tree to grant them a child,' Asha replied.

'But how could they be mothers?' It was Valerie who protested this time.

Asha the Apostate had regained her composure. 'The institutions of Ashagad are not unlike those of Maya Nagar,' she explained politely. 'Those young men had passed all the tests and attained adult status.'

'Why did they pray to a tree?' asked Jyanvi, feeling this was a harmless question.

'In Ashagad, when a youngster passes his first test, he carves himself a wooden doll,' Asha told her. 'It symbolises the baby he hopes to receive from the Tree of Life. Many of the youngsters also carve short, wooden rods, which represent the Tree itself.'

'A charming myth,' Jyanvi murmured.

'It's not a myth,' Asha replied. 'There's a tree in the forest, underneath which we find boy babies. Ask the Matriarch. The mothers of Maya know of it. We call it the Tree of Life.'

For the first time in their acquaintance, Jyanvi saw the Matriarch flinch, but the old woman's voice was steady enough when she answered. 'We call it the Tree of Death.'

Jyanvi and the Blue Donkey were appalled. They had hoped to smooth over differences, not uncover infanticide.

No one knew what to say. Fortunately dinner was served. They were waited upon by two or three of Asha's young men. The visitors found the food delicious. The chapattis were hot and properly layered, the vegetables fresh and suitably spiced. As they ate they felt better tempered. But Saraswati had decided nothing was to be gained by being circumspect.

'I do not wish to offend, she said, 'but are you the only real mother here?'

Asha the Apostate looked at her coldly. 'No. However, to answer you in Mayan terms, I am the only Grade B mother here.'

'And you have borne children?' Saraswati continued. Jyanvi and the Blue Donkey glanced at her. What had got into Saraswati? Didn't she appreciate that she was a foreigner here?

Asha the Apostate replied with cold fury. 'I have borne one daughter. When she was still a baby she was taken away from me.'

The Matriarch put an arm around Asha. 'Gagri is well,' she told her softly. 'Saraswati is a Mayan. Try to be patient with her. She means no harm.'

The Blue Donkey intervened again. 'Gagri the Good is a delightful child,' she said to Asha gently. 'Forgive us for being so clumsy. I think the question that is exercising us all is how you maintain your population.'

Asha looked surprised. 'By stealing from the mothers of Maya, of course.'

Saraswati was amazed. 'You've stolen our children and it has gone unnoticed?'

It was Saraswati whom the Matriarch restrained this time. 'No dear, Asha is referring to the pretty boys.'

'That's right,' Asha told them calmly. 'We steal the pretty boys, the ones left under the Tree whenever there's a surplus.'

'Why?' Saraswati asked. None of it made any sense to her. 'What are they good for?'

'It's the mothers of Maya who produce them,' Asha pointed out, doing her best to be patient with Saraswati.

'Only for the semen.'

Asha the Apostate looked at her sister in exasperation. 'Would you kill one of the daughters of Maya or leave her under the Tree to die?'

'Of course not.'

'Then why are you willing to destroy the pretty boys?'

Saraswati only shook her head. 'It's not the same thing at all,' she said. 'We don't want to kill them. It's simply a matter of keeping down numbers.'

Asha the Apostate gave up then. 'I see,' she said quietly, 'that during my years of exile very little has changed.'

'There has been a terrible upheaval only recently,' Valerie chimed in. 'Your sister, Shyamila, has usurped the throne.'

Asha laughed. 'Who'd have thought that Shyamila had it in her!' She found it hard to take this seriously.

'Sarla Devi egged her on,' Saraswati explained. 'We've all been exiled.'

Asha realised that for the others it was a very serious matter.

'Is this true?' Asha looked to her mother for an explanation.

'And it must be rectified,' Saraswati was persistent. 'Will you help us regain the Matriarchate of Maya?'

Asha the Apostate smiled. 'How and why would I help you do that?'

'With the help of the pretty boys we might succeed,' Saraswati replied. 'As for why you should help us, that depends on you. Perhaps we can give you something in return? A free pardon? The chance to be a Mayan again?'

At this Asha the Apostate laughed openly. 'Now Saraswati, do consider, are you, a loyal Mayan, seriously proposing that we march on Maya with an army of pretty boys?'

Saraswati had the grace to look embarrassed. 'A threat might be enough.' She glanced at Valerie. 'We have received offers of help.'

Asha the Apostate still looked amused. 'And once my pretty boys have helped you regain Maya Nagar, what will you do for them?'

'What would you like?'

'A change in the institutions of Maya and equal rights for boys,' Asha said in a strong voice. 'Boys should also be given a decent education and be allowed to grow up into mothers like everyone else.'

'They're not capable!' Saraswati protested.

'The pretty boys can't become biological mothers, but they're certainly capable of Grade A and Grade C status. We've proved it here in Ashagad.' Asha kept her voice as reasonable as possible.

'That may be as it may be.' Saraswati looked sceptical. She knew her eldest sister had odd ideas. That was why she had been exiled. 'If I may say so,' she said deliberately, 'the internal workings of the Mayan matriarchy have absolutely nothing to do with you.'

Asha the Apostate was still smiling. 'Very well. Then what about a trade agreement between the Matriarchate of Maya and the Fortress of Asha in return for our help?'

'A trade agreement?' Asha's proposal had taken Saraswati by surprise. 'What do you want? Oh yes, of course ...'

'What we want is the Mayan surplus of males,' Asha told her. 'Indeed, why not let us have all of them? In return we'd supply you with semen.'

Saraswati frowned. 'We already have our own supply with very little trouble and expense.'

The Matriarch put a stop to this interchange. 'Asha is having a game with you,' she told Saraswati. 'You're a good Mayan and well brought up, but you're out of your depth. Be quiet.'

It was a snub, but the Matriarch had judged it necessary. She now turned to her other daughter. 'You're older than Saraswati. Stop teasing her. And be serious.'

'Mother,' Asha the Apostate smiled at the Matriarch, 'I was being serious. Indeed, I've now thought of a better plan. We could exchange some of the daughters of Maya for the sons of Ashagad.' Saraswati had annoyed Asha thoroughly and Asha could not resist baiting her.

'What do you mean?' Saraswati interrupted. 'In exchange for us, demand a supply of boys from the Mayans? Haven't you understood? Shyamila has exiled us. She doesn't want us back.'

'You've misunderstood,' Asha replied. 'I meant the straightforward exchange of boys for girls.'

'Never!' Saraswati was on her feet with outrage.

'Be quiet, both of you!' The Matriarch silenced both her daughters.

'Yes, Mother.' Asha the Apostate answered meekly enough, and Saraswati sat down again, but the Matriarch knew that there was a limit to the obedience she could exact from them. She leaned heavily on the Blue Donkey that night as they made their way along the stone corridors.

As for the others, Valerie didn't know whether to be pleased or puzzled; Saraswati was in a bad mood; and Jyanvi was merely anxious.

Jyanvi had a dream that night. The Blue Donkey was ensconced on a throne carved out of the mountainside. Before her were assembled all the creatures, and behind her the mothers of Maya. In the foreground, immediately below her, were dozens and dozens of mewling babies. Jyanvi herself wasn't in the dream. Suddenly a great voice—perhaps it was the goddess—roared out the question: 'Shall these creatures live?' The Blue Donkey looked up in astonishment. 'Yes', she replied. 'Why not? All creatures want to live.' She seemed not to have understood the significance of the question, much less its moral dimension. She got to her feet and ambled away along the slope to nibble grass.

Jyanvi wondered whether to tell the Blue Donkey about her dream, then decided not to.

12
Ashan Babies

Mohan and Madhu were charming—by any standards. Privately Saraswati conceded that. They were well-mannered, eager to please, and deferred to her gratifyingly. They were probably even quite good looking. They had been delegated by Asha to look after the visitors. Asha herself was in conference with the Matriarch and the Blue Donkey. Saraswati had felt a little put out that she too had not been invited to confer, but had decided to make the best of it. She, Jyanvi and Valerie were drinking tea by the great pool which supplied Ashagad with water. The greenness of the pool, the lotus leaves, the small fish darting about, the shady trees and the pleasant patchwork of red earth and green fields in the valley below made it difficult for anyone to remain bad-tempered.

Mohan was answering a question Jyanvi had just asked. 'The group of three that you see over and over again in the carvings are Kurup and Kripa, the first children, and their mother, the goddess.'

'Their mother seems to be angry with them. Why?'

Madhu smiled at Jyanvi. 'We make up stories to explain ourselves. The goddess is angry with the boy, Kurup, because he doesn't look like her and won't grow up into a proper woman. And because she isn't altogether certain whether she wants him or not, she sends him away. That's why he's crying.'

'Why is the goddess angry with the little girl?' Jyanvi wanted to know.

'Because she laughed at Kurup, and said he was useless and would never be able to be a mother at all,' Madhu replied.

Saraswati had been trying to follow the conversation. Madhu's last remark puzzled her. 'Why did that make the goddess angry?' she asked.

Madhu, in turn, looked puzzled. To him the answer was self-evident. 'Because the goddess had made Kurup, after all.'

Jyanvi wanted to know the rest of the story. 'And then what happened?' she prompted.

'Then the goddess cursed the little girl and said that without Kurup's help Kripa would also be barren. That's why she's crying,' Madhu explained.

'Thank you for telling us.' Jyanvi did not comment on the story. Saraswati was also being discreet. It was Valerie who burst out, 'I originally came from a country where the pretty boys rule.'

'Your country must have been like Ashagad.' Mohan said pleasantly. 'Were you their Empress? What did they do after you left?'

'They didn't even notice I'd left,' Valerie told him. 'My country was crowded with many other women, just like me. One more or less didn't matter.'

Mohan looked surprised. 'Mothers always matter,' he said reasonably. 'If there were many other mothers like you, then how can you say that the "pretty boys" ruled? By the way, we'd prefer it if you didn't use that expression. We call ourselves Ashans.'

'Sorry,' Valerie acknowledged the correction. 'It's hard to explain,' she went on. 'You see the "Ashans" and the "Mayans" in my country all lived together. And the "Ashans" bullied the "Mayans".'

Mohan was doing his best to be polite, though it was obvious he thought Valerie was talking a great deal of nonsense. 'Why did the Ashans bully the Mayans?'

Valerie looked at Jyanvi for help, but Jyanvi was staring at the pool. As for Saraswati, she looked as mystified as the Ashans. Valerie struggled on. 'The Ashans wanted the Mayans to bear their children.'

'Only a Mayan can be a biological mother, an Ashan can't. Is that what you mean?' Mohan was frowning with the effort to understand.

'No, I mean that the Ashans enslaved the Mayans and divided

them up among themselves. The more important the Ashan, the more Mayans he owned.' Valerie spaced out the words in the hope that if she said everything slowly it would all become clear.

Now Madhu was frowning. 'For what purpose would Ashans wish to enslave Mayans? How could they? Why didn't the Mayans stop them?'

Valerie was wishing she had kept quiet, but the young men were looking at her. She took a deep breath. 'Only the Ashans mattered, the Mayans didn't,' Valerie clarified.

'Do you mean only the Ashans mattered to the Ashans and only the Mayans mattered to the Mayans?' Madhu asked.

'I mean the Ashans had all the power. Every Ashan thought of himself as a kind of farmer, and of every Mayan as a bit of land or a field which could be his property.'

'What?' Some of Valerie's ideas seemed so outlandish that the two Ashans were having trouble believing their ears.

'His property,' Valerie repeated, 'which could be used for growing babies. Now do you see?'

Madhu shook his head apologetically, but Mohan's face lit up. 'I think I can explain,' he told Madhu eagerly. 'She means that in her country the Ashans find their babies in the fields rather than under a tree as we do here.' He looked pleased with himself.

Valerie gave up. She turned to the Ashans conversationally. 'Have you any babies?'

A fond expression crossed Madhu's face. 'We have both achieved Grade A status. I have a little boy. Mohan is still waiting for his baby.'

'When will he get one?' Jyanvi enquired, feeling she ought to make some contribution.

'As soon as the Tree proves kind,' Mohan replied.

At this point Saraswati put in a question. 'Are the babies you find always pretty boys—I mean, little Ashans?'

'Of course,' Mohan replied.

'What would you do if you found a Mayan baby?' Jyanvi couldn't resist asking.

Mohan and Madhu hesitated. That possibility had never occurred to them. 'Give her back to the Mayans, I suppose,' said Mohan at last. 'Mayans and Ashans don't mix.'

'You have an Empress,' Valerie pointed out.

'She's the First Mother, the representative of the goddess, and there's only one of her,' Mohan replied.

'We could keep her as a sort of Empress-in-training perhaps,' Madhu ventured with a smile.

The Ashans offered them more tea and samosas. Saraswati was just about to make some comment about their system of irrigation, when Valerie, who had suddenly seen a way of making the Ashans understand her, demanded abruptly, 'What would you do if the supply of babies ceased?'

Mohan put down the plate of samosas. 'I suppose we'd ask the Mayans to give us some, please.'

'If the mothers of Maya refused?' Valerie persisted.

'We could offer to pay them for the babies supplied,' Mohan offered.

'What if the mothers of Maya said there wasn't anything you could pay them with?' There was an intensity in Valerie's manner that would not be denied.

'Then I suppose we'd have to make them,' Madhu replied reluctantly.

'How?'

Valerie was looking straight at him. 'By using force, I suppose,' Madhu mumbled. He looked away, he didn't like any of it.

Valerie had got what she wanted. 'Now do you see?' she cried triumphantly.

'See what?' Mohan asked. He tried to keep the annoyance out of his voice. What was this stranger going on about?

'Why the Ashans in my country have enslaved the Mayans,' Valerie replied.

Mohan shook his head. 'No, I don't see.'

'They've enslaved them in order to force them to have their babies.' For a moment Valerie wondered if the Ashans were being wilfully stupid.

Mohan was startled. 'Ashan babies?'

'No, Ashan and Mayan babies who then belong to a particular Ashan,' Valerie explained.

Madhu sighed. It was obvious that Valerie was not going to

let up. She would have to be humoured. 'In what way?' he asked politely.

'The babies are branded by his specific genes,' Valerie told them.

Mohan and Madhu protested. 'How can that be?'

'Because only his semen is used to impregnate the Mayan who belongs to him.' Valerie explained. Mohan and Madhu were already looking a little sick so she omitted the details, but she concluded by saying, 'That's why the exclusive ownership of a Mayan is so important to an Ashan in my society.'

'None of it sounds at all pleasing.' Madhu murmured.

'Who then is the mother of the baby?' Mohan asked.

'An Ashan is always the Grade A mother, and a Mayan is always the Grade B mother,' Valerie said, 'but the Ashan delegates his duties to the Mayan. Sometimes, if they're rich, they hire a number of Mayans and occasionally an Ashan or two to function as Grade C's.'

Mohan had had enough. He rose to his feet. 'Thank you for explaining all this to us. It was very interesting. Now, would you like to see our fields?'

'Yes, please,' Jyanvi and Saraswati replied instantly. Valerie felt upset though she tried to hide it. It seemed to her that Saraswati and the Ashans looked down on her for having come from a mixed society.

Valerie walked away ahead of the others. Madhu sensed her mood. 'Come,' he said. 'We have lunch prepared for you by one of the canals in the valley below. We'll roast fresh grain. I think you'll like it.' He linked arms with her. Valerie sighed. She had forgotten how many years it was since she had walked arm in arm with a handsome young male; but to this young one she was, she supposed, no more than a friendly creature from another species. It was, as Mohan had said, all very interesting. She felt lonely.

13
Loathsome Reptile

Asha the Apostate entered Madhu's chambers. They were sparsely furnished and beautifully proportioned. Some of the furniture had been cut from the stone and on the right hand wall was an unfinished carving of an enormous neem tree. Each one of the leaves was carefully delineated, right down to the serrated edges. Asha glanced at it and smiled at Madhu. 'It's coming along nicely. Mohan must be pleased with it. Have you a moment?'

Madhu smiled back. 'Yes, Mother, but we'll have to be quiet. I've just managed to make Balu sleep...'

He carried the baby to its little cot and tucked it in. They stood side by side and watched the sleeping baby.

'It's his teeth,' Asha murmured. 'Is he all right otherwise?'

Madhu nodded. 'I think so. A bit cranky.'

Asha patted Madhu's shoulder. 'You look tired.'

Madhu smiled. 'I am a little. Balu cried most of the night.' He waited for his mother to sit, then sat down wearily.

Asha looked at him sitting there in his blue sarong and white kurta. Whatever the mothers of Maya thought, he was clever and graceful. And he was beautiful. She was proud of him. 'Would you like to live in Maya Nagar?' she asked him.

'If you'd asked me yesterday, I might have said "Yes", or "I don't know", but now I think not.'

'Did our visitors put you off?' Asha inquired. She was only mildly concerned.

'They were perfectly pleasant,' Madhu replied. 'It's just that one of them described a society in which Ashans and Mayans lived together. It was horrible!' Madhu grimaced. 'She talked about slavery and other unimaginable practices.'

Asha smiled at Madhu reassuringly. 'I didn't mean would you like to live in Maya as one of their "pretty boys". I meant would you like to live in Maya as a fellow Mayan—as their equal?'

'I suppose so,' Madhu sounded doubtful. 'In the society Valerie described, the Mayans were the slaves and we owned them.'

Asha looked at him sharply. 'Who is "we"?'

'Ashans, of course.' Madhu looked surprised.

Asha sat up. 'I'm sorry to hear that our guests have been putting such rubbish into your head. Valerie is an outsider—not a Mayan.'

The disapproval in Asha's voice was evident, but Madhu didn't respond to it. He was trying to formulate a question. At last he said, 'Mother, are you an Ashan or a Mayan?'

It took Asha by surprise. 'What do you mean? I was born in Maya. I grew up in Maya, and I rule in Ashagad. If you must use these ridiculous labels, then I'm both.'

'Can I be both?' Madhu was frowning with the effort to think the matter through. 'I don't see how I can call myself a Mayan.'

'What if you can't?' Asha replied briskly. 'How does it matter?'

'It would matter if the Ashans and Mayans fought one another,' Madhu said slowly.

Asha stared at him. 'Why would we fight each other? What an extraordinary idea! Only this morning, when we were discussing the possibility of a trade agreement, one of the problems we came up against was that Mayans and Ashans have little in common.'

Madhu said in a troubled voice, 'Mother, everyone knows that the Mayans have something we want—Ashan babies. If the supply dried up, we'd have to fight them.'

Asha felt a tremendous sadness. Was this what it had come to? She had better find out just where these ideas had led Madhu. She wrapped her sari firmly about her shoulders.

'Is this what the Mayans have been telling you?'

'Not exactly.' Madhu tried to explain. 'It's just that I realised clearly, for the first time, that for our supply of babies we are dependent on Mayans.'

Asha leaned across and ruffled Madhu's hair. 'It was you who made up the story of Kripa and Kurup,' she told him gently. 'You're needed as well.'

Madhu only looked more troubled. 'No, Mother. Ashans aren't needed. The Mayans have their own supply of captive Ashans. They call them the "pretty boys"—Peebies.' He added hesitantly, 'Mother, what if we had our own supply of captive Mayans to make Ashan babies for us? Then we wouldn't be dependent on them.'

Asha recoiled in anger. 'I'm ashamed of you. I didn't know you were capable of such a disgusting idea!'

Madhu apologised. 'I didn't really mean it. I was only trying to work things out. Besides, it's not my own idea. It's Valerie's.'

'Valerie's?'

'Valerie said that where she came from, the Ashans owned the Mayans and made them make babies for them.'

Asha didn't know what to make of this. 'Did she explain why?' she asked Madhu.

'No, but when Mohan and I discussed it with the others, Mohan suggested that if it were really true that the Ashans and Mayans lived together, then it would be the only way to make the Mayans bear a lot of Ashans.' He looked at Asha. 'That must be why.'

'Why,' Asha asked carefully, 'would anyone want to force the Mayans to bear more Ashans?'

'So that then there would be more of us!' He went on reasonably, 'We worked out that to make babies, a large number of Ashans simply aren't needed. The Mayans would probably want to make more Mayans. They wouldn't be bothered making Ashans.' He glanced involuntarily at his own child.

'So you've been discussing all this among yourselves. Do you realise how much harm you've done!'

Madhu had never seen his mother quite so angry. 'We were only tossing ideas about,' he protested. 'They're only ideas. What harm can they do?'

'And you call yourself a poet!' Madhu winced under the

contempt in Asha's voice. She went on more quietly, 'You'd better tell me the rest.'

Madhu looked shamefaced. 'Well,' he blurted out, 'Mohan suggested the idea of "war".'

Asha could hardly believe her ears. 'Are you saying that Mohan wanted to make war on the Mayans?'

'No, no,' Madhu replied. 'He just wanted to think it through.'

'And his conclusions?'

It was obvious Asha was very angry. Madhu almost wished he hadn't said anything; but the ideas disturbed him and he had wanted to know what his mother thought. 'It was simply that the logical conclusion was war, Mother. To be absolutely certain of a supply of babies, we'd have to enslave a few Mayans. And to do that we'd have to make war.'

'Since we're being logical,' Asha replied, 'did anyone point out that rather a large number of Mayans would be needed?'

'Yes,' Madhu mumbled.

Asha went on relentlessly. 'And did anyone go on to point out that if you made war on the Mayans and killed them, you'd be left with a shortage of Mayans and in consequence of babies?'

Madhu was feeling more and more uncomfortable, but he replied truthfully. 'We sent someone off to ask Valerie about it, but she got upset. We didn't really understand her properly. She seemed to be saying that in order to subdue and humiliate Mayans, and to make more babies, the Ashans impregnated them.'

'What!'

'It didn't make sense,' Madhu said wretchedly. 'And anyway, there was another idea which several of us found more interesting, and that was being able to stamp our own babies genetically.' He glanced at Balu's cot and continued painfully, 'I love Balu, but if I knew that he carried half my genes, then I think I might feel differently. Perhaps love him more? There's something about the idea that is so seductive …' He glanced at Asha. 'And at the same time all these ideas are so revolting!' He stopped and looked helpless.

Asha remained unmoved by his misery. 'What did you conclude? To make war or not to make war?' she enquired coldly.

'Oh Mother, we concluded nothing. It was simply a matter

of logic. We were only kicking ideas around. We meant no harm,' Madhu pleaded.

Asha stood up. 'Nonetheless, you may have done a great deal of harm. You and Mohan have behaved like a pair of irresponsible children. How could you? You who have the status of a mother? This isn't a game. I'll send someone to look after Balu. Pull yourself together. Take two guards with you and place Valerie in solitary confinement. Tell her that this is being done for her own protection. Then send Mohan to me. And Madhu —'

'Yes, Mother?'

'Grow up.'

It was late at night. Jyanvi had been woken up and summoned to the Matriarch's chambers. She stared at the Matriarch, Saraswati and the Blue Donkey. 'Did Valerie corrupt the morals of the Ashans?' She repeated the Matriarch's question stupidly.

'Well?' said the Matriarch. 'Did she? Why is Asha so furious? What did Valerie say to the Ashans?'

'Valerie tried to explain the customs of her own country—I mean where she grew up—but Madhu and Mohan didn't understand, and so she got a bit excited. That's all,' Jyanvi replied.

Saraswati cleared her throat. 'The charge seems to be that Valerie incited Madhu and Mohan to declare war on Maya.'

Jyanvi was puzzled. 'She didn't. You heard her. In any case I thought we were looking for allies to regain Maya. Is the Apostate really upset?'

'Yes,' responded Asha, sweeping into the Matriarch's chambers, 'your friend has been teaching my poor innocent boys to make war on all women. Apparently, that is the practice in the country she comes from.'

Up to this point Jyanvi had thought that there had been some absurd misunderstanding, but now she looked at the Blue Donkey uneasily. The Blue Donkey returned her gaze and said to her in a low voice, 'You see, Valerie has acquainted the young Ashans with the concepts of slavery, rape and war.'

'And the Ashans?' asked Jyanvi.

'Are fascinated.'

Jyanvi was beginning to have some idea of what had happened.

She heard the Matriarch speaking to her. 'Go and see Valerie and persuade her to recant.'

Jyanvi was about to protest that Valerie wouldn't understand what she was talking about, but the look in the Matriarch's eye made her realise that that wasn't the point. 'Yes, Aisaheb,' she said meekly, 'I'll go immediately.' Asha the Apostate accompanied her.

They strode down the corridors. As soon as Valerie saw them, she sprang to her feet and demanded to know why she was being treated in this way.

Asha looked at her with distaste. It was obvious that any proximity to Valerie was unpleasant to her. 'You'd better talk to her,' she said to Jyanvi and left them.

Jyanvi entered the cell and sat down. Valerie had worked herself up into a state. The first step was to calm her down.

'It's not a question of justice or injustice, only of perspective,' Jyanvi began. 'You've got to look at it from their point of view.'

'At what?' Valerie was almost shouting. 'What is it I'm supposed to have done? And why does Asha look at me as though I was a reptile?'

Suddenly Jyanvi had an idea. She would explain everything to Valerie in terms Valerie would understand. 'From Asha's point of view, you're the serpent in her Garden of Eden. You've made her boys eat of the fruit of the tree of knowledge, and now they're corrupted.'

Valerie stared at Jyanvi incredulously. 'Did Asha the Apostate say all that?'

'Of course not,' Jyanvi replied. 'She's never heard of the Garden of Eden. I was just trying to make you understand. Calm down and listen for a moment.' Jyanvi patted Valerie's arm. 'You told the Ashans about the norms of a heterosexual patriarchy. Isn't that right?'

'So what? They seemed revolted,' Valerie said bitterly.

'They were, but they were also fascinated. Don't you see, you gave them knowledge. Knowledge that things might be other than they are. You put ideas into their heads.'

'What ideas?' asked Valerie. She felt baffled.

'The ideas of rape, slavery and war,' Jyanvi replied.

'I did nothing of the sort!' Valerie cried.

'You described these concepts. And what you didn't describe, they worked out for themselves.'

'I didn't say that any of these ideas were good,' Valerie protested. 'I meant no harm. I left that society and those norms. I suffered from them!' Valerie was finding it hard to believe that she had been so misconstrued.

'The serpent suffered, too,' Jyanvi pointed out. 'Can't you imagine a conversation in which the serpent is told that what might have proved too much for sensitive serpents would do very well for ordinary men?'

Valerie stared at Jyanvi in horror. 'What are you saying?'

'I'm saying,' Jyanvi told her, 'that you described a society in which there were male masters and female slaves. For you to say that it was a horrible place makes perfect sense from your point of view, but it doesn't necessarily do so from the point of view of the Ashans.'

'Mohan and Madhu were both so nice,' Valerie wailed. 'You're not saying they want to rape and kill …'

'No,' Jyanvi replied. 'Just artificial insemination and enslavement probably.'

'Are you saying that the Ashans have actually worked all this out?'

'No, but there's speculation, and a natural concern about their self-interest.'

'What are we to do?' Valerie had lost her sense of outrage. She sounded fearful.

'Find a way of convincing males that a male-dominated society is not in their interests.' Jyanvi felt sorry for Valerie. In explaining the problem, she had understood it only too well herself.

'Is that possible?' Valerie asked.

'I don't know,' Jyanvi muttered. She added more gently, 'Try to sleep now and get some rest.'

14
It's a Privilege

The following morning the helicopter landed. The Mayans and the Ashans had been holding a meeting in the Council Chamber when a dozen soldiers sprang out of the machine, burst into the Chamber and covered everyone with machine guns. 'We come in peace,' announced the leader.

Asha the Apostate recovered first. 'Put down those guns, you fool!' she shouted.

'Put down yours first,' the leader replied.

'We haven't got any guns!' Asha told him. 'Put away those guns before you manage to hurt someone.'

'Okay,' the leader agreed. 'Since you haven't got any guns, we'll put away ours.' The soldiers stopped pointing their machine guns at the Ashans and the Mayans.

'Who are you? Why have you come and how did you get here?' Asha the Apostate asked the leader.

'We're Traders. We've come to trade, and we got here by tuning in on an SOS beam.'

Asha stared at him. There had been something almost mechanical about his speech. 'An SOS beam?' she queried.

'Yeah, you've got a hostage here who's in jeopardy,' the leader informed her. 'One of our jobs is to free citizens.'

There was some murmuring among the Ashans and Mayans.

At last Jyanvi suggested to Asha that perhaps they were talking about Valerie and that she be sent for. This was done. Asha turned to the Trader. 'We do have a prisoner of sorts, but she's hardly a hostage. She has only been confined for her own good. Did she send you a signal?'

'Yeah. Quite a while ago all citizens from the west who went abroad were automatically equipped with automatic beepers. When they're convinced that their lives are in danger, the beepers beep. Then we rescue them.'

Just then Valerie was brought in. She looked pale and tired. When she saw the soldiers, she shrank back, but the leader called out, 'We've come to rescue you.'

'I don't want to be rescued,' Valerie answered.

'Yes, you do. You sent out a signal. We've come to rescue you,' the leader persisted.

The Matriarch took pity on Valerie. 'If she has said she doesn't want to be rescued, do you have to rescue her?'

'Well, no,' The Trader paused. 'But we'd sure like to.'

'You can't,' the Matriarch told him firmly. 'Now, what else do you want?'

'We really came to trade and recruit,' he muttered.

'Right,' said Asha the Apostate who had come to a few conclusions of her own. 'Let's start with the recruitment. Who are you recruiting?'

'What about those two boys over there? They look pretty bright.' The leader pointed to Madhu and Mohan.

'We're Ashans,' Madhu protested. 'Why should we want to be recruited by you?'

'Because,' Asha the Apostate pronounced each word distinctly, 'you could then have the Ashan privileges in a mixed society that Valerie the Outsider was talking about.'

Madhu turned to Valerie. 'Is that true?'

'Well,' she said, 'I suppose it's true.'

Mohan was looking at the soldiers doubtfully. 'Who are these people?' he asked Valerie. 'Are they Ashans or Mayans?'

'They're Ashans of the type I described to you,' Valerie said reluctantly.

The leader was getting impatient. 'Are you joining or aren't you?'

'What are you offering them?' Asha put in.

'We're not offering anything,' he replied. 'It's a privilege. We've got all we want. It's just that these two fellows looked pretty good to me. I was doing them a favour.'

'If we were to join you, what would happen to us?' Mohan demanded.

The Trader grinned encouragingly. 'Why, given a little time, you'd become one of us.'

'You mean we'd be your fellow Ashans in your society?' Mohan persisted.

'I guess so. What does he mean?' the leader asked Valerie.

'He means would they be treated like men in a male-dominated society.' Valerie spelled it out.

'Sure.' He addressed the others, 'There seems to be some misunderstanding though. We're not men.'

'Are you women?' Saraswati burst out. She sounded horrified.

'Who're you calling women? That's an insult!' the soldier roared. 'No, we're male androids built to a specific stereotype.'

'What is he saying?' Madhu asked.

'He's saying that the real Ashans have stayed behind,' Valerie replied. 'You have to call them men,' she added helpfully.

'Then the real men aren't like you?' Mohan asked.

'Hell, no. We're almost perfect.' The leader strutted a little. 'We're the stereotype to which the real men try to approximate. We're the best.'

'Will we be allowed to become full-fledged mothers right away?' Mohan enquired.

The Trader stared at him. 'What do you mean?'

'Will we be proper mothers with grade A status just like you and get our babies right away?' Mohan repeated his question.

In response the leader opened his mouth and closed it again. 'You've got to be kidding,' he said at last. 'Now, for the last time, what do you say?'

'No, thank you,' Madhu replied.

'You sure? You're passing up a great chance.' The leader was finding it hard to believe that anyone would refuse such an opportunity.

'We're quite sure.' Mohan put his arm around Madhu's shoulder.

The leader frowned. 'Say, are you two gay boys?'

'What is "gay"?' Mohan asked.

'You know, "homos".' When Madhu and Mohan still looked puzzled, the leader went on, 'Do you act like girls? I mean what was all that stuff about wanting to be mothers?'

Mohan looked astonished. 'Everybody wants to be a mother,' he said.

'You've got to be crazy,' the leader decided. 'Forget that I asked you. You can't join us. You're not proper men.'

'We don't want to join you,' Madhu said.

'That doesn't matter,' the leader replied. 'What I'm saying is that even if you wanted to join us, you wouldn't be allowed to. A proper man doesn't want to be a mother.'

'What does he want then?' asked Madhu politely.

'I guess he just wants a mother in the home—where she belongs,' the leader told him. 'You know, just some place to rest after all that fighting and struggling. Mothering's for the birds. It's women's work.'

At this point Asha the Apostate intervened. She had achieved her purpose, and was beginning to find the leader tedious. 'Since recruitment seems to be out of the question, why don't we take the time to refresh ourselves and then discuss the question of trade?'

'We're androids, we don't need refreshments,' the leader growled. 'We'll wait right here in your Council Chamber until you're ready to negotiate. You've got half an hour.'

The Mayans and Ashans trooped out into the brilliant sunshine. Here there were more soldiers. Some were lounging about, some were chewing gum, some were reading comic books and some were standing guard beside the helicopter. Out of curiosity, Madhu peered at the cover of one of the comic books. It portrayed a large metal male rampaging about, while two or three diminutive females, who appeared to be made of flesh and blood, clung to him. 'What does it mean?' Madhu asked, but the soldier only set his jaw until his resemblance to the metal monster became even more marked.

Madhu joined the others who were all standing in a loose

group. Asha the Apostate was saying, 'Then it's agreed that we want to get rid of these androids as quickly as possible. I'll do my best. The rest of you must help.'

'It may not be easy,' the Matriarch told her. 'Maya Diip has always been treated as forbidden territory. They've been wanting a foothold for a long time. With Valerie's distress signal, they think they've got it. They won't give it up without a fight of some sort.'

'I'm sorry,' said Valerie.

'It wasn't your fault.' The Matriarch spoke kindly.

'In a way it was ours,' Madhu put in. 'We're sorry, too.'

Asha the Apostate was secretly pleased, but all she said was, 'That's fine. What is it that the traders want?'

'I don't know,' replied the Matriarch, 'but I think the whole of Maya Diip is in serious danger. We should send a warning to the mothers of Maya.'

It seemed absurd to Saraswati to be thinking of trying to help Shyamila and Sarla Devi. On the other hand, the situation kept changing so rapidly that it was difficult to keep track of who might be an ally and who mightn't. She felt uncertain about what to say, and so said nothing. It was the Blue Donkey who queried the Matriarch. 'Why are you taking them so seriously? It's true that they take themselves seriously, but surely we needn't?'

'Because stupidity is dangerous,' the Matriarch replied. 'They're automated. Any opposition would trigger their machine guns.'

'Couldn't we try to disarm them?' Mohan asked.

'Yes, and seize the helicopter,' Saraswati added.

'I suspect,' the Matriarch told them quietly, 'that the automated response would be almost instantaneous. I think it would be wiser to find out a little more.'

They returned to the Council Chamber. 'Well,' said the leader, 'are you ready to trade?'

'What do you wish to trade in?' asked the Apostate.

'What are you selling?' the android countered.

'We aren't selling anything,' Asha replied.

'You've got to sell,' the leader remonstrated. 'How else do you think you're going to get dollars? Shiny dollars.' He held up a coin for Asha's benefit.

'We don't want shiny dollars. What would we do with them?'

'Buy guns.' The response was immediate.

'Guns?'

'Yeah. Guns.' The leader decided Asha was slow. He gesticulated with his hands. 'You know, guns, rockets, Big Bangs.'

'We don't want shiny dollars,' said the Matriarch.

'Everybody wants shiny dollars,' the leader replied. 'But if you're refusing to trade with us, why we'll just refuse to trade with you.'

'That's fine then,' Asha seized her chance quickly. 'We are, in fact, refusing to trade, and so it follows that you're refusing as well. You can go home now. It's all over.'

'Wait a minute,' the leader returned. 'You're holding one of our nationals. We can't leave here till you let her go.'

'She's free to go.' Asha was indifferent.

'I don't want to go,' Valerie protested.

The leader said nothing at all, but he signalled to the soldiers and the machine guns were trained once again on the Ashans and Mayans. For a minute nobody spoke and nobody moved.

Then the leader waved his gun at Asha. 'You're the leader, aren't you? Well, you're deposed for obstructing the causes of democracy and justice. We're appointing a new government that'll be more cooperative and loyal to us.'

'I see,' said Asha. 'Well, now that that's done, we'll carry on.'

She started to leave the Council Chamber, but was halted by the leader.

'Stop!' he shouted. 'You're under arrest. And you and you,' he added, pointing to the Matriarch and the other women. 'Take them to the 'copter.' He then informed Madhu, that he, Madhu, was in charge until such time as the androids returned, and that he hoped that the young man appreciated that it wasn't okay to be ruled by women. The leader told Valerie that as a good citizen it was her duty to keep an eye on Madhu. They were taking their prisoners to headquarters, but they'd be back soon. Madhu would have protested, but Asha restrained him. 'I think we can handle them,' she whispered. 'Look after things here.'

The Matriarch and her daughters and Jyanvi and the Blue Donkey were herded into the helicopter. As soon as the doors closed and the rotors began spinning, the androids flung themselves against the walls and plugged themselves in. To the astonishment of the prisoners, they heard the helicopter croon, 'My pretty ones, my babies, are you tired and hungry? ' and they heard the androids reply, 'Oooh, yes, Mother, we're hungry and tired and want to lie down.'

15
The Helicopter Shuddered

After the androids had recovered from their binge, they rose to their feet and stowed themselves inside the cabin, but the senior android seated himself and stretched his legs. He wanted to chat. 'Well,' he began, 'you must have guessed we're not really taking you to a western base.'

'Yes,' Asha replied.

The Matriarch and the Blue Donkey had decided that it would be just as well to find out more. 'Tell me,' the Blue Donkey sounded fascinated, and she was, in fact, genuinely interested, 'why did you refuse refreshments on Ashagad, and yet, as soon as we entered the 'copter, you immediately proceeded to feed yourselves? That was what you were doing, wasn't it?'

'Sure, but the 'copter's juices are different. I mean what the 'copter gives is mother's milk to us.' He looked a little shy. 'You see, the 'copter's our mother, and we're her babies.'

The Matriarch felt the metal struts under her surreptitiously. It was hard to think of the helicopter as a fellow mother, but she said politely, 'Please present our compliments to your mother. When can we have the opportunity to speak with her?'

'Oh, Mom doesn't talk, at least not much,' the leader replied.

'Why not?' enquired the Matriarch.

'I don't know. I guess she's always been too busy feeding us and foraging for us and carrying us about.'

'What about the others?' asked the Blue Donkey.

'Oh, nobody talks much,' the leader replied. 'Just me.'

'And why is that?'

'I don't know,' answered the android. 'I guess I'm exceptional. I don't mean different. I just mean more of everything the others are. I'm Mom's favourite. I've always had double rations.'

'But if the others don't talk, how did you manage to learn to talk?' Jyanvi put in.

The android seemed to be enjoying talking about himself. 'The same way I learned everything else. Don't you understand?'

They shook their heads.

'I've got that on tape. Hang on a second.' The android paused and then reeled off the following speech: 'The truth is we're an Abandoned Experiment. Once we were abandoned we had only two choices: either to disintegrate or to try in some way to shape ourselves. Our mother, the helicopter, in whose belly we were abandoned, chose the latter course. There was an enormous library of videotapes on board and, of course, we were always able to suck in more. This, so to speak, was our pabulum. With this she fed us and shaped us and turned us into men, but not ordinary men; we are modelled on TV heroes.'

'What is TV?' Saraswati wanted to know.

'Something I banned on Maya Diip around about the time you were born,' the Matriarch replied.

Jyanvi leaned forward. 'I know what you mean about the TV heroes. You remind me of them. But since you're not on television and you're not a man, who are you? I mean, when you're not repeating television lines, what do you think and say?'

The android looked puzzled. 'I can only say the lines I know. I mean how can I say the lines I don't already know? But if you're asking what we call ourselves, well, I've already told you—we're Traders.'

'Why did you want the two young men?' Asha interjected.

'We were recruiting. There's a lot of wear and tear. We need replacements. We thought that if we could turn ourselves into TV heroes, then we could probably turn those boys into real life androids.'

'I see. And what about us?' Saraswati enquired.

'We're going to sell you,' the android replied. 'You're not one of us. You're females.'

'Why are you going to sell us?' Saraswati persisted.

The android was getting cross. 'Because that's our trade. I've already told you. We had to have an occupation. It's part of our identity.'

Saraswati was doing her best to remain patient. 'In return for selling us what will you gain?'

'Dollars.'

'What do you do with the dollars?'

'We eat them, of course.'

'What?'

'That's right. And when we need them again, we cough them up.' The android stood up. These females didn't know anything. 'You'll see,' he told them. 'We're nearly there.'

Saraswati ventured one more question. 'Where are you taking us?'

'To Paradise. Look, you're making me tired. I need a little feed. Ahhh. I feel ... wonderful!' The android had staggered to the nearest outlet and had begun to consume quadruple rations.

The engine coughed and restarted, then coughed and spluttered again. The old machine had over-extended herself; she was going to attempt a forced landing. Jyanvi and the others looked down at the sea and at the shoreline in the near distance. They checked the emergency exits and inflated their life jackets. The other androids were stirring now. When they saw the leader gorging himself, they dived towards the remaining outlets and plugged themselves in. It was heyday and holiday. They seemed to be in ecstasy. The helicopter shuddered and plunged downwards.

PART III

'We've decided that you should be nice to us,' the Looking Glass creatures informed Alice.

'Why?'

'Because!' they replied triumphantly.

16
Will You Have Us?

'And is this Paradise?' Saraswati asked.

'Yes,' Jyanvi replied and kissed her.

After the interior of the helicopter, it was pleasant to lie on the sandy beach. It had been easy enough to swim ashore. The 'copter had been close to land and had hovered on the water for a minute or two like a great brooding bird before sinking with her cargo of metal children. Jyanvi and Saraswati were resting in the shade of some coconut trees, while the waves broke against the shore. Presumably this was Paradise, and soon they would have to meet the inhabitants thereof, but for the moment they could relax while their clothes dried in the sun.

The others were sitting some distance away. Asha had one arm around the neck of the Blue Donkey and the other around the Matriarch. It was a great luxury for her to be with her mother again.

After a while Asha said, 'About armies, Mother ...'

'Yes?'

'Ought we to have one?'

The Matriarch glanced at her eldest curiously. 'What makes you ask?'

'The androids,' Asha replied. 'I told Madhu that we'd be all right, but I had no real plan in my head. The androids were stupid, but they had the guns and we did what they said.' She sounded annoyed with herself.

'That bothered me as well,' the Blue Donkey murmured. 'The problem is, I dislike killing ...'

'Killing?' Asha wasn't sure she had heard right.

'Yes, killing,' the Blue Donkey repeated firmly. 'There's no point in having guns, or an army, or wooden rods, or even a strong pair of hind legs, if one isn't willing to use them.'

'These aren't all the same thing,' Asha protested. 'Besides, what good would your hind legs have been against their guns?'

'I don't know,' the Blue Donkey answered.

Asha turned to the Matriarch. 'Mother?'

'I don't know either,' answered the Matriarch. 'When you were very little and you kicked and screamed, I used to pick you up bodily and set you down in another room ... No one got hurt.'

Asha looked at her mother in astonishment. 'Do you want to be as strong as that in relation to everyone and everything else?'

Her mother smiled. 'Like the Blue Donkey, I don't want to kill.'

'It's one thing to refrain from killing and another thing to be helpless. I mean, could you have killed?' enquired the Blue Donkey. 'Could you have stopped Shyamila, for example? Or the pretty boys? Or the androids?'

'Yes,' said the Matriarch.

Asha and the Blue Donkey stared at her. 'How?' they both asked.

'With a bigger and better gun,' the Matriarch replied. 'It blows up everything for miles around.'

'Including us?' the Blue Donkey said, half incredulous.

The Matriarch smiled, 'Perhaps.'

Asha the Apostate looked at the Matriarch in some perplexity. 'Mother, what are you talking about?'

'The defences of Maya—one of the prerogatives of the Mayan Matriarch,' the Matriarch told her. 'It's all a matter of pressing buttons.'

'What do you mean?'

'There are bombs planted all over the island. There are also means of transporting the bombs. Why do you suppose Maya is forbidden?' The Matriarch sounded weary.

Asha and the Blue Donkey drew away and looked at her in horror. At last Asha asked, 'Why didn't you use them?'

Her mother replied, 'I told you, I find it distasteful.'

For a while, nobody said anything.

'Do you suppose,' the Blue Donkey muttered, 'that murder is an acquired skill and has to be taught, or that it comes naturally?'

Suddenly Asha turned on her mother. 'But you killed my pretty boys!' she said wonderingly.

'My dear!' It was hard to read the Matriarch. Was she merely distressed by the breach of decorum?

They fell silent again. Then the Blue Donkey asked, 'Does Shyamila know?'

'No, she doesn't know.'

'Then hadn't we better get back before she finds out?'

'Perhaps,' replied the Matriarch. 'But it's unlikely that she will; the computers respond to my codes and my combinations. In the Matriarchy of Maya that's the power behind the throne.'

The Blue Donkey looked at the Matriarch. 'Why didn't you use it?'

The Matriarch merely looked back at the Blue Donkey, until at last the Blue Donkey dropped her eyes. Then the Matriarch smiled. 'Tell me,' she said briskly, 'Who do you think I should appoint as my Successor, the woman who would willingly use the power or the one who would not?'

Asha and the Blue Donkey looked away uneasily.

The Matriarch relented. 'Come. Let's discuss something else—the art of poetry, or the blueness of the sea or the inhabitants of Paradise. Look, here come two of them.' They could see two figures running towards them. When the runners reached the little group, one of them cried, 'I'm Madhu and she's Mala. Welcome to Paradise. Are you Mothers and can we have you?'

The Matriarch was taken aback, but she answered civilly. 'This is the Blue Donkey, and yes, we're Mothers from Maya. Are you the inhabitants of Paradise?'

'Yes,' replied Madhu. 'I thought you might be Mothers. Can we have you or are you spoken for?'

'What do you mean?'

But just then Jyanvi and Saraswati strolled up. 'Are they Mothers, too?' Mala asked.

'Saraswati is,' the Matriarch replied.

'And the other?'

'The other is her lover,' the Blue Donkey told them.

'Oh, too bad. She's not available. But will you have us?' Madhu asked.

Madhu was kneeling at the Matriarch's feet and Mala was kneeling at Asha's. 'Have you as what?' Asha gazed at them in perplexity.

'As your Gallants, your suitors and supplicants—as your children as it were,' Mala explained.

'But you're grown ups!'.

Mala smiled at Asha sweetly. 'Of course,' she said. 'In Paradise there are no real children.'

'How do you propagate?' Jyanvi cut in.

'Immigration. Lots of people apply to come to Paradise. We only take the fully grown. After all, everything is plentiful in Paradise, except, of course, Mothers. Are you sure you're not a Mother?' Mala smiled at Jyanvi hopefully.

'No, I'm not,' Jyanvi replied brusquely. 'If you're all grown ups, why do you want Mothers?'

'Don't you want a Mother?' Mala looked at her hopefully.

'No!'

'Then can we have her?'

'Who?'

Mala pointed to Saraswati.

'No!'

The Blue Donkey intervened. 'Your customs are strange to us,' she said peaceably. 'Are we to understand that you're making a request of the Matriarch and Asha?'

'Oh, yes,' Madhu replied. 'We saw the 'copter crash and ran to the beach in order to be first.'

'Would it be in order for the Matriarch and for Asha to refuse your request?' continued the Blue Donkey.

'The longer they refuse, the longer we can woo them,' Madhu told her gleefully. 'That's the best part.'

'Very well,' said the Blue Donkey. 'They both refuse you at present. Now would you please lead us to some food and shelter and give us a chance to recover ourselves?'

'Of course,' cried Madhu. 'Our pleasure is to serve them—and their friends.'

'It's our duty to suffer in the cause of love,' Mala added.

The Blue Donkey stared at them. 'Are you suffering?'

They nodded vigorously. 'Oh yes!'

'They're mad!' snorted the Blue Donkey.

'They're not mad,' Jyanvi corrected. 'Just romantic.'

'They're certainly childish. Five of them sang all night long outside my window,' Saraswati told them. 'They said they were serenading.'

'I thought that since you have Jyanvi, you were out of the running ...' The Blue Donkey's voice trailed away.

'Oh no.' Jyanvi explained. 'The fact that she's seemingly inaccessible only makes her more attractive. They're like mosquitoes. But I've made sure that they won't bother me.'

'How?' asked the Blue Donkey.

Jyanvi grinned. 'When one or two of them approached me, I told them that I wasn't in the least bit interested in mothering them, but that if they were interested in mothering me ...'

'What happened?'

'They fled.'

Saraswati shook her head at Jyanvi. 'That was unkind. They mean no harm. They only want a little attention, in return for which—'

'What do they offer?' Jyanvi asked.

'Their need.'

There was an awkward pause.

Then Jyanvi said, 'In this society there are two categories—Mothers and Gallants. I don't in the least wish to be a Mother; but as for the Gallants—I despise them!'

Jyanvi had spoken with such vehemence that the Blue Donkey gave her a sharp look, but contented herself with saying, 'Let's go and see if the Matriarch and Asha are awake yet.'

They had each of them been given separate cabins within the compound of a large garden near the beach. The entrance to the Matriarch's cabin was partly blocked by a mountain of paper. There was a similar mountain outside Asha's cabin. Madhu and Mala were helping the two Mayans pick up the paper.

'What is it?' the Blue Donkey asked.

The Matriarch smiled at her, 'It appears to be poetry.'

'Are the inhabitants of Paradise lovers of poetry?' Jyanvi enquired.

'We write it all the time,' replied Madhu.

When they had finished picking up the poetry and had stacked it away, Mala said, 'There are dozens of Gallants outside the garden gates awaiting your pleasure. They want to know what would please you and would be glad to gratify any whim. They've waited all night for just a glimpse of you. Perhaps you'd be kind and grant each one an interview?'

The Blue Donkey came to the Matriarch's rescue. 'Let's discuss the matter,' she said firmly, 'over breakfast.'

The sun shone down on them. The Ranisaheb, Asha the Apostate and Saraswati had each been set up in a striped deck chair under separate palm trees. Long queues trailed away from them towards the ocean. For breakfast, Madhu and Mala had offered the castaways a bit of coconut and an orange or two. They seemed to think this was sufficient. Then they had begged them to see their suitors. The Matriarch and her daughters were doing so, while Jyanvi and the Blue Donkey looked on.

After a while Jyanvi and the Blue Donkey approached Mala. 'Please,' the Blue Donkey said, 'our friends are exhausted. This must stop.'

'We don't mean any harm,' Mala protested. 'Look at the queues. They come from miles around just to be with the Mothers for a short moment. There's a great shortage of Mothers in Paradise.' She looked at Jyanvi doubtfully. 'You don't think you could be one just to help out?'

'No!' replied Jyanvi violently. 'Tell me, why is there a shortage of Mothers? Is there some reluctance to take on that role?'

'Yes, there is reluctance,' Mala scowled, 'and I don't know why and what's more, I don't want to talk about it. As for the queues, I'll see what I can do. I'll try to arrange for an interval.'

Just then they heard a low purring, quite distinct from the crashing of waves. Twelve Rolls Royces were gliding across the sands towards the Matriarch. The chauffeurs got out and stood at attention. Their leader knelt and declared solemnly, 'The Queen of Paradise sends greetings to the Matriarch of Maya and begs that the Distinguished Visitor and her Entourage will honour her by being her guests.'

'Thank you,' responded the Matriarch and let the poem with which the hundredth suitor had just presented her slide off her lap.

'We will escort you,' went on the Queen's Representative. 'For your transport the Queen has sent a fleet of Rolls. Will they be suitable?'

'Yes, thank you,' replied the Matriarch again, and in no time at all the others were summoned and they prepared to set off. For some reason, instead of being disappointed, the suitors regarded this as an occasion for celebration. They cheered and whistled and garlanded the cars; then, amid much singing and dancing and merry making, they accompanied the procession on its way to the palace.

17
The Poetic Thing

The Queen of Paradise turned out to be a sensible person. The Blue Donkey sighed with relief, as did Jyanvi and the others. She greeted them cheerfully, saw to it that they were comfortably settled and gave them a chance to rest before dinner. 'I would have been happier to see you under better circumstances,' she told them. 'The truth is, there's a crisis in Paradise and I am in desperate need of help, but more of that later.'

Their chambers were oddly furnished, their bath water was tepid and the dinner itself was barely edible. None of this surprised them greatly. They had learnt already that in Paradise, very little worked. The procession had broken down several times and two of the cars had had to be pushed. At least they were rid of the suitors for the time being, and for this they were indebted to the Queen. She had seen to it that the palace doors were firmly shut. They felt sorry for her. After dinner, she confided in them.

'You will have guessed at the problems of Paradise,' she began.

Jyanvi thought that she would now speak of the shortage of Mothers. The Blue Donkey thought that she would say something about the inefficiency of the system, and the others thought that she would express her concern over the childishness of the Gallants. What she actually said startled them all: 'The Children of Paradise are killing themselves.'

'Do you mean that literally?' the Matriarch enquired.

'Yes. Let me give you an example. Do you remember the two young people you first encountered on the beach?'

'Yes, of course. Madhu and Mala.'

'Well, Mala is dead. She threw herself off one of the turrets soon after you arrived here.'

The Matriarch was horrified. 'The poor child!' she cried out. 'Why did she do such a thing?'

The Queen shrugged. 'For me, these things have become everyday occurrences and have lost their horror. She left the usual Suicide Poem behind.'

'What is a Suicide Poem?' Jyanvi asked.

'When the Gallants commit suicide, they leave behind a couplet, sometimes a quatrain.' The Queen shrugged. 'It has become a custom, a tradition—the poetic thing to do—to die with a song on your lips.'

'What did Mala's note say?' asked the Matriarch.

'Forgive me if I tell you that I cannot remember exactly. It was like hundreds of others. Something like:

"Now that I have seen her at last,
My life is done, my pleasures past." '

'What does it mean?' asked the Blue Donkey.

'I think it's supposed to be a tribute to beauty,' Jyanvi whispered to her.

'Whose beauty?' the Blue Donkey whispered back.

'Ideal beauty—as well as yours, of course.' The Queen nodded in the direction of Asha. 'According to our legends Paradise was founded by a Princess of Maya who sailed away in search of happiness. Do you know the tale? An extreme idealism is fundamental to Paradise.'

'If the Children of Paradise are willing to die for their ideals, what is the problem?' The Blue Donkey was genuinely puzzled.

The Queen of Paradise turned to her. 'The problem is they won't live for them. Perhaps you will understand Paradise better if I tell you the tale of the Princess Jaya and her Shobha Rani.'

Both Asha and Saraswati let out an exclamation. It was Saraswati who spoke. 'The story of the Runaway Princess and her Beauty

Queen is a well-known cautionary tale. She was the one who was debarred from the throne for being such a fool, wasn't she?'

The Queen of Paradise smiled and threw a reassuring glance at the Matriarch as though to say, 'It's all right, the child hasn't offended me.' She explained to Saraswati, 'According to the legends of Paradise, the Princess Jaya nobly spurned the throne of Maya Diip for the sake of Beauty.'

'Was Beauty another Mayan Princess?' asked the Blue Donkey, who was trying to keep the story clear in her head.

'No, Beauty was a statue!' Saraswati replied scornfully.

'That's right,' the Queen of Paradise agreed. 'The Victorious Princess and the Beauty Queen sailed away with no money at all and a fair wind, and landed in Paradise.'

'What did she do with the statue?' the Blue Donkey whispered.

'Worshipped it,' Jyanvi whispered back.

'That's right,' the Queen of Paradise said. 'She worshipped it, and then the Beauty Queen came to life, and the Victorious Princess took her in her arms.'

'And then?'

'And then they both died.' The Queen of Paradise finished the tale.

'Why?' demanded the Blue Donkey indignantly.

'That was the penalty,' replied the Queen. 'It's part of the story. You have to understand that for the Children of Paradise, death is definitive.'

The Blue Donkey thought it over. 'What about the Mothers?' she asked.

'The Mothers, according to legend must be worshipped,' the Queen told her. 'As you see, our society is neatly divided into Mothers and Gallants.'

'The Mothers aren't real mothers, of course,' Asha the Apostate interjected.

The Queen of Paradise raised her eyebrows. 'What do you mean?'

'We were told,' Asha said carefully, 'that there are no real children in Paradise.'

'Of course there aren't,' the Queen replied. 'That would spoil everything.'

'Surely being a Mother *vis- à -vis* a Gallant must be a very different thing from looking after a real child?' Asha insisted.

'What's your experience?' the Queen of Paradise countered. 'A Gallant, after all, is a grown-up person, whose first duty is service.'

'But there seems to be a problem?' Asha suggested.

'Yes, there is.' The Queen's voice had acquired a certain sharpness. 'In the absence of real children, the Gallants have become increasingly childish. In my experience, mothering childish grown-ups is at least as arduous as any other mothering.'

'Are the rewards as great?' asked Jyanvi suddenly.

'Obviously not,' replied the Queen. 'As you can see, there's a surplus of Gallants and a shortage of Mothers in Paradise.'

The Matriarch had been listening to this interchange thoughtfully. 'Are immigrants to Paradise given a choice?' she enquired.

'Oh yes,' answered the Queen. 'The Pursuit of Beauty, Love, Freedom and Happiness—these are the inalienable rights of the citizens of Paradise. So naturally they have a choice. When they first enter Paradise, they choose their role for the next ten years. After that they must change roles. It's usually at that point that they commit suicide.'

'Is the suicide rate of the young ones the problem, or is the problem the shortage of mothers?' asked the Blue Donkey, trying to get it straight.

'Both,' said the Queen of Paradise. 'I think they're connected. The Gallants despair of winning a Mother for themselves before they have to take on the job of mothering.'

'Can't the Gallants pair with one another? Then if we could somehow prevent them from killing themselves—or each other—we'll have solved the problem.' The Blue Donkey sounded hopeful.

'In Paradise,' the Queen explained, 'the roles are clearly differentiated and two of a kind may not pair. That would be wrong. I know that the customs of Maya are entirely different. On your island there are only Mothers and no Gallants, so things are otherwise ... I must say I was a little surprised when I was told that a member of your party professed to be a Gallant.' She threw a glance at Jyanvi.

Jyanvi frowned. 'I didn't say I was a Gallant,' she mumbled. 'I just said I didn't want to be a Mother.'

The Matriarch intervened. 'If the numbers of Gallants and Mothers were more or less equal, would the number of suicides drop, do you think?'

'I think so,' replied the Queen of Paradise. 'According to the Suicide Poems most of them are killing themselves out of unrequited love.'

'Is that true?' Jyanvi put in.

'It may be,' Saraswati responded. 'It's only another way of saying that they haven't been coddled and mothered enough.' Jyanvi looked at her sharply.

'I'm a little confused about the gender of the Gallants.' Asha the Apostate broached the subject hesitantly. 'Are they male or female? I mean would my Ashans be welcome here?'

The Queen of Paradise seemed surprised. 'Of course they'd be welcome, particularly if they were willing to start out as Mothers. Since Paradise was founded by a Mayan Princess we use the feminine gender for everyone. In Paradise that's not a matter of any consequence. In Paradise it's whether you're a Gallant or a Mother that makes the real difference. Would your Ashans like to come here as Mothers by any chance?'

'The problem is,' Asha said awkwardly, 'my Ashans want real children.'

The Queen of Paradise shook her head. 'That won't do at all.'

The Blue Donkey spoke suddenly, 'Even as we sit here talking, are thousands of Gallants killing themselves?'

'Yes.'

'Couldn't you order them to stop? As Queen of Paradise many of them must owe you allegiance.'

'I've done that already,' the Queen told her.

'And the effect?'

'It has reduced the numbers.' The Queen shrugged. 'Some kill themselves anyway and make a point of the paradox. Others just sulk. Meanwhile, the systems of Paradise are in dissolution and Paradise must soon fall apart.'

'What do you mean?' asked Saraswati.

'The Gallants of Paradise only work when inspired,' the Queen explained, 'and the few remaining Mothers are on the point of collapse.'

'Why don't you order the Gallants to work?' Saraswati suggested. 'Isn't "service" their motto? And aren't they supposed to be gratified when they find an opportunity of serving you?'

The Queen looked at them helplessly. 'I've tried that as well, but it means having to issue an order for every single bit of work; and then having to spend time afterwards acknowledging the service and doling out favours. It's tedious—and inefficient. The Princess Jaya called this Paradise because the soil was so fertile, the climate so balmy; but to live here does require a little work.'

'There's only one solution.' The Matriarch looked directly at the Queen.

The Queen hesitated. 'We have thought of it,' she said at last, 'but it would mean that Paradise would cease to be paradisial.'

She sighed. 'People would no longer be able to devote themselves exclusively to the Pursuit of Beauty and Freedom and Love and Happiness.'

'At least they'd survive,' the Matriarch retorted.

'What are they talking about?' Jyanvi whispered.

'I think they're talking about bringing in real children,' the Blue Donkey whispered back.

'That would make for a different set of problems!' Jyanvi exclaimed.

'Yes,' the Blue Donkey murmured, 'that's what the Queen of Paradise is saying.'

When they eventually retired for the night, Saraswati said that she had a headache and would prefer to sleep alone. Jyanvi merely nodded. She wasn't going to be forced into being a Mother, but she'd be damned if she'd beg like any Gallant in Paradise.

18
What's Your Part?

Jyanvi woke to the sound of bugles. The Blue Donkey was shaking her. 'Wake up! The Queen of Paradise and the Matriarch are up to something. They're out there on the ramparts addressing a crowd of cheering Gallants. Hurry! I want to hear what they're saying.'

Jyanvi tumbled out of bed and rushed after the Blue Donkey. Saraswati and Asha were already in the corridor wanting to know what was happening.

They got there just in time to hear the Matriarch shouting, 'Are you brave and trusty Gallants?'

An enthusiastic cheer rose from below. 'Yaaay!'

'Do you adore the Queen of Paradise?'

'Yaaay!'

The Queen of Paradise stepped forward and addressed them next. 'Do you adore the Mother of the Mayan Isle?'

'Yaaay!'

'But she's in danger.'

'Nooo.'

'Yes, she is. Will you defend her with your lives?'

'Yaaay!'

'Are you brave and trusty Gallants?'

'Yaaay!'

'Are you willing to fight?'

'Yaaay!'

'Then you must go with her and help her to regain her lost birthright.'

The cheers had been growing progressively louder, and this last suggestion was received with the greatest enthusiasm.

Below them the Gallants cheered and roared and stamped their feet. Jyanvi and the Blue Donkey looked at one another. 'Why are they so pleased?' Jyanvi asked.

'I think,' replied the Blue Donkey, 'it's because they've finally found a glorious way of killing themselves.'

All that morning Jyanvi and the Blue Donkey roamed the corridors in the hope of having a word with the Matriarch, or at least with the Queen of Paradise. But the palace was in an uproar and the two queens were busy. Each was constantly surrounded by a group of Gallants, who would listen attentively and then scurry away, intent on business. As these groups dispersed they were immediately replaced by other Gallants. Towards mid-day the Blue Donkey noticed that the Gallants were beginning to form their own groups. Despairing of ever getting close to the Matriarch, Jyanvi and the Blue Donkey approached one of these groups.

Madhu was at the centre and she was earnestly addressing a dozen Gallants. 'We are the Avians. I'm your Chief, and you're my captains. Do you understand?' She glared into their faces. 'Our colours are scarlet and black. We are the élite of the corps. We shall descend on Maya Diip like the silver rain. None can resist us. The Mayan Queen shall reign again. We are her warriors.'

'What are you going on about?' asked the Blue Donkey when the cheering had died. 'Who are you fighting and what are you fighting for?'

'Don't you know?' Madhu looked surprised. Then she assumed an exalted expression. 'We're fighting for Justice and Peace. We're fighting to restore the Mayan Queen to the Mayan throne.'

The Blue Donkey looked at her curiously. 'How do you propose to do all that?'

'With fire, air and water,' Madhu replied grandly. 'We're the Warriors of Air. We shall fight with the most dazzling display of light and colour.'

'War isn't a game,' Jyanvi put it mildly.

'Life is a game,' responded Madhu gaily. 'We are Gallants.' With that she tossed a plumed hat high into the air and her captains followed suit.

The Blue Donkey hesitated. She wanted to warn the young woman, to make her come to her senses. 'Look, Madhu,' she said gently, 'have you thought about what you're doing? Can't you see that you're only striking an attitude and that it's dangerous?'

That tore it. Madhu drew herself up and looked down on the Blue Donkey and on Jyanvi with immense disdain. 'It's you we're protecting,' she said coldly. 'You ought to be grateful.' She turned her back on them while the Avian captains shouldered them out.

'We must do something,' the Blue Donkey muttered.

Jyanvi looked uncertain. 'But if this is the Matriarch's doing —' she began.

'Of course it's the Matriarch's doing,' the Blue Donkey interrupted. 'The Queen of Paradise and the Ranisaheb have thought of this scheme between them. It gives the Gallants a sense of purpose. They're actually working. They have something to do. That group there is talking about transport. That one in the corner is talking about communications. They've been given a cause.'

'That's good, isn't it?' Jyanvi responded. 'The suicide rate will drop. And if some of these Gallants march away to Maya Diip, that will reduce the population imbalance.'

'Of course, there are some good effects,' the Blue Donkey muttered. 'That's why they thought of it.'

'Then what's your objection?' Jyanvi asked.

The Blue Donkey frowned. 'It's obvious. I'm thinking of the wasted lives of the young Gallants.'

'They won't necessarily get killed,' Jyanvi pointed out.

'That's true. I'm certain that the Matriarch will do everything she can to avoid an actual confrontation,' the Blue Donkey replied thoughtfully. 'I doubt very much that she wants the Gallants on Mayan soil ...'

'And the Queen of Paradise doesn't want them here,' Jyanvi murmured. 'But I wonder what the two intend to do with them once they've served their purpose?'

This had the effect of making the Blue Donkey look sadder than ever. 'Let's see if we can find Saraswati and Asha the Apostate,' she muttered. 'Perhaps they'll have a better idea of what's going on.'

They found Saraswati and Asha enthroned on a platform in one of the great halls. Gallants were rushing to and fro. The procedure seemed to be that a Gallant would approach, kneel before the two women, speak briefly and add to the pile of documents that lay before them. Jyanvi and the Blue Donkey pushed their way through the throng. When they got to the platform, a guard halted them.

'Kneel before the Mothers of Maya,' the guard commanded.

'Nonsense,' replied the Blue Donkey. The guard began to beat her down.

Luckily, Asha the Apostate noticed the commotion. 'It's all right,' she called out. 'Let them approach.'

'What's going on?' demanded the Blue Donkey when at last they had reached Saraswati and Asha.

Jyanvi eyed the pile of documents. 'Are they giving you more poems?'

Saraswati answered her, 'No, those are lists.' She sounded tired.

'Lists?'

'Yes. They may contain a poem or two, but they're mostly lists of the materials and preparations needed for the war,' Saraswati told her.

'The war?'

'Don't parrot everything I say,' Saraswati snapped. 'Surely you've realised that the Gallants have decided to come to our rescue and to march on Maya? I'm sorry,' she added. 'I didn't mean to snap. It's just that all this—' she indicated the scene around her—'is a bit much.'

'What's your part in it?' the Blue Donkey wanted to know.

Asha looked at her steadily. 'We've been set up.'

'Can't you stop it?' the Blue Donkey protested.

'I don't think so,' Asha replied. 'Not once the machinery has been set in motion. Besides, do we want to stop it?'

'What are you going to do?' The Blue Donkey's voice was troubled.

'I'm going to join in and try to control it in order to ensure minimal damage,' Asha the Apostate answered grimly. 'You'd better do the same.'

'I don't like killing.' The Blue Donkey said obstinately.

'In that case it's as well you're in charge of the food supplies and the medical wing. You've been appointed Supplier General and Chief of the Medical Corps.'

The Blue Donkey took in the news. 'What if I refuse?'

'What would be the point?' Asha indicated a pile of documents and a group of Gallants. 'They're your concern. At least you'll be able to help them. Better get to work.'

The Blue Donkey hesitated, but then she slowly cleared a space for herself and summoned the Gallants. She got down to work.

Jyanvi watched in silence. 'What about me?' she asked at last. 'Haven't I got a job?'

'Of course you have,' Asha replied. 'You are the Commander-in-Chief of the Allied Forces of Air, Fire and Water.'

'Me? Why me?' Jyanvi was taken by surprise.

'That's what the Matriarch and the Queen decided. Perhaps it's because out of all of us, you're most like the Gallants.'

Saraswati said this without any sarcasm, but it hurt Jyanvi.

'I'm not a swashbuckler!' she responded angrily.

'That's just as well,' Asha soothed her. 'Perhaps you'll be able to keep them from harm.'

'What's my job?' Jyanvi demanded.

'Your first duty is to look magnificent,' Asha informed her. 'A suitable costume has been designed for you. As soon as you're able, put it on.' Jyanvi grimaced and was about to protest, but Asha continued relentlessly, 'Your next duty is to make sure that the Gallants think highly of themselves. So they, too, must be dressed splendidly. Check their uniforms and inspect them daily. Make sure they parade themselves.'

Jyanvi glanced at the Gallants in the hall. 'They already think well of themselves.'

'Yes,' Asha agreed. 'Your job should be easy.'

'Is that all I have to do?' Jyanvi asked.

'No,' Asha told her. 'You have to work out a strategy.'

'A strategy?'

'That's right, a strategy,' Asha repeated. 'For reinstating the Matriarch. And when that's done, for disposing of the Gallants.'

'I see,' said Jyanvi thoughtfully. 'Well, perhaps I'd better begin. Where are the Chiefs of Air, Fire and Water?' She didn't feel entirely happy about her job, but at least she had one. It occurred to her that Madhu would have to be more respectful in future.

'I think,' Asha suggested gently, 'that you'd better put on your costume first.'

'Why?'

'Because without it, it's highly unlikely that they'll obey your commands,' Asha pointed out. She smiled to take the sting out of her remark.

Jyanvi went off to change. The Blue Donkey drudged on. And Asha and Saraswati sat there, patiently receiving adulation.

For the next fortnight, everyone was busy. There was no time for conversation. It seemed to Jyanvi that the others, especially the Matriarch and the Blue Donkey, were avoiding her. When she mentioned this to the Blue Donkey, the Blue Donkey said that the Matriarch was avoiding everyone. But surely tonight, Jyanvi thought, after the Grand Parade the Matriarch would agree to a council of war, at least to some sort of discussion. After all, they were setting off tomorrow. Meanwhile, Jyanvi sweltered in her grand uniform as she watched the display of the Allied Forces.

The Avians, the Fire Throwers and the Water Workers had competed eagerly. The weapons they had thought of were many and ingenious. Some were secret, like the Great Magnifying Glass. The idea was that the Avians were to extend it over Maya Nagar and thus reduce the city to cinders. Then there was the plan that the Water Workers had conceived of producing a tidal wave that would inundate the island. These were, of course, as the designers had insisted, ultimate weapons, only to be used as a last resort, only as threats ... There were, they admitted, still flaws in the designs—the tidal wave was not properly directional, the magnifying glass needed to be made of some lightweight material—but they were working on them.

Jyanvi squirmed under her cloak. More and more she had come

to hate trying to behave like an Arch-Gallant. What was she to do? When the time came, how was she going to control the Forces? The Fire Throwers and the Water Workers were putting on a show, which, in spite of herself, she found beautiful. Jets of fire and jets of water arched and intersected and swung around with military precision. She glanced at Saraswati, but Saraswati was absorbed in the spectacle. Of late, Saraswati had had less and less to say to her. Only Asha and the Blue Donkey had been kind, but they too had been busy. Jyanvi suppressed a sigh. She straightened her shoulders, held up her chin and tried to look fierce and confident.

She glanced around her. In the royal box, the Queen of Paradise was smiling down upon the Gallants. In the distance, scarlet blimps with black markings stood out against a blue sky. She knew that each blimp was tethered to a motorboat rocking in the harbour. This was to be their means of transport. Tomorrow, they would set off for Maya Diip. But surely before that the Matriarch must speak to her, must give her some private instructions? Dinner would be a formal occasion, and the Allied Chiefs would all be present. But surely after dinner?

Dinner came and went and nothing happened. Jyanvi went to bed in an uneasy frame of mind. When at last she fell asleep, she had an unpleasant dream. The mothers of Maya had pricked the blimps with little needles. This had released a rain of blood, which covered the island like paint. The blood stank and was sticky. The nausea woke her. It was already five in the morning. She might as well get up. She sat down on the floor in the lotus position and breathed deeply in an effort to calm down. Then she put on the uniform which defined her position.

19
Write a Poem

In spite of herself, Jyanvi felt her spirits rising. The shehnai sounded triumphant and sensual. The drums thundered. The Mothers of Paradise cheered the Gallants, as did the Gallants who stayed behind (for necessary war work). The Queen of Paradise shed her blessings on everyone. The Gallants themselves looked happy and gay in their pretty uniforms. For a moment, Jyanvi felt a surge of pride that she was to be the leader of this grand expedition. Then her heart sank again. And then she decided to suspend thought for the next little while. The blimps were lowered, the Gallants mounted, flags fluttered and by noon, the process of loading was done. The green motorboats with the scarlet stripe were within the provenance of the Water Workers. They were in readiness, and in no time at all the first of these set off with the flagship in tow. The rest followed in formation.

In addition to the regular crew, the flagship carried the Matriarch of Maya, Asha the Apostate, the Princess Saraswati, the Blue Donkey and Her Excellency, Jyanvi, the Commander-in-Chief of the Allied Forces. It was about the size of a blue whale. Above them the clouds scudded by, below them the sea was a peaceful and sequinned blue. It would take them two hours to reach Maya Diip. Jyanvi wondered if the Matriarch would talk to her now. There was no one else in the cabin at the moment. Jyanvi glanced in the Matriarch's direction without much hope and the

Matriarch actually smiled at her. Jyanvi smiled back tentatively. The Matriarch patted the seat beside her. 'Come and sit down,' she said. 'You look anxious.'

Jyanvi sat down.

'Now,' said the Matriarch pleasantly, 'what's the matter?'

Jyanvi thought for a second. 'It's our strategy that's worrying me. The Giant Magnifying Glass and the Directional Tidal Wave haven't been perfected yet, though they're working on them. I suppose we could bluff and use them as a threat?' Her voice became anxious. 'Or there are the atomic devices you control. Those would be a genuine threat. We're going to use threats, aren't we?' She looked at the Matriarch doubtfully.

The Matriarch smiled. 'No,' she replied, 'we're not going to use threats, atomic or otherwise.'

'But what are we going to do?' By now Jyanvi was in a state of considerable distress. 'I don't want to kill the Mayan mothers or the Gallants of Paradise!' she cried. 'Don't you see? There's going to be the most horrifying bloodshed.'

Jyanvi sobbed and for a minute or two the Matriarch comforted her against her breast. 'It's all right,' she consoled. 'You're relieved of your command, or rather, superseded. I'll take over. Now, there are only two tasks you have to perform.'

'What?' Jyanvi asked through her tears.

'The first is to make sure that the communications system is in working order,' the Matriarch told her.

'It is,' Jyanvi replied. 'But I'll make sure.'

'And the second is to write a poem.'

'What?' Jyanvi exclaimed, incredulous. Was the Matriarch making fun of her? 'At a time like this?'

'Yes.' The Matriarch appeared to be serious. 'It's necessary.'

'What sort of poem?' Jyanvi asked feebly.

'It will have to be an epic, I think,' the Matriarch said casually.

'And it must describe the valour and splendour of the Gallants.'

'An epic!' Jyanvi stared. Had the Matriarch suddenly become irresponsible? 'How long do I have to complete it?'

'Nearly an hour,' replied the Matriarch. 'It must be ready before we arrive above Maya Diip.'

'It can't be done.' Jyanvi was definite.

'Yes, it can.' The Matriarch instructed her. 'Begin with a description of each of the blimps, then of their pilot boats, then of the heroic attributes of the chiefs, the captains and the other officers. Embroider and embellish and carry on in this way. The remaining sections can be left blank. They're to be the chapters of a Voyage of Discovery. Surely you have an outfit of Slogan Writers? Give them the outline and tell them to fill it in later.' Jyanvi gaped at the Matriarch. 'But you've already given me the outline.'

'Yes. That should make your task easier. Now, go.' She patted Jyanvi's shoulder. 'Get to work.'

Jyanvi went away and settled down with a piece of paper.

'Of the ships that sailed from Paradise,' she began, 'these were the emblems that distinguished each one ...'

As they approached Maya Diip, the Matriarch took her place at the helm. Her daughters flanked her, and Jyanvi and the Blue Donkey stood just behind.

'Are the amplifiers ready? Good. Switch on the communications.' The Matriarch's orders were promptly relayed and carried out. 'Now navigate us so that we remain stationary just above the Great Cave Temple. Tell the rest of the fleet to remain offshore in an arrow formation which points to us.'

Jyanvi wondered what the red arrow must look like to the Mayans on the ground. The Matriarch had begun to speak. Her voice must be rolling through the Mayan streets. The amplifiers had been set for maximum volume.

'O Mothers of Maya,' the Matriarch's voice thundered down, 'your Matriarch has been on a state visit to the Queen of Paradise. Now she returns. She brings with her two Mayan daughters, the Princess Saraswati and the Princess Asha. They are escorted by the Gallants of Paradise. Bid them welcome.' A great cheer rose up from the ground. The Mayans had been told that the Matriarch had gone to the forest. That she had been to Paradise instead and was now back with a friendly armada was even better. They were glad to have her back. The rule of Shyamila the Civil and Sarla Devi had not been popular.

The Matriarch spoke again. 'I am glad to be back.' Below her, the Mayans cheered.

'Let my daughters Pramila and Shyamila ascend the platform so that they may be reunited with their mother. And let Sarla Devi, the Chief of the Guild of the Great Goddess, accompany them so that all the rites may be properly observed.'

The crowd cheered. Jyanvi watched the platform from which the Matriarch had addressed the crowd on the Day of Oracles. There was some activity there, but Shyamila and Sarla had not appeared.

'What if they hold Gagri the Good and Sona as hostages?' Jyanvi blurted out.

The three Mayans looked at her, but did not answer. It was the sort of look that made Jyanvi shrink back.

'What was so bad about what I said?' she whispered to the Blue Donkey.

'From the Mayan point of view,' the Blue Donkey whispered back, 'I think you thought the unthinkable.'

There was movement on the platform now. Shyamila and Sarla Devi had presented themselves. Behind them were two other women accompanied by children. It was the expression on Saraswati's face that made Jyanvi realise that the child clinging to Malini Devi's hand was Sona and that the other child, who seemed to be trying to wrap herself in Pramila's sari, was Gagri the Good.

'Shall we haul them up?' Jyanvi enquired.

'No, we'll descend.'

'Yes, Your Majesty.' It seemed appropriate now to address her so. The Matriarch smiled at Jyanvi kindly. 'You and the Blue Donkey must remain on board a little longer. Give the fleet the necessary orders to keep them occupied for a day or two. Then join us.'

Jyanvi and the Blue Donkey said they would do so. 'Your Majesty—' the Blue Donkey hesitated. 'Will you be taking an escort with you?'

'An escort?'

'Well, a troop of Gallants.'

The Matriarch shook her head. 'No,' she said. 'I think this time we'll be all right. I'll take precautions.'

Asha the Apostate smiled reassuringly. 'We'll look after her, and soon, you'll be with us.'

Shortly afterwards, the three Mayans left the ship. As the Matriarch descended, the Mayans cheered and shouted their welcome. They liked their Ranisaheb and thought that this aerial descent was worthy of her.

On the flagship the Blue Donkey turned to Jyanvi, 'How will you keep the Gallants amused?'

'It's easy,' Jyanvi replied. 'I shall encourage them to prance and strut.'

'What do you mean?'

But Jyanvi was already issuing orders to the Allied Chiefs to meet her on board in precisely an hour. The Blue Donkey busied herself with making sure that the supplies they carried were in good order. Jyanvi spent the next little while relaying the outline of her epic poem to the Slogan Writers. Then, she brushed her uniform and smartened herself up. At the appointed time, the Chiefs of the Allied Forces were welcomed aboard with military honours. They in turn saluted their Commander with proper deference.

'O Chiefs,' Jyanvi told them, 'the pleasure of the Mothers is the code in accordance with which we have lived our lives. Now the eyes of the Matriarch of Maya and of all the Mayan Mothers are upon us. For two days and nights can you put on a display of fire and water and aerial skills that does honour to them and is worthy of us?'

'Yes,' cried the Chiefs all in chorus. 'Yes, we can.'

'Then do so,' commanded Jyanvi, and dismissed them with an appropriate gesture.

For the next forty-eight hours, the Gallants of Paradise put on a most spectacular show of waterworks and fireworks in the Mayan sky. The mothers of Maya were generous in their praise, as were Jyanvi and the Blue Donkey and the Mayan royalty, when affairs of state permitted them to look up.

20
Is That What You Mean?

Perhaps nothing had changed, Jyanvi thought. Perhaps the exile and the wandering had only been a diversion. Shyamila the Civil had not been locked up. Sarla Devi, though no longer a Chief, was still at liberty to walk about. Valerie, of course, was still absent. When she had tried to warn the Mayans about the Trader Robots, they had refused to believe her. The tale was incredible. And so, she had returned to Ashagad in the hope of somehow establishing their existence. The only other difference was Asha's presence—that and the fireworks in the sky. But otherwise it could have been any other evening. Dinner was over, and here they all were, sitting around. Any moment now Jyanvi expected the Matriarch to say, 'Amuse me.' But she was wrong. Within the next fifteen minutes, Jyanvi realised that nothing was going to be the same any more.

The Matriarch was addressing Shyamila, 'Tell me, what is it you really want?'

Shyamila forced herself to meet her mother's eyes. 'Mother, why do you mock me?' She spoke with some impatience. 'I admit that I conspired against you. Punish me and be done.'

'Answer me.' The Matriarch was adamant. 'What do you want?'

'Very well,' Shyamila answered, 'if we must play this game. I want what I've always wanted. I want to rule.'

To everyone's astonishment, the Matriarch smiled, 'Yes, you do, don't you? Well, you are appointed the Supreme Mother of the

Armada of the Gallants.' 'They're unruly children,' she added as an afterthought. 'Perhaps you can give them a sense of direction.'

'Me?' Shyamila was caught off-balance. 'You want me to lead the Gallants? But what am I to do with them?'

'Rule them,' the Matriarch replied serenely. 'Sarla Devi will accompany you. The two of you must lead the Gallants on a voyage of discovery.'

Shyamila stared at the Matriarch in disbelief. 'Mother, doesn't it occur to you that we could use the Armada against Maya Diip and thus gain power? Is this a trap?'

The Matriarch did not hide her weariness. 'Shyamila, the Gallants are children with toy balloons, capable of destruction, but to what purpose? You're a good administrator. I think you'll find the Gallants more challenging than the mothers of Maya. Go where you're needed. Help them to make something of themselves.'

There had been no unkindness in the Matriarch's voice. Wasn't her mother angry with her? Shyamila the Civil didn't know what to say.

The Matriarch then turned to Pramila the Poet. 'Will you go with your sister as Principal Poet?'

'What would be my duties?'

'Your principal duty,' the Matriarch told her, 'would be to glorify the Gallants and define their quest.'

Pramila was uncertain. 'What about my responsibilities here on Maya?'

'You're relieved of them.'

The words startled Pramila. She tried to decide whether what had just happened was good or bad. She decided that it was bad. 'Mother,' she said quickly. 'I've changed my mind. I want to stay.'

'All right,' returned the Matriarch. 'Stay then.'

'What would you do if I asked to stay?' Shyamila asked suddenly.

The Matriarch looked at her. 'Do you want to stay?'

'No.'

'Then go with my blessings.'

Shyamila faltered for a moment. Could her mother dismiss her so easily? Then she stood up, walked over to her mother, touched her feet and left the room. Soon afterwards Pramila mumbled that she had a headache and made her excuses.

It was difficult to know what the Matriarch was thinking. Had Shyamila's departure made her sad? She looked tired, but her features were composed. Jyanvi watched her every movement. The Matriarch gave her attention to her remaining daughters and to Jyanvi and the Blue Donkey. They waited.

'It remains only to dispose of the Matriarchy of Maya,' she said.

They absorbed her words. Asha and Saraswati were too stunned to speak, but Jyanvi cried out. 'Why?' she begged. 'The Matriarchy of Maya is safe in your hands, and all is well.'

The Ranisaheb was shaking her head. 'I've abdicated,' she told them calmly. 'Tomorrow I shall return to the forest.'

The words sank in. 'It's not yet time,' Saraswati protested. Asha said nothing. To have found her mother and to lose her so soon? She kept her grief to herself.

The Matriarch spoke gently, but her resolve was unshakeable. 'It's time.'

'Who's to be the next Matriarch?' Saraswati pleaded. It seemed to Jyanvi that Saraswati still hoped that her mother would take charge.

The Matriarch's reply disabused them. 'That's a matter that it's best you agree upon among yourselves. The three of you must decide with the Blue Donkey's help.'

She rose to her feet and the others stood up. The three women touched her feet as Shyamila had done. Then she embraced each one of them, including Jyanvi. Nobody wept. They were formal and seemly, though they knew they were saying farewell. When she had gone, they looked at one another. They felt bereft. Outside the palace, the sky was lit up by the fireworks of the Gallants. They turned to the Blue Donkey.

'Sleep on it,' the Blue Donkey advised them.

The next morning the sky was still crowded with the displays of the Gallants. The two Mayan princesses and Jyanvi faced the Blue Donkey in the rose garden. The three women were sitting on a bench. All in a row, almost like schoolgirls, the Blue Donkey thought.

'Well,' she began, 'which of you would like to be the Matriarch of Maya?'

It was Saraswati who spoke first. 'It's not so much for my own sake as for the sake of my daughter, Sona, that I feel it's right that I should be the next Matriarch.'

Asha the Apostate stared at her. 'What has any of this to do with your daughter? I also have a daughter, Gagri, whom I hardly know. But surely, even if you are the next Matriarch, it's been established for years that Gagri the Good will be your successor.'

Saraswati looked stubborn. 'That's not so.'

'Well then,' Asha the Apostate announced hastily, 'I claim the throne on behalf of my own daughter.'

'What about you?' the Blue Donkey looked at Jyanvi, but Jyanvi shook her head.

Saraswati was indignant. 'Aren't you going to support my claim?' she asked Jyanvi.

Jyanvi seemed to be in a daze. 'What claim?' she mumbled.

'Don't you remember?' Saraswati was annoyed that Jyanvi and the Blue Donkey had to be reminded. 'On the Day of Oracles I was declared the true heir.

'She who shall reign in the goddess' name must suffer change, yet stay the same.'

'That describes me!' Asha exclaimed. 'I was exiled, not you.'

'At the time the Oracle was interpreted differently,' Saraswati replied coldly. 'And in any case, how can you reign? You committed heresy against Maya.'

'And you're such a true Mayan that you've lost the ability to think for yourself!' Asha retorted.

The Blue Donkey stopped the altercation. 'Since the two of you can't agree, shall we consider the third candidate?'

'The third candidate?' Asha and Saraswati both looked surprised. 'Are you in the running?' Saraswati enquired.

The Blue Donkey shook her head. 'No, I mean to join the Matriarch in the forest.'

'Do you mean Jyanvi?' Asha the Apostate asked suddenly. 'But you don't want to reign, do you?' Asha continued, addressing Jyanvi.

Jyanvi had been shaken by the news that the Blue Donkey was

also leaving her. 'Don't leave me!' she wanted to cry out to the Matriarch and the Blue Donkey. 'Or take me with you into the forest. I'll look after you and find berries for you. I will be good.' She was close to tears. 'What?' she asked when she realised that Asha the Apostate had been speaking to her.

Asha repeated the question. 'Do you want to reign?'

'No,' Jyanvi replied. 'No, I never wanted to reign.'

Asha the Apostate looked at her intently. 'Would you if asked?'

'How can she make a good Matriarch if she doesn't even want to reign?' Saraswati interjected.

'Perhaps that's the best qualification,' Asha murmured. She looked straight at Jyanvi. 'I must return to Ashagad. They need me there. But I must first look after Gagri's interests. Will you look after Gagri for me?'

Jyanvi evaded the question. She turned on the Blue Donkey. 'Why don't you and the Matriarch remain in Maya?'

'No,' replied the Blue Donkey. 'The Matriarch has gone and I must follow soon. Are you willing to take her place?'

'How can I?' returned Jyanvi. She stood up in exasperation and glanced at Saraswati in the hope that Saraswati would back her up.

But Saraswati had become thoughtful. She spoke slowly, 'When I first knew you, there were many things you didn't know. I now realise that there are many things I don't know. If you choose to be Matriarch, you have my support.'

'The oracle doesn't fit,' Jyanvi protested.

'Yes, it does. You've changed, haven't you?' Saraswati replied.

Jyanvi tried another tack. 'The mothers of Maya would never accept me,' she explained to the others, 'I'm not even a native Mayan, let alone a Mayan princess.'

'As Gagri's Guardian and my Consort, they would accept you,' Saraswati told her quietly.

'Will you look after Gagri the Good for me?' Asha repeated.

Jyanvi looked at them helplessly. 'I'm unfit,' she pleaded.

'Yes,' agreed the Blue Donkey equably. 'There's that.'

They waited for Jyanvi's reply in silence. In the sky overhead, there was a sudden burst of noise and colour. Sarla Devi and Shyamila the Civil were ascending heavenward.

Jyanvi pointed to them. 'Is that what you mean?'

Asha the Apostate replied steadily, 'No, that's not what we mean.'

Jyanvi turned to the Blue Donkey. Surely the Blue Donkey would come to her rescue? But the Blue Donkey seemed to be fading away as though already halfway to the forest. She put her arm on the Blue Donkey's neck. 'Why me?' she begged.

'By default.' The Blue Donkey's answer when it reached her ears was clear and dispassionate.

Jyanvi turned away ruefully. 'All right,' she said to her friends at last. 'Come on, then.'

Shupi's Choices

'*Shupi's Choices*' and '*Kumbh*' overlap the narrative of '*Bad People*' in *Dangerous Pursuits*, and are best read together; but sometimes manuscripts don't get written in an orderly fashion. Ravana Dada, Shurpanakha and Kumbhakarna wake up in the twenty-first century and with the help of Grandma Ketumati's balm, manage to make the world veer from its destructive course. Though the three siblings are generally seen as villains, they are, after all, epic figures. And, in these stories, they are also slightly comical. Leading one's life in accordance with epic norms isn't really good sense. Shupi and Kumbh are more aware of this than their big brother, but each has to work out what makes sense. While their narratives reflect on notions of the 'heroic', they also show up some of the silliness and snobbery of our own times.

Contents

1
Not His Baa-lambs

Dada would say that he, Kumbh and I saved the world, with a bit of help from Leela and the others. He sees himself as a man of action, though now he's busy writing his opera. Is he not—was he not—Ten Headed Ravana, the Astonishing King of the Golden Isle? And did he not outwit and out-manoeuvre the wicked politician, who would have prevented us from giving the Golden Balm to all mankind? Sometimes I think he's still fighting ancient wars. Pieces of the past cling to him. That's probably true of all of us. And that is why the world has been reprieved, not saved, not set on a safe course that will lead us ever onward and upward.

My grandmother, Ketumati Ma, had given me the balm. It healed people. It also made them fairer and kinder, more sane. It wouldn't have occurred to Dada that making people better was a worthy cause if Kumbh and I had not suggested it to him. He went along with it to indulge us, and also because it was something to do in this strange new world. Gradually he realised it was worthwhile. I wonder why Ketumati Ma gave me the balm and the recipe? I didn't need it—not then. I was a pretty child, and later, I think, a good looking young woman. Some people even said that I was beautiful. Not my mother's friends, of course. They said I was too tall and not at all well-behaved. Perhaps Ketumati Ma wanted to improve me? Help me fit in? The balm doesn't reshape people. It makes them better-tempered, kinder. By now we've all used it –

Dada, Kumbh, me, almost the whole world. But the world is still flawed. I suppose it all depends on the starting point.

The balm is definitely medicinal. It helped me to heal Dada and Kumbh. After that epic battle in which Dada was defeated, I carried what was left of them to a secret cave with the help of several rakshasas. There, I pieced my brothers together and hoped that the balm would restore them. It took a long time. They slept for centuries. Most of the time, I slept too. Eventually, we emerged from the cave. Kumbh and I realised quite early that this new world was about to annihilate itself, and that human beings were responsible for most of the problems—global warming, the pollution of the oceans, the extinction of species. A miracle was needed. Ketumati Ma's Golden Balm could be that miracle—if it were made available to everyone. Leela, the snake charmer's daughter, whom we met at a fair and the three of us, set about manufacturing it. The balm bought us time. It improved people; but it did not change human beings radically.

This doesn't seem to bother Dada; or if it does, he doesn't say so. He and Vijju are happy enough. I think he feels we should rest on our laurels. And Kumbh? It's hard to know what Kumbh feels. He and Leela fell in love. She asked Dada to give them his blessing, which he did. But I worry about Kumbh. They're supposed to be living happily ever after. That is the end of every quest—at least Leela seems to think it is. Every now and then, she urges me to marry. Dada agrees. Kumbh has his Leela, and I should set about finding a suitable partner—one he approves of, of course.

Dada patronises us. As he sees it, Kumbh is a dreamer and has to be looked after. And he thinks I'm inclined to be impetuous, to think too much and to say what I think. I too have to be kept out of trouble. He means well. I can hear him thinking at me, 'Why can't you be happy? The world is a better place now. Most human beings are better people.' Better than what? Besides, I am quite happy, that doesn't mean I have to be stupid. It's just that I do not think I live in paradise. To this, he would reply that he does not think so either.

If I were to say to Dada that he behaves like a nanny fussing over two small children, he'd be highly offended, so I don't say it. He doesn't realise that both Kumbh and I are capable of making up our own minds. His attempts at finding suitors for me would be sweet, possibly funny, if they weren't such a nuisance. 'Well, what do you want?' he once asked in exasperation.

He has written an account of how we emerged from the cave, distributed the balm, defeated our enemies... With heavy irony he has called it *Bad People*. Dada thinks of himself as heroic, whatever the century. He can't help it. But there are things he knows nothing about. What happened to him isn't the same as what happened to Kumbh and to me. And how we experienced what happened isn't the same either. We shared the same childhood; but the expectations, the inhibitions and the limitations were different. It's hard for me to look back on the past. I question the labels stuck on us. Kumbh wasn't a lumpish giant. Dada wasn't the embodiment of evil, and I wasn't a she-demon. Who was I then? And now?

In some ways this brave new world is easier to live in—at least for me. The colour of the ink from my pen—royal blue—is the colour of the sea this morning. I'm not altogether sure whether who I've become is an improvement on who I've been. Is Ms Shupi better off than Shurpanakha the erstwhile princess? And aside from being better off, is she, at least, better?

Kumbh and I both love Dada, but we don't want to be defined just as his siblings. I could tease Dada and tell him that we are not his baa-lambs. If we were, that would make him a mother sheep, but I'll save that for another time.

2
Is the Sister of a King an Important Person?

I was born a princess; not a grand princess. My father was not king of the world, he wasn't even a princeling, he was merely a sage. As I had been born in a patriarchy, my privileges were limited. My mother was a princess. She wasn't particularly fond of me. Perhaps I bored her? Or perhaps she was envious. Envious of what? My father ignored me, just as he ignored everyone. To make up for my parents, there was Ravana Dada. As my elder brother, he took his duties seriously. He made time for me; though he was occasionally impatient, wanting me to do things I couldn't do yet—fly a kite, string a bow, behave myself. And there was Kumbh, not quite as attentive to everyone as he ought to be; but I knew I could count on him. He slept a lot as though he was hiding from something, avoiding something—being alive perhaps. Our parents didn't have much use for him, only Ravana Dada mattered. Dada had been bred for greatness, earthshaking victories were expected of him. In his heart, though, father seemed to prefer Kubera, and mother liked Vibhishana better. I understood at an early age that unless I married well, I was of no account. Luckily, my grandmother, Ketumati Ma, loved all three of us, and that made a difference.

I enjoyed my status for what it was worth. It was nice to be bowed down to, have people scurrying about and falling at my feet, though I was never sure why they were doing it. I had very little power. What could I do? Curry favour for them with members of the family? The illusion of power is as good as power—except when it's seen through, then the lack of it is humiliating. The King of the Rakshasas was my grandfather, a bluff old man, nice to his grandchildren, and that was about it.

I grew like Topsy. A princess, grew like a slave child? Children grow in many ways. What's common to them is that they do grow. My playmates were the children of servants. That was fine; though I did not look at their lives too deeply. Sometimes I played with Kumbh and his friends. They liked running about, hitting things and scuffling with each other. I considered them puerile. I suppose they couldn't help it, they were boys. I liked being with Dada best. He was a scholar, he taught me music and mathematics, and slokas as well though he got frustrated occasionally.

I watched, I waited. I wondered what was in store for me. Not much, it appeared. No proposals of marriage were forthcoming. For my part, having to say, 'Yes, Sir,' and 'No, Sir,' to someone for no reason other than that he was male and married to me, didn't appeal. 'She's beautiful, but not biddable,' my mother's friends said. I didn't care. And my parents didn't care either, which is to their credit or discredit, depending on how you look at it. Another of her friends said, 'She has studied too much. A man doesn't like to think that his wife is more learned than he is. And should she also be cleverer—Heaven forbid!' I ignored that as well, but a third remark unsettled me: 'She's not really a princess. She is only the daughter of a princess.' Not even a princess? What about when Ravana Dada became King of Sri Lanka? Is the sister of a king a princess? At least an important person? Only if he likes her. Dada did like me, but I didn't want to shine in reflected effulgence. I was young, I was beautiful (if not biddable) and I had a few powers of my own. And I was strong and healthy. I could make it on my own. I would walk out of the palace, out of the kingdom and seek my fortune. I would be someone in my own right. It was a stupid idea, dangerous and silly; but it was better than living at home and being nobody.

Another thing my mother's friends said, when explaining sympathetically why no suitors came: 'She's a foot taller than any of the men, except her brothers. It won't do and that's the truth of it.' Why wouldn't it do? Nobody made remarks about Ravana

Dada or Kumbh being tall, well, they did about Kumbh. But if Dada could be magnificent, why couldn't I? I didn't want suitors anyway; though it would have felt good turning down one or two. I could have held my head higher. This is silly. I am half rakshasa, and therefore a shape-shifter. I could have shortened myself by a foot or two. I didn't see why I should.

Over the centuries, when I've woken up intermittently, I've sneaked out of the cave and learnt this and that. There's a story about a knight who is supposed to find out what women want most. An 'ugly' woman provides the answer, and so he has to marry her. When they go to bed, she tells him she can be beautiful by day or beautiful by night—it's his choice. He's a clever knight and lets her decide. As a result, the knight gets his reward: she is beautiful by day and by night. A happy ending? Why should I be someone else's reward? I am my own reward. And my own punishment? I've just understood what underlies the story: what men most desire is sovereignty. I'm not sure that is what I want.

Some other things my mother's friends said: 'She scowls too much. She's argumentative.' And worst of all—'Disobedient.' They should have sent me to Charm School to learn how to please. Eventually, I taught myself. Why batter people with logic when you can win them over with a pleasing smile? And why not coax people into thinking that what you want is actually their own idea? It allows them to feel good about themselves. Women's wiles? Everybody's wiles.

My mother's friends weren't wrong. I wanted to do what I wanted to do, and I didn't want to be who I was supposed to be. I walked out. I changed my appearance, changed my gender. I looked like an ordinary young man. It was safer. And I decided to look poor, which was more inconspicuous. I didn't tell the family any of my plans. They were worried and angry; they sent people in search of me. I eluded them and only got in touch after I had made a home for myself and was a splendid success.

None of this is true. It was only a daydream. I did consider walking out, but it wasn't sensible. When I asked one or two of the servants whether they would follow me, they turned me down. They didn't think much of my chances. What I did was ask permission to visit my brother, Ravana, who by then was King of Sri Lanka. I said I longed to see the Golden Isle and that Ravana Dada had always said I was welcome. Such a request was acceptable. My mother didn't object. My father, the sage, couldn't be disturbed. And my grandfather, Sumali, the King of the Rakshasas, said he would, of course, provide me with an escort; but it was not all right for a woman of my rank to travel alone. Bodyguards didn't count. Fortunately, Kumbh told grandfather he wanted to go too. The only person who minded about my leaving was my grandmother, Ketumati Ma.

'Beti,' she said to me, 'why are you going? What do you want?'

'Not what's on offer, which is to marry someone, hope he's all right, and have a few children.'

'Is that so bad?'

'What if this husband turns out to be a fool? Or worse? It's too chancy.'

'A woman alone cannot survive.'

'Can a man survive if not supported by an entire network?'

'You too have support.'

'It's a mesh imprisoning me, a set of ropes around my body.'

Ketumati Ma looked at me. 'Do you want to be celibate, live alone all your life?'

I wanted to point out that I could live alone and not be celibate. But that might have been improper and therefore rude. I did not want to be rude to her. I had wanted to ask about her marriage. Had she been happy? That too wouldn't have been respectful. And so, without saying anything, I touched her feet and asked for her blessing.

She said, 'Go with my blessing, child. You have strength, intelligence and courage. Use them well.' I noticed she didn't say anything about my charm or my beauty and using them well. I was pleased. I wanted to make my way on merit alone, not inveigle my way past obstacles; but that's not the way the world works. Perhaps charm is another application of intelligence and insight?

I was sad leaving her, I wasn't sure I would see her again. I didn't. The world looked stable, but it didn't feel stable. Did I want things to go on as they were? Did I want change? Did I want a fight? I wasn't bloodthirsty. I didn't understand why boys loved their war games so. I didn't want war and I wasn't a warrior. I was about to see the world for myself. Then I could offer suggestions for improvement. I even wrote a poem about it, as though the world was something I could hold in my hand, as though I, myself, wasn't very young.

Poor old world.
Like a bruised melon
it wobbles and whirls and wobbles
and whirls as though it was still
very young.

Today I would write a different poem. Perhaps something like this:

Poor, old world,
it spins all the while
on its path through space,
and perched on its back
like a small insect
I too am eroded.

I'm not going to make the mistake Dada made and show him what I've written. For the time being this account is for me alone to revise and revisit. I want to understand who I've been and what I might become. And I'm not taking on labels—Shurpanakha the Demoness, Shurpanakha of the Slit Nose, Shurpanakha the Maimed. How resist? Words mean what everyone thinks they mean. I'll change words and I'll switch words. I'll metamorphose into Shupi the Gentle, Young-Eyed Shupi, Shupi the Able. Can words change us or does time do that? I did change. I became charming (when it suited me). I grew confident and then in time I learnt to be humble. Is time a friend or an enemy? Madame Mutability, who personifies the effects of time, reminds me of my mother's friends—a scratch here, a cut there, and the constant, relentless erosion.

About the mutilation I suffered? I shall tell you about that another time.

3

I Liked Who I Was When I Was with Him

If we had asked in time, Ravana Dada would have sent his flying chariot, Pushpaka. We'd have flown to Sri Lanka in style. I've flown first class once or twice recently, but Pushpaka was better than a gigantic private jet with all the frills. Not that I cared about frills, I wanted the journey. I sent Dada a messenger and asked that we be met in a month's time at Kanya Kumari, where the seas meet. We had a couple of chariots, twenty bodyguards, tents and horses. As we travelled, Kumbh and I got to know each other better. There were hardships—insects, cold water baths, inclement weather, sore muscles; but nothing really bad happened. Who would attack us with Kumbh around? Even the bodyguards relaxed. They felt safe with him, though they knew very well that they were supposed to protect him, not the other way round. Kumbh didn't do anything that was at all frightening. He didn't even carry a weapon. It was just that he was so much stronger and larger than everyone else. In the mornings he would meditate, and sometimes a bird or two would perch on his shoulder. He didn't seem to mind. We travelled by day. At night, before going to sleep, we would sit around a fire and tell stories. It was a happy time, I like remembering it.

One evening, Bhau, an old bodyguard, who had looked after Kumbh when Kumbh was little, said to him, 'Baba, you are a warrior and the descendant of a long line of warriors. Why do you never carry a sword or a bow?'

Kumbh replied, 'I don't want to kill anyone.'

'What if they attack you?' Bhau asked.

Kumbh smiled. 'Shanti, my beloved elephant, told me a story about what happened to her once. This is how it goes.

CROSS ELEPHANT

She was angry with herself. Elephants don't fight, freeze or flee. Elephants aren't frightened, nor are they ferocious. Elephants just stand there. Should an intrepid tiger choose to attack, the tiger bounces off the elephant's back. The tiger isn't hurt. Should a tree choose to cross an elephant's path, the elephant does her best to avoid the tree. At worst a branch or two is broken, but no serious damage occurs. Should a mouse choose to tickle an elephant's foot, the elephant—well, obviously, she just stands there.

What had got to her, of course, was the mighty hunter. Nevertheless, plunging the hunter and his bow into the river repeatedly had been excessive. Now she'd have to hurry and get some medicine. Elephants don't hurry, and on the whole they are good-tempered; but if that hunter died, she was going to be furious.'

'That's all very well –' Bhau hesitated. He didn't want to say to Kumbh that he wasn't an elephant, it wasn't his place. 'Elephants don't tell stories,' he blurted out.

'Sometimes they do,' Kumbh replied.

'Did the hunter die?' I asked Kumbh.

Kumbh shook his head. 'She got help in time.'

The soldiers only half-liked the story. I liked it a lot. It told me something about my brother. I didn't want to kill people either, but then, as a woman, I wasn't expected to. Are women more gentle by nature? I don't think I'm more gentle than Kumbh. Remembering Shanti and Kumbh makes me smile. Other people had dogs who followed them, or sometimes even a cheetah on a leash; Kumbh and Shanti had each other. They used to ramble about the countryside being careful not to trample on crops. In the long saga in which Dada is made chief villain, heroic warriors are often described as 'rutting elephants' ... Each to his taste?

I don't think I can be described as the villainess– that diminutive again—of that soap-saga. I'm not important enough. But I do figure in it. As an ogress? Words can vilify you. Suppose I cross out words? ~~Ogress~~. And substitute other words? Sweet, simple, gentle Shurpanakha. I can be sweet and gentle sometimes. But simple? And yet, I must have been simple. Otherwise, later, when Kumbh wasn't with me, how could I have been treated as though I was nothing, no, worse than nothing, as someone to be scorned, mocked and then mutilated?

On this trip, a young maidservant called Mala accompanied me. Her job was to take care of my clothes, press my legs if they ached, comb my hair, and tell me a bedtime story if I wanted one. She was supposed to look after me and attend to my needs. And she did. She was quiet, subservient and self-effacing. I had no complaints, but one day I couldn't help noticing she was crying. I tried to ignore it. It was probably something minor. But the sniffling continued. In the end, I had to ask her what was wrong. At first, she wouldn't say. I was expected to coax her. I coaxed her. At last it came out. The men had been harassing her, especially when she went to the toilet. There were two or three of them who were particularly troublesome. It was a nuisance. I would have to deal with it. I didn't want to. It was embarrassing. I suggested that she keep out of the men's way, go to the toilet nearer our tent very early in the morning, while it was still dark and before the men were up. If she took proper precautions, she wouldn't be bothered. She hung her head, nodded and tried to stop crying. When I look back, I feel ashamed. I was young, I wanted to have a nice time and to understand things, not have to deal with other people's pain. I must have thought servants didn't matter, or didn't matter much. This is an account, not a confession; nevertheless, the least I can do is admit to my obtuseness.

As we travelled south, a party of Danavas confronted us. The Danavas were the enemies of the rakshasas. Our bodyguards drew their swords, readied their spears and strung their bows. It wasn't necessary. A handsome young man, completely unarmed, stepped forward and bowed to us both. I liked that, the fact that he bowed to me as well to Kumbh.

'I am Vidyutjihva of the Kalkeya clan. May I and my men escort you, at least part of the way, as you travel to visit your illustrious brother, His Magnificence the King of Sri Lanka, Sri Ravana?' he asked humbly, bowing yet again.

How could we help liking him? 'Perhaps it's a trap,' the senior guard cautioned. We were wary at first, but there was no trap. His men were well-behaved, he was charming, and they had brought along ample provisions. What did he want? It turned out he wanted me. I was flattered. He got along well with Kumbh, but then everyone gets on with Kumbh. Vidyutjihva was suave, sophisticated and pleasing. Did I love him? I liked who I was when I was with him. I felt clever and beautiful and capable of accomplishing great things. I knew Dada wouldn't like our having an affair, and so I married Vidyutjihva. I thought that would be considered preferable.

Eventually we got to Kanya Kumari. Pushpaka was waiting for us. We piled in—tents, horses, bodyguards, everyone—and once we got to Dada's court, I presented my new husband. Dada was furious. Mandodari, my sister-in-law, persuaded him to calm down. Later, before leaving Sri Lanka, I gave Mala to her. Gave? Mala was a servant, not a slave; but when someone's choices are limited, what difference does it make? All I can say is, I thought she'd be safe. Mandodari was a nice woman. She once said to me. 'The trouble is, Shupi, you think you're entitled.'

'Entitled?'

'Yes, to the same privileges as men. That's not how the world works.'

She was trying to be helpful and she was helpful. Thanks to her, my husband and I were expected to live happily forever. Sometimes I think my life has been like the action thrillers and domestic dramas they show on television these days. I went to live with my husband. Dada visited, and Vidyutjihva tried to kill Dada. Fortunately, Dada killed him first. It was upsetting of course. Do I sound blasé? It turned out he had married me to get at Dada. We had a son. The Danavas took him away. I have grieved for the child, but not for my erstwhile husband.

I was free now and Dada gave Kumbh and me a province to govern. Pashan was on the mainland, near Sri Lanka. Kumbh and I were delighted and eager to put our ideas into action. We didn't do well. We were inexperienced. There was the additional problem that Kumbh had to sleep for six months of the year—Brahma's 'boon'. We had to hurry to get things done.

Our first diktat was compulsory education for girls, boys, brahmins, shudras, everyone. It wasn't popular. The brahmins objected because education was their birthright, and they didn't want to share it. The kshatriyas objected to its being compulsory: some liked to read, others didn't. The vaishyas waited for the fuss to be over. And the shudras were nonplussed—when were they supposed to find the time?

We forced the measure through. We appointed teachers. Then we appointed tax collectors to pay for the teachers. This made the people ready to revolt, so we abandoned taxes, and asked for donations. Unfortunately, many of the teachers didn't show up, and often the students didn't either. It was a shambles. Kumbh and I told one another that we ought not to expect instant results.

Next, we tried to improve the lot of women. We decreed that brahmin women were allowed to be priests. The men instantly said that women's brains were not suited for the priesthood, it would harm the poor things, and this though there had already been women sages. Most of the women didn't argue. One or two attempted to be priests; no one supported them. It was hard going. For the kshatriyas we decreed that if a woman happened to be the first born, then she should succeed to the farm, the estate, or the kingdom. Most of the women abdicated gracefully. To claim their rights was too dangerous. For the vaishyas we made a similar provision. If a woman happened to be the best at business, then she was to run the family firm. 'That's all very well,' the vaishyas said, 'but rather than have a woman lead, we will go bankrupt.' As for the abolition of untouchability, we explained to the other castes that beatings and rape would be punishable and no one could be harmed with impunity. I don't think they understood. No one came forward to report breaches of the law. Kumbh and I knew that just because nothing was reported, it did not mean nothing had happened. We explained this to the officers, who scratched their heads and claimed they couldn't understand it, it was all too difficult.

We kept trying. People mostly ignored the new measures or got around them, though Kumbh and I like to think that they did work in a limited way. Our subjects put up with us without too much grumbling, chiefly I suspect because they were afraid of Dada.

And finally, we abolished the caste system. That was when riots broke out. There were mass protests, disorderly demonstrations and a spate of ugly incidents—people were beaten up for saying that caste didn't matter. The brahmins maintained an outraged silence. The kshatriyas shouted that they weren't brahmins and didn't want to be brahmins. The vaishyas said the same about the kshatriyas. And the shudras said that if we wanted to be helpful, could they please have their own kingdom? Everyone had had enough of us. Urgent messages were sent to Ravana Dada to do something. He sent troops. They quelled the unrest, we were recalled, our decrees repealed, and law and order reigned again.

When we were talking about it recently, Kumbh said to Dada that we had wanted to appeal to their best instincts. Dada explained that it was more expedient to appeal to their worst instincts. I hope that's not true. That may have changed since we introduced the Golden Balm. Men and women aren't quite as nasty to one another. As for the caste system, it seems to be dissolving, though I wonder sometimes whether other classifications are replacing it.

Kumbh had been at the start of his waking cycle when we got to Pashan. He was now ready to sleep again. He found a clearing in the forest, stretched out and fell asleep. I was sure no one would disturb him. He was so large and looked so strong that he frightened people. They didn't know how gentle he was.

I headed south with a few bodyguards to join Ravana Dada. As I *journeyed*, I looked around. I wanted to see what there was to see. What I saw was a beautiful man, and his brother. How can I explain what happened to me? It was not that I knew nothing at all. I had been married to Vidyutjihva. What I felt now made no sense. And that it made no sense didn't matter. For the first time in my life, I was wholeheartedly in love. It happens to people. I don't need to explain myself. It seemed to me that they were like gods, especially the older one. I wrote poems about them, about him, scolding myself, telling myself not to hope.

If a very handsome young man should smile at you,
say to yourself, 'This is not uncommon.
His nature is gentle, he often smiles.'

And if this handsome man should seek conversation
and your knees tremble—in your heart you're convinced
he's a god disguised—be circumspect.

When a god condescends, anything could happen.
You could turn to stone, or vanish unawares,
or wake to sunrise in his mirroring eyes.

Not that he ever smiled at me. He wasn't even aware I existed. I would watch them from afar, hide behind trees. I wished they would notice me. But how could they if I was hidden? And there was a beautiful woman with them. Would she mind if I approached? She was probably a goddess. Should one approach gods and goddesses? I left flowers for them– parijatak with their white petals and orange stems—not in a heap, but casually strewn. He and his brother walked past them or even stepped on them, but she didn't. I saw her pick them up once and smile because of their fragility and their quiet perfume. I wondered whether she could ever be friends with me.

The more I saw of them, the more I wanted to join them, to be with them, especially with him. I felt light-headed—like a tree with the wind blowing through her and the birds distracting her.

My thoughts fly in and out like birds
in a tree, and the tree doesn't know
who she is or what she ought to do.
Her leaves are trembling.

I wondered if I could write my poem on a leaf and leave it in the clearing. Would he find it? Read it? What would he make of it? Would they all read it? Then what would happen? Often, I felt that there was no hope at all. They were so complete in themselves, as though they belonged in a charmed circle. And then I despaired of ever pleasing him.

Sometimes I want to be
stupid like a tree,
and let the storm howl,
and let the wind wail,
and not care at all
where I put my feet.

Writing poems was all very well, but what good was it if he didn't know that I had written them? Was I being cowardly hiding from him? What was the worst that could happen? That I would be rebuffed? At least I would know. I would not be cowardly. I would go to them, show myself to them and ask for their goodwill as an equal, but with true humility. That would be all right, wouldn't it? Would it? I had made up my mind, but I was afraid.

When a fledgling steps into air
will the wings hold? Will grass or water
cushion her fall?

One day I did approach them. And they were outraged. What was my crime? Is it so very wrong for a woman to consider a man beautiful and to want him? Was I ugly? I did not think I was ugly. Would it have been different if they had thought me beautiful?

Why did they mock me? I turned towards her, but the younger brother slashed my face and disfigured me. If they were gods, how could they do this? If they were human, why did they mutilate a fellow human being? I would not have injured them, I worshipped them.

Pain? Yes, there was pain. But there are worse things. When people are hurt in this way, there is a double desecration—the physical harm, and the deeper harm done to the soul.

4
It Was I Who Had Been Hurt, But I Felt Ashamed.

What comes next is a blank. On it you can inscribe your own humiliation, the times in your life when you felt you were nothing, or worse than nothing, a scrap of flesh, torn and broken. Dive into the pain. Explore fear.

In the dark the last of the monsters,
waiting to rise,
like a coiled dragon, but not a dragon, like a
worm eaten corpse,
but not a corpse, like a sleeping giant,
but not a giant
as yet unawakened, like an un-nameable One.
Yes, not 'like'-
that's who—No-Name himself/herself.
No, not the Cyclops,
the authentic monster: teeth bared,
beard bristling
breasts leaking—blood, not milk—probably
cannibal,
almost certainly cruel, and as ever, un-
mistakably human.

Use it to explore your own trembling when even death seemed preferable. Look into yourself and explore darkness. Did they see me as something monstrous? Was that what I saw—the face of fear? What happened to me is not for your delectation.

I stumbled back to the camp. I had covered my head, but I was dripping blood. The bodyguards were horrified. How could they have let this happen to me? They would be punished, though it wasn't their fault. I waved them away and stumbled to my tent. I couldn't move, couldn't think. Eventually I called for water, tried to clean myself and put the balm on my wounds. It stopped the bleeding. The guards didn't know what to do. They remembered that a hermit called Prithviji lived nearby. They carried me to her on a makeshift stretcher. She took me in. The guards were told to camp at a distance.

I allowed Prithviji to look after me. Allowed? Who was doing whom a favour? That only occurred to me much later. It wasn't what she said that made me trust her. She didn't want to know who I was, where I came from or what had happened to me. I didn't mind that she saw my torn face. In front of anyone else I would have felt vulnerable. Her care was unobtrusive, almost casual. I remember she fed me a spoonful at a time. She sat with me and let me heal.

I'm not sure how many days passed. I was getting better, though my face was still scarred. The balm was working, but the wounds were deep. After a while Prithviji and I began to sit outside. I still covered my face if anyone approached, but most of the time it was just the two of us. She meditated and I sat with her and watched the birds. They were unafraid and came quite close, though they weren't particularly interested in me, except perhaps two myna birds. They glanced at me from time to time. I wondered about their lives—no politics, no greed, no grief. Enviable. No, that wasn't true. It wouldn't necessarily be better to be a crow or a sparrow or a myna. They got shot at too if someone suddenly felt like it, and not even for food. I wasn't thinking clearly. I couldn't convince myself that the birds had any fellow feeling for me, but I had some for them. At least they left me alone.

I mended slowly. I told myself that if I kept the left side of my head covered and my face half veiled, people wouldn't know anything had happened. When it was time, I took leave of Prithviji and thanked her. 'Now that I have Ketumati Ma's blessing as well as yours, I feel safer.'

She smiled. 'One day,' she told me, 'you will be able to bless everyone, including yourself.'

Now, even in these more peaceful times, I don't know whether I can bless myself, let alone everyone and everything. Perhaps I can—occasionally. My body has healed and there are times when I am at peace.

It's hard to describe Prithviji: her eyes blazed in a lined face. When there was no one to comfort me, when I needed her most, she was there for me. She was sanctuary.

I tried to keep what happened secret, but the men whispered among themselves. The news and the gossip preceded me to Sri Lanka. Everybody knew. They pointed and gaped. Dada was already bent on revenge. I had not hurt anyone. It was I who had been hurt, but I felt ashamed. And perhaps he felt shamed because of me? When I look back, I don't think Dada was angry only because of family honour. I hoped that in part he was angry because he cared about me.

I retired to a secluded mansion which belonged to Dada. I hardly saw anyone. People weren't kind. Some mocked me. Some said I was the cause of the impending war. They needed to blame someone.

In revenge, Dada decided to abduct the lady in the forest—the wife of the older brother. That would teach them! What would it teach them? How would it help to harm yet another woman? At least he treated her with respect. He gave her one of his mansions to live in, similar to mine. Perhaps Dada had an ulterior motive? He wanted to make war, extend his boundaries. That is what Conquering Heroes do. Men! Sometimes I think they actually like fighting. And sometimes they say it's because of women, or because of a woman. But that does not mean that it is our fault. It has to do with how they think.

There was a war. What happened is recounted at length in The Slaughterhouse Saga. The other side raised an army of bears and monkeys. Dada summoned his warriors. And the slaughter ensued. Dada's Revenge, The Reaction to That, The Army of Monkeys and Bears, Kumbh Being Woken Up, The Glorious War, Almost Everyone Slaughtered, Kumbh Dismembered, Dada Killed, The Children Killed—the story has been told over and over in different ways, but however it's told, such bloodshed makes no sense. They say that the bodies of the dead covered the ground in such numbers that no soil was visible. It's true. When it was over, I went with a few rakshasas who still remained to try to save those we could. Night after night I led them to the battlefield. It was mostly a matter of matching body parts. Finding pieces of Kumbh wasn't difficult; he was much larger than anyone else. Finding pieces of Ravana Dada was also possible; he was more magnificent than anyone else. But the rest... I don't know how we did it, how we waded through the bodies, the gore and the stench. In the end, we only managed to save a few who hadn't been badly wounded, and we carried away Dada and Kumbh by cart and by boat, their hacked bodies wrapped in sacks. The rakshasas set down the sacks in a cave close to Prithviji's ashram and left.

How describe piecing a body together? Like doing a puzzle in three dimensions? Prithtviji and I reassembled my brothers, slowly, carefully, joining the body parts with applications of Ma's balm. I didn't feel sane, or even sentient. When it was done, Prithviji said, 'Now sleep. In time, all of you will heal.' I did sleep. I woke from time to time, saw that Dada and Kumbh were breathing quietly and fell asleep again. Eventually I woke more and more often. The other two were still healing. Sometimes I crept out, tried to understand the world I was in and learn what I could. At last, a day came when all of us were awake. Dada was ready to battle again. Kumbh was passive. I had to explain to them that centuries had passed.

Once Dada had understood that the war was over, the first thing he said was, 'We lost, I suppose?'

I nodded.

'Is there anyone left?'

'Just the three of us.'

'Well, the three of us could still fight.' He considered. 'If we used guerrilla tactics, continued to hide, made sudden sorties, we might succeed.'

'Dada, the war is over. It all happened long ago,' I tried to explain. 'You don't have to fight.'

'I'm a warrior,' he retorted.

'You don't have to be a warrior,' I told him. 'You could be someone else.'

That silenced him for a minute or two and Kumbh spoke up. 'I could go back to sleep. It's what I do.'

Both Ravana Dada and I turned on him. 'No, you can't go back to sleep.'

'Why not?'

'Because you're alive,' I said. 'You can't abdicate.'

'Abdicate from what?'

'From being yourself.'

5
And You Must Be Lucky.

There's a secret Kumbh and I share. I found out about it when I was trying to persuade Dada and Kumbh to leave the cave. Neither of them wanted to. The world they knew had vanished. What was the point in starting again? I jolted Dada into making an effort by saying he ought not to be cowardly. What? Ravana the Redoubtable, cowardly? It was unthinkable. He would march into the new world, march into hell/ heaven, anywhere. He was *not* cowardly. Pressing Dada's buttons is relatively easy. His memes form a well- known pattern. He changed gradually, but it took time. Kumbh was harder to persuade. Telling him it was cowardly to give up wouldn't have worked. He'd have smiled and said, 'Possibly you're right.' In the end it wasn't I who persuaded him. It was two myna birds. That's how I discovered he understood the language of birds.

They couldn't have been the same two mynas I had seen near Prithviji's hut, but they looked at me in the same way. It wasn't a friendly look, but it wasn't hostile. With Kumbh they were different. They scolded, they chattered and they played with him. One morning when I was trying to persuade Kumbh not to go back to sleep, we heard the mynas. As far as I was concerned it was just a noise, but it made Kumbh sit up. He was listening. Eventually he got to his feet, washed and dressed and said to me, 'Come on. Let's go outside.'

'What made you change your mind?' I asked.

'The mynas,' he replied. 'Can't you hear them? They're saying that if I don't come out soon, they'll do something drastic.'

'What can mynas do?' I was sceptical.

Kumbh cocked his head. 'One of them is saying that she'll fly round and round my head until I feel so dizzy that I fall down.'

'And the other?'

Kumbh grinned. 'You don't want to know.'

We went outside and sure enough, the mynas were waiting for us.

'About time!' One of them squawked. I hadn't yet learned the language of birds, but what that myna was saying was obvious. The other flew around Kumbh's head, settled on his shoulder and crooned in his ear.

'Stop it!' shouted Kumbh, shaking his head. 'You're deafening me!'

'We thought you were deaf,' the bird retorted. 'We've been calling you for ages.'

'What are their names?' I asked Kumbh.

'Heckle and Grackle,' the one on his shoulder retorted. 'I'm Grackle. We like silly jokes. And it's rude to talk about people instead of talking to them when they are present.'

'We are people. And we're myna birds,' Heckle offered.

I didn't know what to make of this, so I kept quiet.

'Are you dumbstruck?' inquired Grackle.

'I'm a bit surprised,' I admitted. 'But not shocked. Ought I to be?'

'No, definitely not,' Heckle stated. 'Nor surprised. Anyone could be anyone.'

Before I could think of a reply to this, Kumbh interrupted, 'Listen, you two. My sister and I are hungry. Do you think you could get us some breakfast?'

'We don't do work,' Grackle demurred.

'We're ornamental,' Heckle added.

'Can you at least tell us where we can find something to eat?' Kumbh asked. 'Then we can get our own breakfast.'

'Oh yes. Follow us.'

They led us to a jamboon tree and left us there, saying they had to get on with their myna bird lives.

'What do mynas do?' I asked, but they had flown away.

'They do what all living creatures do,' Kumbh replied. 'Eat, sleep, love, seek happiness, suffer pain, suffer loss and one day they die.'

As we walked back with a bagful of jamboons I said to Kumbh, 'I always suspected that you and Shanti the elephant had long conversations. How did you learn the language of birds?'

'How did you learn it?' he retorted. 'You've just been talking to them.'

That was true. 'I don't know how it happened,' I told him. 'I wasn't expecting it.'

'That's part of it,' Kumbh replied.

Before he could say anything further, I decided to confide in him. 'I've always wanted to be friends with birds, but never succeeded. They've looked back at me with beady eyes and remained alien. I wrote a poem about it once. Do you want to hear it?'

When Kumbh nodded, I made him sit on a rock, thought back for a moment and recited.

BIRDS

Look, but don't touch.
And don't look too long.

I try to observe the sheen of each feather,
wish I could paint, buy a camera,
and recall
that the great man himself used to wire them up.
I understand.
I must keep my distance.
One day they leave.
'They have flown heavenwards!
To join their cousins!
Birds are angels!'
I know, of course, I've got it wrong.
Birds eat snails,

mate as lavishly as any emperor.
And sooner or later
they abandon their young.
But the flight of the albatross,
the courtship of cranes—
I wish my own life
were a tenth as surreal.
The birds look askance,
their eyes glassy
like the eyes of toy birds.

Kumbh smiled. 'What's a camera? And who was the great man?'

I explained about Audubon and cameras and waited for him to say something more. He didn't. We walked on. At last I blurted out, 'Did you like it?'

'What?'

He was being deliberately dense. 'My poem!'

'I liked it very much,' he replied. 'But it's not about birds. It's about you. By the way, I know why you were able to understand the mynas.'

I waited. He went on. 'You met the four conditions for understanding other creatures.

1. You must believe it's possible. You did. You were sure the mynas were squawking at me.
2. You mustn't be over eager. You weren't thinking about yourself. You were watching them.
3. You must be willing to listen.
4. And you must be lucky. Mynas are mischievous. They happened to be in the right mood.'

That was a long speech for Kumbh. 'Are you saying, that in order to get something, you have to not want it?' I demanded.

Before he could answer, we were back. Ravana Dada was sitting on a rock waiting for us. The two mynas were perched on a babul. They had a sardonic gleam in their eyes. I heard one of them say, 'I bet you she doesn't tell Ravana Dada she's been spending her time talking to birds.'

They were right. I had no intention of saying anything to Dada right then; but I knew I had stumbled on something important. If a creature could speak, then it could say all sorts of things. It could say. 'Hey! I'm here. I matter. Don't hurt me!' No, that wasn't quite right. Creatures did speak. The point was to listen. The mynas sat there nodding sagely. I knew they were mocking me. I didn't mind. They were the first birds who had spoken to me directly. I wouldn't go so far as to say I felt honoured—that would give them swollen heads—but I was pleased.

Dada wanted to know where we'd been. We showed him the jamboons. He ate one and smiled. 'These are nice, but they won't be enough. Perhaps I can get some game. When you brought us to the cave, did you, by any chance, bring my weapons?'

Kumbh and I looked at each other. What was I to say? As a matter of fact, I had brought them.

'I'm not sure, Dada. And if I did, I can't think where I put them,' I lied.

'I think I saw them lying in a corner. I'll go look.' He was back in no time with a long bow and a few arrows.

'It's an arid landscape,' Kumbh said to him. 'I don't think you'll find anything here.'

The area around us was barren: a few twisted thorn trees, dry grass and rocks strewn about.

'I might get a rabbit or two or perhaps a deer. If all else fails, I can always shoot a few myna birds,' Dada replied. He glanced at Heckle and Grackle perched on their babul.

'I don't think myna birds taste good, Dada,' I interposed hastily.

'We taste terrible,' Grackle screeched.

'And you wanted to make friends with us!' Heckle added. 'It's not all right to eat your friends. It's probably not all right to eat anyone.'

'Dada, why don't you relax? I'll go to the nearest village and bring back something to eat,' Kumbh suggested.

'And I'll go to a different village and bring back something too,' I put in quickly.

'We'll all go,' Dada announced in his lordly way, 'and meet here in an hour or two.'

'Why are you so gutless?' Heckle squawked. 'Why don't you tell him it's wrong to kill myna birds?'

'Dada, please don't kill any myna birds,' I pleaded with him.

Ravana Dada laughed. 'I was only joking. I don't think mynas are edible.'

'Huh! We probably taste delicious!' Grackle tweeted. 'Don't tell him. He might believe it.'

Kumbh and I got back first. He had brought back a sackful of chikkus and guavas, and I had a dozen loaves of bread and vegetable patties.

'How did you get all that?' I asked Kumbh, pointing to the fruit.

'Stole it,' he replied. 'What else could I do? How did you get the bakeries?'

'Cheated,' I replied. 'I produced some money out of thin air and gave it to the shopkeeper.'

Grackle and Heckle were flying by. I heard one of them say to the other. 'Oh dear, what else could she do? Oh dear...' Cheeky things.

Just then we saw Dada approaching. He was holding a bag. I dreaded finding out what was in it. He began to rummage. Whatever was in there was wriggling. Oh no, he hadn't even killed it properly. He pulled it out. It was a baby rabbit.

'It came up to me.' He looked sheepish. 'He thinks I'm his mother, so I brought him home.'

I could hear Heckle and Grackle cackling: 'Oh dear, what else could he do? Oh dear, what else did you expect? Oh dear...'

6

A Lover of Rabbits on Tuesdays and a Slayer of Monkeys on Saturdays

I'm not saying that Bittoo—that's what Dada called the rabbit—was important in himself, but Dada's extraordinary fondness for him intrigued me. How did I know he was male? I didn't. To give him a gender seemed less uncaring. Not that Bittoo and I liked each other. Ensconced in Dada's arms, he usually glared at me. I glared back. For one thing, he scattered his droppings everywhere. When I complained about this, Dada said he would sweep them up, and he did. Mighty Ravana, the Conqueror of a Dozen Kingdoms, Very Nearly the Lord of Both Heaven and Earth, cleaning up after a baby rabbit!

I asked him, 'Have you ever looked after a baby, Dada?'

He looked surprised. 'That's women's work.'

'And men don't do women's work?' I asked.

'It wouldn't be seemly. Our spheres are different.'

'Women are inferior?'

'Weaker!' he retorted gruffly. He was getting annoyed, but I wasn't letting go, not just yet.

'Only physically. Dada, what I really wanted to ask you was—why are you looking after a baby rabbit?'

He was genuinely surprised. 'Why not?'

'Is it in keeping with your dignity?'

He shrugged. 'I'm Ravana,' he informed me. 'I'll do what I please!'

And that was the end of that conversation at least for the time being.

It bothered me. Was he a Lover of Rabbits on Tuesdays and a Slayer of Monkeys on Saturdays? I was inconsistent too: I tried to ingratiate myself with myna birds, but disliked baby rabbits. And Kumbh? He wanted to be kind to all creatures, but most of all he wanted to sleep. Wasn't that inconsistent? To wish to be kind, but at the same time not wish to make an effort?

And if we were all really so inconsistent, then human existence should be chaotic. It was chaotic. We lurched from one war to another, from one disaster to the next. If we were so self-evidently inconsistent, why did we pretend we weren't? Why did we deal with each other as though we were dealing with the same human being day in and day out? Because it was convenient? Because it was too difficult to reassess the nature of things all the time, moment by moment? And there was literature, teaching us that villains were villainous and heroes were heroic. Small concessions were sometimes made to the villainy of heroes and the heroism of villains, but we usually knew which one was who, and what was what.

Baby Bittoo would change, he'd grow up. I asked Dada what he'd do then?

'I'd let him go. He could frolic in the fields in the way rabbits are supposed to do.'

'How do you know that is the function of rabbits? Perhaps it's their function to get eaten?'

He didn't like the idea. 'You're silly, Shupi.' He frowned at me and stroked Bittoo.

I let that go and thought about the difference between rigidity and consistency. If Bittoo remained Bittoo for the rest of his life, I suppose he would be consistently Bittoo, but hardly sane? As we live in time, perhaps we are supposed to change consistently? And as we live in space, perhaps we are supposed to adapt to the space we inhabit? And so, if Dada had come across Bittoo when he was Lord of Sri Lanka, he would not have have swept up Bittoo's droppings. He would have ordered one of the servants to do so. Would that have been in keeping with who he was, or at least, with who he was supposed to be?

We live our lives only more or less consistently, fit in with our surroundings, fit in with what's expected, and call that sanity. We muddle through, and often we don't muddle through.

I decided not to think too much about consistency. It was too difficult, though it did make me realise that I could be anyone—within limits. Shape-changing wasn't just a trick we rakshasas could use when it was expedient. It was more fundamental. If we could change ourselves, we could change the world. I decided to give up on speculation and take action. If I looked like someone else, then I would be treated like someone else and would therefore have to behave like someone else. I wouldn't be quite so wedded to my own identity. I decided to change myself into Prince Supratim, Shupo for short. I thought Dada and Kumbh would be shocked, or at least surprised. They weren't, they were puzzled.

'Why have you changed into boy's clothes?' Kumbh asked. 'And why such splendid ones? Are we going somewhere?'

'I'm not just wearing boy's clothes,' I told him. 'You now have an extra brother.'

'But Shupi –,' Ravana Dada began.

I interrupted him. 'Shupo, not Shupi. Short for Prince Supratim. If you can change from Ravana the Rakshasa to Nursemaid to Bittoo, then I can change from Shupi to Shupo. My metamorphosis is relatively trivial, and it's only for the afternoon. Come on. I want to see how I get on in the world.'

Dada and Kumbh glanced at each other. 'All right,' Dada agreed, 'though it might be sensible to wear ordinary clothes. All this finery is too conspicuous. We don't know much about this world yet.'

I had quite fancied myself in princely clothes. I didn't just want to be an ordinary person. 'These are fine,' I told Dada, and we set out.

There were some fields in the distance. A farmhouse or a hut might be nearby; we could ask for information. For company we had Baby Bittoo, his head poking out of Dada's pocket, and the two mynas. 'My, my,' they said, as they flew around me, eyeing my glitter.

We had walked about a mile or two when we thought we heard a cry. We ran towards the sound. It was coming from a well. I peered in. 'There's somebody down there,' I told the others. 'Must have fallen in. I think the well is dry. We'll have to get him out.'

'How?' asked Ravana Dada.

We looked around and saw a coil of rope under a banyan. 'You two hang on to one end of the rope,' I told my brothers. 'As I'm the lightest, I'll go down.' I was quite enjoying myself as Prince Supratim.

I slid down the rope. At the bottom of the well I found a pretty young woman, sitting on a chair. She looked quite at ease. 'Ah, you've come to rescue me,' she said. 'Hello.'

'You don't seem at all distressed,' I said to her. 'Why were you shouting so pitifully?'

'How else would you have known I needed help?'

'You're sitting on a chair,' I pointed out.

'Of course.'

'Do you always carry a chair when you fall down a well?' I was puzzled and beginning to wonder if this was a trap.

'Of course not. When my father sent me down, he put it there so that I would be comfortable.'

I was taking that in when I heard Kumbh, 'Hey Shupo, are you all right? What's happening down there?'

'Just a minute,' I replied. I pointed to the rope. 'Climb up,' I told the young woman. 'My brothers have the other end.'

'I don't do rope climbing,' she told me. 'It isn't ladylike and I wasn't taught. Why don't you tie me securely to the chair, and then your brothers can pull me up.'

It was a nuisance, but I knew Kumbh could haul up a dozen chairs with a dozen young women sitting on them. I tied her to the chair and shouted to Kumbh to haul her up. He did, and after that I climbed up. The young woman looked us over.

'Three for the price of one!' she exclaimed. 'My father will be pleased. Come on. I'll take you to him.'

'You want to take us to your father?' I protested. 'Wasn't he the one who put you down the well?'

'Only to find me a good husband,' she told us, 'one capable of pulling me out. He has my best interests at heart. You're all fine specimens, any one of you will do. Do come along.'

'I'm old enough to be your grandfather or even a distant ancestor,' Ravana Dada told her. 'I couldn't possibly marry you. It's out of the question.'

'Nor could I,' Kumbh added quickly. 'I took a vow of celibacy a long time ago.'

'Oh well, you'll do,' she said cheerfully, turning to me. 'After all, you're the one who found me. And you're very well dressed. Better than them.'

I had to think fast. 'Oh no,' I told her. 'I'm gay. I wouldn't do at all.' Under the circumstances and by some definition I probably was.

'Don't be silly,' she said taking my arm. 'That doesn't matter. We could come to an arrangement. I myself... '

I appealed to Kumbh and Dada, but they were trying to keep a straight face. And I could see Heckle and Grackle laughing so hard that they almost fell off their perch.

'Listen,' I informed the young woman. 'I'm sure you mean well, and I'm sure your father means well, but I definitely cannot marry you. I'm only playing at being a prince. I'm really a woman.'

That didn't faze her. 'Ah, then we'd be talking about Same Sex Marriage. It's perfectly legal in many countries. Of course, in a rural community it might be awkward. Still, if you're a prince, you're probably rich. We could live with your family—or emigrate.'

By now I was almost shouting. 'I AM NOT A PRINCE! I was only pretending. I don't want to marry you or anyone!'

'Well, if you're sure. With those attitudes you probably wouldn't be suitable.' She sounded annoyed.

'Marriage isn't the only option,' I informed her. 'Why don't you work for a living?'

'Marriage is work!' she retorted. 'You don't know anything, do you?' She turned to Kumbh and Dada. 'Please tie me to the chair and lower me down. Once you've done that, coil the rope and put it where it was.'

'You're resetting the trap!' I accused her.

'Of course,' she answered. 'You, my dear, were a great disappointment. You don't know who you are; and you can't even keep up the pretence of being someone else.'

I let her have the last word. I let Heckle and Grackle snigger. I let Ravana Dada and Kumbh hide their smiles. I didn't feel I had much choice. When we got back to the cave, I wrote a poem about Prince Supratim.

Change who you are, tell those you meet
your heroic exploits
led you across the seven seas:
you've walked on waves,
dined with mermaids, been one of them.
Or get grandiose
and speak of galaxies, of planets consisting
of a single solitaire,
or of Goldilocks planets, providing
heart's ease;
and so taste the kernel of your dream.

I told myself that once in a while it was all right to be silly.

7
Elbowing the universe

I wasn't the only one thinking about choice and change. The next day Dada, Kumbh and I decided to be less arrogant, dress like poor people and learn what we could. I took the form of an old woman, ventured into the village and got baited by the village boys. This made me so cross that I hung them up by the seat of their pants on a tamarind tree. I gave Dada and Kumbh an account of this and confessed I hadn't done well at all. What I didn't tell them was that as I was walking back, I felt another woman walking beside me. Ketumati Ma? Prithviji? I could not look at her directly.

'How are you feeling?' she asked.

'Angry and defeated,' I replied.

'What should you have done differently?'

That elicited a bitter reply. 'I couldn't change the boys instantly into civilized, well-behaved, kind hearted beings with a purpose in life. Look at the lives they lead—the lack of opportunity, the dirt, the poverty and the utter neglect!'

'It takes time,' my companion murmured. 'They need education, training—a better life.'

'You can take a horse to water, or a boy to school, but you can't make them drink. Even the willingness to learn takes time. Should I have ridden in there as Prince Supratim with a dozen followers, given the boys a few coins each and enlisted them all as trainee soldiers? That would have given them employment, got them out of their idle ways, and instilled some discipline and purpose into their lives. Of course, I'd have had to find a war or start a war to engage them in. Would that have been better?'

'No, of course not.'

'People are awful because of their circumstances; and the circumstances are awful because of people, and nothing changes.'

'There is always change,' the old woman protested.

'Mutations!' I retorted. 'Different forms of awfulness!'

There was a silence. 'It's like walking,' she said at last.

'What is like walking?' I felt impatient. What was she on about?

'Progress,' she answered.

'There's no such thing,' I told her. 'And even if there were, it would be like crawling, not walking.'

'Well, the attempt at progress then. Walking is a better analogy. First the left foot forward—you change yourself. Then the right foot forward—you change the world. Then the left –'

I interrupted her. 'You want me to change myself?'

'It helps.'

Having given me what she thought was good advice, the old woman disappeared. I plodded on. I didn't think trying to change the world was going to be easy. Should I change myself? Be less impatient? More thoughtful? Less intolerant? Listen to what people were actually saying? Just then Heckle and Grackle appeared. A welcome interruption. I was tired of finding fault with myself.

'Hello Heckle, hello Grackle' I called out cheerily. 'Why aren't you with Kumbh?'

'We like you better,' Heckle replied.

'And today our names are Push and Shove,' Grackle added.

'It's because you're more entertaining,' Heckle went on. 'Always getting into the most amazing messes.'

I had had enough. 'If you think my function in life is to entertain you, you can think again! Get out now, before I clip your wings!'

'Temper, temper,' Heckle cooed.

'You'd never catch us,' Grackle retorted. 'Don't be so bad tempered. We are your friends really. We've come to help you.'

Being bad tempered, that's another fault I have. 'You've come to help me?' I asked. 'How?'

'Before you start improving yourself or reshaping the world, you should try to understand a little about yourself. The problem is, you're perverse. You don't even know how to help yourself,' Heckle informed me.

I didn't know what she was getting at. She carried on, 'What did you think of that woman in the well?'

'She was silly!'

'Not as silly as you. At least she knew what she wanted!' Grackle said this triumphantly as though she had scored an irrefutable point.

'You think I should set myself up as bait and hunt for a husband?'

'Why not?' Heckle replied. 'That's how many stories end—finding a prince or a princess and living happily ever after.'

'Are you saying I should have agreed to marry the woman in the well?' I couldn't believe that even the mynas could be suggesting that seriously.

'No,' Grackle said soothingly. 'But suppose the person in the well had been Prince Supratim—a handsome young man in real trouble—things could have been different then.'

I considered walking away from the mynas; but I had just resolved to listen better. That didn't mean I had to listen to nonsense. 'Are you saying that I should marry myself or look for Prince Charming?'

'You would be lonely by yourself,' Heckle pointed out. 'The trouble is you don't think anyone is good enough for you.'

'No,' Grackle interrupted. 'The trouble is you don't know what's good for you—just like the rest of your species!'

That startled me. 'What do you mean like the rest of my species?' I asked. Perhaps I could get them to change the subject.

'Oh that,' Heckle shrugged, as though stating the obvious. 'There's global destruction going on and you just don't stop, or even pause. You carry on burning fossil fuels, polluting the air, clogging the oceans and all in the name of progress. You're insane!'

'And you've sent up a load of space junk to circle the planet!' Grackle continued.

'I know about global warming,' I muttered feebly. 'We're doing our best.'

'No, you're not!' they both squawked.

'Well, what should we do?'

'Give up being Boss Species, proceed cautiously. AND UNDERSTAND THAT THE UNIVERSE WAS NOT CONSTRUCTED SOLELY FOR YOU!' Grackle shouted.

She was beyond exasperation. She sounded despairing and that silenced me.

After a while Heckle said more gently, 'Do you know the story of the Five Monkeys? Listen and learn.'

ALAS, POOR MONKEY

Five monkeys, who were whooping it up in the middle of the night, fell into a well. The well was dry, but they were bruised and frightened. They began to blame each other.

'You led us into this!' they shouted at the monkey who had fallen in first.

'You had the torch. If you had pointed it at the ground instead of at the sky, this wouldn't have happened. And anyway, when you saw me fall, you shouldn't have followed,' retorted the first monkey.

And so it went on. By the second day they were hungry and thirsty. They realized they had a problem. They used up that day arguing about the nature of the well, why it had it appeared, and whether it had always been there.

By the third day they understood they had a serious problem. They spent that day arguing about the best solution.

And on the fourth day, they agreed on a solution they thought would work. They estimated the depth of the well. They carefully calculated the height of each monkey. And they concluded that if they stood on each other's shoulders, the monkey on top would be able to leap out and fetch a rope.

This time they argued about who would be on top and who at the bottom. They argued so endlessly that the rains came, and they all drowned.'

'Let that be a lesson to you!' Grackle added. As they prepared to leave, they had the satisfied look of a pair of mynas who had done their best to help the benighted.

'Good Bye, Shove. Good Bye, Push.' I waved to them as they shoved off and pushed off respectively.

I didn't feel annoyed with them despite their lecturing me. They weren't wrong—not about the global problem. I had learnt quite a bit while waiting for Dada and Kumbh to wake up. But as for their advice to me personally, had they just been having a go at me?

I couldn't help thinking we had come down in the world. Dada's companion was a baby rabbit. I had a pair of cheeky myna birds. It was a far cry from Kumbh and Shanti roaming the countryside. Kumbh didn't seem to have a companion. I was mistaken. When I discovered later who it was, I admit I was repelled. Dada was too, but he hid his feelings. My revulsion bothered me. If, as Heckle and Grackle had implied, the universe was constructed for everyone, did that mean that I had to take the interests of bed bugs into account? I made a note to ask Heckle and Grackle what they lived on. What I really wanted to know was whether they ate insects.

As Dada, Kumbh and I had no idea how we were going to live, we decided to try our luck at a nearby fair. The mynas appeared as soon as we had finished setting up a tent. We had been hoping to raise money by getting people to engage with Kumbh in contests of strength. There hadn't been many takers.

'Hey, Shupi,' Heckle called. 'You're not getting anywhere. Why don't you come with us? We'll have some fun.'

Grackle interpreted the look on my face. 'We're not going to try to improve you. We thought you might like to fly around.'

Fly! My heart lifted. 'How?' I stammered.

'Turn into a myna. It would be an improvement on the other identity you tried recently,' Heckle replied.

That was true. Prince Supratim had been a wimp. I made up my mind and turned into a myna.

'Now there are three of us!' Heckle chortled. 'We're a Girl Gang!'

'Do I have to be part of a girl gang?' I asked hesitantly.

'What you call yourself is up to you. We ourselves are gender-fluid,' Grackle informed me. 'It makes labelling impractical, probably impossible.'

'That's arbitrary,' I protested.

'You changed your gender,' Heckle pointed out. 'Why shouldn't we change our labels? Now then, are you going to help us terrorise a few people or are you not?'

'Terrorise?' I asked feebly. We were perched side by side on a convenient neem tree.

'Yeah,' Grackle replied, trying to sound tough. 'We'll just annoy a few people. Start a fire here. Flip a switch there. Cause small accidents.'

'You're confused,' I replied. 'That's what terrorists do, not Girl Gangs.'

'All right.' Grackle shrugged. 'See that group of men eating jalebis? Let's fly in formation and peck their eyes out.'

I dug in my claws. 'I'm not pecking out anyone's eyes.'

Grackle looked disgusted. 'You don't understand anything. We're not really going to peck out their eyes; but just look at those jalebis dripping with syrup. Mynas don't do terrorism. That's reserved for human beings. But if we frighten those men enough, we'll be able to make off with a jalebi or two. Are you coming or not?'

Heckle and Grackle took off at full speed. I fluttered after them. I don't think I contributed much to the air raid, but Heckle managed to grab a whole jalebi. She brought it back to the branch we had been sitting on and shared it with us. I suppose in order to succeed at anything you have to have conviction. I didn't know how I felt about the jalebi. I considered the facts. I hadn't contributed towards getting it. It was stolen goods. I had gone along with them—after a fashion. It was also a fact that the jalebi was delicious. We ate every scrap. Was it possible to eat jalebis and be serious about global warming?

'Look,' I said, 'though the raid was successful, I don't think I want to be a Girl Gangster. I'm an honourable person.'

'All right. Let's be Girl Scouts and do good deeds,' Grackle replied, deciding to be agreeable. 'Do you see that rich little boy eating ice-cream? Let's steal his ice-cream cone and give it to the beggar boy watching him.'

Before I could reply, they were away. I sat on the branch like a feathered blob. They were back in no time. Beneath us I heard cries of 'Thieves! Thieves! Stop the thieves!' and the sound of people running.

'How was that for a good deed?' Heckle asked me looking pleased with herself.

I hoped we were well-hidden by the leaves. 'Now look what you've done,' I scolded. 'They're after us.'

Grackle sighed. 'The redistribution of wealth,' she said sadly, 'isn't popular.'

I didn't know what to say. Finally, I muttered, 'This is all a bit childish. Can't we do better than that?'

'Sure. Let's be goddesses or at least powerful females. I could be Medusa. Turn people into stone. A sculptor of sorts,' Heckle giggled.

'I could be Ate, the goddess of ruin.' Grackle put in. 'Homer says, "Her feet are tender because she walks upon the heads of men."'

'Where did you pick that up?' I asked.

'We get about.' Grackle shrugged.

'And you,' they added, cackling at me, 'could be yourself—Shurpanakha the Demoness. Just your name terrifies children.'

That hurt. That hurt so much that I hopped off the branch, stopped being a myna and hid in the tent. Heckle and Grackle had gone too far. I decided I'd watch and wait and just be an ordinary woman. Meeting Leela at the fair had been a lucky chance. I would copy her.

8
Who Wants to Be Called 'Nails like Winnowing Fans'?

I didn't know how to go about learning from Leela. How make girl-talk? Fit in with one's peers? Which questions were proper, which not? Could I be sure that Leela was a good role model? I decided not to tell her my real name. I would pretend that my name was 'Shupi', that it had always been 'Shupi'.

I asked Ketumati Ma once, 'Why Shurpanakha? Why not Sundari? Or Suvarnarekha or Sudarshini or something splendid? Who wants to be called "nails like winnowing fans"? It's ridiculous!' She smiled and said I was someone splendid and names didn't matter. They do matter. I examined my nails. They were ordinary—possibly like winnowing fans. They weren't claws, whatever people said.

I found Leela sitting on her own by the Ferris wheel, watching it go round. I asked if I could join her.

'We're new around here,' I began. 'I wondered if you could tell me what women are wearing these days. What is fashionable?' I thought this was a good ploy. This was girl-talk. Ordinary young women talked about clothes. And why not? What you looked like was who you were.

Leela seemed surprised by my question. 'It depends on who you are,' she replied. 'The women in the villages no longer wear nine-yard saris. Young women and even older women mostly wear salwar kameez—like the ones we are wearing. And the very rich wear anything. Whatever it is, it costs a lot.'

I wasn't sure what to ask next.

'These Salwar-Kameez Women,' I ventured, 'what do they think about?'

'About getting by, I suppose. I think about making a million, no, a billion rupees. Then I could do what I liked.'

'What would you like?' I asked. Perhaps here was a woman who knew her mind.

'Once I've made the billion, I'll have time to find out,' Leela replied. 'I'm not against luxuries. Good things to eat—exquisite meat dishes, delicate sweetmeats, fine clothes, silks and brocades. Some luxuries would definitely be on my list. What do you think about?'

'About who I am,' I said at once. 'And also about letting go who I am.'

'Don't you know who you are? I'm the Snake Charmer's Daughter. And you're Kumbh's Sister,' Leela tossed off.

I was normally known as Ravana Dada's sister. Why did she think of me as Kumbh's sister? Was she particularly interested in Kumbh?

'I want to be someone in my own right,' I stated, rather daringly I thought.

She only said, 'We all exist in relation to each other.'

When I didn't reply to that, she went on, 'Your brother, Kumbh, he's strong, isn't he? And gentle?'

The penny dropped—girl-talk was about boys.

'He's a good person,' I replied. 'He's been through a lot.' When she didn't say anything, I suddenly asked, 'What about happiness? Don't ordinary women think about happiness?'

'Of course,' she replied. 'To fall in love, to marry the man of your choice, have children, live happily—who wouldn't want that? But many settle for what is possible, for what their parents arrange for them.'

I didn't know whether it would be all right to ask the question that floated between us. Before I could decide, she said diffidently, 'Have you ever been in love?' I didn't want to answer, or to remember. I hope my face betrayed nothing. She seemed very vulnerable. I suddenly realised that I was much older than Leela, however competent and self-possessed she usually was.

Fortunately, Kumbh came up to us just then, looking worried. He greeted Leela, then turned to me.

'Shupi, have you seen Bugzee?' he asked.

'Who's Bugzee?' I replied.

'A friend,' Kumbh answered. 'Like Heckle and Grackle. I thought they'd told you about him.'

Just then I saw a bedbug on my arm. I hate bedbugs. I know I should not hate any creature, but I draw the line at bedbugs. I was about to flick it off when Kumbh stopped me. 'No, no!' he cried. 'That's Bugzee. Don't hurt him.'

'Bugzee?'

Kumbh took the bug from me and placed him on the palm of his hand. The bug reared up on his hind legs. 'Yes, Bugzee,' he informed us. 'I chose the name myself. Do you like it? I hope to make it to Hollywood and become a superstar.'

Leela had been listening to this in disbelief. I couldn't read her expression, but I didn't think she was charmed. She made an excuse and hurried off. Kumbh also wandered away in the same direction. I sat there thinking that this time Kumbh, in his love of all living creatures, had gone too far. Heckle and Grackle pounced on me.

'Now look what you've done!' they scolded.

I didn't think I had done anything at all. I stared at them.

'Don't you know anything? Kumbh and Leela are in love,' Grackle informed me.

'And we're their go-betweens. We've been carrying messages for them,' Heckle added importantly.

'Well, I'm not against it. I don't know about Ravana Dada. Why are you scolding me?' I replied.

'Because,' Grackle said carefully, using her why-do-I–have-to-explain-this-to-a-stupid-child tone, 'you allowed her to find out that Kumbh keeps a bedbug about his person. She's not sure she could live with a bedbug.'

'Kumbh shouldn't have asked me about Bugzee in front of her,' I retorted.

Grackle looked at me sorrowfully. 'Don't you know your own brother? Kumbh didn't realize that she might mind.'

'You're right,' I said peaceably. I wanted to know what sort of messages Kumbh and Leela had been sending each other. 'I don't suppose you remember any of the messages?' I ventured.

'We remember all of them,' Heckle said proudly, 'and the order in which they were sent. Let's go sit under the neem tree where it's quieter and we'll tell you all about it.'

We settled down, and Grackle began, 'The first message was from Kumbh. It went like this:

When the Queen of Swords frowns,
birds shut up, flowers close up,
and trees hunch over.
The summer recedes and a mild, blue
sky learns to glower.
Someone should tell her.'

'What did Leela say when you repeated that?' I asked. I couldn't help remembering my own foolish verses. It was a long time ago.

Grackle cocked her head at me. 'She made me say it over again. Then she said, 'Tell him, I'm not the Queen of Swords. I'm only a woman. Here's my answer:

The birds are sky writing, the fish
have inscribed their poems
in water. The words slip and slide,
my vision blurs.

I nodded. 'Then what happened?'

'Then Kumbh sent the following:

Dragonflies are making
my heart hover
over green water.'

Heckle shrugged. 'Neither of them has said anything outright. I mean nothing about the moon or the stars or anybody pining, but it's obvious, isn't it? This is what she sent:

The light on water makes shadows tremble
like a memory that will not be still.

'Then Kumbh replied,' Heckle continued.

'Already the past is fading rapidly,
the future is murky,
but the day explodes like a jewel'

'And then?' I asked.

'The messages have stopped,' Grackle said sadly. Did Grackle have a sentimental streak? 'Leela is wondering whether it was all a mistake. And Kumbh doesn't know what has gone wrong.'

'Do you think it's his versification? Exploding jewels are a bit much,' Heckle offered.

'It's all Bugzee's fault,' I told them. 'You can't blame a girl for not wanting to live with Bugzee.'

'I could eat him,' Heckle offered. 'One peck, and hey, presto, no more Bugzee!'

'Don't do that. It would upset Kumbh. He's vegetarian, you know. And Bugzee is Kumbh's friend, or at least Kumbh is his friend,' I warned them.

'We'll have to entice him away to new pastures,' Grackle murmured. She and Heckle were eyeing me.

'No,' I said firmly. 'I will not keep Bugzee about my person, not even to help the course of true love.'

'We can't keep him in a matchbox,' Heckle muttered. 'He wouldn't agree. He needs to feed.'

'We have to get him off Kumbh,' I was definite about that. 'He's not even particularly attached to Kumbh. He wants to go to Hollywood.'

'We could put him on a plane.'

'How?'

'We could introduce him to a rich person, and tell him that such a person was far more likely to go to Hollywood than Kumbh. Or we could point out that Bollywood might be just as good.'

'I don't know any rich people,' I demurred.

'Oh, you will, you will,' Grackle replied with complete conviction.

'Can you read the future?' I asked frowning.

'I know a thing or two.' Grackle sounded smug. 'Just wait. Everything will be fine.'

'Except—' Heckle muttered.

'Except what?'

'Leela isn't vegetarian,' Heckle answered.

'She'll have to change,' Grackle said firmly. 'Kumbh might not want to live with a person who's willing to eat his friends. That's your job, Shupi.'

My job! 'What am I supposed to say? "Look here, if you want to marry my brother, you've got to be vegetarian"?'

I was being sarcastic, but they nodded, 'That might do it.'

'I have to get back to the tent to see how Kumbh and Dada are doing,' I told them. 'We'll talk tomorrow.'

That was the evening Leela concocted her vast plan for manufacturing the balm, marketing it and distributing it. We all needed money to live on; and when Leela understood that I had the recipe for the balm and that the balm actually worked, she saw its potential at once. The next day we headed for the city and got to work. In his account, Dada has described how a wily politician tried to steal the balm and how we defeated him. By then we had realised that the balm was much more than a means of making money, it could help save the world. We had to persuade Leela that we should give away the balm rather than make money out of it. Once she had used the balm, she agreed readily, though I think she would have agreed anyway, or, at least, compromised. Dada, Kumbh and I were delighted. Even the mynas were pleased.

I could see that Kumbh and Leela were preoccupied with their feelings for each other, though they didn't say anything or do anything obvious. Ravana Dada had no idea of what was going on. I asked the mynas whether there had been any new messages.

'None from Leela,' Heckle replied. 'Two or three from Kumbh. All sorrowful.' She recited one.

The white bird of happiness
is made out of paper,
lies flat on the ground,
and the flowers are sulking.

I was sympathetic, but that one made me laugh. I could see Kumbh lying flat on the ground while tall flowers glowered at him. Grackle was indignant. 'Don't laugh. He's suffering. He may have fallen in love rather suddenly, but it's genuine enough. Here, listen to this one.

There is sorrow in every leaf.
The trees are dripping with sorrow.
One day sorrow will vanish,
and I may not notice,
but the leaves
will be a different green.

I quite like the last two lines, don't you? So evocative.'

Was Grackle becoming an aficionada of Kumbh's poetry? Perhaps I ought to have felt more sympathetic about Kumbh's predicament, but I was fairly sure it would end happily.

'And in the very last one he sent, sorrow has turn into grief and resignation,' she went on. 'Listen.

Now grief is exact and falls on the ear like music.
It's grief all right: the daylight dying,
the swans leaving. Always there was pleasure,
and therefore grief.'

'Poor Kumbh. We've got to help him.' Heckle was clearly sorry for him.

'We will be meeting rich people,' I told them. 'Leela has arranged a reception to raise capital. It shouldn't be difficult to get Bugzee to jump ship. But how do I persuade Leela to stop eating meat?'

'Just tell her,' Heckle advised.

'I don't know her well enough.'

'Make up something!' Grackle was getting impatient with me. 'Tell her that when Kumbh was a boy, the cook skinned his pet rabbit and served him for dinner. That traumatised him.' I thought of Bittoo. Before leaving for the city, Dada had set him down in a field. Bittoo had hopped away, but only after giving Dada a reproachful look.

I was impressed by Grackle's story. She had made it up effortlessly.

Just to be awkward I asked the mynas, 'What if Leela gets it into her head to de-traumatise Kumbh?'

They weren't having it. 'That,' they said, 'is your problem. You deal with it.'

I had forgotten about copying Leela. By the time Leela had concocted her plan for making us millionaires, no, billionaires, and had whizzed us through the marketing and the management and the putting together of a business plan, it was clear to all of us that she was very unusual. Still, however extraordinary she was, becoming vegetarian was something she would have to do if she wanted Kumbh. I needn't have worried. It turned out that Leela had turned vegetarian, possibly even vegan, the day after she had met Kumbh.

I'm not sure how the mynas and I had got quite so involved in Kumbh's courtship. Under Leela's direction, Dada, Kumbh and I were setting up a business, an entire industry, with our final aim clearly in mind. The events, which Dada has recounted, were spinning us around rapidly. In spite of us or because of us, the Golden Balm was working its magic.

Helping the mynas help Kumbh and Leela had been a pleasant interlude. The last message from Kumbh the mynas brought was for me. Heckle recited it:

And so the lovers dissemble.
They tell themselves
that's how it is:
rain and sun and ordinary weather.

She added, quite kindly for her, 'He's telling you not to interfere. All's well. They will break the news to Ravana Dada when the time is right.' This they did as soon as they could. Bugzee was no longer a problem. He had left with alacrity at the marketing reception for the very rich. A few weeks later the mynas brought me another message and another poem, this time from Bugzee.

'I know you didn't take to me, but don't judge too hastily. In my last life I was a poet. It was hard work and I couldn't make a living out of it. Being a Superstar beats being a poet and I get some street cred. Here's a poem I wrote about it.

SUPERSTARS

A body of sufficient magnitude clearly bends the space
around it.

If I were to say to an angel, 'It's not your angelic nature,
but the particular sheen of iridescent blue on the edge of your wings
that draws me to you so that I seek acquaintance,' would the angel
snub me, or look bemused and peer over its shoulder to examine
its feathers? They don't understand what I admire so. They think
it's their prowess, or their amazing innocence. They are insouciant.
They think I'm confused. And in my heart I know I probably am.'

The message went on, 'I'm doing well, and you and the mynas are welcome to drop in for a cup of tea or something stronger. Yours irrepressibly, Bugzee.'

I was glad he was enjoying being glamorous. Perhaps we would drop in for a cup of tea.

Things were sorting themselves out. Bugzee was successful. Dada and Vijju were happy, they suited each other. Leela and Kumbh had got together, and soon afterwards, they began the work of cleaning up the oceans. As for saving the world and distributing Ketumati Ma's balm, that too had gone smoothly. There was still danger from global warming, but people were working together now to try to prevent it. Goodwill and common sense had prevailed. We had changed the world, and along the way, we ourselves had changed.

I thought I would philosophise a little, and conclude my tale of how it was for me. I had wanted to find out who I was in my own right as opposed to just being Dada's sister. My only revelation—if it can be called that—was that I was of as much importance, or as little, as anybody else. I thought I would meditate, and instead of insisting on being someone, let go of such considerations. It seemed to me a good way to finish this account—suitably modest and with a tinge of wisdom. But my saying this has made Heckle and Grackle flap about and threaten me with unspeakable consequences—of their devising. They see my wanting to withdraw to meditate as a cop out. They want me 'to live happily ever after', or failing that, to do something, be someone. I could ask, 'Why?' And they would answer, 'Why not?' Arguing with them is not a good idea.

'You modest!' Heckle heckles. 'And wise?'

'And what about us?' Grackle protests.

'We have ideas of our own, you know!'

9
What They Want Isn't What They Need.

Heckle and Grackle don't care about the truth. They've gone around bragging about our matchmaking skills and saying what a wonderful team the three of us make. The result is: I've been set up as an Agony Aunt. Though this new world has the benefits of the Golden Balm, people still agonise over who loves them and who does not. They still want what they cannot have, or are grieving over what they once had, or are worrying about what they ought to have. And now, all because of Heckle and Grackle, my desk is flooded with cries for help. The mynas have told the world how the three of us sorted out Kumbh's problems and brought Leela and Kumbh together. We didn't, but people believe what they want to believe. The emails and the cheeps are flooding in, and Heckle and Grackle are preening themselves. We have become media stars. They've even asked Bugzee and Leela and Kumbh to make guest appearances. Dada and Vijju refused point blank.

'I don't know why you're so bothered,' Heckle says to me. 'All you have to do is supply the answers. We'll do the work.'

We'll send out messages, manage your image and deal with the publicity,' Grackle puts in. '

I glare at them.

'You were young once,' Heckle coaxes. 'Don't you want to help people who are in trouble?'

The answer is, 'No, I don't want to help,' but that's churlish. I should at least give it a try. I want Kumbh and Leela to be happy.

There's even a small part of me that's a little envious. That does not mean I want to advise the lovelorn.

'Come here,' I say to Heckle and Grackle. I clutch Heckle in my left hand and Grackle in my right hand. 'You, Heckle, will read the questions, and you, Grackle, will type the answers.'

'All right,' Heckle grumbles. 'Stop squeezing us to death. Here's the first question. *I love someone, but she says she does not love me at all. What shall I do?*'

'Write,' I command Grackle. '*Here are your choices: 1. Pester her to death. 2. Pine away and hope that you'll be remembered for your fidelity. 3. Accept her answer, take up meditation, exercise hard and think about something else. Remember, Aunt Shupi always answers a question with another question. That is her trademark. Now, which of these choices do you think is best?*'

Grackle hesitates. 'You want me to write all that? It will upset him.'

'He's upset already. He needs something bracing. Next question.'

Heckle reads. '*I'm good looking, charming and extremely lovable, but no one has fallen in love with me. Why has that happened? I mean, why hasn't that happened?*'

'Right.' I turn to Grackle. 'The same format. Choices. *1. Accept the fact that you are too good for this world. 2. Get a new mirror. 3. Be content that you love yourself so much, you don't need anyone else. Now, which of these choices etc.* Next.'

Heckle looks glazed and Grackle wants to say something, but she's busy typing. Heckle reads: '*I think I might love someone, but I do not think he is worthy of me, and my family objects. Should I marry him?*'

'Choices,' I dictate. '*1. Yes/ No. 2. Find someone worthy of you. 3. Get your family to solve the problem. Now, which of these choices...*'

Heckle hops away from the desk. Grackle stops pecking at the keys. 'Shupi,' Grackle says. 'They want answers, not questions. Couldn't you just offer sensible advice?'

'Answering questions with questions is what psychiatrists do. It's best practice,' I tell her. 'Besides, read the subtext. My advice contains a grain of common sense.'

'Shupi,' Heckle says in her why-must I-explain-this-to-a-stupid-child manner, 'what they want is sympathy, not gnomic wisecracks.'

'What they want isn't what they need,' I retort.

'But we're in the business of giving people what they want,' Grackle pleads. 'At this rate, Aunt Shupi's Bureau will have to shut down.'

I feel triumphant. 'Exactly,' I reply.

'Don't you want to supply answers?'

'No.'

'And have a host of followers?'

'No. It's what you want.'

'Nobody would accept us as Agony Aunts,' the mynas protest.

'They might,' I tell them. 'Why don't you set yourselves up as Heckle and Grackle, the Mystic Mynas? It sounds good. People could come to you with offerings of food and money. You could look deep into a bowl filled with rice, dive in suddenly and emerge with just one grain of rice held in your beak. Then you could give them the grain of rice and tell them that the answer they seek is written on it.'

'They'll say they can't read it,' Heckle objects.

'You must read it for them for which you can make a further charge.'

'What shall we say?' Grackle asks.

'Keep the epics handy. Stick your beak in and pick a sentence at random. Tell your clients that if they think about that sentence long and hard, they'll achieve clarity.'

'You're good at this,' Heckle says with respect in her voice. 'Are you sure you don't want to join us?'

'Quite sure,' I reply.

Kumbh, who has come in to ask whether we're going to accept Bugzee's invitation, overhears some of this conversation. 'How can you set yourselves up as counsellors when you missed the most difficult problem Leela and I have?' he says.

We stare at him.

'You don't even know what it is, do you?'

When we don't answer, he tells us. 'My sleeping habits!'

Of course! 'You're right,' I tell him. 'We should have thought of it. What is Leela supposed to do during the six months when you're fast asleep?'

Heckle and Grackle are listening with their beaks open.

'That's right,' Kumbh says. 'And during the six months when I'm wide awake, what am I supposed to do while Leela sleeps night after night?'

'We should have thought of it,' Heckle mutters.

'Perhaps we're not that good,' Grackle admits. 'What are you going to do?' she asks Kumbh.

'We're working on it,' Kumbh replies.

For a full minute, the mynas look abashed.

Luckily, they stop pestering me. That still leaves me at a loose end, and therefore the target of benign interference. The truth is, I'm happy as I am, but Dada wants to know if I would like to help him with his opera—not to write it, but perhaps to get together some of the props, help with research—and the funding... And Kumbh and Leela offer to take me on their next trip. It's a worthy cause, and I like being at sea; but find I'm expected to spend all my time collecting plastic. It doesn't appeal. Perhaps I'm not as worthy as I ought to be.

Then, one day, a delegation arrives on my doorstep. The government has decided that it would be helpful if at least one member of the family were to join the cabinet—they say our illustrious lineage, our vast experience and above all, the inestimable gift of the Golden Balm would add lustre to their proceedings. I decline. It turns out they weren't asking me. They want me to persuade Dada. Clearly, vestiges of the patriarchy still persist. Dada declines. He says he prefers music to machinations, and poetry to politics. They try Kumbh. He says he hasn't got time. The planet is still in need of saving. Global warming has slowed down, but it hasn't halted; the oceans are still polluted, and the production of rubbish hasn't stopped. They then ask me whether I would join the cabinet. Dada twists my right arm. Kumbh twists my left arm, they both point out that as at the moment I have nothing better to do, it is clearly my duty. I give in.

'What is my remit?' I ask the ministers.

'Oh, Shupaji, as we have already distributed all the portfolios, you will be the Minister Without Portfolio,' they tell me.

'Well, then what is my function?' I ask.

'Madam,'—and they look so pleased with themselves as they tell me this—'your function is to solve all the problems we cannot solve.'

The first problem they hand over to me has to do with education. They have schools. The children go to them. They even have teachers. What there's no agreement about is which history should be taught and in what language.

I don't know the answer to that. I summon Heckle and Grackle. I ask them what they think, and I send a message to Bugzee. Bugzee replies, 'Abolish history. Let them start afresh. As for language—teach them every language that has ever existed other than the one they already know. Too many, you say? It will keep them busy and out of trouble.'

I send a message to Dada and get an instant reply: 'Give them a diet of poetry exclusively. Poetry is beauty and beauty is truth. It is all they need to know...' I suspect he hasn't even read my message and that this is his current standard reply. I turn to the mynas, who immediately contradict each other.

'Teach them their own history,' Grackle says firmly.

'No, teach them everyone else's,' Heckle interrupts.

'And in their mother tongue,' Grackle goes on.

'No, in the lingua franca,' Heckle insists.

'Right,' I tell them. 'You've given me the answer.'

I tell the ministers they have to do both—what Grackle says as well as what Heckle says. They don't like it. 'It's contradictory and unsatisfactory,' they point out.

'So is life.' I shrug. 'Besides, I'm expected to spend most of my time collecting plastic: and as for languages, the brain can accommodate several of them.'

They go away, grumbling. A few days later they're back with a different problem. They want to know whether the laws that apply to individuals should apply to nations? One of their pundits thinks it's a good idea. 'Let's discuss it,' I say to the ministers. 'Murder is a crime, therefore war would be prohibited.'

'Yes,' they agree.

'Theft isn't allowed, therefore conquest would be banned.'

'Agreed,' they say.

'And if a needy individual were to knock on the door of a private individual and ask for shelter, should the private individual keep the door shut?'

'That's up to the individuals.' The ministers shrug.

'Well, then what about refugees?'

'It depends,' say the ministers.

'There you are then. There is your answer. The laws that apply to individuals apply to states, but sometimes they don't.'

The ministers go away looking unhappy. I decide to resign. They want definite answers and I have none. But in no time at all, the ministers are back.

'We have decided that the best thing to do is to institute World Government, but there are groups here and there who feel that this would deprive them of their independence, what should we do?'

'You should,' I tell them wearily, 'institute the World Government, leave the independents alone, and let them join when they choose to.'

'Is that sensible?' they ask.

'I don't know,' I reply. 'Please accept my resignation.'

'Why?'

'Because I don't have all the answers.'

'Nor have we. Should we resign?'

'That's up to you.'

I remember Pashan, which Kumbh and I attempted to govern, and feel I've failed again. When Kumbh, Leela, the mynas and I go to tea at Bugzee's, I'm not at my most cheerful. Success has made Bugzee affable. He lives in a pleasant flat and has minions at his beck and call. He provides us with a splendid tea—cakes and sandwiches as well as pakoras and samosas of various sorts. His latest animation film—a rags to riches story—has been a hit.

'What's the matter, Shupi?' he asks.

'Didn't do well as Minister Without Portfolio,' I mumble.

'Nobody could have,' Leela says.

They're all nice to me and I feel better.

'What are your plans?' Bugzee wants to know. 'I could get you into films if you would like me to. Bittu was in touch and he has a part in the new animation. He's a waif on the streets.'

'He'd be good at looking lost and forlorn,' I reply. 'Thanks for the offer, Bugzee, but I don't want to be a film star. I don't think I'd be good at it.'

'Oh, I wasn't offering a star part,' Bugzee demurs.

So much for my ego, but I don't really mind. 'I thought I would lead a quiet life,' I say meekly.

'Yes,' Heckle and Grackle say loudly. 'The three of us are going to live quietly beside the sea.' I hadn't realised the mynas were thinking of moving in with me.

'Sounds good, but I overheard Dada,' Kumbh warns. 'Watch out. He has something in mind for you. I overheard him consulting Leela.' When I try to catch Leela's eye, she looks away.

10
If People Want to Be Awful, That is Their Inalienable Right

Just as I'm about to tender my resignation yet again, the phone rings. It's the ministers. 'You can resign later if you want to,' they tell me. 'Right now, we have an emergency. We're sending an armoured car for you.'

It turns our there's a riot in progress and I'm expected to quell it. 'Why me?' I ask.

'Because it has to do with the Golden Balm,' they answer. 'The moderates are saying they do not want to be led to heaven. They want to earn their own merit points. The extremists, however, are accusing us of the worst kind of abuse—brain washing by means of drugs.'

'Right,' I say to them, pretending I have all the answers. 'Employ water cannon, but lace the water with a concentrate of Golden Balm. That will calm them down.'

It doesn't work. The demonstrators have thought of that and are well equipped with umbrellas and waterproof clothes. In fact, it makes matters worse. The rioters gain strength and are now joined by broad-minded liberals. If people want to be awful, they say, that is their inalienable right. This time the ministers accept my resignation. They need a scapegoat.

When I return home, Dada phones. Would I please come to see him, he has an important proposition. 'Please Dada,' I plead with him. 'I'm looking forward to hearing your opera once it's finished, but I don't want to be in it. I'm not a good singer.'

First it was the mynas, then the government, now Dada. I don't want them to find an occupation for me. It turns out that what Dada wants has nothing to do with his opera. He has decided he has been a negligent big brother and ought to have taken a more active part in finding me a husband. He has been working on it.

'Dada,' I protest. 'I'm not interested in getting married. If I wanted to get married, I expect I could find someone.'

'Shupi,' Dada says. 'Getting married isn't just a matter of finding someone. A search has to be instituted, the matter advertised. Unsuitable suitors have to be weeded out, a short list made, which in turn has to be further shortened. It's a long and arduous process. And I've done it for you in accordance with the best modern practice. At least come and look.'

I give in. Dada is at his desk with a pile of papers. As I come in, Vijju gives me a sympathetic smile. She sits there and doesn't intervene.

'First things first,' Dada says. 'Here's the ad I sent out for you. He reads it out:

Caste, class, creed, colour no objection. No, I crossed out 'colour.' These days everyone's fair. *Wealth or the lack of it also not a problem. A suitable partner is required for Rajkumari Shurpanakha, sister of Maharaj-adhiraj Ravana the Serene, the Inestimable Ruler of Shri Lanka, and descendant of Pulastya and Sumali, King of the Rakshasas.* Then in order to be modern, I also added that *gender, sexual orientation, and the incompatibility of horoscopes also not a barrier.*' He looks pleased with himself. 'What do you think?'

What can I say? 'It's very non-discriminatory, Dada,' I tell him, 'but I would like to exercise a little discrimination—in the best sense, of course.'

'Of course!' Dada agrees. 'That's where the sifting process comes in. I used the computer to sort out those who said they would like to meet you before making an offer. I deleted them.'

'Why?' I ask. I don't want to get involved in this, but I am curious.

'How dare they want to meet you! The fact that you are my

sister should be good enough for them,' Dada replies. 'That still left a great many applications. To narrow things down further, I asked all the applicants to tell me in ten words or less why they wanted to marry you. I don't want a brother-in-law who talks too much. That cut it down to twenty suitors. Still too many. I reduced the number further by asking them to give me their reasons in five words or less. And now I have a shortlist of four suitors.' He smiles at me hopefully. 'That's good, isn't it? And it's all based on motive, which is surely important.'

Do I want to know why anyone would wish to marry me? I'm so taken aback that I don't say anything.

Dada continues. 'Here are their answers. *1. Because she's iconic. 2. Because she's epic. 3. Because my parents want it. 4. Because she's related to you.* What do you think? I quite like the fourth chap—he's astute.'

'How do you know it's a man,' I say, just to mix things up. 'All you have are the initials. Anyway, I couldn't possibly marry four people.'

'No.' Dada nods. 'That's why I sent them another question: What do you hope to get out of this marriage? Here are their answers: *1. A son. 2. A dozen sons. 3. Good cooking and a comfortable life. 4. Useful contacts thanks to your connections.* Which ones do you think we should delete?'

He's entirely serious. I decide to have a little fun with him. 'Dada, I have a simple multiple choice question of my own.'

'Fine. I'll send it out right away.' He's happy I'm taking some interest.

'Here it is,' I dictate, '*Would you consider Princess Shurpanakha an "unsuitable" match? A. If she smoked cigarettes? B. If she didn't speak English? C. If she failed to address you in the second person plural when not speaking English?*'

Dada gives me a sharp look, but he sends out my query. There's a resounding silence. All my suitors have disappeared.

Dada looks crestfallen. 'There is one other suitor. I wasn't quite sure about him.'

We wait. 'He says he has no ulterior motive,' Dada continues. 'According to him you would be a prize worth winning, a trophy worth having—a feather in his cap. What do you think? He wants you for yourself.'

'No, Dada, he wants me for himself,' I retort.

I'm beginning to get exasperated when Vijju, who has been listening to the proceedings, puts her hand on Dada's shoulder. 'Be sensible,' she tells him.

And Dada, to give him his due, is sensible. After a minute or two he apologises to me. 'Sorry,' he says, 'I thought it might work. I didn't mean any harm, Shupi. I happened to read this story in one of Vijju's feminist magazines.'

AN HONEST TO GOODNESS FAIRY TALE

Once upon a time, there was a charming woman who liked being flattered. (Who doesn't?) She was also very rich, so she thought she might as well get herself the sort of partner she would really like. She advertised: 'Half my riches and my hand in marriage to the suitor who pays me the best compliment. Caste, class, colour, creed or anything like that not an impediment.'

Dada interrupts himself to say, 'You see, she reminded me of you.' He goes on.

'Suitors came from far and near in all sorts of colours, sizes and shapes. And some were clever and some were downright stupid. "The greatest compliment I can offer you is to make you my wife," one of them said. She suppressed a giggle and turned to the next one. This one threatened to commit suicide. She said that wasn't a good idea, but if he insisted on it, would he do it elsewhere please? And a third offered to weigh her in gold, which implied that the plumper she was, the more worthwhile—it didn't feel right. Then there were the poets with their sheaves of similes, some so outlandish that she was flabbergasted rather than pleased. For example, the magnitude of her attraction was compared to a black hole at the centre of a galaxy. She didn't like it. And of course, there were hundreds of frogs who claimed they were princes in deep disguise.

She withdrew the ad, realised she'd been silly, and said that this time she would give half her wealth and her hand in marriage to whoever courted her with the greatest honesty. This also was an error, because now she was subjected to a battery of insults. The suitors thought that the ruder they were, the more honest they were being. The least insulting were the ones who merely said they were marrying her for her money.

She began to wonder whether it might be best not to marry. Then one day, an old friend said to her, 'I've loved you for a long time.' She paused. 'The only thing is I'm no good at contests, so if you're going to hold another one, tell me now, so that I can go away and break my heart in peace.'

And it was then that the charming and rich (and beautiful) woman suddenly realised that to be loved and to love was the best thing of all and so they got married.'

'I didn't understand the story completely,' Dada admits. 'And we can ignore the bit about same sex marriages; but it occurred to me you might be lonely, and I thought a loving companion might be just what you need.' Here he can't help glancing at Vijju.

Poor old Dada. He means well. 'It's all right.' I smile at him. 'You might be right, but such a companion will be of my own choosing.'

Relieved that I've dealt with the problem of having to be Mrs Shupi Somebody, I return to my house by the sea. It's near Dada and Vijju, and it's reasonably quiet, though Heckle and Grackle have moved in. How do I manage? We made a little bit of money from Ketumati's Balm, and the house has a small garden in which I grow vegetables more or less successfully.

I've given an account of what I achieved. I wasn't very good at being Prince Supratim, or an Agony Aunt or a Cabinet Minister, but I don't have to justify my existence. No one does. I listen to the waves crashing on the sand over and over again, and try to understand what it all means. We construct myths and then deconstruct them, again and again. We do that with ourselves. It's an occupation. Sometimes we call it progress. With the help of Ketumati Ma's balm the world avoided imminent disaster; but there's the road ahead. 'Surely to try to meditate is permissible, at least for a time?' I say this aloud to Heckle and Grackle, but it's Leela, who answers.

'Only for a time.' She has just dropped by. I suspect her of having conspired with Dada.

Heckle and Grackle break in suddenly. They don't like having to be quiet for too long. 'Our function,' they inform Leela, 'is to keep Shupi tethered in case she floats away like a hot air balloon.'

'You exaggerate,' I tell them. 'I'm not in any danger of rising above it all. But it's true, you do keep me grounded.'

Heckle and Grackle nod. 'We do more than that,' they claim. 'Please tell the world we're teaching you to fly.'

Leela rolls her eyes, but Heckle and Grackle ignore her.

'Do you think we could set up a small bureau? "Lessons in Levitation and The Telling of Tall Tales—while perched on a cloud"?' they ask.

'I haven't been lying,' I protest.

'No,' they retort, 'you've been telling the truth while making it sound like a fairy tale.'

'That would require a happy ending,' Leela says. 'The trouble with you, Shupi, is that you want the impossible. How are we going to find you a suitable partner?'

'It's not compulsory,' I smile.

'And it's hardly an ultimate goal,' Heckle puts in.

I stare at the mynas. 'I thought you agreed with Dada and Leela? Whose side are you on?'

'We are always on your side, Shupi,' Grackle says patiently. 'Now about that plan we were discussing, perhaps we should set it up as two separate businesses? Lessons in Lying and in Levitation?'

'You're absurd!' Leela bursts out.

'No, we're not,' Grackle says smugly. 'We're a pair of mynas. In a fairy tale, much is possible.'

'Well, whatever you say, someday I think she will, you know,' Leela insists.

'No, she won't,' the mynas reply.

'Yes, she will.'

'What?' I confront them.

'Find a partner!'

They carry on back and forth. I listen to their voices. Beyond them, I can hear the sea. Nothing really ends. These are everyday sounds, and for the time being I am content.

Kumbh

Though I knew they were the 'bad people', as a child I felt sorry for the three siblings, especially for Shupi and Kumbh. It didn't seem fair that Shurpanakha had to have her nose cut off and that Kumbhakarna had to spend six months of the year asleep. In this narrative, Kumbh doesn't want to fight, not because he might get hurt, but because he might hurt someone. He doesn't want to sleep either, even though he's a dreamer. In some ways, he reflects my own guilt about wanting to dream and to write poems and fables rather than work more actively towards a better world.

Kumbh

The child is mortal; but Poor Child
Creeps through centuries of bone
Untransient as the channelling worm
Or water making sand of stone.
Poor child, what have they done to you?

Jay Macpherson
Poor Child, The Boatman and other poems

Contents

1
The Leaves in the Wind Lecture

People think I am innocent, guileless, a little gullible, incapable of harming anyone—in short, a gentle giant. I am large; it doesn't follow I am simple. Sometimes I want to disabuse people—pick them up gently, look them in the eye, and say: 'I'm not a nice guy! I have appetites and needs and fits of bad temper—just like you!' It wouldn't do, much easier to fit into the role set out for me, though that's not altogether true either. I'm Dada's Younger Brother, Shri Ravana's Shadow and Shupi's Sibling. Is Dada more important to me than Shupi? She's only a girl. She'd have my head for saying 'only'. As children, we both looked up to Dada. We followed him about. Were Shupi and I rivals? She's only a woman—there I go again—and I am strong, stronger even than Dada. Do I love my sister? I would fight for her, and for Dada. I love myself best, of course, but that is human.

Dada has written his memoirs. Shupi is writing hers. My turn now. I don't think we'll repeat each other. What we each thought and felt was different. It would be comforting to think that it was sometimes the same, or similar, that we understood each other.

I was the also-ran son. Kubera was the eldest. Vibhisana was the favoured one, the 'good' son. Ravana Dada was the 'designer' son, born to do great things, and I was the extra. Shupi was Ketumati Ma's favourite, so was Ravana Dada. Dada was looked up to and admired by everyone. I wasn't disliked, but I wasn't important and I wasn't anybody's favourite, except Shanti's. Shanti was the Elephant Matriarch; I was closer to her than to anyone else. Because I was a prince of sorts, I was able to go where the elephants were stabled and ask the mahouts to let me ride her. We'd walk about the gardens, even go into the countryside. Nobody bothered us. They didn't want to cross the king's grandson. At the time we lived with our grandfather, Sumali, King of the Rakshasas. And we were careful; we did our best not to trample crops. It wasn't because I was gentle and kind, which is what everyone thinks—Kumbh the Gentle, Kumbh-Wouldn't-Hurt-A-Fly. It was because we didn't want trouble. If our wanderings came to my grandfather's notice or to my mother's attention, they might be stopped. Shanti, on the other hand, really was kind, at least to me.

Now when I remember some of the things she said, I understand them differently from what they meant to me then. Once, when I was quite young, I asked her point blank, 'Who do you love best? Dada or me?'

I half-expected a lecture on how that wasn't a sensible question. But she wrapped her trunk around me and set me on her back. 'You, of course,' she told me.

It made me feel I was king of the universe, and all that euphoria made me say, 'It's because I'm better, isn't it?'

She reached back with her trunk and patted my shoulder. 'I'll tell you a story. In my last incarnation, I was an African elephant.'

'What is an African elephant? Where do they live?'

'In Africa. It's a place like India, only bigger. And African elephants are like Indian elephants, only bigger. The females have tusks.'

'Were you the Matriarch of the elephants there?'

'Of course, and as such, I had to settle a dispute once for some birds called oxpeckers. They were arguing about which was better—to be useful or to be beautiful?'

It seemed like a silly question to me—why not be both? But I knew this was going to be a moral tale, I had better be quiet. Shanti began:

A red-billed oxpecker and a yellow-billed oxpecker, who were perched on buffaloes standing next to each other, got talking.

'I caught and ate thirteen fleas yesterday,' Yellow Bill boasted. 'How many did you get?'

'Only two,' Red Bill admitted. 'That's because I keep my buffalo so clean that she hardly has any on her.' 'Anyway,' she went on, preening herself, 'I think looking good is far more important than being useful.'

Other oxpeckers overheard them, and soon a great argument broke out about which was better: to be useful or to be ornamental.

As the discussion grew heated, they asked the lead buffalo what he liked best—their usefulness or their beauty?

'Your usefulness, of course!' he snorted. 'You might look great perched on my spreading horns, but I can't see you when you're sitting on them.'

'Hurrah!' shouted the Useful Party. 'We won! We won!'

But the others insisted on consulting a hippopotamus.

'I don't care about fleas and ticks and suchlike. I just plunge into the water and drown them all,' the hippopotamus told them smugly. 'And if one or two are still not dead, I roll in the mud and that does for them.'

After that, the hippopotamus seemed to doze off, but the Ornamental Party clamoured to know what he thought about their looks.

'Well, now,' the hippopotamus declared, 'on a lazy afternoon when I'm wallowing in the river, the sight of an antelope, stooping for a drink with Yellow Bills and Red Bills perched on his antlers sure breaks the tedium.'

The Ornamentals were triumphant.

'We won! We won!' they shouted, but the Usefuls did their best to shout them down. They made such a racket that they disturbed the elephants.

The Elephant Matriarch ambled up to them. The elephants behind her trumpeted for silence.

The Matriarch spoke. 'Being useful is good. And being ornamental is good. You are both, and that is best. Therefore, be quiet.'

Then she had an afterthought. 'What is best of all is to combine usefulness with beauty and both with strength. That is truly magnificent, but that is given only to elephants.' She walked away and the other elephants followed.

The oxpeckers were too stunned to say anything. Then a Yellow Bill twittered, 'Being both is best.' And a Red Bill tweeted, 'We're second only to elephants.' And for a while that satisfied them.

I wasn't quite sure what to make of this story. I said to Shanti, 'It means both Dada and I are excellent, doesn't it?'

'Of course, you are,' Shanti replied.

I wish she could have come with us, got into the cave and woken up when we did. She was the best thing in my life.

I'm not saying that people were unkind or that Kaikesi Ma was a bad mother. Her children bored her, even Ravana Dada, who was destined to do great things, but ended up fighting a losing war. As for her husband, he was a sage, absorbed in meditation; she resented that. She was born for greater things than rattling about in her father's palace. I don't know how Dada and Shupi felt, they didn't say much. I felt I was a nuisance.

Every now and then, Shupi would try to mother me and I would let her; though at the time I wasn't really willing to listen to her. She saved our lives. After what she calls The Colossal Carnage, she dragged us off the battlefield and hid us in a cave. She had to put us together piece by piece with Ketumati Ma's healing balm. Our maternal grandmother, Ketumati Ma, was kind. I loved her, though I wasn't her favourite. Why do I always come second, or even third?

I remember what Shupi said after Dada read her some of his memoirs: 'Stop whining, Ravana Dada!' I should stop too. It isn't something kshatriyas do. Am I kshatriya? Or a man-eating demon? Or a scholarly brahmin? I'm recounting my youth, and the truth is I did often feel sorry for myself.

Besides Dada and Shupi, I had two other friends, Dev and Dagadu. It hurts to talk about them. I'll say it outright: *I killed them.* Dev was a brahmin. His father was a clerk in my grandfather's service. Dagadu's people were in charge of the weaponry. They were hunters. Dagadu was a tribal. (Later, when Leela read this, she objected to my tone. I had to cross it out. I told her that my grandfather didn't care about caste, to which she replied, 'Why would he?') All this was a long time ago; but what happened between us changed everything.

While we were playing together, Dev and Dagadu started teasing me about how huge I was. I picked them up and knocked their heads together. They were so fragile. They fell into a coma. All I could think of was how to revive them. I had done a lot of meditating, and my concentration was good. Ketumati Ma explained that if I sat with them day after day and tried to get through to them, I might succeed. It took six months. In the end they revived and were able to speak, but they never spoke to me again.

That was when I began to sleep a lot. My brain felt tired and I wanted to avoid dealing with people. I got called Slugabed. Also, Greedy Guts because I ate so much when I was awake. What did they expect me to do? Nibble at food? I was a giant.

I liked being with Shupi and Ravana Dada, but other than that life at home wasn't much fun. Shanti made up for everything. She cared about me and set me right when necessary. I remember one occasion when I went to her complaining about Dada yet again. I had picked a fight with Dada in order to prove I was his equal, or more than his equal. I had tried it before. Dada had always smiled in his lofty way, asked what was the matter and patted my shoulder. This time I was determined to make him fight. 'Dada,' I said to him in the fiercest tone I could muster, 'I bet I'm stronger than you. I challenge you to fight.'

Dada had smiled, as usual, in big brother fashion. 'What for? You're being silly.' He'd gone on doing whatever he was doing—polishing his armour probably—but I pestered him so much that at last, he gave in to keep me quiet.

'Right,' he said. 'With what do you want to fight?'

The thought of hurting him was unbearable. 'We'll wrestle,' I replied firmly.

Within two minutes I was flat on my back. I couldn't understand it. I knew I was stronger. I got to my feet. I wanted to know how he had done it. 'Wrestling, too, is an art,' he told me.

I had meant to look good and had ended up looking foolish. Upset and confused, I went to Shanti for consolation. That was when I got The Leaves in the Wind Lecture. It went like this.

'Dear Kumbh, you are trying so hard to discover who you want to be, or who you should be, or who you can be, or who you are. You even try to define yourself by who you are not. And you do this by snatching at labels that fly past you like leaves in the wind. NOT-RAVANA DADA. DADA IS FIERCE. I WILL BE THE OPPOSITE. I AM GENTLE. I AM THE GENTLE GIANT. NOT THE GENTLE GIANT. I EAT PEOPLE. I AM A RAKSHASA. I AM A BRAHMIN. I AM VEGETARIAN. MY NAME IS GOBBLE GUTS. I AM NOT-SHUPI. SHUPI IS A GIRL. I AM A BOY. BAD BOY. I HURT MY FRIENDS. MY NAME IS SLUGABED. I AM A HERO. I AM AN EXTRA. I AM A WINNER. NO, I CAME THIRD. I AM THE ELEPHANT BOY. I AM DADA'S TAIL/ FOLLOWER/ HERO WORSHIPPER. I AM LOVED. UNLOVED. WANTED. UNWANTED. A NUISANCE. A KILLER. A SAVIOUR. A SLEEPER. A DREAMER. A TRIER. A FOOL. AN ENTITY CAPABLE OF LEARNING.

These labels are only words written on leaves. Some stick to you, some are stuck on you, some are carried away and some crumble and fall down. If you didn't have the labels, you wouldn't cease to be. They aren't even useful for keeping out the cold. You don't have to be afraid. But if you are afraid, you will be able to face your fear. That is my blessing. Carry it with you.'

Her words, or the way she said them, made me want to cry. I did cry. It felt like a farewell. A year later, when the chance came to visit Ravana Dada, who by then had become King of Sri Lanka, I jumped at it. I wanted to see the world, learn what I could. They wouldn't let Shanti go with me. Her place, they said, was with the other elephants. According to The Slaughterhouse Saga—Shupi's appellation—it needed a thousand elephants to walk over me in order to wake me and summon me to battle. That may be so, but they didn't send Shanti. I do carry her blessing with me. It protects me, not so much because it has kept me safe, as because it has kept me sane. I wonder what happens to a ~~boy~~ child who has no one's blessing?

2
So? I'm a Tall Woman.

Once I was awake, Shupi had trouble persuading me to leave the cave. That was when we heard the mynas calling. Shupi was impressed that I understood them. 'You understand the language of birds? Of animals? Teach it to me!' She was excited. She learnt it quickly and easily. Understanding other creatures isn't difficult. It's a matter of wanting to understand and be understood. As it turned out, Heckle and Grackle, the two mynas, preferred Shupi to me and tended to keep her company. I didn't mind. I didn't want to make friends with anyone, especially not with talkative mynas. My mind felt as though a large chunk of it had been shorn off. My family, my life, my world, all that I had known, had vanished thousands of years ago. I had Dada and Shupi and my own thoughts. For the time being, that was all I could deal with.

Shupi had been awake longer and more often than Dada and me. She was eager to explore the new world. With any luck, it would be better than the world she had grown up in—kinder to women. For Shupi, that is always a primary concern. As I write this I can hear her scolding: 'And it should be a primary concern for you as well!' But I am not a woman. Do I have to be a woman for the welfare of women to matter to me?

I hadn't meant to upset her. I had decided long ago not to argue with Shupi and Dada. I could always slip in what I really thought. Unluckily, I made the mistake of letting Shupi see what

I had written. She pounced on me at once. 'That last bit: "what happens to a boy who has no one's blessing?"—Kumbh, don't you ever think about the implications of what you're saying?'

I was amazed. 'What's wrong with thinking about other people?'

'You weren't thinking about other *people*,' she retorted. 'Just about boys and men. What about girls and women?'

'I could hardly say, "I wonder what happens to a girl who has no one's blessing?" It wouldn't have sounded right coming from me. I happen to be a boy.'

She wasn't having it. 'You could have said "child". Change it!'

I changed it. Simpler not to argue. She still wasn't satisfied.

'And what do you mean by asking: "Do I have to be a woman for the welfare of women to matter to me?" Of course, the welfare of women should matter to you whether you're a boy, a man or a sparrow!' she raged.

'Sparrow?' I asked feebly.

That made her smile and she let the matter drop. I decided not to show Shupi what I had been writing and to keep my head down. She had enough on her hands persuading Dada that we ought to be more egalitarian. I backed her over that. It felt right and I wanted to find out where it would lead. It led to Shupi being tormented by a bunch of small boys, to Dada being beaten by an old man and to me being bullied by an old woman. I'm not sure how much good that did us.

I was already in trouble with Shupi. It was all because she changed herself into Prince Supratim and nearly got trapped by a woman in a well. Dada and I did our best not to laugh, but she caught me smiling that evening.

'What are you smiling at?' she demanded.

'At the thought of the Woman in the Well wanting to kidnap you,' I replied truthfully. I didn't think she'd mind.

She was annoyed. 'At least I had the guts to try to find out what it feels like to be a man. Why don't you try it? You'd understand then that we women and girls are also human, and you wouldn't have to ask yourself whether what happens to us should matter to you. You're so trapped in what you think of as your own identity!'

She flounced off without giving me a chance to say anything.

That night I lay awake, thinking about what it would be like to be a woman. Should I try? An hour or two passed. I was still wide awake, so I crept out of the cave and set about my transformation. I turned myself into a beautiful woman—might as well be beautiful, I thought—and gave myself a gorgeous sari. I copied one of Shupi's. I decided I would be Gajra Devi, the Flower Lady. Suddenly I wished I had Shanti with me. I put the thought aside and walked into the night.

I realised at once that silk saris weren't meant for tramping through the countryside. I heard the fabric tear, but I ignored that and carried on towards a light. It looked like a campfire. 'Human beings,' I thought. 'Companionship. A chance to talk and find out things.' There was a half moon in the sky. I could more or less see where I was going. I walked along a riverbank and then up a hillside to a small shrine. Three people were sitting in the courtyard around a fire: a boy, a middle-aged man and an old man. I must have startled them, coming as I did out of the darkness and into the firelight. At the sight of me, the old man fell on his face.

'It's the Devi,' he whispered. 'She's come to punish us for desecrating her shrine.'

They were probably drunk. I could smell the liquor. 'I am not a goddess,' I told them in a reassuring a voice. 'Do sit up. I want to ask you some questions about your world.'

The old man sat up, but kept his distance. 'Are you a *bhoot* then?' the boy asked, looking at me warily.

'I'm not a ghost,' I replied. 'I'm a flesh and blood woman. I want to know whether in the world today, men and women are treated as equals?'

That made them gawp. Then the middle-aged man laughed. 'Of course not! Men rule. Women obey. Women are there for our convenience.' He was clearly feeling bolder.

'Unless, of course, the women belong to powerful families. Then if we tried to touch them, their men folk would slaughter us,' the old man added. 'Who are you? And where do you come from? Are you really a woman? Where are your people?'

'Of course, I'm a woman!' I replied indignantly. 'I come from far away.'

'You're very tall for a woman,' the boy said uncertainly.

'So? I'm a tall woman,' I informed him.

The middle-aged one stretched out an arm to touch me tentatively. He nodded at the others. 'She's real.'

Suddenly, he got very friendly. 'Here, come and sit beside me. Get warm by the fire.' He made room for me.

I didn't want to appear unfriendly, so I sat down beside him. He stank! I felt ashamed of myself for thinking that, so I didn't move away. After all, they were being friendly. The old man offered me the bottle they'd been drinking from. It was vile, but I pretended to drink from it.

'Could you tell me if I could get some work around here?' I asked.

'What sort of work could you do, I wonder,' the old man said, screwing up his eyes and looking canny. Then he laughed and elbowed the boy. 'I'm sure we could all find some work for her, couldn't we?'

The middle-aged man agreed. 'I'm sure we could. Come lie down beside me, and spend the night here. Tomorrow we'll find something for you.' He tugged at my sari and tried to push me down. I didn't move. I glanced at the other two. Their expressions had changed. The more he pawed me, the more avid they looked. 'She's luscious. And alone. We could all have her. Nobody would know. And if necessary, we could kill her afterwards.' It wasn't difficult to read their thoughts, just surprising. Foolish of me to think I could just join them, chat for a while and be friends.

The middle-aged man kept trying to push me. I continued to sit. That made him angry. He began to hit me and then kicked me. When this had no effect, the others joined in.

'Why are you doing this?' I asked.

'You're a bad woman or you wouldn't be here,' the boy said.

'You're fair game,' the old man added.

'We're going to rape you and teach you a lesson,' the middle one told me.

'And if I complain against you?' I asked.

'You'll be dead.'

'You wouldn't dare.'

'No one would believe you. And anyway, you would be dishonoured. They'd want to know what you were doing wandering about at this hour of the night.'

In between kicking and punching me, they started using their knives. Then the boy seized a burning stick and tried to gouge my eyes. I had had enough. I got to my feet, picked up all three of them and tossed them in the river. There wasn't much water in it. I don't think they drowned.

As I strode back, the moon was behind a cloud. My fine clothes got caught in the bushes. I didn't care where I walked or what I trampled. I was on the side of women. I was definitely on the side of women, though I might not admit it to Shupi right away. She was awake when I got back. I was covered in blood. She got some water quickly and dressed my wounds. My account of what had happened was brief. 'I tried to find out what it was like being a woman. I went for a walk. I met some men. I wanted to be friends. They tried to rape me.'

Shupi didn't say anything. She touched my cheek briefly.

'I threw them into the river,' I went on. 'You know, Shupi, the whole damn problem would be solved if women were as strong as men. That's all it would take. That's all we care about—brute force—who can bash whom.'

When she still didn't say anything, I added, 'At least, now I know what it feels like to be a woman.'

'No,' she replied. 'You know what it feels like to be treated like a woman. No ordinary woman would have approached three drunk men in the middle of the night.'

I was tired, but I had trouble sleeping. Something bit me. I slapped my arm and heard a voice protest, 'Hey! Don't bash me! I mean no harm.' I got up, went to the cave entrance and examined my arm. There was a bedbug standing on it, gesticulating.

'My name is Bugzee. Please don't squash me just because you can. All I want is a fraction of a fraction of a drop of your blood. You wouldn't even notice it,' the bedbug pleaded. 'Please let me live? I wouldn't hurt you. And if you were feeling lonely, I could talk to you.'

'I don't want to be talked to!' I growled at Bugzee. 'You can stay the night. But no more biting. I need to sleep.'

After that, Bugzee was so quiet that the next morning I forgot to evict him. He stayed with me for a few days, and only moved when he found better lodgings. In The Slaughterhouse Saga I'm sometimes described as a Man Eating Monster. In Dada's and Shupi's version of me I'm a mild, biddable chap who wouldn't say, 'Boo!' to a bedbug.

3
Even Your Blood Tastes Sweeter!

We had realised we needed a way of making a living and had decided to try our luck at a nearby fair. Dada would sing. He had a fine voice. Shupi would tell fortunes and I would be the strong man. That was where I met Leela, the snake charmer's daughter. She was good looking and had such charm, and was so forthright, I couldn't keep my eyes off her. I did, of course, keep my eyes off her. It's not that I'm shy with women. In the old days I had two wives, and sons by them; but that world is long gone. I stayed in the background and didn't say much beyond being grateful for the help she gave us. But then one day, she smiled at me and everything changed.

There's something wrong with that sentence. Not the last one, but the one before that: 'And anyway, when it comes to women...' I have a feeling Shupi wouldn't like it. She would say, 'Kumbh, women are not a bowl of cherries to be picked at and picked over. They are human beings with lives and wishes and needs of their own.' Now that I look at that sentence again, it does seem wrong. I'll delete it. I only wanted to say that at first I thought Leela was just being kind to strangers. There was no reason to assume she was interested in me; and yet, she was. We began to exchange verses with Heckle and Grackle serving as willing messengers.

I don't know for sure, Leela may have been impressed by my strength. Quite by chance, she saw me lift an enormous boulder and put it down in front of our tent, though I had tried to do it as unobtrusively as possible. Our plan was to challenge young men to try to move it. That evening she caught me just before supper.

'I saw you,' she said. 'Are all the men as strong as you in the country you come from? Can they all lift gigantic boulders?'

'I'm probably exceptionally strong,' I muttered.

For a moment or two, neither of us knew what to say. Then I remembered something I had seen her do that had impressed me greatly. 'Are all the women where you come from as brave as you?' I asked.

'What do you mean?'

'One of your father's cobras got loose. I saw you scoop it up and put it in its basket without even stopping to think. I don't think I'd have had the nerve,' I told her.

'I'm used to the snakes,' she replied. 'It was nothing.' But I could see she was pleased by the compliment. Shupi joined us and overheard the last bit of the conversation.

She couldn't resist making a point. 'See Kumbh. Women are as brave as men, and as good as men. Probably better.'

'Shupi,' I said reasonably, 'I don't think we should argue about who is better. I'll tell you a story Shanti once told me.' I wanted to impress Leela, so I told the girls, I mean the women, about the African oxpeckers.

They listened attentively, but when I was done, Shupi said, 'You've missed the point, Kumbh.'

'What do you mean?' If anyone understood Shanti, I thought I did.

Shupi explained. 'It's clear, isn't it? Judgement depends on the nature of the judge.'

I didn't know what to make of that. Did she mean that men did the judging, and so... I let it go and went off to buy some food.

Leela and her father ate with us. That was the evening she came up with her idea for making millions. We would manufacture Ketumati Ma's balm and save the world. The bit about saving the world was put in by Shupi and me; we were sure we could soon persuade the others. I was filled with admiration for Leela's genius.

I lay awake hardly daring to believe that someone as enterprising and capable as Leela could care about me. Perhaps she wouldn't when she found out who I was—Kumbhakarna, Dada's Giant Younger Brother. She was going to find out sooner or later. I considered turning into a snake and eavesdropping on her. But what if she caught me and put me in a basket with the other snakes? I didn't like the idea of slithering and sliding about with them. I was almost asleep when Bugzee bit me.

'What do you think you're doing?' I said crossly. 'You're only allowed a fraction of a fraction of a drop of blood!'

Bugzee was unabashed. 'Who's a lucky boy then!' he crowed. He was wide awake and wanted a chat.

'What do you mean?'

'Leela. She was making a dead set at you!'

'And what would you know about that?' I growled.

'More than you think. I've been talking to Heckle and Grackle. And you've changed too. Even your blood tastes sweeter!'

'You should know,' I muttered. I didn't really like his drinking my blood, but what could I say? According to him, his life depended on it.

It suddenly occurred to me that Bugzee could find out what Leela thought. I could hear Leela and Shupi laughing and talking inside the tent. Dada and I were sleeping outside and I couldn't make out what they were saying. 'Bugzee,' I said urgently. 'Could you do me a favour?'

'What?'

'I want you to crawl into the tent and eavesdrop on the girls.'

He came straight to the point. 'What will you give me?'

'What do you want?'

'You haven't been very appreciative lately. I want you to write a poem in my praise.'

'In praise of you? Will a poem in praise of insects do?'

'All right. And I want you to go on a jaunt with me—as an insect.'

That took me aback, but I wanted to know what Leela thought. 'All right,' I agreed. 'Go!'

It took him a while to return. I suppose for a little chap like him it was a long way. I had time to compose the poem he'd asked for and a dozen more.

'Well?' I demanded, when he finally returned and climbed up my arm. 'What did Leela say about me?'

'Nothing,' he replied. 'They weren't talking about you. Shupi was telling Leela a story called "The Daughters of Perfection".'

'Was it any good?'

'Yes, but it was feminist.'

'I'm a feminist too,' I said firmly, but I felt disappointed.

Bugzee wasn't interested. 'Where's my poem?' he wanted to know.

I recited it to him.

INSECT LIFE

There are days when I think
even insect life
might not baffle me. I could slip
under doors,
lift my own weight;
and when annoyed,
bite or sting,
get away with it.
And my slippery soul,
sliding and gliding,
would escape from myself,
from all
my selves, from everything
I've done and been.

'That's not about me,' he protested. 'That's about you.'

'What do you expect?' I retorted. 'I wrote it. It does praise insects; it says they're strong and can fight back.'

'All right,' Bugzee replied. There wasn't much he could do about it. 'What about the other part of the bargain? You said you would change into a bedbug and go on a jaunt with me.'

'I agreed to turn into an "insect", not necessarily into a bedbug.

We're not going anywhere tonight. I'll consider it when we get to the city.'

Bugzee had to be content with that. Leela was masterminding the setting up of a company to make the balm; and Dada, Shupi and I were running about doing what she said. That didn't stop Bugzee from pestering me. As soon as we got to the city, he wanted us to go out and stand on the pavement. He was hoping to crawl onto somebody's trouser leg.

'That's how we'll get about. We'll just use people as our taxis,' Bugzee explained. 'Come on. You said you would turn into a bug and go with me.'

'If I'm going to change into anything,' I told him firmly, 'it will be a Diabolical Ironclad Beetle. But just standing on the kerb, hoping for a lift, is stupid. We could get lost, or get into trouble—anything could happen.'

'That's the fun of it!' Bugzee grinned. 'What's a Diabolical Ironclad?'

'Probably the toughest insect on earth,' I replied. 'I read about it somewhere. It said, "New research reveals that getting run over by a car is not even a near-death experience for this bug." That way I'll be able to protect myself and you.'

'I don't need protection,' Bugzee answered. 'Why can't we go tonight?'

'All right,' I agreed in desperation. 'Leela has organized a reception at a grand hotel for some important people. They will be shown what the balm can do. After the reception we could latch onto someone's coat tails, and see what there's to see and learn what there's to learn.'

I only said that to keep him quiet, but to my astonishment Bugzee thought it was a brilliant idea. 'That's really clever,' he enthused. 'I didn't know you had it in you. That way we could pick up somebody worthwhile. To get rich you have to mix with the rich.'

'Is that what all this is about?' I asked. 'You want to get rich?'

'Yes,' he said simply. 'And famous.'

The evening at the grand hotel was a hectic affair. We had to work hard and stay alert. I muttered something about staying on to look around after the reception. Leela raised an eyebrow, but didn't demur. She was busy deploying her troops—telling us exactly what to do and whom to charm. I worked hard, chatted nicely with this one and that, intervened quickly when required, and stood there awkwardly while the women gazed at Dada and me after they'd been shown how the balm worked. All through this I had Bugzee perched behind my ear making comments about the people.

He was trying to decide which one to jump on. 'That one,' he said at last. 'The bald man in the shiny suit and the loud tie.'

I looked around. Many of the men were bald, one or two had shiny suits and several wore florid ties. 'Which one?' I whispered.

'That one in the corner being chatted up by a group of people. Don't you know anything? His name is Multi Moghul. Every single film he has made has been a blockbuster. He's called Multi because all his films are shown multiple times in multiplex cinemas. Get closer to him.'

There was no point in arguing. I moved closer. Just then Multi Moghul decided to leave. 'Now!' cried Bugzee and leapt from my ear to his collar. A promise is a promise. I metamorphosed into Diabolo, hung onto Multi's shoelace and started on my journey upward. Meanwhile, Multi got into his car and was driven to his flat by the sea. There he let himself in, poured a drink and sat down.

'Now's our chance,' Bugzee whispered. 'Jump on the table near his glass so that he'll see us. And don't fall into his drink!'

Multi saw me all right! He picked me up, flung me on the floor and stepped on me. I could hear my armour plates give. Then they slid back into place again. I was glad I had changed into Diabolical Ironclad, but I wasn't going to take any more chances. I changed back into my usual self, startling poor Multi. Now he had a giant towering over him and a bedbug perched near his whisky.

'Please,' I said gently. 'We mean no harm. I am Kumbhakarna.'

'Out of the epic?'

'Yes,' I said. What else could I say?

'And I am Bugzee, out of nowhere,' Bugzee introduced himself. 'Might we talk to you please?'

'Why not? Sit down. Have a drink,' Multi replied.

He poured me a whisky and gave Bugzee a drop of it. He wasn't sure whether we were real or not and didn't care. He allowed Bugzee to explain to him why it would be a good idea to have him, Bugzee, star in an animated feature film—how much money it would save, and what a great job he, Bugzee, could do. We had more whisky. Multi was feeling expansive.

'I could give you a role too?' he said waving his glass at me.

What me? The hero of a blockbuster? I admit that for a moment I quite fancied myself. Before I could reply, he went on, 'There are always bit parts for giants.'

Well, I hadn't really wanted to be an actor. I finished my third drink and said I had to get back. They barely noticed. I teleported myself to the house Leela had rented and got there just before the others arrived. No one said anything. We were all busy thinking about money and talking about money. I noticed though that when I was near her, Leela's nose twitched. The whisky? I didn't feel I could tell her it was all Bugzee's fault.

4
Can Men be Beautiful?

I was up early the next morning hoping to catch Leela before the others came down. I thought I might be able to explain where I had gone. She was early too. 'About last night-,' I began.

She interrupted me. 'All Bugzee's fault. I know.' She was smiling at me.

'How do you know?' I asked.

'Shupi told me,' Leela replied. 'She was keeping an eye on you and saw what happened.'

'And you don't mind about Bugzee, even though –'

'Even though he's a bedbug? Of course not. I'm not squeamish. Besides, he's your friend. I'd like to meet him sometime.'

What a woman! 'I'm afraid he's moved up the social ladder.' I told her about how well he had got on with Multi.

'Ah, but you are Prince Kumbhakarna and the brother of Shri Ravana!'

Was she teasing me? I knew that Dada had told her who we were. 'It's a stupid name,' I said. 'I don't know anyone else called "Kumbhakarna". It means "pot-ears".'

'You don't have pot-ears,' Leela replied. 'They're beautiful—like seashells.' She was teasing me. She went on to say, 'And what about me? Do you think I have exquisite, shell-like ears?'

'I think you're altogether beautiful!' I burst out.

'So that's all you care about!' She laughed. 'My mind and soul don't matter?'

'Of course, they do,' I replied. 'And do mine matter?'

'I think you are beautiful!'

'And my mind and soul?'

'Of no consequence!'

She only said it to shock me. Can men be beautiful? The truth is: I was shocked. I wasn't sure women were supposed to call men beautiful. It made me glow all over. And it gave me the courage to kiss her.

I had never considered myself good looking. Giants usually aren't. And no one had told me I was, but Leela made me feel extremely handsome. When I told her that she said I was silly and it was just as well I didn't know how very handsome I was.

Suddenly she changed the subject.

'Who's Shanti?' she asked.

I was startled. 'She was my dearest friend in all the world,' I began. 'I loved her very much.' I was going to say more; but Shupi came in, and Leela went away to fetch something. She returned a few minutes later. We didn't continue our conversation. There was general talk. And then the phone rang and we received the Chief Minister's summons.

The Chief Minister offered us a huge sum of money for The Golden Balm. When we declined, he threw us into prison. Dada then challenged the CM to a combat, and the CM agreed to a game of poker. Dada won, whereupon he reneged. In his memoirs, Dada has described how we finally managed to outwit the Chief Minister. Astonishingly, despite all the excitement, Shupi and I had another argument.

We had returned to the cave to escape from the hitmen the CM sent after us. Dada had gone to bed. Shupi, Leela and I were talking over the day's events. I was proud of Dada.

'That was a glorious victory!' I exclaimed. 'In its own way as remarkable as his military exploits.'

'It didn't work,' Leela pointed out.

'That's because the CM was dishonourable. Dada won,' I maintained.

'By cheating,' Shupi interposed. 'He substituted the Queen of Hearts for the Queen of Spades.'

'All's fair in love and war,' I said defensively.

'Are you saying,' Shupi demanded, 'that in war right and wrong don't really matter, one's own side is always right?'

'That's the sensible way to look at it, isn't it?' Leela queried.

I was feeling nettled. 'I'll tell you a story Shanti once told me about a bower bird. What Dada did wasn't wrong. There is a difference between "immoral" and "illegal",' I informed them.

'What is a bower bird?' Leela asked. 'What are they known for?'

'Their bowers. The male bird builds a bower for his mate and adorns it with blue objects.'

'Is this true?' Leela wanted to know.

'I think so. It lives in New Guinea and parts of Australia. Shall I begin?'

'Yes, do. Is your story long?'

I saw her suppress a yawn. I forgave her. It was late, and we were all tired. I began at once.

THE BOWER BIRD

The bower bird had gone too far. People were willing to forgive the bird his habit of snapping up blue trifles, but this time he had snatched a sapphire necklace belonging to the Queen. And now the Queen's soldiers were after him.

The bower bird's friends gathered around.

'What shall I do?' he wailed plaintively.

'You could give it back,' suggested one friend.

'Or give it to me,' suggested another.

'Or you could make off with it and go and live in some far country.'

'Or you could hide it.'

Of all these suggestions, the bower bird liked the last one best.

'Hide it where?' he asked.

'You could bury it in the ground,' put in one friend.

'Or hang it on the tallest branch of a tall tree,' added another.

'Or give it to me,' offered a third.

The bower bird and his friends had taken so much time discussing the matter that before they knew it, the queen's soldiers were upon them.

In his fright, the bower bird dropped the necklace. It lay there, glittering among bits of blue glass, scraps of blue paper, brilliant blue feathers and other bits of blue stuff that the bower bird had gathered.

The queen's soldiers demanded that the bower bird return the necklace.

'I didn't steal a necklace,' the bower bird replied. 'It must have been somebody else.'

The soldiers scratched their heads. As far as they were concerned one bower bird looked very like another. They glanced at the hoard of blue stuff the bird had collected, didn't spot the necklace and went on to the next bower bird and the next. In the evening they returned to the Queen empty handed.

The Queen thought hard. The following morning she displayed another pretty necklace on her window sill. This one was made of blue glass. It glittered even more brilliantly than the other one had done. She waited. Sure enough, the bower bird returned. He had been hoping there might be another necklace. Just as he was about to pick it up, the Queen stopped him.

'Just a minute,' she said. 'You can have this one if you give back my old one.'

'Why?' asked the bower bird.

'Because I like that one better and you like this one better,' the Queen replied.

This seemed so reasonable that the bird agreed. The Queen got her sapphires back and the bower bird's bower became even more resplendent. They were all set to live happily ever after, when the King heard about it.

'Look here,' he scolded, 'what you've done might have been practical, but it isn't moral.'

'Sorry,' said the Queen.

The next day she hung out another scintillating necklace made of blue glass and sure enough the bower bird appeared.

'Look here,' she said to the bower bird, 'What we've done might have been practical, but it wasn't moral.'

The bower bird didn't know what 'practical' meant and he wasn't very sure about 'moral'.

'What should we do?' asked the bower bird. 'And can I have this necklace?'

'What you have to do,' explained the Queen, 'is bring me every

single jewel you happen to find, and in exchange I will give you a bigger and bluer glass crystal.'

'Okay,' agreed the bower bird. It seemed like a good deal to him. 'Can I have this necklace please?'

'Only when you bring a sapphire one in exchange.'

Over the years the bird brought her many jewels. They were mostly sapphires with bits of lapis lazuli and turquoise thrown in. The King and Queen got exceedingly rich. They used to put the jewels in a Lost and Found box and if nobody claimed them within twenty-four hours, they would transfer them to their own coffers.

One day the bower bird said to the Queen happily, 'Now what we're doing is both moral and practical, isn't it?'

'I don't know about that,' replied the Queen, 'but it is legal and that is always useful.'

Leela smiled politely. 'Yes,' she agreed, 'Being legal is useful.' That wasn't quite what I had meant. Had I bored her? Soon afterwards she excused herself.

I looked at Shupi. 'Well?' I asked.

'I take your point, Kumbh,' she replied, smiling at me. 'But have you considered mine?'

'No,' I said. 'What point was that?'

'The possibility,' she said, 'that war is always immoral.'

What could I say? Shupi has an amazing ability to wrong foot me, even when I agree with her.

I didn't sleep well that night despite Bugzee's absence, not because of Shupi so much, but because of Leela. A tiny doubt had crept into my mind. Were we entirely suited to one another? I brushed aside the thought. The Chief Minister was still after us. It was best to sleep while I could. The next day was eventful. We managed to evade the CM and set up a way of making and distributing The Golden Balm. It was also the day on which Leela asked Dada for permission to marry me.

I was taken aback. I had meant to say something to Dada, but had put it off. Suddenly that evening there was Shupi signalling to me to go and join Dada and Leela. When Dada asked me how I felt, I could hardly say, 'No, I don't want to marry Leela.' As for my doubts about being the right person for her, I thought they would dissipate. Here she was, taking the lead and putting our relationship on a firm basis. And she had used The Golden Balm. She hadn't changed radically. She was still a Doer and a Goer, but I didn't have to convince her that saving the world was important.

And it's here that I intended to close my memoirs with the two of us buying a boat, trawling the seas to rid them of plastic and living happily if not ever after, then at least for a good long time. We did buy a boat, also a house, right next to Shupi's and we trawled the seas, but we never got around to getting married. There was always something or the other to do, repairing the boats, going somewhere. And we all saw each other quite often, Bugzee especially was a frequent visitor.

He was a double star now as Bugzee the Bed Bug in animation films and as Bugzee, the debonair hero of romantic comedies. Leela liked him. He not only entertained her, he also helped her hugely in the empire she was building. Once Leela was convinced that saving the planet was a more worthwhile task than making money, she set about it with her customary energy. In no time at all, she had a fleet of boats that trawled the seven seas, an army of beachcombers that walked the beaches and a battery of recycling plants that converted the plastic into something useful. I have to confess that I may have been something of a disappointment to her. I was not attentive enough, not in the way she would have liked. She said I always seemed to be thinking of something else. I did care about cleaning up the oceans, but not quite in the way she did. Sometimes I think that had she been born into a beehive, not only would she have been the queen bee, but the hardest worker of them all.

Bugzee, meanwhile, had turned into a suave and sophisticated human being, who was also eminently efficient. He and Leela made a good team. He too had taken the need to clean the oceans seriously and soon they entered into a partnership. He no longer wanted blood from me. Not that I had minded giving him a bit. After all, by giving away a few drops, I could contribute to the food chain without actually killing someone. He told me that he considered me his best friend. 'It's all because you taught me how to metamorphose.' He had asked me once how it was done. I had told him that he must have a clear idea of who he wanted to be. And I had also explained that the more comfortable he was in his new shape, the longer he'd be able to maintain it.

In his human form, he cut quite a figure. He and Leela were often thrown together and I couldn't help noticing how good they looked. For one thing, they were of a size. I towered over Leela, but then I had always towered over everyone. I wasn't surprised when they finally discovered that they had fallen in love. They came to me and asked for my forgiveness, and then for my blessing. I gave both freely. Leela, Bugzee and I remained friends; even though they couldn't understand why I liked sitting still and looking at the sea and I couldn't understand why they didn't.

This happy ending belongs to them. Mine is yet to come.

5

In a Dream I Enlisted Whales and Dolphins.

Dada, Shupi and I are happy enough: Shupi quietly, Dada noisily and me uncertainly. Shupi likes dreaming and meditating. It suits her. Dada is immersed in his music. Vijju indulges him, and he adores her. And I'm looking for something, I'm not sure what. I like being at sea. Sometimes I dive into the water and disentangle the plastic with my hands. If I start running out of air, I turn into a dolphin or a small whale, a humpback or a minkie. The water suits me. It's a shape shifter's element: forms dissolve and form again continuously. Shupi joins me sometimes and so does Dada. Bugzee and Leela don't like the water even though they own a fleet of boats. They say it's too wet, it flows out of their hands.

When I'm on shore I sometimes walk with the beachcombers, or I just watch them. This morning, as Shupi and I are having a cup of tea together, Leela drops by. She sees me holding a piece of paper.

'Oh good,' she says. 'You're keeping an eye on the beachcombers.'

She stretches out her hand. I give her the paper, and she reads from it.

BEACHCOMBER

The beachcomber stranded on shore
knows she can't swim,
not like a dolphin. She walks
along the beach

and observes how the sea
is awash with time,
how it thrashes about -
doesn't mind the waste.
And so she gathers driftwood, turns it
into sculpture,
and, in casual emulation,
tosses it down.

Leela frowns, struggling to find the right words. At last she says, 'Kumbh, I know you often work with the beachcombers. Both Bugzee and I admire your approach; but it would be good if you could see yourself in a more supervisory capacity. The beachcombers are supposed to collect debris, not throw it back.'

'It's a poem,' Shupi intervenes, 'questioning whether art matters, given that it too is ephemeral.'

Leela is appeased. 'Oh well, in that case, I agree with the poem. Art makes nothing happen.'

Shupi and I don't say anything, Leela carries on. 'Kumbh, I was wondering—would you like to go on a reconnaissance mission? Huge amounts of rubbish are dumped in the Southern Indian Ocean, but no specific garbage patch has yet been found. It would be good to know where the rubbish goes.'

I leap at the suggestion. 'A splendid idea,' I reply. 'I've been trying to devise ways of scooping up the flotsam, perhaps by diving for it and manually setting up vast fishing nets.'

Leela opens her mouth and closes it again. She was about to tell me my idea wouldn't work, but has decided against it. She wants me to go and I want to go. At least we agree about that. Leela loses no time. She arranges for a boat, which I decline. 'I'll swim,' I tell her; she says that would take too long. I give in.

'Do you really want to go?' Shupi asks me later.

'I desperately want to go,' I tell her. 'I didn't want to tell you in front of Leela. But in a dream I enlisted whales and dolphins to help me with the nets, and the smaller fish to protect marine life.'

Shupi smiles. 'A good omen,' she says. 'Dada and I might join you.'

What I don't tell her is that Shanti was also a part of the dream, not as an elephant, but as a blue whale. It was a good dream. When the whales spouted, it felt like a celebration as fountains rose across the ocean.

I don't know what Shupi said to Dada; he has informed me that Shupi and he are coming along. He might have asked permission, but that's not his way. He said he wanted to record underwater sounds. It sounded plausible. And Shupi says she likes to feel the water streaming against her. That may be true, but I have a feeling they're into Big Brother mode and Big Sister mode. When I ask again why they're coming, they just smile and say, 'It's an adventure.'

'There are sharks,' I warn them.

'We'll turn into whales,' Dada replies in his lordly fashion.

A few days later, we set off. It has been a while since the three of us have been on our own together. It feels good. The crew prefer their own company and keep to themselves; that suits us. Dada has brought equipment along to capture sounds. He edits his recordings, and plays them to us in the evenings. He wants to write music for a ballet in which the dancers defy gravity. 'In the way fishes do,' he explains. Shupi and I nod as though we agree and don't point out that even fish know which way is down.

'That deep pulsing sound the blue whales make is their A call,' Dada tells us. 'The low sweeping sound is the B call, and the short drum beats are D calls. Some of the sounds are so deep that the human ear can't cope with them.' I may not be able to hear them, but I can feel the vibrations. I love listening to this music. Shupi listens too, but as she listens, I can feel her watching me. I think she has guessed that I'm listening for a particular sound, a voice I'll recognise. And I am, of course. I've heard it when I'm swimming underwater. It's faint. Dada's microphones haven't caught it yet.

During the day Shupi often sits on the deck and meditates. Sometimes she joins me in the sea, so does Dada. If a pod of dolphins comes along, we turn into dolphins, and play with them. Once, when we were playing with the dolphins, I heard that special sound. I nudged the dolphin next to me. 'Where is that sound coming from? Who is making it?'

He seemed surprised that I should have to ask. 'It's coming

from the south. It's the signature of an especially large blue. She's called—I can't remember what she's called. Something to do with peace. The Peaceful One! That's it.' He dives under my belly and expects me to chase him.

It is Shanti then. The dolphin has only confirmed what I already knew. It's her sound—that's what I've been hearing. That's why the dream. That's why this trip. It all makes sense. And at the same time, it doesn't make sense. What reason have I to believe that in this incarnation, Shanti has become a blue whale? No reason, just my instinct. I asked her once, 'If you weren't yourself, who would you like to be?' 'I like being myself,' she replied. I can't remember now if I pressed her further. And yet, if she left the land for the sea, it seems logical that she would have become a blue whale—she was so large, so serene, so gentle. Or perhaps this is just another of what Leela calls my stupid daydreams, born out of need. Leela is too polite to use the word 'stupid'. Kumbh the Sleeper, Kumbh the Dreamer, Kumbh who writes the occasional poem—is that all I am good for?

The portion of my dream in which whales and dolphins help to catch rubbish in a vast net isn't going to work. The worst of the rubbish is micro-plastic. A net fine enough for that would trap even the most miniscule fish. It would destroy marine life. The best that Dada, Shupi and I can do is swim about with butterfly nets. We gather large bits of flotsam, which the crew then stuff into the hold. It's not much of an accomplishment—a boatload of rubbish. We'll return with it and Bugzee and Leela will recycle it, but getting rid of such a small amount isn't enough.

We need to stop throwing rubbish into the sea, and to use skimmer boats to siphon it away at the mouths of great rivers. And we need to build recycling centres. Leela is right. There's work to be done! And I don't want to do any of it. What's wrong with me? And the information she asked for? Where does the rubbish go?

We've been sailing south and have Africa to the west and Australia to the east. Both Dada and Shupi are reasonably certain that the rubbish swirls around the tip of Africa and seeps into the Atlantic. They've hinted gently that it's time to turn back. I cannot turn back. I have to head south.

That evening I feel a thunderstorm coming. I decide to slip away once the storm breaks. I could tell Dada and Shupi what I'm planning, but I'm afraid they'll try to dissuade me. I'm as cheerful and normal as possible in their company, and hide my thoughts even from myself. We retire as usual. The boat rocks quite a bit, but none of us minds that. Between thunderclaps, I can hear Dada's snores, Shupi's too. I creep to the upper deck. It's raining hard and the deck is slippery. I stagger to the railing and look down at the sea. I love looking at the shapes the waves make. As I'm about to go over the side, I realise that Shupi and Dada are standing beside me.

'Let me go with you?' Dada asks.

I can't look at him. I keep staring at the sea. I shake my head.

'Will you come back?' Shupi asks.

What can I say? I cannot say 'No'. But what if I said 'Yes,' and it turned out to be a lie? Without answering, I dive overboard. The water receives me as though I belonged there. I turn into a dolphin and head south. I'm free! I feel euphoric—and sad. I become aware of two dolphins swimming beside me. I hear Dada's reassuring voice inside my head, 'It's all right. I've told the crew to take the boat back.' They're coming with me! They're not angry! Suddenly the three of us leap into the air and race each other through the dark sea.

We swim at a steady pace. Occasionally, I can hear Shanti's voice. It may be my imagination, but it seems less faint. We keep swimming. After a while Shupi offers a four line poem.

There were always days when the wind whimpered.
We slipped into the water and quickly dissolved.
We had turned into seals. We slithered and swam,
were limpid and cool and felt absolved.

I'm thinking about of how much I prefer this to being on shore. I respond to Shupi.

Everyone wittering,
withering
on the branch: the parrot seeking a loftier

perch, the skylark wanting a steadier
life, the eagle soaring, the bulbul
roaring, wherever you look, endless
aspiration—and why shouldn't they want
a better life?

Then Dada sings.

The trees are sighing in the wind
pretending to be people;
the stones, obdurate and dumb,
are making it clear
they are stoical;
And the particles—
dust, dirt, torn molecules
are merging and melting
and turning into something
meaningful.

We laugh, we sing, we dream and we hope that our dolphin brains will keep us afloat as we head southward. I must have been swimming in my sleep. I wake with a start. Dada and Shupi are still beside me, but Shanti's voice is so faint that I'm not sure whether she's still there. I can't let her go beyond my hearing. I increase my speed and lunge ahead. I can hear Dada warning me not to swim that fast, I'll tire myself out. I pay no attention. Eventually I hear Shanti's voice more clearly. I call out to her; and though I'm gasping for breath, I swim harder and harder. She has turned back! She's swimming towards us! I can hear Dada roaring in my head, 'Slow down! You can't keep that up!' I do slow down. I intend to let Dada and Shupi catch up with me; but something slashes my flank. There's blood in the water. 'Sharks,' my brain tells me. I make a break for it. We're close to the coast of Australia. I fling myself out of the water and land on rocks. The sharks don't follow, though one makes an effort, twists in mid-air and falls back.

6
Monsters Can't Mince

I don't know how long I lie there. I drift in and out of consciousness. The sun beats down. I continue to bleed. It rains a little. I open my mouth to let water dribble in. 'You may have landed on one of the Montebello Islands,' my brain informs me. 'Is that good?' I ask my brain. No answer. I black out or perhaps I don't. A large bird approaches officiously, and pecks my shoulder. 'Stupid boy,' it says with each peck. 'Stupid boy! Stupid boy!'

'Stop it,' I tell the bird.

'The sunnnnn!' the bird squawks. 'Get out of the sun.'

'Can't,' I reply. 'Can't move. Get help.'

'Only us sooty oystercatchers here, and some curlews. You're too big. Can't help.'

'All right, I'll try to slide back. Is there shade behind me?'

'A bit.'

I ignore the pain in my leg and drag myself back until I'm under an acacia bush.

'That's better,' the oystercatcher says approvingly, 'But you're still stupid.'

'Why?'

'Look at the mess you're in!'

'Perhaps I'm just unfortunate, not stupid,' I protest. 'Can't you help me instead of lecturing me?'

'Can't help you,' the oystercatcher says. 'I'm only a bird. Besides, there's nobody around.'

Just then another oystercatcher walks up. 'Don't help him,' he tells his friend. 'Bad Boy, Kumbh,' he says, pecking at me with each word.

I half raise myself. 'How do you know I'm Kumbh? How do you know I'm stupid? How do you know I'm bad?' I roar at him, but my voice comes out as a hoarse whisper, and as I fall back my head hits a stone.

Are they really walking about me? Peering at me? Pecking at me? Are there two of them? Twelve? Twenty? And why are they singing? 'We know a lot./ Put that in your pot./ We know –'

'You are bad, stupid birds!' I yell at them.

Suddenly it's quiet. Half a dozen curlews stroll up. The oystercatchers make way for them. The curlews form a semicircle. The Head Curlew addresses the birds. 'No lynching here, no mob justice. Due procedure must be followed.'

'Now then,' he says to the two oystercatchers. 'Why were you willing to kill him?'

'Not kill him,' protests the first oystercatcher. 'I don't think we could. He's too big. We were just going to let him die.'

'Why?'

'Because he's stupid.'

'Because he's bad.'

'Stupidity is not culpable, though, I concede, it is annoying. We cannot condemn him just for that,' the chief curlew pronounces. The other curlews murmur deferentially. 'However, an account of his stupidity would be of interest.'

The oystercatchers reply immediately.

'He exceeded his strength.'

'He left his friends behind.'

'He got caught by sharks.'

'He followed a sound without being sure he was hearing what he was hearing.'

'He said he wanted to save the world as though he knew how.'

'But he only wants to save himself.'

'And now he's lying here and doesn't know what to do.'

'You are right. He is stupid. Should the stupid be helped? There is no case law on the subject,' the Head Curlew tells them.

I raise myself on my elbows. 'If you don't help me, you won't have a defendant when you start your trial.'

'That is a good point.' The Head Curlew instructs the oystercatchers to bring me water. 'What else do you need?'

I don't want to eat regurgitated food. 'Berries,' I say, 'Berries on the branch.' I hope that whatever they bring won't poison me.

Birds aren't built to be water carriers. They spill most of it from their folded leaf cups, but I manage to drink some and dab a little over my wounds. After I've eaten a few berries, I feel better and reasonably sure I haven't been poisoned.

'Now, you must stand trial. If you can't stand, sit up,' the Head Curlew orders. He turns to the oystercatchers. 'What are your grounds for complaining that he is not only stupid, but also bad, a more serious charge.'

'He doesn't like to work,' offers one oystercatcher.

'I don't mind working,' I reply. 'But there are better things to do than collecting garbage and sending it home by the boatload.'

'Such as?' demands the Head Curlew dangerously.

'Stopping the generation of so much rubbish and finding better ways of dealing with it.'

'And you're willing to do this?' the Head Curlew demands.

'I suppose so,' I mumble.

The Head Curlew addresses the oystercatchers regretfully, 'You haven't made your case. Unless someone can come up with a further charge, I will have to let him off.'

A curlew flaps her wings and presents herself before the judge. 'There is indeed, a further, graver charge. I charge him with being himself. My Lord, I charge him with being a monster.'

The Head Curlew draws in his breath. 'A monster! That's more like it. And how do you propose to make your case?'

'With a poem, My Lord.'

'A poem you have written?'

'No, My Lord. With one of his own poems. You shall see how out of his own mouth he convicts himself!' The curlew can barely contain her glee. 'My Lord, not only does he say, he is a monster, he even suggests that everyone is a monster.'

There's another intake of breath and a murmur among the birds.

'Proceed,' says the Head Curlew in a solemn voice.

The prosecuting curlew closes her eyes and recites:

I will make you a gallery of monsters,
I will make you portraits
and hold them up as mirrors to my face,
and mirrors to your face,
and I will watch and you will watch
as they make faces at their faces
and attempt to deface what
they cannot repair.

Crookedness is ugly,
the bent back is ugly.
The hurt dribbling, the blood spilling,
all that is ugly.
They might be battered,
but they are not beautiful.
These gentle monsters, who are not gentle,
are sick with despair.

'Look at him, My Lord,' the curlew continues. 'He's sick, he's bleeding, he's monstrous. If you let him get up, he'll step on everyone.'

'No, I won't!' I attempt to roar.

'Yes, he will,' the curlew insists. 'Monsters can't mince. Ask him what he truly wants.'

'What do you truly want?' the Head Curlew demands.

I've had enough. 'I want to be shot of you, and shot of trying to do what I think I ought. I want to roam the oceans with Shanti and the whales. And I want to dream better dreams and write my poems.' There, I've said it. Now they can do what they damn well like.

The birds leap into the air and dive at me. They screech. 'Poetry isn't work!' 'Dreams are something to do in your sleep!' 'Roaming through the oceans is roaming around!' 'He's a bad boy!' 'He's a monster!' 'And he wants to step on us!' 'Guilty! Guilty! Guilty!' Thankfully, I black out.

When I'm awake again the Milky Way is clearly visible and the stars are brighter than I've ever seen them. There's light enough to see by. I'm still under the acacia bush. The Head Curlew is perched beside me. Underneath us, I can see a lizard and a grasshopper. The oystercatchers are guarding them. To the left there are some curlews. One of them says: 'Be upstanding. The Judge has woken up.'

'What's that bunch of curlews doing?' I ask the Head Curlew.

'We are not a bunch, My Lord,' one of them says. 'We are a skein, a curfew or a salon.'

'They are the jurors,' the Head Curlew explains patiently. 'You are the judge. And those are the defendants down there. Please sit up.'

'I didn't ask to be judge,' I protest.

'You did in a way,' the Head Curlew says. 'You were angry about having to defend yourself. So, we thought we'd make you the judge. We don't really mind who's what. It's quiet down here. A trial makes a change, and this way we get two trials. Don't worry. I'll help you. I am your Assistant Judge.'

'Wild and wonderful,' I think sourly. I hope I'm dreaming or hallucinating. 'Where are the defendants?' I ask.

'There,' he says, pointing to the lizard and the grasshopper.

'And what are their names?'

'Leela and Bugzee,' the Assistant Judge answers.

'WHAT?'

'I don't know why you're surprised. You arraigned them,' the Head Curlew murmurs.

'How can I be the judge and the accuser?' I demand.

'It's efficient. Makes for an open and shut case,' the curlew responds. 'I can't understand why you're so cross.'

'What is the charge?' I ask feebly.

'They don't understand poetry,' the Assistant Judge states.

'What?'

'They do not understand poetry,' he repeats. 'And if asked, they would probably admit that they don't even like it.' He sounds impatient.

'And that's what I've accused them of?' If this is a dream, and I'm sure it is, then it's a highly improbable one.

'Of course,' the Head Curlew replies. 'You secretly believe that any creature who can't write a poem or tell a story shouldn't be allowed to live.'

'I think no such thing,' I retort. 'And even if I did, I would never say so! Release them at once.'

'No!' shouts Leela. 'We want our day in court.'

'No!' shouts Bugzee. 'We want to have our say.'

'I see.' I try to sound judicious. 'How do you plead?'

'Not guilty!' Leela roars. 'My Lord, when you and I were madly in love, I wrote you several poems.'

I don't know where to look or what to say. Fortunately, one of the curlews flaps his wings and raises an objection. He must be the prosecutor.

'Not valid, My Lord. Everyone writes poems when they're in love.'

I nod sagely. 'And how do you plead?' I ask Bugzee.

'I don't know, My Lord,' Bugzee replies.

'What?' I must stop saying 'What'. 'You are either guilty or you are not. As it seems unclear, it's the duty of this court to find out if you are. Now then, do you or don't you understand poetry?'

'Sometimes, My Lord,' Bugzee mumbles.

'Not very well, My Lord,' Leela mutters.

'Speak up. Just "Yes" or "No".'

'No, My Lord.'

'Then you are clearly guilty!' I say cheerfully. This isn't real, I tell myself. This isn't something I would say or even think about my friends. This is something the curlews have made up. I carry on. 'Have you anything to say in extenuation?'

'We were badly taught, My Lord,' Leela offers.

'Besides, poems are misleading, My Lord. So are stories. Birds don't talk. And giants are mythical,' Bugzee points out.

'It is not the function of poetry to provide you with information.'

'Sorry, My Lord.' Leela hangs her head. 'Poetry is for the elite. We are ordinary folk. We have had no time to understand these things, My Lord.'

'Can you write poetry?'

'No, My Lord.'

'Have you ever tried to?'

'We refuse to answer, My Lord, on the grounds that the answer might incriminate us.'

'Well, if you don't understand it, and can't write it, do you at least wish you could?'

'What for, My Lord? No one can make a living writing poems.'

'GUILTY!' I roar. I turn to the Assistant Judge. 'There. That's done.'

'Now you must pass sentence and spell out the nature and duration of their punishment,' the curlew tells me.

'It's a Life Sentence,' I pronounce. 'They must write ten lines of poetry every day for the rest of their lives. And if they can't make them up, they must copy them.'

'That's tyranny!' Bugzee shouts.

'Who are you to say what we have to like?' Leela protests.

'Contempt of court!' the jurors yell.

'Silence!' bawls the Assistant Judge.

There's an uproar, and while it's going on, Bugzee and Leela slip away.

'The Court is adjourned!' I declare as loudly as I can. The birds disperse. I heave a sigh of relief and fall back into the acacia. Definitely a dream and one I'll never repeat to anyone—not ever. Perhaps it wasn't even my dream. It was the curlew's. But then why was I made to be in it?

Just as I'm about to fall asleep again, the lizard and the grasshopper creep up to me. They begin whispering in my ears, one on each side.

'Bad Boy Kumbh.'

'Bad Boy Kumbh.'

'Do you really think—'

'I look like a lizard?'

'Do you really think -'

'I'm a lightweight bug?'

'Why blame the curlew?'

'What did he do?'

Why am I being subjected to antiphonal whispering? 'Shut up!' I want to scream at them, but do I have the right?

'Will this do, Kumbh?'

'Boom. Boom. Boom.'

'We're trying to do a rap.'

'Aren't you going to clap?'

'Bad Boy—'

'Stop!' I shout at them. 'I recant. I repent. I take it all back. Poetry matters, but it doesn't matter more than everything else.'

That doesn't stop them.

'He says it doesn't matter -'

'How much we pitter-patter.'

'We think it serves him right.'

'We'll carry on all night -'

'UNTIL WE FIND A POEM!'

My brain has been pecked at until it's bleeding. If only I could black out: no sound and no pictures. At last I do black out and there's silence, a deep, soothing silence—almost. The last thing I hear is Bugzee's whisper, 'No poetry without silence.' I don't even try to answer. He's right, of course.

7
Who Wants to Be a Damsel in Distress? Or a Beached Whale?

When I open my eyes, I'm lying under a yellow sun in a blue sky. A red helicopter is circling overhead. The sea is a flat blue, with pretty waves embroidered on it. About a mile offshore, a pod of whales is lolling in the water. The setting looks so simple and harmless, like a child's drawing. Am I being mocked?

The curlews and oystercatchers are still around, wading in the shallows, pretending to be sheep in a pastoral of sorts. They look incapable of an unkind thought. Underneath the water, their beaks are jabbing at unwary crustaceans. What am I in for? As the red helicopter begins its descent, my anxiety increases. The curlews and oystercatchers continue to feed. I try to sit up, I can't. The helicopter lands. Two figures leap out and sprint towards me. Bugzee and Leela! They have the clean cut look of action heroes. I wish I could crawl under the acacia. Is this the third dream in a three act drama?

I do not want to face Leela and Bugzee. Do they want revenge? Or is this a totally different dream? Perhaps they'll attempt a rescue, and demonstrate that Doers are superior to Dreamers. They'll show the world that though I condemned them, they are forgiving. I do not want to dream this dream. Who wants to be a damsel in distress? Or a beached whale? But dreams have their rules. However much I will it, I don't disappear, nor do they. Leela is holding a flask to my lips. She's sobbing, 'Kumbh, oh Kumbh! We thought you were lost!' Bugzee is tending my leg, rubbing it gently with The Golden Balm. Ministering Angels! And I took it upon myself to judge and condemn them! Bad Boy Kumbh! A clear verdict.

They may not know about the trial. I hope the curlews keep quiet. These are different curlews. Were those unreal curlews? Are these the real ones? I can feel the tears coming and screw my eyes shut, but the tears leak out. Leela and Bugzee become even more solicitous. Leela wipes my eyes. Bugzee apologises for hurting me as he bandages my leg. They think my leg is making me cry. Shame upon shame. These are my friends and I disowned them.

'How did you find me?' I ask.

Bugzee points at the sky. Two sea eagles are gliding overhead.

'Ravana Bhaiya and Shupi,' Leela tells me.

Her voice is so kind, I'm afraid I'll blubber again. I let my head fall back. As I try to pull myself together, I hear Shanti's voice inside my head. 'It's all right, Kumbh.'

'What is all right?' I rage at her.

'You are all right.' Her voice is soothing, as though she's talking to a small child.

'I'm not a small child! I'm supposed to be grown up.'

'You're both,' her voice continues.

'Both what?' I demand.

'A child and a grown up. A doer and a dreamer. You belong to the land and to the sea.'

'And you?'

'Me too. We're all many things. This isn't the time for a long discussion. Listen to what Leela is saying.'

I open my eyes. 'Ravana Bhaiya and Shupi sent us a message saying you had disappeared off the west coast of Australia,' Leela is explaining. 'We caught a plane and hired a helicopter. We've been searching the islands ever since.'

High overhead, the eagles have seen us, they land close by. The curlews and the oystercatchers vanish instantly. They needn't have worried. It's Shupi and Dada. They rush up to me. Shupi strokes my hair and kisses my cheek. Dada puts his arm around my shoulders and helps me to sit up. A part of me is enjoying the attention. If this is a dream, it's better than the others. So far, nothing bad has happened. Leela fetches a large hamper and spoonfeeds me, and Bugzee sets up a tent-like structure to give us shade. None of them seem to be angry with me. All I can read is joy and relief.

'How did you know where to look for me?' I ask Dada.

'Shanti. She could hear you calling. She tracked you here, but she couldn't reach you. The water is too shallow. She called. You didn't answer. You were in a deep sleep or else unconscious. She and her pod searched for us and told us what had happened.' Dada grins at me. 'The rest was simple. We went ashore, signalled Leela and Bugzee, turned into eagles and came looking for you.'

'That was quite a burst of speed you put on,' Shupi says to me. 'You must have knocked yourself out.'

Is she scolding me? Admiring me? Or just waiting for me to explain myself?

'I caught Shanti's voice,' I tell them. 'I didn't want to lose her.'

Dada nods. 'That's what we thought. We followed you, but couldn't keep up.'

Shupi strokes my hair. 'I'm glad you're back.' She's never been so affectionate before. I'm sorry I worried them, but this is turning out to be quite enjoyable.

Leela and Bugzee have brought food and wine. We eat and drink.

'What will you do once your leg mends?' Dada asks.

I'm in it for it now.

What should I say? This needs courage. I take a deep breath and face them. 'I'd like to return to the ocean and join Shanti's pod for six months of the year –'

Before I can finish, Dada thumps me on the back. 'We'll come with you!' he says with huge enthusiasm. 'Shupi and I have been talking about it.'

I glance across at Shupi. She's smiling.

'We want to come too,' Bugzee says diffidently, 'if you'll help us.'

'But Bugzee, you can't swim!' I blurt out.

'I can now,' he replies. He sounds shy, quite unlike himself. 'I've been taking lessons.'

'And I'm learning to metamorphose, and to write poetry,' Leela adds.

I can hardly believe it. Are they having a go at me? Do they know about the dream? I scrutinise their faces. I can't detect a hidden agenda. Perhaps I'm not dreaming? How can I tell?

'Shanti?' I query.

She replies instantly. 'Pull yourself together. You're being allowed to be happy. Be grateful!'

I return my attention to Leela and Bugzee.

'Leela is doing really well!' He sounds proud. 'I'll recite one of her poems for you.'

If a god came along and said to me,
'You are so beautiful,
I will turn you into a tree,'
what could I do?
How resist a stupid deity?
I might offer nicely
to be less beautiful,
but he wouldn't like it.
'Metamorphosis,' he'd say,
'is the province
of the gods.' He'd be wrong,
of course.
Even as a tree I'd still age,
albeit more slowly.

We laugh and clap. Leela looks pleased.

'And I'll recite one of Bugzee's.' Leela offers.

To be lowly and downtrodden
pitiful as a worm,
looked down upon,
attacked from on high
by those who are beautiful
and have dominion;
and then to change,
become one of them,

though more fragile,
wayward and wavering,
not as cruel,
and glorious among creatures—
I cannot know or imagine
how this may be.

This one makes me catch my breath. Brash Bugzee, capable of understanding humility?

'It's an insect poem.' Bugzee grins.

I clap him on the back. 'Are you coming with us now to join the whales?'

'What about your leg?' Dada protests.

'The balm worked. It's fine,' I reply. 'Shanti and her pod are waiting.'

'We have to take the helicopter back,' Bugzee replies regretfully.

'But we'll meet you in a month,' Leela puts in. 'We'll swim with whales.'

'Play with dolphins.'

'Roam the oceans.'

'Write poems.'

'Dream dreams.'

'Be lotus-eaters.'

And Shupi interjects,

'Lotus Eaters are not druggies and addicts,
dropouts and derelicts.
They stretch time and make themselves
a hammock out of it.'

I put my arms around Dada and Shupi, Leela and Bugzee. I have my friends and my siblings, and my oldest friend is out there, waiting for me.

'It's a glorious ending!' I tell Shanti.

'Almost.' Shanti's voice booms in our heads. 'The oceans still need to be cleaned.'

'We'll work on the land and in the seas,' Dada declares.

The red helicopter rises in the sky. The three of us dive into the water. We metamorphose. The oystercatchers watch, the curlews offer sage advice. I call to Dada and Shupi, 'Are we awake or dreaming?'

'Both!' they shout. And we breach.

Scan QR code to access the
Penguin Random House India website